PRAISE FOR *THE MAZE MAKER*

"*The Maze Maker* . . . is proof of the power of classical myths to rekindle the interest and imagination of a 20th-century mind."

THE NEW YORK TIMES

"It tells a story, rich with incident and description and dialogue. It portrays characters who can be described and judged; it is poetic and exciting, imaginative and sometimes didactic. English critics have already praised it highly as a novel, rightly so."

NEW YORK REVIEW OF BOOKS

"*The Maze Maker* is a book of rich texture and memorable qualities. It belongs with the word of such other fine modern interpreters of myth as Mary Renault and Robert Graves. It speaks to all of us about our nature and our time. It is also an artist's book, speaking to artists over the heads of other readers. The mystery of making, of creation is its heart."

THE WALL STREET JOURNAL

"Extraordinary, both profoundly and poignantly ruminative, *The Maze Maker* is a parable about the nobility available to man during his few "insect minutes" in the amazing macrocosm. . . . It makes a great deal of contemporary British fiction look banal and trivial."

BOOK WORLD

"This original novel should blaze a brilliant place for itself. . . . Mr. Ayrton, sculptor turn novelist, makes the world of mythology a superbly real place with a relevance to our technological society that is inescapable in this beautiful, cruel, and fascinating re-creation of the Daedalus-Icarus myth."

PUBLISHER'S WEEKLY

T0373408

"Mr. Ayrton's sustained achievement is remarkable. There is no tell-tale ridge to show where the molten grandeur and terror of this archaic has blended with the modern idiom. . . . It is poetry in a unique manifestation."

CHRISTIAN SCIENCE MONITOR

"Here, at last, mythology is acknowledged and accepted in all its beauty, brutality, unreason, and terror. Mr. Ayrton has written a unique book."

WILLIAM GOLDING

"The fabulous Minotaur is superbly described, and Daedalus's journeys into the misty land of myth and magic are wonderfully imaginative."

SATURDAY REVIEW

THE MAZE MAKER

THE
MAZE MAKER

A NOVEL BY

MICHAEL AYRTON

THE UNIVERSITY OF CHICAGO PRESS
CHICAGO AND LONDON

The University of Chicago Press, Chicago 60637
The University of Chicago Press, Ltd., London

© 1967 by Michael Ayrton
All rights reserved.

First published by Holt, Rinehart and Winston in 1967
University of Chicago Press edition 2015
Printed and bound by CPI Group (UK) Ltd, Croydon, CR0 4YY

24 23 22 21 20 19 18 17 16 15   1 2 3 4 5

ISBN-13: 978-0-226-04243-5 (paper)
ISBN-13: 978-0-226-04257-2 (e-book)
DOI: 10.7208/chicago/9780226042572.001.0001

Library of Congress Cataloging-in-Publication Data
Ayrton, Michael, 1921–1975, author.
  The maze maker : a novel / by Michael Ayrton.
    pages cm
  ISBN 978-0-226-04243-5 (pbk. : alk. paper) — ISBN 978-0-226-04257-2 (ebook)
  I. Title.
  PR6051.Y7M39 2015
  823'.914—dc23

                                        2015008738

♾ This paper meets the requirements of ANSI/NISO Z39.48-1992 (Permanence
of Paper).

FOR MAURICE DRUON

This is the way Daedalus rose.
This is the way the sun rejects the shadow.

MICHELANGELO: *FRAGMENT*

The 'Erechtheid Line'

Hephaistos = Gaia (divine ancestors)

Erechtheus

(semi-divine: a man, a serpent & a wind, related to Pytho & Delphyne; twin snakes destroyed by Apollo)

Orneus — Metion = Iphinoë — Pandorus — Cecrops

Sisyon — Perdix = ? — Daedalus = Naucrate — Eupalamos — Pandion

Talos — Icarus — Nisus (of Megara) — Aegeus (of Athens) — Lycus (of Euboea) — Pallas (of Sounion)

Theseus

The Minoan Line

The first Minos, King of Crete, was the son of Zeus in bull form, and the nymph Europa. His queen, Pasiphaë, was the daughter of Helios, the sun god deposed by Apollo, and the nymph Crete. The royal names became generic, as did many of the names of their children. Thus it is uncertain which Minos and which Pasiphaë were the parents of Glaukos, father of Deiphobe, the Cumaean Sybil. The line as relevant to this narration is:

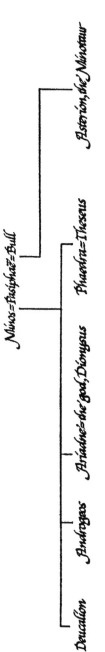

Minos = Pasiphaë = Bull

Deucalion Androgeos Ariadne = the god Dionysus Phaedra = Theseus Asterion, the Minotaur

PART ONE

I write in the time of the Ram, when the time of the Bull **1** is passed, and I address you across more than three thousand years, you who live at the conjunction of the Fish and the Water-carrier. You, in your time, have completed much that I began and your technical achievements make mine seem trivial and perhaps childish. Nevertheless, I have done things no man before me has ever done and I have made marvels which no man before me could make. With my son I have crossed the sky, where no man before has ever been.

I make these boasts as I begin to write, and counter them with the admission that I am a coward and that I never understood the pattern of my life so that I have blundered through it in a maze. I did not know until now that in places the walls of this maze were cunningly polished so that the perils I have endured, my fears and hopes, and the joy I have taken in my tasks have time and again been reflected in one another. I did not know that those I have loved and hated have been mirrored images of one another. In all my life I never learned from one experience how to encounter its reflected twin.

Above all I have been the creature of a god and endured his relentless persecution. He it was who drove me in terror to hide in the womb of his consort, in the labyrinths I made. He it was who killed my son and who has driven me to be what I have been and what I am. The demigods and kings, the monsters and mysteries which have peopled my life, he has directed; the power they had, he gave them. The power I have he gave me. What I have felt of love, endured of pain, seen of death and fought in terror, he imposed upon me. He is the sun and his consort is the earth. I do not speak of them as symbols.

11

I am Apollo's thing, born in his consort Gaia to whom I shall presently return. If other gods have been concerned with me, their concern has been idle. If they have watched me, they have done little more than watch and if they have seen me crawling through my maze, it is possible they found me no more interesting than those who have crawled before me and those who will come after.

Each man's life is a labyrinth at the center of which lies his death, and even after death it may be that he passes through a final maze before it is all ended for him. Within the great maze of a man's life are many smaller ones, each seemingly complete in itself, and in passing through each one he dies in part, for in each he leaves behind him a part of his life and it lies dead behind him. It is a paradox of the labyrinth that its center appears to be the way to freedom.

My name is Daedalus and I am a technician. This I chose to be. I have made many things in many places and done so cunningly, for that is the meaning of my name. I have constructed buildings and planned fortifications. I am proficient in stone carving and I can make the forms of gods in wood, competently joined. I have made many tools to do these things and invented others to make the work simpler and have it better done. Also I can paint images and I am adept at mechanical contrivance. All these things I can do as well as any other, be he who he may.

Above all, I am skilled in metal working and if I can boast of the intricacy of my mind, I should compare it to skilled metal working, to the delicate and perilous process which begins with the forming of the wax, burns fiercely in the long pour of the molten metal and ends cool and complete with speculation carried into considered action. What I do here is to write down what I remember of my life before it is ended and cooled, so that when you break away the mantle of the years you will find the bronze of Daedalus well cast and find that I have made myself properly. I do not forget that Apollo heated the metal.

This much is simple. I am not. I am no ordinary man, but

one who has always sought order above all things, that order which is beyond even the caprice of gods to disturb. Do not think I am unaware of the irony. I am a god's insect, yet I seek a harmony beyond the reach of gods. Therefore I write to unwind my own labyrinth and to defeat my own conviction that this order I crave does not exist despite the passion of my belief in it. Time is part of the problem. What I mean by time as I write of it, is the liquid in which legend is suspended. What I write here you will read as though it concerns matters sunk many thousand years into the past, yet clearly I am writing it today. I address you man to man.

In the liquid which contains our communication there are no problems of depth nor is the sea measurably bounded. It cannot be plumbed and soundings taken in it are illusory. You, who hang high in these tidal waters, where there seems to be light, may look up and see in the blue cavern which becomes the darkness of space, shreds of cloud moving across the sky or you may look down and discern the shifting shreds of memory swaying like weeds in the darkness of the deep past. It is for you to decide which way up you hang, because you too swim suspended in this solution of memory and are dragged about capriciously by the tides.

First, then, I shall describe myself as I now seem to be and try to explain how I was formed. I would wish you to know me and I do not wish you to think me more remarkable than I am simply because I have become a legend. I am an Athenian of the royal house of the Erechtheids. The legendary founder of this house was thought to be a serpent with a human head and also a great wind. Both these characteristics are present in me, although I hope neither is too apparent, but anyhow by convention I wear the serpent amulet. A sacred snake is kept in the Erechtheum on the Athenian acropolis and we are, as a family, under the aegis of Athena, who, contrary to report, has taken precious little notice of me personally. Snakes, on the other hand, are well suited to

13

labyrinths by their form and nature and they have played a considerable part in my life.

Being royal and a member of a family which has spent itself in futile and bloody strife among its members, my normal role would have been to learn the arts of warfare and murder and spend my life in arms chasing my relatives out of Attica with that enthusiasm for killing, burning and brave destruction usually thought to be the proper way of life for an aristocrat. This I early declined to do and for this reason I have been distrusted all my life. Being distrusted, I have learned to act accordingly. I am not called "the cunning maker" for nothing.

Physically I am a thickset man, inclined to run to fat. My legs are weak and I am a little lame in one of them. This is characteristic of craftsmen and most suitable. My shoulders are very powerful. I am not remarkable to look at.

I was born in Athens, on the rock, soon after my father Metion and his brother Orneus defeated first my uncle Cecrops and then my uncle Pandorus, both of whom fled to exile in Euboea. My childhood was much occupied with being guarded against the extravagant, if natural, ambition of my uncles and my father to destroy each other and each other's kindred, so that my early recollections are of warriors being bandaged by my mother, Iphinoë. In particular, I remember one who had lost the forefinger of his right hand in a scuffle with the supporters of Pandorus, near Eleusis. The finger stump bled freely and two things occurred to me as I gazed at it. Although I cannot have been more than six years old, I realized that the slashing sword, which required the forefinger across the guard to manage it, was an ill-designed weapon. Any man who used it risked his opponent's blade running up his own and taking off the finger, as in this case it had. I also realized with absolute certainty that while a warrior hero could well sport a finger stump to prove his valor, my hands must be preserved intact or I was nothing.

It was not that I had, as a child, any ambition to become something better than a warrior, but I showed no promise with weapons. I was a fat boy and lazy, and I was usually defeated by my brothers and cousins. Since I early developed some craft and would avenge myself unexpectedly by taking advantage of circumstance, I was not respected but I was feared. By the time I was eight years old I was much left alone.

My father was Metion and not Eupalamos, as some have reported. Metion was an ambitious but unwary man who had some affection for me but clearly found me unpromising. I had nothing of the hero about me and heroism is a quality most admired by those who make nothing practical. My father made nothing whatever, but war. He also smelled bad. I remember him most for his goat smell but I do not otherwise remember much of note about him. He was covered with scars which he revealed importantly. Those maimed but still active are much admired and every physical imperfection gained by mutilation is considered an honorable display. A man with one eye, the other lost in some raid, a man with one arm, the other hacked off in some scrimmage, such men are held in high esteem, providing they can still maim others. I could make no sense of it then. Nor can I now.

When I was ten, my father took me with him to Delphi to consult the oracle. Characteristically, he delayed so long that we arrived, in early but fierce winter, in what I believe to have been Apollo's absence, so there is no sure way of knowing if the Pythia spoke with Apollo's voice. However, my father received some oracle. Elliptically, the Pythia spoke to him and the priests translated her words. This they did in a manner which could be variously interpreted, or so I presume, for I never learned the prophecy to Metion. Clearly, the easiest reading of it must have meant that my father would presently die, for like an honorable and conventional man he forthwith returned to Athens and did so, without undue fuss. Before this, however, before we left Delphi, I began to know the pattern of my life, for though my memories of my earlier childhood are many of them vivid, none now seems significant. At Delphi I entered the first intricacy of my labyrinth. It was at Delphi that I made my first clear choice because at Delphi, in that winter before my father went home to die, I witnessed two events, or rather two parts of one event, which showed me power in two forms, one acceptable, the other empty.

Greece, as you will call it, was then, as it is now, a land of many kingdoms each differently named, but there are certain sacred places shared by those numerous Greek-speaking kingdoms. These places are not contested by men, but they are disputed by gods, and when I was a child the sky-god Apollo had long contested at Delphi with Pytho, the serpent of the earth, a servant of the Mother. Therefore male god joined battle with the female earth and it was no simple matter, although overtly the victory, as you know, lay with Apollo.

In my time all Greece stood in awe of the Cretans simply because they were civilized. From them we learned our arts and sciences and from them we learned the mastery of the sea. Our kings, forever grasping at each other's kingdoms, graceless in power as curs, puffed with the importance of each pig-sty realm they fought for, accepted without admiration or understanding a Cretan supremacy in the fabrication of all things material. So much did they accept this state of affairs and so bitterly were they divided among themselves that they had not thought of general rebellion. They spent their lives contesting for petty power and filled each other's middens with the blood and offal of their gutted ambitions.

Only in one particular was Greece secretly united against Crete and that was among the sky-gods. Even this was not simple, for the contest lay not only between sky and earth but between male and female, and the sky-gods were not uninhibited by their female consorts. We of the mainland gave our worship to the male sky coupled uneasily with the female earth. The earth alone was constant in its sex and Crete was constant to the Mother.

Gaia, the earth, has many aspects and such is her power that she holds the moon as part of her. Therefore those dedicated to the moon are dedicated to the female. At one time even the sun

16

was hers, but this long ago became the province of the sky-god Apollo, her adversary; her adversary and yet her lover, a situation not uncommon in human affairs. The moon is constant in that although she menstrually waxes and wanes she does not fail in the winter of the year and grow dim, vacating her place to rain and snow clouds. For three months in each thirteen, Apollo's strength fails and he withdraws from Delphi. In that time Dionysus sits in his place and among other things, the women eat the king. It was in that time when Dionysus changes place with Apollo, that my father took me to Delphi, and when we entered the gray pass above the sacred place, the snow had closed the sky.

We went down through the storm into a black trough filled with driving whiteness, sheltering from the worst, when we could, in the shallow crevices of the enclosing rocks. We went down into the stone niche which contains the sanctuary and I have never since seen a day so empty of Apollo, except those days which I have spent within the earth herself, and as I remember it the road to Delphi was more fearful in its icy darkness than any part of the inner earth. The screaming wind swung around the rocky bowl like water whirled to wash a kylix and in the rush of snow my father and his followers, huddled in sheepskins, looked like a lost flock. Over the wind a scream, high and joyful, throstled like a gigantic flute cadence, a cadence of rising notes and then another. These sounds circled echoing, a spiral of high laughter repeatedly cutting the snow sound's thickness and the wind-howl.

Half a mile below the pass, we halted because of these sounds and because at my father's feet, tripping him so that he floundered on the ice-slide surface of the stone, lay the head and, separately, part of the trunk of a boy. The blood was not frozen where the nose and cheeks had been torn away from the face, nor where the guts poured from the ripped thorax. As my father struggled to his feet in the drift and gathered me to him, I saw, in one clear moment, two women, naked but for fawn skins tied below their breasts, with streams of ivy waving from

17

their hair. Each carried a bough tipped with a pine cone and bound with leaves, and they ran as surely on the ice as girls run through hay-fields in high summer. One picked up the child's head by an ear, the other jerked the torn torso into the air and caught it in the rib cage on her hand so that blood ran down her arm and over her shoulders. This I saw and then my father covered my face with his sheepskin.

What happened next is not clear to me except that we ran, sliding and falling, down toward the temenos and hid in a cave near the spot where the Castalian Spring poured through a necklace of ice. In the cave, my father and his followers drew their swords and waited, and I remember wondering how much good the King of Athens thought his sword would do him. The laughter and the cries went on and on but they grew fainter.

Later, the men lit a fire and crouched around it, gazing fearfully out into the narrow gorge. The night came down and they hung skins over the entrance to the cave and waited for morning. I suppose I slept and dreamed, for I saw a sweet and dissolute face, its brow horned like a goat, then like a bull, change smiling before my eyes, into an animal mask and vanish into the dark. I saw the high and broad brow of this great beast ringed with ivy in which the small black serpents of Crete were twined. Those were the snakes which the merchants brought from Crete in stoppered bulls' horns, sleeping; the Erechtheid snakes which we kept beneath stones, near the doors of our houses, and fed with milk, to guard us from sickness. One snake in the smiling creature's crown had my father's face and that too smiled at me before it twisted behind the horns. Then I remember the smell, the feral lion-smell mingled with the stench of Athenian sheepskins and my father's foolish sword clanging on the rock wall as he beat at nothing.

Next day the storm had died and the sanctuary lay white and quiet and my father went down to the oracle, but I remained in the cave with his followers who, out of fear, waved their weapons about and engaged in mock fights to warm them and talked of what they would have done with the women had they

18

caught them, but they did not speak of the fragments of the boy. He had been much of an age with me.

When my father returned he told us nothing of the oracle but he said that Pytho was no longer absolute. "The snake is dead," he said, "and the sun will come again and speak through her skin."

I could make nothing of this at the time, nor when I have thought about it since can I understand who spoke through the oracle, Apollo being absent. I fear my father was tricked.

"It is no longer the Mother," he said. "It is Apollo who now speaks the oracle."

"Where is Apollo?" I asked, looking at the leaden sky.

"He is in the dark with the body of the snake," replied my father doubtfully.

"Why?"

"Because I tell you so."

"What will he do there? When will he come out?"

"When he is ready."

"Can we go now?"

I by no means believed my father. I thought Apollo was dead.

"Can we go now?" I asked again.

He looked old and tired and said, "We can go now and I shall soon go further still. The goat trembled quickly." It was warmer and we went up into the pass through gray slush among dripping trees.

"The oracle spoke quickly, King?" I asked. I did not know what he meant about the goat. I thought he must be speaking of himself by his nickname.

"Quickly, little, but enough," said my father. "You and your brothers must hold the power in Athens."

"Why?"

"You ask foolish questions," said my father angrily, "and you will be useless to the deme. It is fortunate you are my youngest son. Your brothers will rule." He hunched his shoulders, backing a step or two. He was very like a goat.

19

"What shall I do?"

"Make war," said my father abruptly as though the answer were too obvious to mention. "What else?"

"Why?"

My father then hit me with the flat of his sword.

"To hold the power," he said.

I said no more, not wishing to feel the flat of his sword again, but I could see no point in what he called power. This so-called power was empty.

Presently I asked him the meaning of what we had seen, of the wild women and the dead child and the horned one.

"You saw nothing," was all my father would reply, "and you will say nothing," and he raised his sword again.

So I said nothing but I began to think. Power did not lie with men who waved swords about and slashed at each other, with men who foolishly lost their forefingers. It lay with those who had no need of swords. If power then lay with gods who needed no weapons and carried them only for show, what power could I gain when I was grown, which would be adequate to a man who had no skill with weapons?

I do not say I knew then that I should make the choice I did when, five years later, my mother and I were forced to leave Athens because my cousin Aegeus drove out my brothers and deprived them of their power. They went elsewhere to take other, similar power by precisely the same means as it had been won from them, and we went into Euboea and took refuge with Lycus, Aegeus' brother, and he in turn was exiled from Euboea and took refuge with Sarpedon, so that these years were filled with a pointless trekking from those who wished for power over men and lost it, or won it, spending their lives in its pursuit. But it was at Delphi, the first time I went there, that I began to perceive how a man can make his own power only by disdaining power over other men, how he need only fear other men's power if he is no more than another man and how he can become more than other men by gaining power over things which are not men, for thus he goes beyond men.

The solution, as it gradually came to me, is that a man must move carefully between men and the gods, recognizing that they are much alike and seeking to know how they differ. Thus he will learn from the gods, which most men fear to do. In this way he will not invariably avoid enemies but he will have mastered skills which will make him too valuable to destroy carelessly. Also, he will inspire awe and seem more like a god than a mere king does, in that he will seem to have some power which is not man's. Providing he avoids hubris he may live long by refusing rivalry.

My father, who had spent his life in rivalry, fell ill on his way home from Delphi. South of Thebes, on the road, he began to shake and fell down, shaking, in the cold mud of the track. "The goat trembled quickly," he said. Now I understood him, because I remembered that the goat sacrifice must tremble in every limb before the Pythia can follow, and she in turn must tremble before she speaks. I did not then know how the goat was made to tremble, nor why my father, in his sheepskins, should tremble like a goat, but he did and clutched at his sword. Now he looked like a sick goat. The men picked him up and carried him and as we reached Eleusis and bargained for a free passage through it, the sun came out and shone wanly upon the place. My father smiled and said, "The god, the god," and then he said nothing more so that we went on to Athens in silence.

Rivalry is of all conditions the most distracting to a man who seeks order and needs no stimulation beyond the urge to master intractable materials. And rivalry I had observed in full measure before I was ten years old and went to Delphi with my father. Minimal or murderous, it was the mainspring of every member of the house of the Erechtheids. My relatives, hating one another, grouped and re-grouped their allegiances from childhood to old age, and as a result, little is memorable about any one of them, although each one believed he was earning immortal fame in the achievement of his simple desires. My brothers, like my uncles, believed in the virtues of simplicity. This was all they could believe in since they were themselves simple, and after my father's death they carried his tradition of murderous simplicity before them like a standard, deviating in no way from the pattern which had enslaved him and all his forefathers. They were dull, narrow men and although each believed himself ambitious, their ambitions extended nowhere beyond the effort to enlarge the boundaries of that with which they were each already familiar, without changing the pattern. Moreover, they were outraged if any member of the family behaved differently or expressed views at variance with their code of conquest. It was the insecure security upon which they based their lives.

When I was thirteen, my cousin Aegeus raised a force of Laconians, hard fighting men, tattooed from neck to knees, and unseated my brother Sicyon, who, since my father's death, had ruled in Athens. This operation was carried out in the usual way, for the Athenian acropolis, upon which our palace stood, was impregnable and therefore treachery was the invariable method of conquering the palace. My cousin Aegeus brought gifts in the name of his father Pandion, the ruler of Megara, and my brother Sicyon feasted him. Aegeus, seeing Sicyon drunk with his followers, after two days of feasting, signaled to his Laconians, who straightway killed everyone within reach and took possession of the palace. Aegeus took the power.

This tale is one which you will have heard a hundred times told about a hundred kings in a hundred places. It is an example of the monotony of simplicity and I believe my brother Sicyon found it quite normal, although I am told he looked surprised when Aegeus knifed him. My brother Eupalamos escaped. I do not know what became of him.

For myself, I hid and when the Laconians came for my mother she and I were apparently dead, as I had taken the precaution of pouring bull's blood over both of us. We lay sprawled in her megaron, I with a sword conspicuously buried between my arm and my side. The Laconians did not look carefully. There were other women screaming satisfactorily in adjoining rooms.

It was the same pattern of events as that which marked the overthrow of my uncle Cecrops except that my father had failed to kill him when he took Athens, before I was born.

It is possible that you will find my description of the fall and death of my brother Sicyon cynical and lacking in drama as I tell it, but you must realize that any drama fails to grip if it is performed too frequently, and, besides, it was all a mere family matter. Also, I disliked my brothers. What will be unfamiliar to you, in your time, is not the pattern but the scale. You are used to your contemporary treacheries and defeats taking place with less bloodshed if it is a family matter and very much more if it is a national one.

One recollection stands out clearly in my mind from this trivial shambles where so many honorable men cut each other to pieces with such treachery. My clearest recollection is even more trivial than the shambles, but it played a great part in making me what I have become. As my mother and I lay motionless in our pools of bull's blood, I watched one of the Laconians, a broad, dark, red-faced, plethoric man, clearly less concerned with lechery than with gain, loot my mother's possessions. She had a gold cup, of very fragile Cretan workmanship, and, among various gold ornaments, six gold grasshoppers which she wore in her hair. This broad and red-faced man put the grasshoppers in the cup and then pressed the cup between his red hands so that both cup and golden insects became, in one spasm of his grip, a shapeless lump of metal. This he thrust into his belt, and picking up my mother's ivory pyxis, he crushed that too between his hands. He had no reason to smash that. He simply enjoyed doing it and grinned like an idiot at the fragments.

There is perhaps nothing unusual in such a moment. Those

23

who assist kings to power may take what they can get on the way and destroy what they enjoy destroying. But I had watched the Cretan who made the cup and two others who had made the grasshoppers and I had known the cow suckling her calf, carved on the ivory pyxis, all my life. They mattered more to me than my brother Sicyon, who to me was much like the Laconian, broad, dark and red-faced. I knew the long days and weeks these things had taken to fashion and was not at that time aware that it had been any trouble to fashion Sicyon although later my mother wept for him.

I remember the gold lump under the Laconian's bronze-studded belt. To him gold was shapeless gold whereas to me, even then, gold was a material to shape. I had seen it done. That difference of attitude is absolute. When the Laconians and my cousins had become drunk enough and were either asleep or setting fire to parts of the palace, my mother and I left.

In Euboea we lived with my kinsman Lycus for two years. Lycus was a remarkable man. At least, unlike **3** the rest of my male relatives, he had several interests rather than one. Of course, he plotted the overthrow of Aegeus by a trick which involved visiting him with gifts and killing him while they feasted on the impregnable acropolis at Athens. On the other hand, Lycus was deeply religious and initiate in the mysteries of the Mother in her aspect of Demeter. He also possessed some power of prophecy and was the one Erechtheid with any sense of order. To my surprise, he was not a little wizened man, as my family would expect of any member of it not wholly pledged to warfare; he was tall and powerfully built, regal in carriage, and showed a commanding presence. He was the first man to discuss with me the relationship between humans and the gods.

Lycus was not complicated, he was dual. He kept the two

sides of his life separate and when he spoke of power in political terms he was only a little more imaginative than the rest of our house. He believed that man's destiny was conquest and at feasts he would boast of his bravery in arms, the number of his captured cattle and other mundane achievements of this sort. Secretly they bored him. His other nature, which he kept carefully hidden for social reasons, was no less practical upon a different level. He was concerned to understand the gods and his natural fear of them was tempered with a recognition of their fallibility, so that he earnestly sought to adapt himself to their caprices with a view to his personal advantage.

As I have said, I was not myself respected by my family. Even my mother, although she loved me, was a little ashamed of finding me unconventional. That Lycus was attracted to me was in part due to my apparent strangeness and in part it was physical, for I had lost much of my childish fat and was presentable. Lycus had no feeling for women, but was, I presume, bored with budding hoplites. He preferred Cretan manners to Hellene forcefulness. Furthermore, he washed frequently.

Life for an exile, even a princely one, is empty and humiliating. One has no place, no function and no prestige as a refugee, unless one can show some special ability in arms. I was thus much alone and spent my time in watching Lycus' *demiorgoi* at their work. He was not satisfied with mere loot; heaps of battered treasure were not enough for him. He therefore employed Cretan goldsmiths, potters, carpenters and stone carvers, but he did not accept Cretan bronze work, recognizing, as few men then did, that the Cretans are skilled beyond measure in the art of inlaying bronze with other metals but remarkably inept in the craft of working bronze itself. Their sculpture in this metal is as abject as their large stone images of the goddess. Their genius lies in the perfection of small and precious objects. Lycus obtained, with great difficulty, a skilled bronze master from far to the east, beyond the Copper Island, and this man taught me the first skills I gained.

Lycus was both shocked and intrigued to find an Erechtheid

25

prince pouring metal under instruction from a barbarian smith. He was surprised and I think gratified to find me promising in the Cretan crafts as well. In those two years I served my apprenticeship in the mastery of true power.

My master in this, a man who seemed close-mouthed and yet spoke a great deal to the point, was one who had changed his name so frequently that he found it difficult to recall the one in current use. He belonged originally to the people called the Hurri and was, he gave me to understand, much traveled in the service of the Hittites, a warlike people to whose arsenals of armor and bronze weapons he had constantly and tediously been called upon to contribute. His real interest lay in bronze sculpture and he was a master of the techniques developed at Ugarit. He had at one time been a slave of the Mitanni, had escaped into Egypt and briefly had set up at Pharos as an armorer. From there he had journeyed to Crete where he had greatly improved the design of swords, which brought him into high regard at the palace of Knossos.

The Cretan sword, before he improved it, had one great weakness, aside of course from the general Cretan inability to cast a flawless bronze blade; it had a short handle-tang so that the blade would often snap off at the hilt in combat. My master extended the tang into a slim, flat plate long enough to hold four rivets. This long tang was flanged at each side to hold a grip of ivory or wood and these flanges were extended laterally to form a guard. Hilt and blade being therefore integral and the guard adequate to protect the hand, the Cretans and subsequently Lycus' men in Euboea seldom lost their forefingers. Many even kept their lives. I was much taken with this device. My master regarded it as a trifle, but acknowledged that as an invention it had been valuable to his career.

"The Cretans," he said, "are the most accomplished craftsmen, the most skilled architects and in general the best-mannered men I have encountered anywhere. They are more inventive than the Egyptians, who, incidentally, are also poor bronze workers. To understand bronze you must go east.

26

Where the Egyptians are superior to all others is in the use of stone. No one can rival them, but of course they have unlimited access to it." Naturally he did not allow his views to be heard in their entirety by Lycus' Cretans for he was both courteous and wary.

His wariness was even more pronounced than his courtesy. No one knew his true name. This is not uncommon among craftsmen, who often believe that their magic is weakened if their names are spoken openly. He called himself, at that time, Dactylos, after the Dactyls of Ida who are thought to have invented bronze. This name was Cretan and he felt it to be sufficiently strange, foreign and curious to give him status in Euboea. In Crete he had, I believe, called himself Hattusis to indicate his Hittite origins and before that in Egypt he bore a Canaanite name which I never learned. Dactylos believed in being foreign wherever he was. It gave him mystery, which is always useful to technicians. He was a slender man with a leathery skin, much wrinkled, and despite or because of his many names he achieved a timeless, immemorable, anonymous persona as if, when he was there, he was not actually present but had just left. Impersonal and usually silent, he could and did move about the world at once unnoticed and revered, itinerant and valuable. He had power over no one but himself and he would die only by accident or of old age. He had no rivals and kept his pride secret.

Lycus, who was fond of nicknames, called him Ptah because he had been in Egypt and Ptah is the Egyptian Hephaistos who, for some strange reason, is often portrayed there as mummified. Dactylos, I suspect, resented this nickname. It drew attention to his appearance and furthermore his name, Dactylos, being already a nickname of his own choosing—it means "finger man"—he did not wish another chosen for him. Lycus and Ptah-Dactylos seemed however to be on excellent terms and spent much time together discussing religion. Both were inclined toward the Mother in one aspect or another, for not only were both influenced by Cretan thought but the Euboean goddess Graia was patroness of Lycus' city. It was a time when the rivalry between the male sky and the female earth was intense. Despite their real sympathies, both Lycus and Dactylos were openly responsive to the cults of Zeus and Apollo.

Dactylos adopted Athena as his tutelary goddess. He admired her wisdom and especially her practicality. It was a shrewd choice in view of Athena's obvious identification with the Cretan snake goddess. Lycus was much flattered. Athena in this form has, among her primary attributes, a snake which surely gives her Erechtheid associations. It was tactful of Dactylos and typical of him. He continually, if briefly, praised Athena, giving her credit for all the skills he himself had so patiently acquired. I suspect that this public avowal of divine responsibility for his excellence in the techniques he practiced, served to turn away the potential envy of the Cretans, his fellow craftsmen. I think also that it was the origin of the fable which evolved in after years, that I had learned my skills from Athena herself. Nothing is further from the truth.

Dactylos ate enormously. It was his sole indulgence apart from his remarkably procreative enjoyment of the women of Lycus' court. His prowess in this, like everything else about him, remained deeply secret until it became apparent that no less than sixteen boys and seven girls, all born within a year of one another, closely resembled him. This similarity did not emerge until Dactylos had left Euboea. The women themselves were in general either the widows of men killed in battle or refugees from one or other of the warring states in the neighborhood. Therefore no one pursued him.

I like to think that Dactylos, who created where other men destroyed, carried his vocation so far that he created human beings upon the relics of men destroyed by one another.

"Be silent," he told me, "or at least be quiet and watch. Watch the lesser men, the warriors and the kings. Watch the gods and flatter them but without ostentation. Do not dispute with them, for although they are greater than men they behave by habit and training much as men do and their caprices are more dangerous and incomprehensible than those of men. Athena of course is an exception," he added piously, "and so are Zeus and Apollo." The habit of caution was strong in him.

Another time he said to me that we were the keepers of memory. "Our work will live when the warriors lie in their tombs and our work lies with them," he said. "They will be dust and what we make will lie among their bones as whole as when we made it." I asked him what good that would do us and he replied, "What are we but our work and who are they but their work and since both will lie in the tomb and their work will be dust. . . ." He did not finish. Unsatisfied, I pressed him. "Surely the singers will praise heroes long after they are dead?" "Words," he said, "are air. Who engraves them?" "You have done," I said stupidly. "Memory," said Dactylos, "is a curious thing. Men do not utterly lose it, they cover it with dust and then hope to blow the dust away with words. But we leave proofs."

"In tombs? Who will see them there? Besides, they will take their goods with them. Who will dare to look in tombs for what we do? They would be cursed."

He smiled and said no more. You will understand him, but I was very young then. I was not satisfied but I was so flattered that he coupled us together as craftsmen that I left the matter there.

I remember, too, among many things he said so cryptically that for the most part I could make nothing of them, one statement that has come into my mind many times. These were his exact words: "The sole dishonor is to die with work unfinished so that those who see it cannot know what was meant. Time itself will work to confuse and distort one's intentions and one can do no more than leave the meaning clear when one leaves it. The sole dishonor is to die with work on hand. Do not stumble rashly onto the sword blade, especially the sword you have made yourself, when it is placed in another's hand."

Dactylos, my master, I wonder what became of you.

Lycus, my protector, was a most talkative man who **4** said very little. He liked to gather people around him to help him reconcile his orthodox, kingly views with his taste for speculation which continually led him into doubt. His manners were free and Cretan. The women of his household moved as freely as the men and were welcome at his table and welcome to express their opinions. He treated them with special courtesy because he did not care for them.

He called me "Tectamus," being fond of nicknames, and made it clear that I was favored. I found Lycus very impressive at that time and although my regard for his intellect may have depreciated, I still admire the effort he made to exercise it. At supper he was invariably filled with burning questions and these he liked to answer himself after courteously leading all those present to voice their opinions. He listened with especial patience to the opinions of women, but seldom gave the company the benefit of his own views until all females had withdrawn. When they did, by a coincidence often remarked but not then fully understood, Dactylos also withdrew, pleading the weight of his labors.

Those who were left then were perhaps a dozen warriors, who fell asleep at once, the priests of Zeus and Apollo, a number of palace officials and myself. The Cretans found the talk unconventional and tiresome, although Greek was then coming into general use in Crete as a second language. Also I fear they found the conversation unsophisticated and did not approve of Lycus' regard for the sky-gods whom they found unpleasantly novel. They seldom came to meals and kept themselves apart.

"Our Cretans," said Lycus, "are set in their ways. They will accept Zeus only because he was born among them. Otherwise they find the gods vulgar and obstreperous. They refuse to recognize, as we must, that although the Mother will ever be held in honor, in whatever aspects she manifests, there must come a time, and I believe it has already arrived, when the gods will rule over all." He sat back to allow us to consider the weight of his words. "It has been long in coming but I must tell you that my grandfather actually witnessed the contest between the young Apollo and the serpent Pythia—our own serpent, mark you—at Delphi, and he was in no doubt of the outcome. She was vanquished. The god triumphed and indeed my grandfather maintained that far from slaying her he possessed her by an act of rape."

"But surely. . . ." began one of the priests.

"You will remember," continued Lycus, "that when Zeus had possessed Leto, the jealous Hera sent Pythia to pursue her and this the serpent did with unstinted vigor. Hera swore that the offspring of Zeus and Leto, who had coupled in the form of two quails, should not be born in any place where the sun shone, yet in fact Apollo was born on Delos after nine days of labor and the serpent was powerless to prevent it. The sun shines continually upon Delos. One must deduce from this that Hera, however powerful we know her to be, was thus defeated by Zeus. Apollo, then, in his conquest of Pythia maintained the tradition set by Zeus and further defeated the serpent who, as we know, now speaks her oracles under the repeated blows of Apollo's vigor."

Since the priestesses of the Mother, who had been present, had all withdrawn and the priests of Zeus and Apollo were the only religious left at table, Lycus met with the mildest opposition to this explanation.

"My grandfather. . . ." began Lycus.

"My lord," put in the priest of Apollo gently, "the young Apollo, as you will remember, was nurtured by Themis, upon nectar and ambrosia, so we must conclude that the Mother was not in that aspect opposed to him. Furthermore, there is the question of Pytho's sex. He was, we believe, a male serpent and fled from Parnassus to the sanctuary of the Earthmother at Delphi when Apollo pursued him."

"That was not my grandfather's view," replied Lycus.

"The female serpent, Pytho's mate Delphyne, was also at

31

Delphi; indeed, the place takes its name from her," murmured the priest of Apollo. "She, it may be, submitted to Apollo on the death of Pytho and he possessed her." It was a compromise Lycus brushed aside. "Either way," he said, "the Pythia at Delphi was clearly vanquished by Apollo and now submits to him. My grandfather witnessed it. When I was a boy, he told me how he had watched the god descend in the full fire of the sun itself into the cleft of the rock and, taking the snake between his hands, ride her so that the very stones shone with their sweat and clashed together with the rhythm of his thrusting. Then it was that she first spoke under his loins and foretold that the Mother would retreat into the earth forever. That this oracle proved only partially true is not remarkable. Oracles are never as simple as they may seem."

"It is difficult," put in one of the court officials, "to found laws upon oracular utterances," and then he fell into a brooding silence.

"The Cretans maintain that Daphne, whom Apollo violated and who was the priestess of the Mother, fled to Crete where the Mother is still supreme. They say the laurel leaves chewed by the Pythia were left by Daphne at Delphi to assuage the agony of Apollo's fierce penetration," said the priest of Zeus.

"That may be," said Lycus, "and it supports my grandfather's contention. Everything points to victory for the sky-gods and we must be prepared for Crete to suffer for her allegiance. The island has been shaken by Poseidon time after time."

In the silence that ensued, Lycus began to stroke the inside of my left thigh. "You, child," he said, "should go to Crete and learn from them. They have much to teach a boy of your talents and their time is clearly short. The Cretan mother is dying and the future is here. When I have taken Athens from Aegeus we will make it more golden and more splendid than Knossos. We shall exalt Demeter and her daughter there as equal to Athena, and Apollo to Poseidon, and both the sexes will be served."

He was wrong in some ways, although not in all.

"Tectamus," he said, when we were in private, "I am not so

sure of what I say as I must sometimes seem, but this I believe; we must at all costs imitate the gods as women must imitate the Mother in her many forms. It is not hubris I am suggesting, but honor. The gods are pledged to violence, to rape and to destruction and for men to give themselves to other tasks invites their displeasure. You, I know, have already set yourself against manly pursuits and in my heart I honor you, but before you die you will have had a harder life than the most scarred veteran in arms, for you will have set yourself to follow Ouranos whose very son castrated him. If you were destined simply to become a fine craftsman, welcome in any house to work the metals from the storeroom, you might have a good and fruitful life even if you were occasionally mocked as Hephaistos is mocked on Olympus. But you have already made another choice which the gods will resent. They will see it as a challenge to their divinity, as hubris. Creation, Tectamus, is more painful and more hated than murder, if only because it is less common. I envy you in some ways but I am glad I am not in your shoes." And very gently he took off my shoes.

He was not stupid, my kinsman Lycus. He was a little pompous and ineffectual; he never did take Athens from Aegeus, but I remember him as gentle. When he was fully armed and led his men on some useless but noble escapade he always looked slightly embarrassed. Even when there was a sound reason for raiding, such as the need to get metals for his Cretans to work, he still looked embarrassed.

A constant state of feud between the members of a single house is not uncommon in any age and sorts **5** well enough, among those who have nothing better to do, with the general profession of warfare. If, however, a family feud becomes endemic, it tends to lose its impetus. The *oikos* tends to reunite. Aegeus was firmly fixed on the throne of Athens. His brother Nisus seemed content as ruler of Megara, in succession to Pandion, while his younger brother Pallas possessed south Attica in apparent peace. Naturally, they hated each other and raided each other's lands in the slack months between sowing and harvest and they had sufficient regular bloodshed to content them. Lycus joined in and occasionally stole a few cattle and women from the territory of his nearer relatives, but his heart was never in these games despite the conventional side of his nature. My own brother Sicyon was dead and Eupalamos had gone overseas. The sons of Metion, in so far as they menaced the sons of Pandion, were reduced to the single person of myself and although I was sixteen years of age I showed no sign of a talent for battle. The sons of Pandion rested secure in the knowledge that I presented no danger to any one of them. In old age both Nisus and Pallas expressed themselves gratified with my achievements, or so I have heard. At that time they discounted me as a potential rival and rightly. I had no designs upon their little kingdoms.

Aegeus, hearing of my abilities, which he regarded as eccentric, was nevertheless sufficiently intrigued to let it be known that my mother and I would be welcome to return to Athens. Aegeus knew the value of magnanimity. He also felt I might be useful and would be safer under his eyes. My mother was homesick and wished, before she died, as she put it, although she was in excellent health, to see my sister Perdix and her son Talos, my nephew, who had remained undisturbed by the king, largely because Aegeus, for reasons obscure to me, had taken Perdix to his bed regardless of consanguinity. This royal favor had not lasted long but had at least assured Perdix of safety while my mother and I were in exile. Talos was not Aegeus' son but had been born to Perdix' husband, a man who had been killed in a skirmish at Marathon some four years after I was born. I do not remember him. Perdix I remember all too clearly and greatly disliked. As a sister she was fifteen years my elder, for I was born to my mother when Iphinoë was no less than thirty years old, which is doubtless a credit both to my mother and to my father's prolonged interest in her.

34

Perdix, whose name means "partridge," was a woman perfectly named. She exactly resembled this edible but irritating bird. She was plump and small and her legs were red. Her pride in her son, my nephew, was disproportionate and its consequences for me were disastrous. Talos, my nephew, my junior by three years, regarded me with a most flattering awe from the moment my mother and I returned to Athens. He was a good lad and there was no malice in him. He was able with his hands and willing and his sole ambition, within a few months of our return, was to resemble me closely in every particular. I was touched by this and taught him much that Dactylos had taught me, so that for many months we were well content in each other's company and came to love each other.

In the summer of my eighteenth year, Talos and I were together on the shore to the east of Athens. It was the time, just after harvest, when the men are tired, unambitious and well fed so that the chance of a raid was remote. Talos and I lay naked on the sand, lazy after swimming. Within a yard of my head I saw the shell of a crab's claw and picked it up. The two elements of the claw were still joined, as they often are when one finds them, and the shell, smooth and warm to the touch, was sharp in the serrated inner edges of the grip. Idly I opened and closed the pincers and saw in an instant that by crossing two sticks, thrust into the empty segments of the claw, I could make tongs with a toothed grip. I spoke to Talos and he fetched two slivers of driftwood. We packed the claws with sand to hold the wood, crossed the sticks and bound them at the cross with my sandal lace, using one of his to hold one claw to its shaft and a second to bind the other. The device worked badly. We had tied the cross too high. We moved it down the wood, recognizing that the leverage must come as near as possible to the claws themselves. "It will work if we can rivet rather than bind the crossed elements," said Talos. "We'll do that," I said. "We'll cast the thing in bronze and rivet the two elements at this point so that they fold. Pull them apart, so, and they open. Pull them together and they will grip."

"A good idea," said Talos, "but give me back my sandal laces."

I dismantled our crab-claw tongs and gave him back his laces. One of my own still bound the sticks together. Thinking how best to make the tongs, I chewed the short ends of the two tied sticks.

"You look like Marsyas," said Talos, and I blew out my cheeks to imitate the playing of the syrinx. "No wonder Apollo defeated you," he added drowsily.

"I shall reverse the pipes, as Apollo reversed his lyre, and sing and play at once," I said.

"Zeus forbid!"

"Apollo worsted Marsyas with that trick."

"Well, at least don't sing," said Talos and seemed to sleep. The sun was hot enough to make us both lie still and we both slept.

"I shall go in again," said Talos in my ear, and woke me.

We went down to the edge and I stuck one end of my two bound sticks into the packed smooth sand at the water's edge. "Here, Ganymede," I said and pulled him down in the shallows. He fought me and we rolled in the warm water.

"I'll reverse your pipes," he said.

"No, Apollo, I'll reverse your lyre," I said and did so.

As we came out of the sea, Talos bent down and twirled the sticks on the edge, spinning one round on the axis of the other. It made a perfect circle in the sand.

It was a god-blessed day, that day on the seashore under Hymettus. Truly we loved each other, Talos my nephew and I, and in that one day between sleeping and bathing and playing like the gods under the smile of Apollo, we invented three separate tools. On our way up the beach, Talos found the spine of a fish intact and we took it with us so that, on the dusty walk to Athens in that golden evening, we carried the claw of a crab, two sticks bound together and a fish spine. From these flotsam fragments we cast in bronze a pair of tongs with a serrated hold, a pair of compasses and a saw.

Therefore when you hold hot metal, fresh from the furnace, well gripped in your tongs and lay it on the anvil before you strike it, you owe your hold on it to our crab's claw, and when you inscribe the bowl of your kylix, or make graven circles on a breastplate, you owe your compasses to that day's bathing, and when you cut your cypress wood to make the roof tree of your house, you owe it to the fish spine which Talos found on our way up the beach.

Talos and I made these inventions together and share them. Each understood the other's mind as we understood each other's bodies and loved each other. But for Perdix, the jealous partridge chattering in the grass, perhaps we should always have done so.

When I look back on Talos as he was then, with eyes less clouded now than mine were when I loved him, I see that in his mother's malice and his own fundamental simplicity the gods had a weapon to use against me. It was not Talos' fault.

I can see him still, as he walked up the beach on that summer evening, a big-boned strong boy with a short, thick neck. His head was small and neat, a little too small for his body. As I remember it, his face was a trifle uneven to be what is generally thought beautiful. When he was angry he grinned and I do not have so far to look back to see that grin, for I saw it on him many years later. The day he found the fish spine, he was simply smiling in the sun, bronze only in the depth of his sunburn, gleaming only with sweat, so that his heavy shoulders and buttocks and thick muscular thighs looked finely cast in metal.

Talos and I had a workshop outside the propylaeon of the acropolis, where we worked with the metals which Aegeus gave us from his store and where we made various things in wood. Outside, in the courtyard, we also shaped small statues out of *poros* and tried our hand with marble which, in Athens, is easily come by. Talos had no patience with marble. Punching out the forms and smoothing them with the black powder from Naxos, with pumice and fine sand, was too much long labor for him. "If we could cut this stuff like wood, with a sharp edge," he

37

said, "it might be less wearisome." You cannot, however, cut hard stone with bronze chisels unless you have unlimited labor to sharpen and re-temper each tool after one blow. Given a hundred boys, each in charge of one blade, and another hundred to use the abrasives in relays, as, I am told, they work hard stone in Egypt, even Talos might have been patient enough to carve a marble figure. He was not. I was, myself, from time to time, but even I left much unfinished and abandoned various figures soon after they were begun. When one is young one wants to see quick results and shaping a rough marble block with a punch for weeks together, in order finally to grind out of it a statue by further weeks of rubbing, does not produce a quick result.

We did not have two hundred assistants, we had two. One was from Laconia and, like all Laconian freemen, he was intricately tatooed from chest to knees. His name was Laerces and he was built like Talos, big and heavy, but unlike Talos he was clumsy, so clumsy and so like and yet unlike Talos that although I found him manageable enough, Talos had no more patience with him than with the lumps of marble he so soon abandoned. The other man Aegeus spared us was a wiry little Athenian called Endoios. Endoios loved Talos as Talos loved me and for this reason he had precious little love for Talos' lover.

The god manipulated the four of us, as we worked each day below the acropolis, manipulating in our turn all manner of materials and devices with passionate enthusiasm. The god used my friends to set the first of several traps for me. It needed only Perdix to spring it.

Soon after the death of her husband, Perdix came to believe, or at least to maintain, that this dead man, who had been nobody of any great consequence, had not fathered her son. In her partridge form, she insisted, she had been ravished by Zeus in the form of another partridge. Talos was therefore a demigod.

No one took much account of this assertion, least of all Talos.

He used to put on a pair of gilded ox horns when he was drunk and dance about in them proclaiming himself a son of Zeus in bull form, partridge or no partridge, but after a time we found this a dull and perhaps a rash joke. Perdix took it very seriously. It is not uncommon for women, especially those who are unable to explain by date the birth of their children, to cite some god or other as the father. Perdix, however, was unusual. She could perfectly well have conceived Talos in normal intercourse with her unimportant husband, but this she felt to be an inadequate mating to produce so splendid a bull of a son. She had a great conceit of him. My own mother, who might, I have sometimes felt, have claimed some intercourse with Hephaistos in producing me, was far too down-to-earth to do so. She regarded Perdix as absurd. "Your father got Perdix on me," she said, "during the partridge festival, which may account for her appearance, poor thing, but I never had a god and nor did she." I am not absolutely sure of this in my mother's case but my father Metion would certainly have boasted of it if she had been taken by a god, and so I suppose she was not. Nevertheless no one is sure of the extent of divine participation in the partridge dance and some strange offspring have been conceived at its climax, when the male treads his mate. I have seen our people, dressed as partridges, move through the spiral maze marked on the dancing-floor, with more than human speed and sureness, the male hobbling and bowing, wings extended, to the female, who trembles in her plumage and spreads her tail to him. And I have seen the net, dropped on their coupling, jerk with madness.

Such rituals create abundance but they can drive the participants insane even when the dance is demanded, but Perdix and Talos, Laerces, Endoios and myself went through a partridge dance in Athens, all unknowing, which left Laerces dead, Talos in flight and myself in jeopardy. We went through the spiral of the steps and the net fell. Perdix the partridge, the tame bait, escaped the snare and went chattering on. Endoios escaped too and went to Ionia with a store of metal from our workshop, which doubtless set him up there. He was a good bronze founder and an expert carver of ivory, which would have been a help to him in the east. In Ephesus he made a celebrated statue of Artemis in dark vine-wood and in the course of time, like most craftsmen, he came to Crete, where we met again.

The trap took time to set. The net's first knots were made by Perdix' chattering when she put it about that Talos was the leading spirit and the innovator in our mutual works and not I. Tirelessly she gossiped and always to my disadvantage. "Talos, my son," she would say, "inspired by Zeus, his father, has invented a new kind of ball-and-socket joint; Daedalus is wild with jealousy." Then she would puff out her feathers and add, "Talos is as royal as Daedalus and he is more, he is a demigod. Daedalus is fortunate to be allowed to serve him." "What is a ball-and-socket joint?" asked her friends. "An invaluable instrument for making sculpture walk and talk like men," said my sister. The women of Aegeus' household did not quite believe this and rightly, but as the weeks passed they gradually accepted Perdix' evaluation of her son and began to treat me with some disdain. Presently their husbands became mildly insolent and I, at eighteen, did not take even the most veiled insults quietly.

It was all quite gradual. At first Talos would laugh at his mother, then argue with her, then apologize to me for her. I shrugged it off. Then Endoios began to take Talos' side and Laerces to take mine and they would argue together as to which of us was entitled to credit for the compasses, or the tongs, or the saw, or the gold cup I gave to Aegeus or whatever else we had worked on, Talos and I, so harmoniously together. It was all very gradual and we were very young and perhaps it is remarkable that for so long our loyalty to one another withstood this continual whispering, this subtle campaign to antagonize us, which the god had inspired in Perdix. But we grew short-tempered. I would give Laerces the back of my hand for speaking against Talos and he, I daresay, would do the same for Endoios, if Endoios spoke against me. The work began to suffer and each of us refused any share of the blame. Then someone smashed a stone-carving I had spent weeks in shaping and Laerces accused Endoios of doing it deliberately, to please Talos. "It was a rough, awkward thing," said Perdix to my mother, and so it was; it needed much more work on it. "Talos," said Perdix, "would never have left marble so poorly worked."

My mother was angry, but even she had begun to accept Perdix' critical assessments for, as you may have found, anyone who expresses an opinion about an art, continually and at sufficient length, comes to be accepted as a judge of such things. We were gathered together, pecking under the net.

I remembered Lycus' words when he cautioned me that to seek to create angered the gods and I wondered which god had become angry with me.

Talos assured me, and I believe him now, that the breaking of the marble carving was an accident, but he was a little casual about it, too casual. The net completely covered all of us.

One night, near Athena's olive tree by the Erechtheum, the place of our royal serpent, Laerces lost his temper with Endoios and threw him down a flight of steps. Endoios was as lithe as a lizard and not much hurt, but he was a small man, half Laerces' size, and Talos must have thought the attack cowardly. Endoios lay stunned and Talos perhaps though him dead. As for me, I was not even there when it occurred, but came upon Laerces and Talos fighting silently but savagely in the temenos, which in itself was punishable by death. I intervened and received a blow in the belly which laid me next to Endoios and winded me. Trying to breathe, I pulled myself up and went toward them again. The moon came out and I saw them on the edge of the rock itself at a gap in the curtain wall where it was under repair. They were black against the thin light, a clump of struggling limbs. They broke apart and crouched, evenly matched. Both had the same heavy-shouldered, thick-flanked build, both were like young bulls. One, I could not tell which, moved in low. The other hit him on the back of the neck with both hands clasped and then fell backward, his legs pulled out from under him. Clouds shut out the moon. There was no sound except the panting, hissing breath of the antagonists and my own gulping intake, the breath I was trying to regain. Talos crossed Laerces and threw him, unless it went the other way. I could not tell. A body hit the stone. The two figures joined again. I could hear them straining against each other, and the quick stopped gasp, the thick thud of effort. Feet slithered and the smack of flesh on flesh sounded wet, like fat fish slapped on a stone slab. The moon shone suddenly and I could see the single wrenching, swaying mass swing upright and then topple, breaking in two. The figures were separate now and near the very edge of the rock. A hundred feet below, the huts of the thetes crouched against the side of the stronghold. This I could not see but I could picture it. I knew what the fall would mean. "Talos," I shouted, and the cry hurt my guts. Then one figure lifted the other and somersaulted it. It came down on all fours, slithered, scrabbled with its fingers and went over the edge in a shower of loose stones.

The night went black and I heard Talos cry "Laerces" and then nothing. Endoios grunted and began to moan. Talos came up beside me. "He went over," he said, "he went over."

Then there were people coming and going, guards and other men, wakened by Talos' shout or mine or the noise of Laerces falling. Torches flared in various places high in the palace. We went through the wall where Laerces had fallen and crawled down the face of the rock like flies, Endoios moaning until I shut him up. Near the base we came into the scrub. No one saw us. No one seemed to have woken in the huts either. Thetes, men bound to labor for others, sleep heavily. It was dark and silent under the bulk of the citadel except for the sound of the briars tripping and tearing at our shins. It took time to get down to ground level. I recall thinking that Athens was not so impregnable if the guards were so lax. I don't know how long it took to find Laerces, but it was almost dawn when we did.

He had not fallen all the way to the village. He hung on a spur of rock, like Prometheus bound, spreadeagled and looking upward toward the Erechtheum. His eyes were open. He was nearly naked, but not bloody. Only a few scratches, from the pine roots jutting out from the cliff, had marked him. His tattooing, red and blue but black under the moon, made him look at once dressed as a Phrygian dresses, and like a partially skinned lizard. We took him and dragged him into a little cave, a crevice in the rock face, and there we crouched with him while the sun came up and all through the day until it went down again and during all that time none of us spoke much. One was dead and could not. The others had nothing to say, except how Talos must somehow get away.

When it was night again we carried Laerces down and wrapped him in a cloak we stole from a hut. Endoios went in after it. He was small and quick. We wrapped Laerces and bore him out toward Kerameikos, the place for the dead. On the way we talked in whispers, saying enough and only enough to plan what must be said and how Talos must leave. I kissed him and he walked away and I did not see him again for more than fifteen years. He went to our workshop and took his tools, a sword, a little gold and what bronze he could carry and then he went.

The god saw the trap sprung and the partridge bait came chattering and strutting around the net. Next morning she, Perdix, my own sister, came with armed men to our workshop and there she accused me of the murder of Talos, her son. That he was a demigod, it seemed, did not make him an immortal. I had killed him out of envy and there were those who had seen Endoios and myself carrying the body of Talos to the Kerameikos in a sack. What could I say?

"Murderer," screamed the partridge and the guards took me to Aegeus, where he sat in his megaron, and he judged me. Endoios bore partial witness against me and I could not entirely blame him. He was Talos' man and loyal to him and would make his personal demigod neither a murderer nor a victim. He told a long circumstantial tale of the darkness and confusion and how it had been an accident and how Laerces had fled and how he had been compelled to help to carry Talos' body, being too small to fight with me, and so on. As he told it, the whole thing was no one's fault and no one seriously considered pursuing Laerces nor digging up the body of Talos, for this would have been to invite further disaster. It was not for mortal men to disturb the corpse of a possible demigod, even if his entombment had been so hasty and so inadequate. No one pressed for it, not even Perdix. The one factor which would have threatened all our lives was not murder but the act of fighting in the temenos, the sacred place. That was the danger from which Talos fled, not knowing that no one had seen the fight, but only our carrying away of the wrapped body of Laerces. Some god or other guarded us and no one revealed the truth.

Aegeus banished me and exacted all that I had done, all my work and all the materials and tools in the workshop, as a blood tally for Talos. I suppose Perdix got the benefit. It could have been worse. As I went out from Athens, I saw my mother and she smiled at me so that I knew she did not believe the story as Aegeus had heard it. I went down the road toward Sounion, with nothing but a chiton and a pair of sandals to my name, those and my hands and eyes and what I knew I was, even then. I looked back at my mother and she smiled and waved to me as if I had simply gone for an evening stroll. I never saw her again.

Calculated retreat has formed much of the pattern of my life. Sometimes I have made the calculations after the retreat has been forced upon me, sometimes I have calculated the retreat first and chosen the method of withdrawal before I needed to embark on it. Either way, I have spent half my life in flight.

The principal reason for my departure from one place to another has been jealousy. Many have been jealous of my works and this is understandable. Sometimes a tyrant has come to hate me or others have influenced him to do so. False witness has been borne against me frequently. Sometimes with nothing to fear, I have fled from my own fears. At other times I have displeased the many by carrying out exactly what was required of me, when they themselves have failed in foreknowledge of the consequence. Worst of all perhaps, I have carried out, on occasion, more than was required of me, not foreseeing the consequence, and found myself once more in exile. I cannot always let well alone.

When I left Athens on that winter morning, in my nineteenth year, it was my second exile from the same city. I am better equipped to wander than most men. To be *demiorgos* means to work for the people, the people of any deme. One carries one's abilities from place to place and the needs of one people are much like those of another. What they generally lack is not the materials to supply their needs but the means to fabricate serviceable implements for secular or religious purposes.

As I walked toward Sounion, a partridge flew up by the roadside and I hit it with a stone. It was an extraordinary chance shot, one in a thousand, but I brought the bird down. I roasted it there, on a little fire by the road, and ate it, looking out to sea, and I have never enjoyed a meal more.

Sounion is not very far from Athens and my cousin Pallas had his city there, a few miles up the east coast of the promontory and as near as he could comfortably get to his silver mines. Pallas was very rich. His wealth came from silver and he had copper too at his disposal and other metals in his hills. His place, in south Attica, lacked the prestige of Athens and he was dedicated to adjusting this by the splendor of the gifts he made to noble visitors, by making these treasures so rich and notable that they did indeed add to the grandeur of his deme. Nobility and honor were his ruling passions and had he not been at heart a coward, he would doubtless have won even greater renown. It was no surprise to me that he made me welcome, gave me metals in abundance from his storerooms, and anxiously requested me to make marvels as soon as possible. By marvels he meant toys, for he was essentially childish. I made him a life-size silver dog with movable limbs which, after playing with it for several months, he offered to Athena. The goddess accepted it but without, I surmise, much enthusiasm. It was placed in her shrine from which it was eventually stolen.

During my time with Pallas I made various other simple devices for him, to his great delight, which kept him quiet until he had given them away. He did not interfere with me providing I made him toys at frequent intervals from which he could gain prestige. There was nothing interesting about Pallas except his ostentation as a host. As I have said, he was obsessed with the notion of honor. By honor he meant prowess in arms and he had none, but he had the wisdom to see that if you are not physically impressive, nor intelligently devious, nor especially beloved of some god, it is advisable to make the best of what you have before it is taken away from you and to take trouble to see that it is not. Pallas resorted to soothsayers to give him confidence. He was anxious to learn how long he would be allowed to rule in south Attica, while pretending to himself that it would be forever. The soothsayers assured him that it would and in a sense they were right. He died in his bed before anyone could conquer his realm.

In Pallas' house, I was bored but not entirely discontented. I had good employment, respect, renown, and I was generously treated. True, Pallas gave me racehorses and other things of no use to me in order to please me and he expected me continually to produce inventions to delight him in return. Our relations were of course conducted on a lofty plane. Pallas did not reward me for my work as if I were a common man or a mere trader. He made me gifts and I in turn made him gifts. His sense of what was appropriate being limited by his code, he pressed upon me numerous tripods, cauldrons, cups and bowls which are most traditional and honorable as gifts, but almost all of which I could have made better myself. Nor could I melt them down nor remake any of them without offending him. I began to feel myself encumbered with a mass of goods more suited to the house of a resident prince than to the workshop of a transient bronzesmith.

"Take this bowl of silver, of such and such a weight, and rimmed with gold brought by Jason himself from beyond Colchis, the metal from the fleece itself," he would say with great ceremony. "Take it as a gift, Daedalus, for your ancestor Hephaistos himself made it and beat out in the metal the birds and animals which figure it. He it was who gave it to Aphrodite, who gave it to Adonis for love of him, whose blood stained it when Ares, in the form of a boar, slew him on Mount Lebanon. See where the stain discolors the precious surface. It is the blood of Adonis. On Mount Lebanon Cecrops found it and passed it at his death to Pandion, from whom I had it. Take it, Daedalus, that I may honor you."

I would take the thing and thank him with an even longer speech. I would take it to my workshop wondering what to do with yet another tolerable example of Phoenician workmanship which some hero had cut some throat to own and, in due course tiring of it, had given it to Pallas on some honorable occasion. The bloodstain tarnish was real enough.

Within a reasonable period I should tacitly be called upon to go through similar motions. "Pallas, my noble kinsman and host," I should have to say, "I bring you a gift," and then I should be required to make a suitable harangue and he would take my gift and put it happily in his great storehouse. It was a simple way of life between us, but tedious.

Naturally, even I have limitations as an inventor. To content Pallas I should have had to conceive a marvel every month. As a solution I reproduced some of the fabled creations of Hephaistos whom, I may say, I do not for one moment claim as an ancestor. I made models of these toys and made them work, whenever practical. For instance I made one of the three-legged tables, with golden wheels, which would run by themselves to their owner's side when he commanded them, because Hephaistos had had such tables in his workshop. The means I devised was to construct a false wooden floor to occupy the center of the small room where Pallas often rested. This floor I poised delicately upon a central roller so that it seesawed on this pivot no more than an inch, inclining either toward or away from his couch. I then entrusted this device to one of my men who, standing concealed by hangings at the opposite end of the room from the prince, could, with a slender rod, raise or lower the incline. Thus when Pallas called for the table, my servant pulled gently on the rod and the floor inclined sufficiently toward the couch for the table to run smoothly downhill, drawn by its own weight, until it reached the edge of the true floor, where it would stop by his bed. It work equally well the other way. The prince dismissed his table, my servant pushed down on the rod and the table ran back to the wall.

For a while, this simple little trick deceived Pallas and he was delighted when I told him that no one but the owner of the table, the prince himself, could see it run and only when he reclined upon his bed. With anyone else in the room I insisted it would not obey and indeed it would not, for any man's weight on the false floor, apart from disturbing its balance, would have given the game away. Pallas eventually noticed the slight movement of the false floor and I had to soothe him into sharing the joke which he thereafter delighted in playing upon visitors even more simple than he was himself. He would make them stand in the doorway, marveling as he called and dismissed his table. Eventually, of course, Pallas tired of this toy and stored away the table, but when he gave it to Cocalus of Sicily who straightaway took it aboard ship and sailed for home, I have been told it ran so freely about the deck with the movement of the sea that it went overboard whilst Cocalus shouted vainly for its obedience. It was nicely balanced on its three wheels and moved very smoothly because I had placed small sliding weights on a bar beneath the table top to increase its momentum.

My life at this time seemed an interminable monotony. I am no better suited to play the courtier than I am to play the warrior. If I am not to be solitary then I must be among those whose intelligence can stimulate mine. Idle, or occupied with petty matters, I fall into lethargy, grow fat and let my sensuality rule me. For a while I enjoy this as fully as any lord after a good harvest or good plunder, but I am a driven man. I am pricked on by curiosity and by that supreme luxury which outweighs any other, the luxury of the exercise of power. It is because I need to exercise my power that I can bear with those who lack it, whose luxury is conquest, who believe they are in power rather than that it is in them. Such men lay waste the land to prove it theirs. I am not utterly unlike them. I recognize their joy in the acknowledgement of achievement, in the flattery they earn and even in their physical acts which, like the breaking of my mother's ivory pyxis, are a sensual expression of power. But we disdain each other, the warrior princes and I. They, from their molehill fortresses where they can dispense death to their low-born captives, dragged at the horsetail from little skirmishes and the firing of villages, disdain me because they can burn or break what I have made, if they lay hands on it.

I, in my turn, disdain those who have no power to make anything. Yet paradoxically I respond in some degree to praise from these princes and they, whether they admit it or not, are proud to have me among them.

Pallas was in awe of me because I could perform little mechanical tricks for him, Aegeus honored me, and Minos, King of Crete, who above all men was a prince. Minos, who was my one true rival in that lifelong game of power we have both played, Minos I believe loved me. His intelligence fired mine and neither in his house, nor in flight from it, was I in any way idle.

With Pallas I was idle and became rich. I was encumbered with treasures and disdaining them, I still enjoyed their possession.

But for my power, I am no better than the next man. **7**
As to my power, it has become customary to attribute
it to various gods, on the assumption that no ordinary man
exists who proves extraordinary. It will not surprise you to
learn that because I have some reputation I have been given
an ancestry far more splendid than the simple possession of
Erechtheid blood. As I have grown older, my forefathers have
developed by rumor into gods and while I am in no doubt
that gods have manipulated me, I am not so vain as to suppose
that they did so out of family loyalty. I am not, to the best of
my knowledge, related to Athena, who is credited with being
the virgin mother of all mechanical inventions, nor to Hephaistos, the archetypal metalworker. I have followed this god in
his practice, learned from what he achieved and perhaps I
resemble him physically, as those who seek to flatter me have
suggested. I am not, I repeat, a relative of his, nor am I flattered when I am told that we look alike. By report he was
uglier than I am. If it is he who is responsible for my gift, I
am grateful, but he has never shown me any specific sign of his
favor except occasionally to allow some chancy experiment to
succeed where otherwise it might have failed, always suppos-
ing that he actually interceded in the matter.

Apollo is the single god who has given me his serious attention and he, the deity of music and medicine, he whose
maxim is "nothing in excess," has pursued me relentlessly,
demanded more of me and taken more from me than any
other member of his mighty and unruly family. Apollo, it
seems, dislikes metalworkers, for he killed the Cyclopes, but
more than that he is the enemy of the Earth from which I take
all that I make. Apollo attacked her at Delphi and raped her
in her shrine. He destroyed her snake and the blood of the
snake is my blood. He hates the moon, into whose house I
married. He hates me and you will presently learn how he
killed my son, but I have served him more than any other god
in all my life. It is curious, but it may be because he paid more

attention to me than any other god. And so it has also been with Minos, although he never came to hate me. He paid me more attention than any other prince. My vanity makes me smile. It is where I am truly vulnerable. Pride is a wound and vanity is the scab on it. One's life picks at the scab to open that wound again and again. Among men it seldom heals and often grows septic.

Having given me racehorses, tripods, cauldrons and all manner of suitable presents worth so many oxen, Pallas inevitably gave me various women, to him, I suppose, worth so many cows. These I took to bed, as you would expect. Apart from the enjoyment, it is expected of the recipient of gifts to make use of them. These women, who were captured, given, exchanged, conquered and so on, in due course passed into less arduous service in the palace and they are vague memories to me now. They were differently colored, fair or dark, depending upon their origins, and some sought to please while others merely submitted. Prestige, which pleases women as much as men, made some of them regret that they had not been taken by nobles more valiant and virile than I. One, I remember, scorned me because I had no strong instinct to kill other men, calling me unmanly on this count. I have forgotten her name. I have, to tell the truth, forgotten most of their names. Occasionally I remember one or another for the shape of her hips or for some expert caress, but they drift into one another forming a kind of composite experience which serves usefully to provide a variety of stimulating recollections when one is alone and idle. I remember several who taught me their trade, which was their bodies. One I do not forget persuaded me to go with her to Crete.

When I first came to southern Attica, I had thought little of any woman. I had played with women in Athens, for the sake of my vanity and curiosity, but they had not moved me as Talos had moved me nor had they been as Lycus had been to me in Euboea. In all my life men have meant more to me than women, except I suppose for the woman who bore me Icarus and perhaps three others whose grip upon me I shall try to describe in due course. These had some essence of the earth, so that I dreamed of burial in them. Men cannot find that appetite in other men, or at least I cannot.

The quality of earth, like the tidal pull of the moon, swings one downward. That tight yet gaping mouth drags one into the dark. I am aware of the shape of the entrance to that little maze. Who could know it better? Thus those women who remain in my mind when I am wakeful are wound in the earth by the moon. The rest, like Pallas' gifts and pleasure, are toys. They can card and spin strands in my memory when I am drowsy, but the thread unravels into sleep.

I was with Pallas seven years. In the course of that time I trained myself in my practice, learning by trial and error how to do those things which have since made me famous. In silver working especially I made much progress since Pallas had silver in abundance from the mountain behind his palace and copper too. I learned to extract pure metals from sulphide ores by roasting. I learned matting and fire-refining to eliminate the sulphur and the iron from low-grade ores. Tin came overland from the north and was also brought by ship from far to the west by Phoenicians whom Pallas despised as traders, but who taught me much as to the sources of metals and added to the skills I had learned from Dactylos in Euboea. I came to know the effect upon metals of hammering, annealing, oxidation, melting and alloying, of the simple decomposition of ores, their reduction, double decomposition, metathesis and of the miscibility and immiscibility of solutions. I came to know them by instinct, as a good cook comes to know by instinct how to add herbs in proper proportion to a stew or how long it takes to roast meat properly. Metals are perhaps more alarming to those who do not know them than meats because they seem more valuable and more dangerous to manipulate, but although I should not make the fact public for fear of depreciating the public magic of my craft, they are in truth no more remarkable and no more various than foods, if you

52

consider the variety of game and fish. I know, for instance, at what temperature slags will theoretically fuse, at what temperature below that copper, lead and tin will separately melt and I even have some idea of the high heat, above the melting point of slag, at which iron will melt when pure. Much will be made of that fact after my time. Atmospheres differ in oxidizing and reducing and this is almost as important as temperatures because unrestrained temperatures can be a grave disadvantage, producing unexpected changes in materials. All these things I know as I know the movements of my own hands and although you will some of you know innumerable connections between metals and their different structures which are unknown to me, yet it is possible that I possess secrets which you, in your time, might envy me. Do not expect me to reveal them all. It is not the custom among us and by the time I have finished I shall already have revealed much of how we make what we make.

In the seven years I spent with Pallas I learned much and I learned it in solitude. I came to know the friable stones, sandstone and limestone, and how they could be used for carving. I also learned how badly they would weather and how they must be protected if they were to hold their shape. Sandstone is not quite rigid; it will bend fractionally in the block, unlike a stone, and crack and split and powder. It is journeyman stuff, although much in use for building in some places. I learned the different qualities of marble and came to prefer the honey-colored Attic stone to the more celebrated island marbles from Paros and Naxos or the milky stone of Chios. I learned the variations of starring and how under the punch some stones will stun to matt, as their crystalline structure is internally disturbed, and some will sparkle. I learned to choose among woods for carving. I learned the nature of the close-grained fruit-woods and the different purposes to which the pine and the cypress could best be put. I learned where soft woods served better than hard, how to use oil to prevent woods from drying out and how long woods take to season. In all this I was much occupied and Pallas, as time passed, took my presence in his household for granted and left me alone.

Pallas was like a cuttlefish, small and lacking a shell. He would hide from fiercer predators among the rocks of his promontory and occasionally dart out to wrap his soft tentacles around some weaker creature to feed his vanity. Frightened, he would squirt out his wealth like ink and take refuge behind lavish gifts. When in time he came to float belly-upward his remains were devoured by sharks and dogfish. All that was left of him then was a stele, a flat, white, chalky stone shaped like a paddle. Such is the fate of cuttlefish. His tomb was robbed almost before he was cold, and much that was taken from it I had made.

The greatest gift which came to me in his house was not his gift to make. Naucrate came from Crete and was his guest among many who came that year with the Cretan fleet. Her father, an elderly man from Tylissos, in the central province of the island, was too ill to sail further with the fleet and so he and his daughter remained with Pallas who used them first generously and then casually. Naucrate's father presently died and Pallas, remembering vaguely that his guests were subject to Minos and therefore to be treated with judicious ceremony, behaved deferentially toward Naucrate and waited for Minos to reclaim her. No ship came from Crete.

For many weeks Naucrate and her women waited, looking out to sea all day from the rocks above the beach. Pallas lost interest in the high politics surrounding a guest who had so long outstayed her welcome and in time I suppose he forgot who she was. As for me, I watched her from my workshop and she, perhaps because craftsmen were regarded highly in Crete, watched my work from a distance. It passed the time for her when she was not gazing out to sea.

Naucrate seemed made of silver. She seemed to shine in the dark. She seemed unlike any woman I had ever seen. To Pallas she was a handsome girl whose name he could never remember. He confused her with others about his house and came to treat her discourteously, despite the tactful warnings of his more able servants. Then one evening, when he was drunk, he gaped foolishly at her and taking her for an entertainer, called upon her to sing for her supper. Her rage reminded him sharply that the daughters of Cretan noblemen near the king were not chattels to be disposed of by petty tyrants, especially if such daughters are novitiates in the cult of the Mother in her aspect of the Moon. "My name," said Naucrate ominously, "means 'sea power.'"

Pallas thereafter shunned the lady, whose name symbolized the sea power of Crete. Apart from ritual courtesies, not one of his people dared to speak to her. Her loneliness became an agony, and the moon, her mistress, sailed careless of her misery and unresponsive to her entreaties. No ship from Crete put in at Sounion. Naucrate's women and her father's servants dispersed as servants do. Some were given duties in Pallas' household, some stole and fled, some died and were not replaced. Her few slaves merged with those of the palace in that imperceptible fashion which anyone familiar with a great household knows well. Naucrate was too proud to call for redress. She said nothing. Her pride was cold. It broke like ice under the moon's eventual sign and on that night, by chance, I was the only human being within reach of her.

There are occasions, as you know, as you must have seen, when the full moon in all her fat and gleaming pregnancy is suddenly and briefly blotted out by a black and terrible shadow so exactly shaped to her orb that she hangs in the sky as a slender ring of fearful silver spray. When it passes, this transformation does not resemble her normal passage from a slender sickle through fruitfulness into the opposed blade. It is abnormal and unpresaged. She seems to die of cold. Once I have seen this thing happen to Apollo himself. Once I watched his radiance darkened by a similar disk and the world fell into a night at midday.

Waiting for a sign, Naucrate was shown one. The moon was covered as if the thumb of Zeus himself had pressed her into darkness and Naucrate screamed in the courtyard of the palace. Everyone fled from her in terror and hid themselves. Had I not observed such a sign before and found that the world continued unchanged thereafter, I too might have fled. Instead I seized my chance and went to her.

This will not seem remarkable to you, since you no longer recognize the moon's power and do not know the terror of her rule in the empty night, just as you no longer recognize the divine charioteer of the sun. Or perhaps you use different names for what you fear. To us, who are bound to the Mother, the moon is no empty thing and her votaries are not women carelessly to be put on their backs in the warm dark of a palace bed. Her darkness, like her light, can move seas in their beds and it is she who wraps the months around the year and pulls the seasons against Apollo's fiery grip upon the days.

Naucrate, who was silver in the moon's color and whose breasts, jutting from her dress, were marked each with a pale ringed nipple like those pale rings the moon herself discloses when on a clear night she waxes, stared at me in fear and grief. As I saw her then she was not a votary but a votive, an image set in honor of the Mother in the shrine of the night-filled courtyard, a *xoanon* sheathed in the metal of the goddess, so that I closed my eyes and set my fist upon my forehead in reverence.

If she had not sobbed I should have left her and backed away, for my courage ebbed in her presence. There was cold and there was silence and darkness over the silence. But she sobbed and the spell broke. The moon moved out from the fearsome ring and sailed fat into the night and Naucrate wailed like a girl. I saw her face screw up and she bawled like a child whose doll is broken, so that I took my fist from my forehead and put her against my chest and held her there.

When she was fifteen years old, Naucrate gave birth to **8**
my son, whom we called Icarus and whom she dedicated to the moon. His name shows this. She was wrong so to
dedicate him for he grew up to hate the moon and to fear the
dark in which the moon lives and partly from his hatred of
his name I have come to believe he ultimately derived his
death.

I am not sure, I never shall be sure how it all came to be contrived because I am not sure how concerned the gods are with
the behavior of men. In this I am perhaps unusual.

When I took Naucrate, I dared to steal her from the moon
knowing the risk I ran. Pallas was persuaded by his court that I
was a madman and eventually Pallas drove me out. As time
went on he concluded that I had brought his house ill luck
and that my sacrilege menaced his realm, but this did not
occur at once, for several reasons. Firstly, Pallas was incapable
of making up his mind about anything; secondly, he had been
assured by his soothsayers that he was safe in his kingdom; and
thirdly, he was committed to the sky-gods and had himself
abandoned the Mother in his heart. It was a time in which
allegiance was greatly divided. Those who looked to Crete as
the center of their world looked to the Mother whose worship
was the core of Cretan religion. Many mainland kings secretly
wished the overthrow of Crete but lacking any unity among
themselves, they well knew that they lacked the power to challenge Crete in arms. Being male, and believing this to be all
they had in common, they joined only in their new allegiance
to the sky, who we believe is male. Being male they prayed for
the subjection of the female earth. Lacking ships and hating
each other, the little princes left it to the gods to dispose of
Crete, and Poseidon, earth shaker, it seems, listened to them.
Myself, I cannot believe, despite the evidence and the way
that things have gone, that either sky or earth, male or female,
can gain an ultimate victory over each other. They seem to

57

me interdependent. I am, however, aware of the struggle and all my life has been at its mercy, for all my craft.

When I first took Naucrate, Pallas feared Cretan reprisals, but none came. Then typically he became proud of my symbolic conquest of the moon and, absurdly, he showed me great favor, calling it a defeat for the Mother and taking credit for it because it had happened in his house. Then he changed his mind. The reason for this, I discovered, was that Pallas felt the continuing presence of the moon in the sky must mean that the sky-gods were leagued with her or she would have been cast down into the sea. Therefore in challenging the moon, I had rashly thrown out a challenge to the sky in which she moved freely. Therefore the moon was no longer identified with the Mother but, like an Attic prince, had changed sides. Therefore I had flouted the sky. These arguments seemed to me shallow.

Nothing happened. The months rolled on, pulled as usual by the changing but continuing moon, and nothing happened. Nevertheless I became uneasy. Naucrate herself was not. The political implications of her act were not significant to her, nor was she concerned with sky-gods about whom at that time she cared nothing. She went alone at night to worship her goddess, to whom she gave our son, calling him Icarus, since her name for the moon was *Car*. It was all she had to give and I allowed it, but I came to feel that the sun shone differently upon us. I came to feel a malignant heat beat down upon my workshop and upon my shoulders as I worked.

Heat is my most precious tool and heat is Apollo's gift. Heat, in my trade, must be controlled or I cannot practice. I felt my control slipping from me. My work failed, not once but many times, when the temperatures and atmospheres of my kilns would not obey me. I turned from metalwork to stone carving and to building, and apart from jointed wooden dolls I had no tricks to show to Pallas. He lost interest in me. I wasted time and materials and felt the sun burn me dry. Nothing I did succeeded and those about Pallas said that I was cursed. I went from the palace, taking my tools and such metals and other materials as I had, and built a house and workshop on the eastern shore of Attica, below the silver mines. I had no help in this nor any workmen left and I had only Naucrate and our son for company. I melted down Pallas' gifts of tripods and cauldrons. I melted the cup he thought Hephaistos had made and recast it as a votive to the moon. In wax, when I modeled it, I remade Naucrate as I had seen her on the night I took her from the moon and I never made a better image, but the mold burst from abnormal heat and the cast emerged in hopeless fragments, beyond redemption. I made an image of Apollo, remelted the fragments of the moon votive and watched as the pour cooled and contracted so that the metal would not fill the mold. The moon gift refused to be recast in honor of the sun. My craft was thwarted, my skills went for nothing. Earth and sky combined in hatred of me and yet refused each other. All that I had were lumps of unshaped metals, the detritus of power; lumps as ugly as my mother's golden cup and grasshoppers became when they were crumpled between the hands of the Laconian on the day Aegeus took power in Athens.

I melted down every piece of treasure I had had from Pallas, cast the metals into ingots and put them in two baskets. I broke my kilns and let the leather of my bellows perish. I no longer worked in metals even to the extent of casting tools to carve wood and stone, for even these simple things I could no longer make properly. It was a time of shame.

Pallas' men came and burned our house. If I had not hidden the baskets of metal, they would have taken them. It was the spring of my seventh year in southern Attica. I think they would have killed me and taken Naucrate and the child, but the legend of my magic remained to me and of this they were afraid. They did not harm us. That summer we lived in the open, moving between the shore and the hills and moving continually. It was a rich summer; the land and sea fed us. I begged a little and bartered small quantities of metal in the hill villages so that we had a few goats and three donkeys to drive before us. These donkeys carried all I had, my little wealth of metal and my woman and my son. We had no sickness to trouble us except the sickness in my mind with which I tormented myself and my woman. I cannot say it was a hard summer. We ate well enough and Pallas did not pursue or harass us. Probably he forgot.

During the long, hot days of that summer Icarus grew strong, quick in his infant learning and heavy-fleshed. His mother gloried in him and called him "moon ripe," but to me it was the sun who ripened him. I was right although I did not know then how deeply Icarus would come to love the sun. I gave him sea shells to play with and made him little wooden dolls so crudely made that even now I cannot bear to think of them. When he broke them, throwing them down with all his strength from his perch in his mother's lap on the donkey's back, I hated to pick them up and he laughed at me when I crushed them underfoot. Then at the next halt, I would try again to make a respectable toy and fail again and blame Naucrate. She bore with me remarkably. Nothing disturbed her much until she became aware that Icarus feared the dark.

I do not know how we survived the winter. It was mild enough that year but when the fruit was over and the goat's milk ran short, I was afraid. I had come to believe I had lost my power, and despite my weariness of the sun's bludgeoning, I feared the cold would starve us when Apollo went out of the sky. The months to come were those in which Dionysus sat at Delphi and the women ate the king.

We did survive the winter and the next one too, and in the second of those winters my power began to return. In that second winter the cold was terrible. We crouched together in a cave under the eastern slopes of Hymettus and lived because my control of fire came back to me when Apollo had gone into the black clouds for his sojourn in the earth. It was with the earth as hard as stone and the rocks brittle from frost that Daedalus came back into my hands. We had nothing. Donkeys and goats remained to us only in the skins they left to wrap us in. We fed on each animal as it died and used each part of it, bones, sinews and horns, to make the further means to get us food. I brought down birds with a bow strung with the tendons of our goat, whose milk had fattened Icarus.

Naucrate did not seem to feel the cold unduly. She called it the moon's temper and treated it lightly. Icarus was so swaddled in skins that he stayed warm. As for me, I was chilled all that bleak winter, but I had Apollo off my back and was grateful for that. In the second spring of our poverty we found a boat from Crete pulled high up the beach, south of Marathon, and bought our passage on it with the last of all my metal, the gold from the rim of the bowl Hephaistos had not made, but which Pallas had given me.

We paid our passage but I also worked it and I began my work before we rolled the vessel down the beach. She was a *triakonter*, carvel built, ram-bowed, a fighting ship worn and patched as a battle shield and as shapely. Though she lay beached and beaten, her belly scarred and partly stove, she yet reared up her prow and stern like the flexed sinews of a sword arm. Her black prow stared with the great eyes painted on her. Stranded, she was unsubmissive.

I knew nothing of ships beyond the little sailing craft which fish the inshore waters and cling close to the sight of land. Certainly I knew nothing of the build of fighting ships, oared galleys rowed by thirty men, but carpentry is a logical practice and to repair a boat one needs only to know what strains her timbers must bear. In case such matters are unfamiliar to you, poplar and fir are the best woods for shipbuilding. Timbers are shaped with the adze and bent by heating over steaming caldrons. The planks are joined to transverse frames and drilled for pegging. The pegs we call *harmoniae* and it is the sea which makes the harmony for it makes wood swell and hold the pegs in place. I learned shipbuilding, or the rudiments of it, in the days I worked to repair that *triakonter*. My skill, springing back into my fingers, went far to counteract my ignorance.

She was long and slender, that strong vessel, too slender to be stable in a heavy sea, captious to handle as a high-strung mare. Her keel ran curving up to meet the converging of her sides and ended fiercely in a bronze-sheathed beak, below her glaring eyes. Above this ram her bows swept smoothly to the vertical, rising to a short forecastle which reached to the forward rowing bench. The rowers, two abreast, one to each oar, ranged down fifteen benches in her belly, open to the sky, and abaft this her stern stood high above the oar bank and was decked. Under this little deck Naucrate and Icarus could shelter among the meager stores, and on it sat the *keleustes* who kept the rhythm of the rowers constant with even strokes upon his drum. Behind him stood the helmsman, master of the ship, who guided her with two great steering oars.

She carried a single mast, set two-fifths of her length from the bow and on this mast a single, square and shallow sail could be set. I judged this sail of little use in any but a fair wind and even before we embarked I had designed another smaller sail to be set on a second mast raking over the steam and the design of it I scratched on a flat pebble with the point of a knife.

The purpose of this subsidiary sail, I explained to the master, would be to give stability to the vessel and prove useful in an emergency such as the disabling of several oars. He stared at me as if I were a dolt and walked away. I had forgotten that the reputation of Daedalus once stood high among landsmen, at least in Attica, but had not then reached beyond the seas. I had also forgotten that my reputation no longer stood so high even in Attica, until I looked down at the filthy skins in which I was dressed and glancing up, saw Naucrate smiling at me with a touch of malice. I grinned at her, feeling a fool, but I was not such a clown as those seamen may have thought me. Within a decade no Cretan galley sailed out of Amnisos without that second sail rigged on a second mast, raked over the stem.

Twenty days after I had paid our passage we sailed, if **9** that is the term to be used. In fact we rowed and it was backbreaking labor that dragged those first days out from Attica. If my arms and shoulders, which were always powerful, eventually developed the strength to sustain me in flight, I first advanced them toward that pitch behind an oar. Icarus, who came in time to hold a power far greater than I upon his back, sat in the stern and played with sea shells.

Icarus, in that spring, was three years old and I watched in vain for any dexterity in his movements. He was quick and strong but he was clumsy, and clumsy he remained during all his short life. In the large movements of his body he was able enough. Even at that age he would lift weights greater than seemed possible for such a stripling. His chest swelled like a bird's breast and his shoulders were thick and supple. He had the makings of an athlete, but his hands lacked delicacy and his handling, even of his sea-shell toys, lacked precision. What he touched he broke.

I do not think I was an easy father for Icarus to have. I watched him too closely, hoping passionately to find in him my own particular virtues and have him surpass me in them. I was hard on him, trying to make him in my image when I should have known that the image he would make would be his own. I never understood him while he lived. Perhaps it was not possible. Only his death explained the nature of his life.

How much does a man make his own son? How much does he show himself to his child? Did he in his infancy, when I had lived in despair believing my powers drained out of me, sense my mortality, my inferiority to a god, and despise me even then? And when I was myself again and gave him reason to be proud of me among men, why did he never show me cause to be proud of him until he died? Why did he break what he touched? I never knew him. Perhaps when I have written all this out I shall understand where I failed. Sometimes I think nothing I could have been or could have done would have altered him.

"He will be a great warrior," said Naucrate proudly, and I could do nothing but agree with her. I foresaw him growing up to strutting manhood, covered with the blood of those he had killed and boasting of his prowess.

The sailors made a pet of Icarus on that voyage. One man in particular, whose name was Tros and who called himself a Hyperborean, sat next to me on the rowing bench and wooed Icarus to sit upon his shoulders as we rowed. Tros was a large man with thick gold hair like curling wires and great gray eyes so widely spaced that his glance seemed unconcentrated, often blank. I feared him, but Icarus bestrode his shoulders, drummed his heels on Tros' great chest and twined his fingers in that thick gold hair, which made Tros laugh. And when the wind blew steadily and we were under sail, Tros would make toy weapons for Icarus out of fragments of driftwood, beautifully spliced together. His hands were hard as bone, but he could knot a fishnet with the speed of a seamstress.

Tros committed two wanton acts on that voyage which, looking back, I take for omens which I failed to read. In both he was concerned with Icarus and these happenings, although they seemed minor savageries at the time, returned to plague me. Tros was no ordinary brute, his ferocity lay below a solemn calm, and he sheathed himself remotely from companionable men. He did not join the talk of the other oarsmen or compare his weapons or his prowess with theirs. Once we had landed in Crete he was not seen again and no one could say what became of him.

This Tros held aloof from all men but with Icarus he played like a boy with a puppy. Icarus had his treasures and among them was the shell of a chambered nautilus, a grave and harmonious object figured with a rippling red on its white surface which patterned the convolutions of a ram's horn, although the nautilus was shaped to a perfection beyond any horn. This shell I found on the beach and gave to Icarus, showing him how, if he held it to his ear, he could hear the sound of the sea in it. This delighted him and even on our voyage, with the sea itself beating against the ship, he would hold it to his ear and say that he could hear two seas at once.

I do not know what made me try to explain the beauty of the nautilus to Icarus. Perhaps it was merely to hear myself talk, to break the monotony of our passage. "It is a miracle, that shell," I said to him and he held it up to me proudly. "That shell," I said, "holds in its spiral the law of number, the geometry of perfection. It holds *ananke*, the order beyond order, the order even the gods cannot disturb." It was a foolish piece of rhetoric to voice to a child of three and he put the shell to his ear, as he always did, and took no notice of my speech. Tros did. His great gray eyes went blank. "The shell of night," he said, "each chamber holds the night, the cups of dark, each holds a smaller night."

Icarus stared up at him and Tros stared down at Icarus. "The center of the shell, the smallest night. The curling tip holds fast the smallest night." He seemed to be speaking in ritual, chanting nasally like a priest. His face was shut smooth. "In the center of the shell, the night is closed against the morning, forever closed against the morning." This he said quietly, conversationally, and then he shut his eyes. He took the shell gently from Icarus, raised it above his head and smashed it with all his strength against his oar. The splintered shards burst from his hand and sprayed into the air.

Icarus laughed and shouted to see the shards fly shining in the sun but I cried out involuntarily at the sacrilege, at the brute breaking. I saw each private place made bleakly public, each curving hold blank open as the eyes of Tros.

Tros brought his hand down again, bleeding, upon the oar, unclasped his fingers and stared into the ruins of the shell. In the center of his palm the final chamber was unbroken, the tight curled tip still held the last small darkness. Icarus stared owlishly into that bleeding palm and carefully took out the piece of shell intact. "Why did you break my shell?" he said.

Tros brought his heavy gold head laboriously round to look at me. Then stupid as a dazed animal he shifted it to look at Icarus. "Why did you break my nautilus?" said Icarus clutching the little center of the shell. Tros said nothing. At that moment the wind dropped, the sail flapped empty and the *keleustes* began to beat out the rhythm of the stroke. We bent to rowing.

The episode passed and Icarus quickly forgot it, or I assumed he did. He was a little silent for a day or two and stayed more with his mother. But the sun shone and the ship moved bravely toward Crete and Icarus returned to sit between Tros and myself on the rowing bench.

Every night whenever possible we put in at islands and took on food and water. Wherever we landed we were welcomed. The Cretan power was recognized among all the islands and we went ashore under the aegis of that power. The rowers carried arms, bronze swords and javelins. They wore motley pieces of armor to show that they were warriors.

Tros kept himself apart. He never drank with the crew nor went after women with them and I, to whom the islands were unfamiliar, would also leave the men when my absence would not be noticed and go looking for the marble quarries or try to discover what metals were present in the hills. Also, I sought out craftsmen and watched them work. Sometimes I would see Tros in the distance, armed with a bow, and once I came upon him making a lyre from the shell of a tortoise he had found. He did not bring the instrument aboard when he returned.

In all these islands the Mother was supreme and Naucrate, even in her rags, was recognized for what she was. At Syphnos she was clothed in Cretan dress by village women and I, her consort, was treated with a certain respect. I, too, was given clothes. Island courtesy was very different from mainland manners. Our years of poverty in Attica seemed very remote and so did the time before that, the years spent in the little kingdoms of my squabbling family.

66

South of Naxos, Tros committed his second barbarity. It was strangely like the first, yet it was different. The two episodes were connected, but I did not know that then. Near the islands great flocks of seabirds would follow us, scavenging for food. These birds would wheel and scream about us as we rowed and Icarus would reach out, hoping to touch one as it flashed past him. Birds made him gay. He loved to see the pigeons, bred in Crete, which the helmsman would release from time to time to take a bearing. When one leaped clattering from its basket and darted south, Icarus would wave his arms and cheer it on and all the crew would join the cheering. All flight delighted him. All flying things or any object tossed high in the air, which spun or glittered in its fall, delighted him. Once fallen he would let it lie and walk away from it. When I had taken him with me as a baby, in the hungry days, and hunted birds to eat, he would crow to see them fall transfixed by the arrow, but when he could walk and we searched for birds I had brought down in the long grass, or among the rocks, he would not pick them up. I do not think that this was because they were dead. I do not think he made that connection. He would stroke their breasts before Naucrate plucked them for cooking, but he would not touch them when he had seen them fall. Death and food were not connected in his mind then. Flight and fall were, but not fall and death.

That morning out of Naxos, he reached to touch a small dark-feathered bird, a shearwater darting low over his head. It veered from him. Tros moved one hand from his oar, never breaking the rhythm of his stroke, and caught the bird above his head. He moved so fast I never saw him move, but his hand closed over it and crushed it in mid-air. Over his head he held it, at arm's length, his fist clenched with its thin wings stuck askew between his fingers, like a brittle clutch of broken oars, and the beak pointed over his thumb like a little metal ram. The bird did not twitch or flap in that vise. Only the pinion tips flickered in the wind. The blood squeezed out between his fingers and Tros lowered his fist and held it out to

67

Icarus. Then he flung the body high in the air and watched it spin pinwheel into the sea. Icarus stared at it in the sea and watched it spread out and float away. An oar struck it and it sank. The eyes of Tros were quite blank. Icarus put his head down in my lap.

It was odd but neither Tros nor I broke the rhythm of our rowing. The drum kept us unfaltering. The beats were regular and unchanging in their pace.

I expect men to destroy. It is an instinct few of us lack. Cruelty is a game and I have seen men do worse things to animals and to each other than crush out their lives with one quick grip. We can forget the pain of others as, fortunately, we quickly forget our own. The killing of the shearwater remains vivid to me because this savage sleight of hand was unnatural, the speed of it was inhuman. Also, the trick was aimed at Icarus and performed for him. It was not like the trick the Thracian oarsman of the third bench liked to demonstrate: he would kill a dog with his teeth to amuse the crew.

When we sighted Crete it was late summer. Half a day's rowing out from Amnisos we saw more shipping than I had seen in a month below Athens and in a greater variety of shapes than I had ever seen.

As we rowed in I saw that our own vessel was unusual; it was a fighting ship while those about the port were built to carry cargo. They were in general broader and heavier in the water, with more deck space, and they rolled like oxen compared to our greyhound speed.

I had imagined that Minos protected himself with a great fleet of warships but he had no need to do so. No one menaced Crete and we, as I discovered, had sailed in one of no more than a dozen watchdog vessels whose task it was to deal with occasional raiders from the islands. I discovered also that the master of our vessel was not above raiding on his own behalf and that, to a man like myself brought up on the mainland, was what I would have expected. I was amazed that raiding was not the general profession of Cretan sailors; I was amazed to be shown commerce for the first time.

At Amnisos we did not beach our ship and this too amazed me. We sailed into a vast harbor, as congested as a palace on a feast day, and tied up at a stone dock among a hundred broad-beamed boats which jostled for position. Nosed in to the quay, we walked ashore down a plank of wood.

It is ridiculous, after all these years, to think how strange I felt. Icarus and I stood gazing at the turmoil and when Icarus saw a black man and asked if he was real, I replied that I could not be sure. The noise too was new to us, not because it was so loud but because it was dense and unremitting. We had heard at home the rattle of the market, the festival chanting of our own people gathered, the riot of troops, the lowing and lumbering of herds and the wild cries of pain and triumph in war, but the port of Amnisos breathed with a thunderous murmur of talk and it was a great hive hum like a giant swarming of bees. This ceaseless roaring undertone was pricked with the high shouts of porters clearing a way for themselves, but even these sounds were not alarming.

All this great mass of people, all these ships were gathered for a purpose which Aegeus in Athens, or Pallas at Sounion, would have regarded as disgraceful. What we were seeing was not compatible with Attic honor nor did it play any role in the little game of plunder and conquest by which those stunted principalities lived. We were looking, Icarus and I, at trade. Neither of us had ever witnessed it before, on any scale.

On the quay and in the streets behind the harbor, were piled bales and crates a tithe of which would have burst open the walls of Pallas' storerooms or swamped Lycus' treasury. The property my kinsmen fought over and intrigued to gain was no more to Crete than the shell-counters on a children's gaming board or than a handful of knucklebones. Into the port of Amnisos sailed ships from Egypt loaded with stones of every color and every degree of hardness, ships from the Copper Island heavy with ingots and ships from the continent in the east beyond it, loaded not only with gold and tin and more silver than Pallas had in his whole mountain, but such materials as amber, feldspar and lapis, materials so rare in Greece that often they lay virgin in the treasuries because no one was trusted to work them. In time I should come to count these fabled substances as the normal currency and raw materials of my trade and have them in whatever supply I asked. Then, I could not believe so much wealth of stones and metals existed in all the world; nor had I ever seen so many manufactured things together.

You will laugh when I tell you that I saw unloaded, from a ship put in from Byblos, a pile of rolls of a thin white, brittle, stiffened cloth made, I was told, from reeds compressed under water, and I did not know what they were. It was papyrus, which you would call paper, and men drew and wrote on it. At that time I did not know men wrote except on clay or drew except on stone. You would have laughed to see me gape as childishly as Icarus. On that first day in Amnisos, Icarus and I were much of an age. As much was new to me as to him. Naucrate laughed at both of us.

"Where are the warriors?" I asked her. "What is this throng of people doing? Where do they come from?"

"Is that black man real?" said Icarus and both of us looked to Naucrate for the answer to that.

"There are warriors," she said, pointing to two armed men, armed in so far as they carried long bronze rapiers. They wore little else but loinguards and tall headdresses.

"Where are their helmets and their shields?" I said. "How can they protect themselves naked?"

"They do not need to here."

"Not need to?"

"Why is that man all black?" said Icarus.

"He comes from beyond Egypt," said Naucrate, "where all men are black."

"Why?"

"They are black because they are black."

I found that hard to believe, but it was true. I had much to learn in this place.

"Where is the king?" I asked.

"At Knossos."

"Should we go to him? We have no gifts. Will he enslave us?" I asked a hundred such questions and Naucrate patiently answered them. In due course we set off up the road to Knossos, pushing our way among men of many races, avoiding oxcarts and pack animals, moving aside for horse-drawn chariots driven by nearly naked young men and litters containing old ones. I think I saw more kinds and shapes of people on that morning than I had ever seen before. I think at Amnisos I saw more people in one place than I had ever seen before. They frightened Icarus, who cried. As for Naucrate, she walked ahead of us and as she walked her carriage subtly changed. She seemed to throw off the habit of toil. Gradually she stiffened, throwing her shoulders back like a woman carrying water on her head, but different from that, not with the quick hip-swinging, short-stepping motion of a woman carrying a jar in this way. She walked with a long, measured stride and for a time held her arms away from her sides, her hands level with her shoulders, palms inward, like a sculptured figure. Her movement became hieratic and people moved aside for her. We no longer had to push through the crowd. It fell back, murmuring.

We must have been a strange sight. Naucrate was in Cretan dress, but salt-stained and shabby. Her hair had not been dressed according to her rank in four years. And I, carrying Icarus mother-naked, was bearded, shaggy and burnt almost as black as the man from beyond Egypt. Also we were filthy and I was armed like a raider. Even as they made way for us, certain of the more elegant among them wrinkled their noses and looked wary.

It was a long, sweaty pull up the dusty road to Knossos. The landscape, as we passed, was populous and cultivated, so richly tilled that the corn stood thick as though it were already bread and the foliage of fruit-trees lay heavy as a deep, still sea suspended over the earth. It was a landscape which had not been fought over in ten generations. There were no ruined huts; none of the rotten teeth of burned-out buildings stuck up through the dry grass, as you see them everywhere in Attica. The great brindled, golden rocks shouldering above the valley looked edible in themselves, softly crisp as honeycomb. The very dust was new-ground flour, the hills wore fertile woven cloaks, a heavy dark green warp crossed by a pale weft of the silver-foliaged olive. Athena, born from the head of Cretan Zeus, had sewn his birthplace olives wide and if the grape was Dionysus' gift, he too had been prodigal with his vines in Crete.

"I am very hungry," said Icarus. Naucrate in her priestess homecoming did not turn her head. I was surprised at this. "The child is hungry," I said, "and so am I."

"Time enough," she replied shortly.

"They are late with harvest."

"It is the second."

I dropped back and walked behind her again, wondering to myself why a man, why I, should accept such brusqueness from a woman. But I did. Naucrate was changed.

"Why won't she give us food?" asked Icarus peevishly. He too was not used to a Cretan woman on Crete and he was nervous of his mother in her new role.

"Soon, soon," I said to comfort him, and put him astride my shoulders. He always liked to ride high. Figs hung from a tree within his reach and as we passed he pulled one off in each hand and for a time they quieted him.

Travelers' tales can be wearying and in any case it is so long since the palace of Minos was a new marvel to me that it would best be described by someone more recently come to it. I will say only that it was big, bigger than any complex of buildings I had ever seen or have ever seen since. Every hall and chamber of state in it is plastered with gypsum and painted with scenes of ritual or diversion, or with gardens, or with strange animals. Every floor is laid with colored stones set in simple patterns and bedded in red or white plaster. It was this method of mosaic which I exploited when I laid out the dancing floor for Ariadne, but I elaborated the technique. However, that was five years later.

At Knossos the ceremonial is as elaborate as the palace. Every person there performs a certain task in a certain manner and does not vary the sequence nor even the physical movements long established in carrying out his task. These rituals and the solemn pace at which all activity proceeded in the palace became evident to me even before we arrived on that first evening. Hot and foul-smelling we sweated up the hill and I, expecting to see an acropolis bearing great fortifications saw no such thing. There was no rocky hill. There was no towered gateway. There were no fortifications, but so vast was the building that what I had taken to be the rock upon which a citadel is generally set proved to be buildings clustering about the ground floors of the palace.

No one halted us. No guards came forward to interfere with us from among the horde of people who moved slowly about the vast paved courtyards. There was none of the stench, the thronging, greasy spearmen, the rooting pigs or flapping geese to be kicked out of one's path, which make the entrance to an Erechtheid city a lively place. There was no dust, no smoke from cooling cauldrons, no offal on the ground, no snapping dogs to fight over it, no screaming children nor distracted mothers calling after them. All sound was muted and those who paced gravely down the great steps or across the terrace at their summit moved processionally like trained dancers.

Naucrate's hieratic movements, which had seemed so strange to us on the road, now fitted with the pattern of the place and those who walked there knew by her movements that she was at home in it. Despite our disheveled appearance, despite my loutish shambling as I walked behind her, dragging

73

the weary and protesting Icarus along, no one was so discourteous as to interrupt Naucrate's stately progress. They looked at her and averted their eyes from her undesirable retinue. She walked majestically up the steps and entered the building as if she had been absent for several hours rather than several years. We followed her through halls and corridors to which the light penetrated because at intervals there were courtyards surrounded by balconies and open to the sky. This device, the light-well, is a familiar one in Cretan palace architecture. I had never seen it before.

We followed Naucrate up flights of steps and down ramps, moving in her wake as if we were rowing boats tied to the stern of a royal barge, until she came to a halt in the doorway of a small room filled to capacity with women. They were massed and moving with the abrupt rapidity of birds and making the sort of twittering sounds appropriate to an aviary, so that the contrast between their fluttering and the tall sleepwalkers who moved in the public parts of the palace would have been unnerving had not Naucrate's entrance produced a silence and a suspension of movement more unnerving still. She stood in the doorway for a moment, holding her puppet priestess pose and then her shoulders dropped and she burst into tears. The tumult was resumed, redoubled. The bright birds flew to welcome her in a wild flurry until she subsided slowly under the weight of their clamorous affection. Icarus and I stood outside.

"Where are we?" asked Icarus.

"Knossos," I replied absently.

"I want to go back to the boat," said Icarus, tugging at my hand. But the female flood flowed over us at the very moment when Icarus demonstrated his anxiety by watering the elegantly patterned floor. He was instantly gathered up in a smother of flounced skirts and borne off in one direction while I, enveloped in a nest of swan's-neck arms and bouncing breasts, was hustled away in another. I saw Icarus' face, aghast at the indignity, peering from among this flock of self-appointed nurses and then he was gone, wailing, to be bathed, scented, fed, rested, dressed and comforted all at once. That was my fate too and if Icarus found it embarrassing, I enjoyed it greatly.

Among the various interwoven and mutually dependent cults of the Mother to which the ladies of the court at Knossos are dedicated, the cult of the moon is paramount. These mysteries are all intermingled and all intricately conjoined. All have their special symbols, the tree, the snake, the pillar, the bee and various other plants and animals and each of these sisterhoods is subtly competitive. The moon however is supreme and the double axe which symbolizes many things, both male and female, but which is the paramount Cretan sign, represents in its two curved-edged blades the passage of the moon from her sickle-edge announcing the new month, through fullness, to the obverse curve of her waning.

Cretan religion is, however, sophisticated, complex and flexible. The admission of Zeus to the older order was simplified by his courtesy in having elected to be born in a cave on Mount Dikte. The double axe was adapted to him, as his *labrys*, without detracting from its original meaning. It was set up in his shrine and presumably the Mother accepted the compromise. Such arrangements are perfectly possible if enough time is spent on them and the Cretan kingdoms, undisturbed for generations by the need to protect themselves from marauders, had time enough to spend. Theology is the pastime and the ruling passion of the Cretan mind. Nowhere have the divine forces been so cunningly reconciled to one another as in Crete, and nowhere are the superficial caprices of the gods better understood. The price of this concentration upon minute distinctions of ritual and the absorption of the entire court in endless discussion of these niceties is not immediately apparent, but it is a heavy one. Crete is losing her vitality and her arts show it. She is gradually absorbing her own core by continually abrading it with intensive self-examination. The most delicately adjusted balance of flatteries is directed toward every aspect of the deities. The gods, being impatient by nature, grow weary of this soothing game and become restless even if they are sometimes slow to show it.

From my point of view the peculiarities of the Cretan cult of the moon were singularly fortunate. In Crete the moon is no virgin and Artemis, who comes more frigidly to power abroad, demands no personal chastity from her Cretan votaries. Therefore Icarus and I were accepted as Naucrate's possessions and in her homecoming the fact that she had acquired us was not thought disreputable. Cold as the rituals may appear in public, the private life in Crete is warm enough. Furthermore, Naucrate, although born at Tylissos, had become initiate at Knossos and was, to my surprise, regarded as especially favored by the goddess.

No one interfered with my predilections at Knossos. The bland courtesy which the court had shown us on our arrival when, on the first day, Icarus and I had trailed after Naucrate into the palace, was calmly maintained. Should I wish to spend my time in workshops and give my attention to such things as metal casting, that eccentricity was accepted however odd it seemed to many that I took no part in interminable discussions as to Brito's exact rank as mistress of the animals in view of Poseidon's hegemony over horses and Zeus' identification with the bull.

Icarus grew up at Knossos and so in many ways did I. What I had learned from Dactylos in Euboea and from my own experience elsewhere, I joined to what I came to learn in Crete, and there the continual insecurity of my youth eventually proved valuable because my familiarity with violence and change made me continually wary. Cretans, who know nothing of either, are rarely self-reliant. They have never needed to be.

Nowhere I have ever been harbors such a concentration of master craftsmen as there are at Knossos. A quarter of the great palace is given up to them and many others have their shops in the town below. Nor have I ever found elsewhere such a perfection of achievement in the minor skills.

I shall not pretend that I came to match these masters, except in bronze casting. My goldwork and my ivory carving look rude compared to theirs. Those skills require a patience which I lack. Where I surpassed them was in invention and in flexibility. Cretans cannot improvise and their curiosity extends only toward the strangeness of things imported from Egypt and the eastern continent. So many curious treasures reach Crete from abroad that her craftsmen are continually occupied with modifying and adapting foreign luxuries to Cretan taste. That they can take the most exotic jewel from the very edge of the world as a model and transform it into something instantly recognizable as Cretan is a remarkable achievement but not to me an adequate way of spending a lifetime. They are also rigid in their acceptance of convention. As their fathers and grandfathers worked, so they work. They adventure in their methods exactly as far and no farther than their theological sanctions permit, for Cretan craftsmen are as obsessed with these matters as Cretan courtiers. In consequence, when I studied their works, of which they reverently preserved ancient examples, I found that the urgent potency of the antique prototypes had gradually dispersed and where a golden flower smaller than a thumbnail had once burst sap-filled upward, like the force of summer, it now drooped succulent and heavy from its gold-wire stem.

Above all, the Cretans excel in the miniature and in an effeminate delicacy of execution. The male vigor of bronze sculpture defeats them and their votive bronzes lack all tension; they look as soft or as stringy as vegetables. Nor can the Cretans make large sculpture in wood or stone. They can bring the surface of a material to a marvelous smooth perfection but they cannot give dignity to the larger forms and they whittle away the strength of a figure in the pursuit of comeliness. Their arts hang overripe from their minds or go dry like pomegranates whose skins in time reach the brittleness of fine Cretan pottery and crack untouched. The gods will burst out through Crete and spill their red pomegranate seeds on Knossos and Knossos will rot under this autumn weight. I know this. I have seen it begin.

While Icarus and I lived at Knossos I spent my time in one workshop or another and remained an Athenian, but Icarus became a Cretan. He grew up smooth, golden and supple. What of me there was in him seemed concentrated in his chest and shoulders which were, to Cretan eyes, uncouthly powerful. Below, his waist was as narrow and elegant as any bull-leaper and his legs were long and slender as saplings. He played among princes, performed the intricate rites expected of him by his mother and gradually both of them drifted imperceptibly away from me; or it could have been that I, taken up with technicalities which had no significance for Icarus and were to Naucrate the mere fabrication of the implements of ritual, drifted away from them. To both of them my activities seemed insignificant.

I was, now that I look back on it, slightly absurd to everyone at Knossos except the king. The craftsmen found me frivolous. My apparent inability to concentrate my whole life upon a single task made me so and in this judgment they were as shortsighted as I was myself because, as I have discovered, I have in truth given my whole life to making labyrinths. They could not know that then and nor did I, although Minos, the king, knew it from the moment I was presented to him. That prescience was typical of Minos, even if it may be of little use to him in the end.

A Cretan craftsman gives up his life to the perfection of a single intricacy. There was one, a man of incredible skill, whose granulation of gold I have never seen surpassed. It was so exact and so minute that it could only properly be seen when studied under a ground crystal lens and there was an-

78

other man whose forty years had all been spent in grinding crystal lenses, without which the goldsmith would have been unable to see his own work clearly. These two men worked next door to one another and had done so since they were children. They drank together and worshipped together. Their children played together and they greatly respected one another. Neither was interested in the other's craft except from mutual need. That I should try to learn both their trades seemed to each of them impertinent. My father had practiced neither. They were sure of that.

The crystal grinder made lenses by which goldsmiths could work and ground ornamental crystals for jewelry. Painters on ivory used these crystals to magnify their work and mounted their tiny pictures under crystal to enlarge them. The crystal grinder could achieve a magnification to the power of ten, but it did not occur to him that by concentrating the sun's rays through such a crystal a man could light a fire. It did to me and I have carried a ground crystal ever since on a thong about my neck.

In one section of the craftsmen's quarters lived men who ground hard stones for seals. Cretans love seals and each wears one or more about his person, engraved with images relevant to his family, or his pursuits, or his religious partialities. The craftsmen who ground the seal-stones did not engrave images upon them. Others did that and did nothing else, while among those who ground the stones a man who shaped lentoids would not have dreamed of making cylinders. Every man had his separate skill and was content with it. I was not. I should have run mad in a year, to be so specialized.

Being so diverse in my concerns, the craftsmen did not take me seriously as a rival and, as I say, found me frivolous. So did the warriors and the priesthood, the palace officials and those innumerable functionaries whose administrative ability, each in his specific field, maintained the kingdom and deployed its wealth.

Being neither a native-born Cretan, nor a priest, nor a warrior, nor a functionary, I could afford to be absurd providing I did not antagonize any particular section of society. I might easily have done so and found myself once more in exile, but it so happened that Minos did not find me absurd and I came to occupy a place under his aegis where my eccentricity was privileged. It came to be viewed as similar to the mandate extended to clowns, dwarfs, racehorses and well-bred hunting dogs. But this is hindsight and I must return to my first months at Knossos and my first sight of Minos.

Minos, of the line of kings called Minos, which goes back into an age before men spoke Greek, stems from Zeus and Europa and his blood is god's blood. At a point in time, a Minos refused to die on the proper occasion and a resolution or adjustment of this conflict was appropriately contrived in the Cretan fashion: the Mother accepted Zeus as co-regent just as she had permitted his birth in her dark stone womb on Dikte. Minos thus became the incarnate Zeus on Crete and for some time thereafter surrogates died regularly for him. Or so I have been given to understand with a wealth of unmemorable, circumstantial detail. Now Minos as earth's co-regent stands also as the sun in co-regency with the moon and the moon, as Pasiphaë, Minos marries. Minos represents the bull and Pasiphaë the cow, a fact which led the queen into her madness for which I came later to suffer, since the sun couples with the moon in those forms in Cretan theology. The identification of the bull with the sun is, needless to say, not acceptable to Apollo, who despises the moon as an aspect of the Mother and hates all the earth but Delos for denying his own mother a birthplace. Thus Apollo, who overthrew the earth at Delphi, and rides in the sun, rejects Minos as the bull even though Minos descends from Zeus who, like so many gods, has a bull form and is himself the father of Apollo.

The Cretans read all these matters differently and I, having failed to pay proper attention to the complexities of rival doctrines, moved carelessly deeper into the trap which gods prepare for men, or at least for men like myself who are too care-less of protocol.

Dactylos, who took that name from the Dactyls who came to Crete even before Zeus and who worked in metals there for Rhea, would never have moved so blindly toward destruction as I did. He was a cautious man and would have seen to it that he escaped the attention of so heterodox a lord as Minos and one with so many divine enemies. I should have listened more carefully to Dactylos, or pressed him to speak further, but I was young then.

Pasiphaë, the queen, was descended from Helios, whom Apollo had thrown from the sun, and from the nymph Crete, whose name means "ruling goddess." This ancestry did not endear her to Apollo, who liked neither Helios nor any god-dess to rule. Apollo contrives the destruction of Crete itself and he will succeed, if I know anything about him. My own life has been a little episode in his plan and I have been his puppet, Cretan or not.

Cretan ceremonial is a movement of puppets, a dolldance in the greatest dollshouse on earth and there are many who par-ticipate who may, for all I know, be dolls, but Minos was not one of them. Enthroned, armored in gold, buttressed by for-malities so fixed in their order that even his movements were stylized as puppets' movements are, Minos spoke in formulae, as he was called upon formally to respond to formal phrases. Thus, when I stood before him in his throne room, his actions and his speech were mechanical, regulated by the traditional stereotypes of speech and action ossified by endless usage. Priests and courtiers followed prescribed movements, passing ritual objects to and fro, each according to his station.

Minos accepted my reverence. As he spoke, his eyes looked into mine and held me. I had never seen such eyes. He con-templated me for a moment and then the occasion moved laboriously to a close. I was conducted from his presence.

Nothing followed for three days. On the fourth, I was sum-moned again and shown once more the extraordinary contrast

between public and private life in the palace. I was taken to
him by Naucrate and found him alone but for a few servants,
in a small courtyard, its wall painted with frescoes of a boar
hunt. Minos wore nothing but a loinguard; even his hair was
unbound. He kissed Naucrate on the cheek and took both my
hands in his as if I were his brother.

Minos was a small man, compactly built and thicker in the
waist than most Cretans. He had the look of one who keeps his
shape by the attention of others, by massage and a careful
watch upon his diet. Also, he gave the impression of finding
kingship a burden. I did not feel that he enjoyed his state but
rather that he accepted the life decreed for him as one who,
never having known freedom, has yet learned of its existence
and lost the tranquillity of ignorance. He moved about the
sunlit courtyard as if he were caged and yet as if he would fear
to leave his cage. His eyes were black and compelling but
curiously opaque as if their depths were clouded. He would,
when he was not pacing restlessly, seat himself and remain
motionless for moments together, his eyes wide open but
somehow shuttered by a hard and glistening film which barred
the world's entry but allowed him limitless sight. When he
looked directly at me, he shackled my glance and held me in a
translucent chancery so that I felt like a fly in amber.

"I have heard from Naucrate that you are royal and that you
possess extraordinary skills," he said, his voice retaining a trace
of the chanting monotony of the throne room. "Here in Crete
we have no men like you, we are too old, too set in our ways.
We are dying here in Crete." A moment of his enclosed
meditation came upon him then and he looked old and dying,
as if to suit his words. "Crete is a jeweled bone," he said, "a
pair of gilded horns set in a skull—and I am Crete. There are
things which must be done here and you must do them. You
are a builder; you must build. The Earth Shaker rocks us."
Again he paused and I waited. Naucrate moved slightly and
the little bells sewn to her skirt tinkled. In that silence they
sounded like the clash of arms. Minos glanced up and smiled

at her. "Bulls," he said, "and cows, moving without minds in this ancient pasturage; we are a cattle kingdom. What shall we do in the coming drought?" He looked at me and again locked me in his look. "I have had you watched these many months and know how you have spent your time. I do not find it odd as do those who reported on your movements. I do not even find it as strange as Naucrate finds it. When she lived with you across the sea, she was a wild calf. She has re-joined the herd and forgotten the thin fodder you found among the rocks." He beckoned to her and she sat at his feet, in a jangle of bells and bracelets. She put her head against his knee and he stroked her hair. "I know," he went on, "much that passes overseas. I know what brews in Attica and in the country of Pelops. I know the movements of peoples to the edge of the world in the north and in the east. I am a bull better informed than most but," he said smiling, "I am not so well endowed with the other attributes of bulls as were my forbears."

I wondered why he should tell me this on so brief an acquaintance.

"I tell you because I have a task for you," he said, as if I had asked him a question. "Also, since you are a stranger here and reveal nothing of yourself to my servants except the peculiarity of your concern with techniques, no one would believe you if you were to speak of what I am saying to you. No one would believe I should have anything to say to you."

"What would you have me do?" I asked.

"You will build beneath this palace a place so deep, so tortuous beyond its entry, so convoluted in its winding passages, that no one but you and I will know the way to its center. You will build a labyrinth. That is the central purpose of your life. Master of many crafts you may be, but finally you will discover that all your life you have been a maze maker. I set you your first maze to make. You, who have wandered all your life, shall construct a wandering place and when it is done you will take Minos to its center."

It was only when I had left him that I realized I had not asked him the purpose of this maze.

It did not occur to me to disobey him, although I speculated deeply on the nature of the task he had given me. For weeks I explored the foundations of the palace, the innumerable magazines ranged with *pithoi* filled with oil and wine, the cellars crowded with gifts made to former kings and long forgotten, the great stores of grain, the armories stacked with weapons unused for decades, the deep shrines piled with votives left by long-dead votaries. At last, with seven hundred laborers I began to build the labyrinth at Knossos.

No group of men knew what their fellow laborers were doing nor where the passages they tunneled below the palace led. The whole force I divided into fourteen sections and trained an overseer for each. These companies I kept apart, unknown to each other. Some dug, some built great walls, for I encompassed in my scheme the whole existing plan of rooms and passages which lay beneath the palace. I sealed off storerooms from the outside world and connected them through the ground with new vaulted passages. I made false trails that led nowhere and tunnels that doubled back upon themselves to end at blank walls. As I obeyed Minos, so his servants obeyed me, without question.

The task took fifteen years and in all that time I kept the pattern of the maze in my mind. No one knew its plan except Minos and myself. Often in all that time I saw the king, sometimes in the grave processionals of his public life, sometimes alone. He never questioned my progress nor volunteered the reason for my task. I never brought myself to ask him.

As time went on we grew closer to one another. In his lonely authority my own singularity appealed to him and I in turn found my will bound by his. He was the only king that I have ever known who seemed to me a king and not a man covered with panoply, for all that he was more set about with the impedimenta of power and the trappings of ceremony than any other king in my experience. In private, despite his melancholy and his trance-like withdrawals into silence, he was wryly humorous and disarmingly cynical. "Bulls," he once said to me, "are creatures with one set purpose in life and I envy them for it. To be a symbolic bull, as I am, is a role better suited to a simpler man with fewer purposes and none of those clearly set. I must also admit that it is many years since I could act out the role with any degree of singleminded enthusiasm. When I was young I rutted with the best. To name a few, I lay with Paria, whose sons colonized Paros, with Androgeneia, with Britomartis of Gortyna, whose absurd belief that she was mistress of the animals caused me to share her bed with some noisome and painful household pets, with Procris about whom some strange tales are told and with more moon priestesses, whose very names I cannot remember, than would be expected of any but Zeus himself. Had I not done so I should have lost my reputation and you know where worn-out bulls go. They go under the knife or jog their final years away being leaped over by apprentice acrobats. As it is, I have preserved the myth of my potency by all sorts of shifts and I believe my forefathers, all of whom died young of exhaustion from their genuine exertions, did not maintain a greater fertility in Crete than I have done."

"My respect for you is unwavering," I said.

"That is the primary necessity of kingship," said Minos. "The others are guile, foresight and to preserve the myth. I am glad, Daedalus, that you came." He looked at me quizzically as if sharing a secret, but I was none the wiser at that time. I can be very obtuse.

"There is only one person, or I should say goddess, in this land who knows the failure of this sacred bull."

"One?"

"Yes, one."

This could only mean Pasiphaë. I had seen her in public and it would have been better for me had I never been sent to meet her in private.

85

When I say that I spent fifteen years in digging the **12** maze of Minos, I do not mean that burrowing was all I did. I am not a troglodyte, although there are times when tunneling or moving through existing tunnels has seemed my principal function.

Minos did not hurry me. He was no despot so far as I was concerned. Rather he showed me favor but equally he was careful to be circumspect in his generous treatment of me. He allowed me a small workshop in the palace and then a larger one, but not one so large as to provoke comment or envy. Gently and without ostentation I found myself established as a master craftsman at Knossos, well provided with materials and with apprentices, so that when I was not supervising the digging, I practiced my several crafts without interference and with excellent patronage. I was accepted by those who worked for Minos and I was careful to give no cause for jealousy. There was very little ill-feeling among us because there was work enough to content even the most ambitious native Cretan and besides there were already many foreigners at Knossos and little restriction was placed upon their activities.

With the greatest care I kept my urge to experiment within bounds. Nevertheless, it became known that I was impatient of the narrow conventions imposed by the Cretans themselves upon their crafts and gradually the more gifted and restless of the young men came to me as pupils. Two especially dreamed of making sculpture of a kind and on a scale never produced in Crete. These two, Dipoinos and Skyllis, were inseparable and both were remarkably gifted. Dipoinos had been employed in the shop of a fresco painter since his childhood, and had acquired the greatest skill in modeling the stucco reliefs with which Cretan painters build up the forms beneath their paintings. This technique of high, painted relief is greatly favored in Crete. It is as near to large sculpture as they generally allow themselves to get.

Skyllis was first trained as a wood and ivory carver. It was

86

understandable that his resentment of the miniatures his master forced him to carve made him impatient. He was gifted enough. It was simply that he had no great talent for elegant little treasures and yearned only to carve great monumental figures like those he had heard were made in Egypt. Both Dipoinos and Skyllis were obsessed with the idea of Egypt and to them everything grand, daring and inventive was Egyptian. When they first came to my workshop and lingered there, pretending, as young men do, that they had no great desire to remain but had merely been passing the place, they talked to each other of their plans to work their passage on some trading vessel and sail to Pharos, where real sculptors lived. They were very respectful to me because, even if I was not an Egyptian, I was at least a foreigner. And gradually—everything on Crete is gradual—they came to spend their time with me and each neglected his established calling. Eventually, with many protestations and apologies made to their masters, who expressed themselves well rid of such undisciplined assistants, I took them into my shop and Dipoinos and Skyllis became my men. Together we produced the first Cretan monumental sculpture, the figure of Brito holding twin serpents, which stands in the sanctuary near the queen's megaron.

This figure was an amalgam, a *xoanon* sheathed in a variety of different materials. Skyllis and I carved the head and arms of fruitwoods, making each part separately. The body, Dipoinos and Skyllis made by gluing planks of olivewood together until there was bulk enough to carve the torso from them. The legs, hidden by the skirt, were not carved, for we made a great cone of wood by the same method, which was pegged into the torso. Face, breasts, shoulders and arms Skyllis covered with thin plates of ivory, riveted to the wood, as was the jacket of the figure which was made of thin gold sheets, adorned with panels of lapis. The headdress was carved in one piece with the head and plated with gold inlaid with electrum and niello. The tresses of the hair and its sacral knot we cast in bronze and burnished. The eyes were inlaid with shell and onyx and the lips with copper. The skirt and belt were bronze plated and the flounces of the skirt were made from thin bronze sheet cut, pleated and riveted to the wooden cone.

It was, I must say, a most spectacular image and no less than seven feet high. People came from as far off as Phaistos to see it and the queen pronounced it not only noble but a work of deep piety which made Dipoinos, who was a cynical worldling, laugh whenever he thought of it. That the figure was so large outraged conservative opinion; that it was so highly decorative and indeed gaudy, pleased the general Cretan taste. Cretans love brightly colored things, especially if they are made of rare materials. As I say, the queen was much impressed and it was this figure which caused her to send for me and entrust me with the secret work which set in train all that followed and led me to my self-imprisonment and exile.

Having accomplished the large figure of Brito, nothing would content Dipoinos and Skyllis until they had learned to carve in hard stone, for this, to them, was to be truly Egyptian. They pestered me daily with talk of basalt, porphyry, marble and even granite, of which no example I have seen has been satisfactorily worked. Dipoinos insisted that its shaping had long been perfected in Egypt. Perhaps he is right.

Now the Cretans are adept as carvers of hard stones on a small scale. Their rhytons imitating conch shells and lion heads are beautifully made and ground with marvelous patience, but no Cretan has, to my knowledge, attempted a lifesized marble figure until Dipoinos and Skyllis did so. This they did not do on Crete but at Sicyon in the northern Peloponnese where they went after they left me, or rather after I had undertaken the secret work for the queen, in final consequence of which I had been myself removed from them.

In Sicyon, I have been told, they were treated badly and went on to Aetolia, whereupon the Sicyonians were plagued by famine, barrenness and other calamities. The elders of Sicyon sent to Delphi to the Pythia and through her Apollo instructed them to recall Dipoinos and Skyllis so that they could finish the statues in marble of Apollo, Artemis, Heracles and Athena, which they had begun.

I am proud of this story. It shows how high in reputation my pupils have become and that although I taught them only the rudiments of marble carving while they were with me at Knossos, they so far persevered as to obtain the approval of Apollo himself. I am by no means certain that I can say as much. He does not seem to approve of me; but then again he may have preferred Dipoinos and Skyllis as part of his relentless persecution of me. If he did so to make me jealous, he has failed.

There are works by Dipoinos and Skyllis at Ambrakia, Argos and Kleonai, and I have heard that the marble of Paros, which I trained them to carve, has remained their favorite stone. Whether or not they ever reached Egypt, as they so fervently wished, and came to grips with hard stones there, I do not know. They are brave and stalwart and hard-working lads. I wish them well. Skyllis' mother came from Gortyna in the south of the island and had very beautiful buttocks. I wish her well too.

During these years, when I was hard at work in the various ways I have described, I saw less and less of **13** Naucrate and I suppose it was unkind of me that I failed to notice the lack. She withdrew into her mystery and became, as she grew more the priestess, less the wife. Then again she was, by birth, close to the throne and that is a position I find difficult to sustain. My thoughts wander when I am among aristocrats whose main concern is their aristocracy. Religion, too, tends to take me unawares, so far as the monotonous observation of rituals is concerned. It lulls me and I find myself thinking of practical matters. It is not, you understand, that I am impious. I am fully aware of the power of the gods and few have more reason to be. It is simply that I seek to serve them more directly than do those who chant and mumble for them. Naucrate took to chanting and mumbling endlessly, which gained her considerable prestige at court, but wearied me personally.

When I think of her, I feel a certain guilt in my neglect and remember how hardy and admirable she had been in the lean years after Icarus was born. I owed her much. She brought me to Crete by sea, and that her name means "sea power" seems to me very fitting. I hope she is content in her dedication to the moon. When I look into the night sky I remember her with gratitude but she was a trial to live with when she became fully initiate. After a while I took to sleeping in my workshop and she in turn vanished permanently into the horde of women, just as she had vanished briefly on our first day at the palace. In time I saw her only as one of the many painted and superbly dressed ministrants at the shrine to which she was dedicated.

Naucrate grew away from me and Icarus grew up. In doing so he too grew away from me and in my concentration upon matters in hand, I did not notice how much he had grown up and how remote he had become from me, until it was too late. I loved him and upon those I love I suppose I make too few demands. I expected him to love me and asked no proof of it. I showed him no special sign of my love because I felt, and felt wrongly, that he understood its depth and permanence. If he had shown any aptitude for any one of my trades, or any versatility, or any interest in techniques, I imagine we should have been drawn close to one another, but so far as I could tell he grew into a young man interested in the fashionable ways of young men. He became a notable athlete, was admired as a hunter, became proficient in the use of weapons and in sailing small boats about the coast. In a warlike society he would have made a notable warrior, but on Crete he had no one much to fight, except in mock combat. I dutifully attended when he showed off his strength and prowess by severely bruising his contemporaries, but I fear I could not find the enthusiasm for these martial games which he wanted me to show.

I have not been adequate as a husband nor as a father, but then I do not really understand priestesses nor, until my son was dead, did I come to understand the strange nature of heroic aspiration. I am a technician not a hero. The two do not mix.

After several millennia, the abrasive of time which can grind men into archetypes has made me that. I am not unlike the product of the absurd Cretan practice of grinding out of marble a complex sea shell so exact in its verisimilitude that it looks perfectly like a sea shell. It takes a man half a decade to imitate this object which he could as well find on the sea bed for the price of a little diving. Archetype or not, I am no hero. That was my son's chosen role and he played it fully with a proper degree of foolishness mixed with glory.

Heroes are disguised as men until their heroism is revealed. This was one reason why I failed to understand my son; that and his clumsy hands. You will understand how difficult I found that to tolerate. Also he was a fool. That was, of course, inevitable in a hero. Also he was exclusively concerned with himself. That, too, is inevitable in a hero although not always apparent. He preferred posthumous honors to any sensible achievement and he pays for them by remaining a celebrated shadow whose one splendid moment is his monument.

I see that I run on, writing too much of Icarus before it is time, but I cannot help remembering how, in those years at Knossos, Dipoinos and Skyllis were nearer to me than my own son. The contrast comes back to me between Skyllis' slender, flexible hands, which could hold and carve a flake of ivory as fragile as a petal and Icarus whose hands could have crushed the club of Heracles himself, but who could rarely hold a cup without dropping it. Then I can see in my mind Dipoinos' strong, slim shoulders, as he bends over the marble, patiently smoothing it with pumice; and the shoulders of Icarus, thrown back, impatient, holding a fully-armed man above his head. He was forever throwing someone or dropping something, breaking both. Surely it was natural that Dipoinos and Skyllis

91

were more like sons to me than Icarus, at least until I was tested?

Icarus was always in combat, with other young men, with bulls, with horses, with himself, and I, heedless, remained in combat with intractable substances and difficult materials. I love order and measured harmony. The proper conquest is to me the conquest implicit in the making of a satisfactory image or a tool which suits its function. I need no other power. Icarus needed power and although I am proud, his pride eclipsed mine. He was, as I say, a fool. He never became a man although he became an immortal. I do not think he ever discovered who he was. He was disorderly. It was doubtless his careless contempt for order which estranged us; his compulsion toward discord. He resented me, but then he resented everything, even his god, and that resentment is the ichor of the hero. I wish I had grasped this and yet I do not know what I could have done to assuage it.

In those years at Knossos we went our separate ways.

Pasiphaë sent for me in secret. I received her summons at moonrise from a cloaked figure who brought me, as a gift from the queen, a double axe of gold signifying the moon's full month. I took it that she required a month's work from me and I assumed that such a month would have to begin at moonrise despite the fact that I was in bed at the time. There is no end to the petty irritations the great can inflict on one.

I dressed and went with the cloaked figure through the palace, following a roundabout route through cellars and storerooms. It took half an hour to traverse the distance when, had we gone directly, it would have taken ten minutes. We went the darkest way and in the dark I stubbed my bare toe and had to hobble like a mating partridge. At the entrance to the queen's megaron, the cloaked figure departed and I limped into the room. There were guards there dressed in white, the livery of Tauros, and they loomed out of the half-light like stone carvings.

I have not yet spoken of Tauros but then, until that night I had not been concerned with any of the great except the king. Tauros was the king's general and although I did not then know it, he was also the royal surrogate committed to die in place of Minos at the appropriate time. He was a huge man, almost a giant and in appearance, the pattern of the warrior hero. It seemed perfectly possible that he had actually fought in wars at some time or other, although scarcely on Crete. He came from somewhere in the east although he was of Cretan blood. All that I knew of him was that no one would contest with him in the games; he was reputed too formidable. I did not believe we should find we had much in common.

Tauros always wore white, a white loinguard and belt, white sandals and a white cloak. His complicated headdress was of ivory and the large white feathers which have to be imported from Egypt. His dagger hilt and sheath were also of ivory. Unlike a Cretan, his skin too was white and he never went naked in the sun for long if he could help it. He had a bodyguard, also dressed in white which contrived to make them look curiously sheepish, like a flock of armed rams.

Tauros was there, in the queen's megaron, with his bodyguard, standing before the round hearth. I looked at him across the little fire that burned there, and behind him I could just see the queen enthroned. There was no light except from the fire. At the queen's feet, on a little stool, sat Ariadne, her daughter.

Pasiphaë, unlike Minos and contrary to the general practice at Knossos, conducted a private audience with as much ceremonial as a public one. In her megaron, the walls were painted in deep blue and decorated with shoals of dolphins. There she shone dimly like milk at the bottom of a dark jar and seemed as remote as the moon, but then, to be sure, she was the moon incarnate. She did not let one forget it. On the other hand,

93

despite her elaborate formality, she was not immediately impressive. She looked like a cow, a beautiful cow but a cow, and of course that too was proper. She was the cow of cows. Her great dark eyes were wide and placid, her big breasts looked milk-filled and she rested as motionless as a handsome ruminant in a field of deep grass. I almost thought, as she contemplated me, that if I went toward her she would slowly lumber to her feet and shy off in the way cows do when one walks too near them. I almost thought she might be chewing cud and looked away for fear of seeing the slow champing of her lovely jaws. It would have embarrassed me.

Tauros snorted like a bull. It was a habit he had. I switched my gaze from the floor and looked at him living up to his name, a veritable white bull.

"The white bull," he said, unexpectedly. I should think I too looked vacant, drop-jawed, when he said that. The whole roomful of us must have looked like a herd of cattle.

"The white bull contains the god himself in his epiphany. Zeus inhabits him."

I thought he must be describing Minos, the bull of Crete, but why white? Minos was not white, he was golden and dressed in earth-red and gold for preference. I waited.

"In the Messara, with the royal herd," said Tauros impatiently, "there is a great bull, greater, more noble than any natural creature. No one knows where he has come from. He joined the herd five days ago. He is the god himself."

I could not begin to see what this piece of information, true or false, had to do with me, nor why I had been got out of bed to learn it. I said nothing.

"He will not mate in the herd," said Tauros. "The cows offer themselves. He rides none of them."

Stock breeding is an interesting study, but no concern of mine. I wondered foolishly what semi-divine heifer would drop from a cow mated with a divine bull and my glance was automatically drawn to Ariadne. She, of course, would be as near as one could come to imagining such a calving.

"So?" I said.

Tauros snorted again. I thought at any moment he would paw the ground. He looked ridiculous, however formidable, in his pomposity.

"This man understands nothing," he said, turning to the queen.

Pasiphaë shut her eyes and opened them again. She stared at me and her stare caught and held me as immediately and as unbreakably as that of Minos. Both the king and queen could turn one to stone when they cared to. Her eyes, like his, were black and opaque in their depths. Like his, they seemed shuttered until she looked at one and then the glistening film moved and drew one into those depths, drowning the clear function of one's mind.

I heard Tauros speaking in the distance, something about the fertility of the Cretan herds, something about the ritual mating of the sun and moon. He droned on about the symbolic act. Pasiphaë, who said nothing, gave no indication that a symbolic act counted in this mating. Although I could see nothing but her eyes, I knew her whole body shook and her thighs parted. Her tongue flicked across her lips. I felt her heat and scented her. I am sure Tauros explained everything necessary but I did not take in what he said until he began to talk about carpentry. Pasiphaë closed her eyes.

"Of cowhide on a wicker frame," Tauros went on, "the queen will enter it and the herd will be driven to the field. The white bull will come to her there." I then knew perfectly well what I had to make in the month I had for making it.

I looked vaguely at Tauros and then again at Ariadne, who was hunched, crouched low on her little stool and trembling. Pasiphaë had not moved. Her eyes remained shut.

"The month, the solstice, the waxed moon . . ." Tauros talked on.

"I know what I have to do," I said.

I did not know what it would mean to me to do it and how

my own life would be changed. I simply knew I had no alternative. I had to make the thing.

I had one month in which to make a false and hollow cow so perfect that a god would mount her, a cow in travesty ample to contain the queen of Crete. It was not as if I had no other work on hand. Furthermore, I should have to do the job alone. I should never dare to speak of the project, let alone employ others upon it.

Any cunning and sensible man would have somehow avoided the task or waited, hoping the white bull would vanish as gods can. Not I. I am Daedalus, the master obsessed with techniques. I thought of nothing but the technical challenge. Before I had left the queen's apartments I had begun, in my mind, to select materials, consider stresses, calculate the weight of bull which a cow must carry on her pelvis and what resistance to his driving loins must be borne by the structure. There is a singular obtuseness in being a Daedalus.

The next day I apportioned all my other work to trusted men, gave instructions to the overseers of the maze-digging and set my pupils to complete tasks I should otherwise have finished myself. Then I went out of the palace to a disused building far beyond the city to the south. I went by oxcart and carried with me my tools, a load of various woods, lye to bleach hides, salt for tanning, soft leather, oil for working leather, reeds and withies for basket making, horsehair, fine sand, glue and cauldrons for boiling it and for other purposes, four small wheels, dyes, gold leaf, copper rivets and nails. I forget what else.

On my way, people greeted me. No one was surprised to see me pass with my load. Oxcarts in Crete are often drawn by cows. Mine was drawn by two of them and if there were any comments among those I passed on the road, they may have touched upon the exceptional beauty of the two cows I had chosen to pull my cart.

Arrived at my temporary workshop, my cow factory, I slaughtered both beasts, naming them sacrificed to Poseidon with all appropriate formalities. Then I prepared their hides, working them to the necessary softness. I boiled the carcasses, to separate the meat from the bones, until I had the bones clean and white and these I put to dry in the sun. I needed the skull and horns, the vertebrae with attached ribs, the scapulae and the pelvis of one cow. The other's bones were reserved against faulty workmanship or accident.

The story of the cow for Pasiphaë has been told and retold since those days and with ever-increasing inaccuracy. They say I made it of cowhide on a wicker frame, as Tauros proposed, and mounted it on a wheeled platform. It is typical of the sort of tale that is told of me in that it is partly true, but ignores the mechanics of the problem. I did use cowhides, the two hides tailored together from the cows that drew my cart, but the cutting, sewing, padding and general contrivance of this covering was no simple matter of stretching a single skin over a wicker frame. It was not a brute bull I had to delude, but a god. In the retelling of the story even the identity of the god varies. Some say he was Poseidon, others Zeus. I am not sure, but tend to believe he was Poseidon, if only because I cannot believe Tauros could have been right.

No wicker frame would have stood the pounding of a rampant bull when all the power of his hind legs was braced to drive him home. The whole contrivance would have crumpled up. I had to build a frame of hardwood, cypress in fact, a frame splayed outward and braced to make a flattened pyramid of the four legs. I watched the normal mating in the royal herd to know the exact attitude taken by a cow before she is mounted. It is curiously compressed and cramped. The head is thrust forward to the full extent of the neck, all four legs are thrust rigidly apart to take the strain; the back is arched abnormally, the tail upthrust. To fix such a structure to a wheeled platform would be absurd. It would slide away at the first buck of the male. It is true I made such a platform to trundle the cow to the mating place, but we removed it before the white bull came anywhere near.

97

I built the frame of hardwood and braced the hind legs and the spine with bronze. Below this strengthened spine I suspended a great belly made from the ribs of both my cows buttressed with plaited withies and padded with packed horsehair mixed with chaff. I attached the shoulder-blade bones to the hardwood spine and also used the pelvis of one cow, set in thick layers of soft leather, to cushion it. The elongated neck, the udders and other soft parts, I built up in leather and gut, filling the pouched skin with fine sand to give it body. The head I modeled on the skull of one of the cows in clay and coated all with a slow-drying glue which would remain soft under the hide. As the hide dried and shrank it would hold all together compactly. In the breast I left an opening for the queen's breathing, disguising this with flaps of skin where a cow's throat hangs loose.

When this was all completed, there was room in the belly for a woman to kneel crouched uncomfortably. Even queens must suffer occasionally if their pleasures are recondite. She would have to climb into the trunk as it lay on its back, spread her legs and have them cushioned to withstand the brunt she would bear between them. She would have to be sewn in and then the whole structure be raised, turned over and set upon its braced legs. The hooves had bronze spikes driven through them to strike into the earth and hold them from sliding along the ground at the moment of impact.

When this was done I stretched the hide over the whole skeleton of bronze and wood and leather and molded it, kneading it into the glue and modeling it like wax while it was still pliable.

The horns I covered with gold leaf, set eyes of shell and steatite in the sockets of the skull, filled the milk bag with sand and attended to the delicate details of the vital vent, against which the queen's hunger would rest, with the thinnest and most supple skin taken from a newborn lamb. The queen herself I knew would provide the scented lure toward that lamb skin.

All done, I dyed the whole sweet creature red and groomed her coat until it shone. All that I had worked with, save my tools and some bronze and gold leaf, I replaced in the cart. The cart I burned in the courtyard and the smoke of this burning, watched from the palace, was the signal that my work was finished. I had spent exactly one month at the task and pale in the afternoon sky the moon lay like a little pool of milk.

In the evening they came. The priestesses of the **15**
Mother, Tauros and his white retinue, the queen in
her litter, with Ariadne, robed as her priestess, walking by its side. There were musicians with flutes, lyres and sistrums, conches and bull's horns. The women carried garlands as if the cortege were visiting a shrine.

Tauros and his men waited in the courtyard by the smoking ashes of my burnt cart. Inside the building the women reverently raised the queen from her litter. She was flushed, breathing like a woman in a deep sleep, but her eyes were wide open, staring at nothing. They disrobed her and she stood naked and white as cream. They lifted her and laid her in the cow and spread her open. That I, a man, should have been present was only permitted because I had made her bovine bed and was needed to bed her in it. No one spoke, no one regarded me. I was not to them a man watching a naked queen; I was no more than a sexless ministrant performing an ordained rite. But I was a man. When I looked down on Pasiphaë and saw her hunger laid tight against the soft opening in my effigy, I rose hard as a man and shook so that my hands could scarcely arrange even the slight comfort of padding I had prepared for her hips. I fumbled the laces which wrapped the lips of the hide across the belly. In time it was done and together her attendants turned the false cow over and set it on its legs on the wheeled platform. Then to the great noise of the music, Pasiphaë, the moon's earth cow, was

99

trundled, garlanded with flowers, into the plain and the herd of the cattle of Minos fled from her, only to turn and return, as cattle will when human beings come among them. We took her from her wheels and rolled the wheels away. We set her on spiked hooves in the grass.

Poseidon, in bull form, came as night fell, snorting and tossing his great white head. Tauros, standing next to me, snorted in chorus with his superior, but briefly and sounding nothing like a bull. That habit of his seldom made less dramatic hearing. The plain was bleached under the moon and in the black cup of the surrounding mountains, the ground shone like water. On the hillside where we stood, no one stirred. Even Tauros did not dare to snort. The bull came on, trotting slowly, white as a salt pan, head up, his horn-spread swinging. He was tapered from his shoulders, which moved under the mass of his crest like an ocean swell. This silver mountain held the great head high; behind it he fined down greyhound slim and looked not like the heavy, sullen bulls that boys leap in the palace court, but like the boys themselves, slender and strong as spears. He scented her and his own spear slid out, obsidian black. Then from Pasiphaë, bound into her cow, there came a strange long lowing, a note sustained beyond endurance; the cry of the moon herself entreating the earth to breed on her. The god came at her, rose above her, poised like a breaker and fell forward with the weight of the sea. He roared. The male shout, god brazen, thundered down on her female keening and blended into it. Home to his hilt, he struck into her like the blows of an axe and as I watched fearfully the double-braced forelegs of my effigy cracked and gave at the knees. Riven, they folded inward and her outstretched head drove into the earth, breaking at the neck. Still he beat upon her. The liquids of his flood splashed back across his straddled hocks, spuming and drenching his hooves. Then it was over.

I thought, without thinking, that I should have bronze-braced the forelegs and bound the knees with wire. That was the first thought I had. The bull drew off, pouring from his slackening sword. The cow remained stiff as broken sculpture embedded in the ground.

Tauros was gasping and snorting again. I looked at him and saw him clutching at his kilt. Then I felt my own legs wet and as I did so I saw the whole solemn, sacred procession of priestesses, soldiers and musicians running wildly away among the rocks, stumbling, dropping their arms, their instruments, their garlands, flapping and skittering away into the darkness toward the city. Then clouds passed across the moon and the darkness closed out all but Tauros, crouched with his hands in his groin, and Ariadne, sniffling, lowing, vacant as a new-born calf.

She alone went down toward the herd and vanished into the dark. I could not see what she did there, but presently I saw fire and saw my broken cow shrivel and fall in a cloud of sparks. The herd stampeded away, rumbling across the plain. Of the white bull and of the queen and her daughter I saw nothing more.

In the palace the word spread. At once, as news always does, it became distorted. Eye-witnesses swore Tauros was the white bull and had raped the queen. Others would have it that Dionysus had made all drunk and in bull form had passed into Tauros and sent him rutting mad. Tauros was given blame by some and jealous praise by others. I was blamed for contriving the circumstances of the act and by some for instigating it. Being a foreigner I was thought capable of anything, the overthrow of Crete, the destruction of the royal house, anything. Tolerance of foreigners is great in Crete but naturally they must expect trouble in times of crisis. I took refuge among the diggers of the maze, which did me little good. Within a few days word penetrated even to the labyrinth and the hostility of the diggers became uncomfortably apparent.

16

Wherever I may be, I am habitually prepared to leave quickly. What I should need in tools, metals, food and the usual necessities, if escape should be prudent, I always keep ready.

I told only Skyllis and Dipoinos that I must go into hiding. I should have told Icarus and even thought of asking him to come with me, but he was hunting ibex with his companions in the hills to the west and could not be found. Skyllis believed I should be safe in the south of the island and assured me that his mother would take me in. We left by oxcart, six days after the event which caused my leaving, and went south into the Messara, past the building where I had made the cow, and the place where the cow had burned. We did not hurry.

"Was she injured?" asked Skyllis, frowning at the oxen and urging them forward.

"Injured?"

"The queen, was she hurt? How did she survive?"

Had she survived? Until that moment I had not thought about it. In my alarm I had not thought clearly of anything except my own skin.

"I don't know," I said.

"The palace is divided. There are those who say the act was a criminal sacrilege, and others who say the god was in the bull and all Crete will prosper from his seed spilt in the queen."

That was the dispute which had given me time to leave unmolested.

"The king...?" I asked.

"No one knows."

As we trudged on, leading the oxen and making no great pace, I hoped I would not be recognized in my shabby working clothes and I was fortunate. No one looked twice at us and no armed men pursued us.

To this day I do not know what happened to Pasiphaë in the immediate aftermath of her mating with the bull. I often find it difficult to believe I witnessed it or played any part in it.

102

It took three days to reach Gortyna and half another to reach Skyllis' mother's house. It stood by itself and she lived alone in it on the produce of a patch of vegetables, some geese, some goats and a dozen olive trees. I had been in many equally well-hidden forest huts in the days when Naucrate carried Icarus and we escaped from Pallas. We had felt safe in them and I felt safe in this one.

Skyllis stayed three days and then left me, taking the oxcart. He and Cameira, his mother, spoke little to each other while he was there and Cameira asked no questions, being content with his presence and taking mine for granted, as if she housed fugitives regularly. They made no mention of her husband. I never learned how he had died.

The name Cameira means "the sharer out" and no woman was better named. She shared her house, her food and her bed with me, putting no limit on her hospitality. What can I say of her? I have her in my heart. I remained with her eleven months, working in her garden, hunting small game, doing my best to be useful. I repaired her cooking pot, mended her furniture and was happy whenever I forgot to be afraid. When I remembered, I kept watch from among the boulders on the hill and there, to pass the time, I watched the hawks flying, until gradually I found a pattern, a key to the labyrinth of the sky through which these birds wandered with such ease. I learned how they rode the wind and that the currents of the upper air, invisible yet palpable, seemed different in breadth and depth from those encountered near the ground. It seemed to me that the hawks were schooled in the knowledge of a sky-maze in motion and that once they gained the heights, they were carried about in it, without effort, wherever they wished. Up there, their movements looked lazy.

I was not so ingenuous as to believe that no power was needed to gain those heights nor that heavy weather would be easy to fly through. I had seen what it was like when birds beat upwind on gusty days. I also realized that to move in the element of air and be sustained by it required a special structure,

103

a skeleton and musculature essentially different from our own. I built models, cut up dead birds to compare the interleaving of their sinews, and the weight and proportion of their thin and hollow bones with human anatomy. I caught a young kestrel and hawked it on a long twine until it broke loose. Then I contrived a curious object of sapling wands on which I stretched the bladders of wild goats, carefully dried and spread. This thing was shaped like the sting-ray, that flat, long-tailed sea grotesque which fishermen sometimes net, far out. On the first windy day in autumn I ran with this air-fish thing and conjured it up, reeling and playing it on a twine and trying to feel the blowing topography of the air to discover what, if any, consistency or principle governed it.

Cameira looked curiously at me as I scampered up and down with my toy. I suspect she found my romping undignified in a middle-aged man of some reputation. Perhaps she thought I had gone a little mad, but she did not say so. She made no comment and merely brought me a jug of barley water to cool me.

On other days when I lay for hours on my back watching clouds form and disperse and seeking some clue to their behavior, Cameira must have thought I fell into trances. She was very gentle with me and only mildly curious.

"Is Aeolus your god?" she asked me once.

"Perhaps he will be," I replied, little knowing how much I should come to owe the Keeper of the Winds, "but for the moment Demeter commands me, in all her harvest." And I took Cameira and kissed her breasts and sowed her and was harvested: and she, "the sharer," shared herself with me. As I say, when I was not afraid, I was happy during those months.

Through the winter she became thin as Demeter does and so did I, but we did not starve. I ventured into Gortyna and mended pots and pans, which I did well enough to gain a local reputation as a competent tinker. Then, one day late in the spring, this gentle and fruitful life ended.

I was beating out the dents in a bronze bowl, the **17**
heirloom treasure of a cattle-drover and his most
prized, if battered, possession when Endoios came into this
drover's yard; Endoios, whom I had last heard in Athens speaking against me to Aegeus about the death of Talos, when it was
Laerces who was dead. I had long forgiven him that.

"Where have you been?" I asked him lightly. I was alarmed
but tried not to show it. His sudden appearance was a shock
and being recognized was disconcerting.

"I was in Ephesus for a time," he said, "and then Tegea and
various places. For the last year I have been looking for you."

"Why?"

"Because of Talos, because I am ashamed of what I said of
you in Athens and because you are my master in what I would
be."

"You were Talos' man," I said. "You never liked me much."

"Talos is mad."

"Mad? How do you know? Where is he? What became of
him?"

I got to my feet, dropping the bronze bowl. I picked it up,
dropped my hammer and picked that up.

"He is in Crete. I came to warn you," said Endoios, putting down his pack.

"Where? Where is his workshop? Where is he?"

"He no longer needs a workshop. He is changed."

Endoios himself had not changed. Little wiry men don't
seem to change or age.

"How do you mean Talos is changed? Why should I need
to be warned?"

"He has gone mad. He believes himself made of bronze
and that he made himself bronze. He has become a warrior
made of bronze."

"Talos?"

"Yes."

"Why?"

"No one knows for sure. When he left Athens it is said that he became an armorer, but no one knows where he went. Now he is in Crete and his mind is gone."

It was only at this point that it occurred to me to ask how Endoios had known where I was.

"Skyllis told me. When he heard I was looking for you, he told me where to find you to warn you that Talos is searching for you."

"But I should welcome Talos."

"I tell you he is mad. He believes you murdered him."

"You mean he believes he is dead?"

"Yes, and remade in bronze."

"But why?"

Endoios shrugged. "The mad are mad," he said.

"I see," I said, but I did not see. "Come, let's go and eat," I said, and we went into the drover's house and I took my pay in bread and wine and beef and we shared it. Then we went out onto the hillside and I watched a kestrel swinging along the wind. It had become a habit with me. "What now?" I asked Endoios, watching the hawk.

"What are you doing in this place?"

"Have you come from Knossos?"

"But why are you here, doing tinker's work?"

We looked at each other and laughed. It was all questions and no answers from either of us.

"Tell me," I said, "and then I'll tell you what there is to tell."

"I've been at Knossos. I came here from the palace. I told you Skyllis sent me."

"Did he tell you why I was here?"

"He said you had simply been taken with the urge to leave the palace."

"Did he say I was hiding?"

"No. Are you? Why?"

I was not sure what to make of this. Was there no pursuit? Was I hiding from imaginary perils?

"Did you see Minos and the queen at Knossos? Are they in good health?"

"I have seen Minos enthroned. The queen was pregnant when I first reached the palace. Before I came here she gave birth to a son. There were strange stories circulating about him. He is not normal."

"You mean the child is deformed."

Endoios looked at me and didn't reply directly. "They say Pasiphaë bore a calf. I don't know if it can be true. No one has seen her, nor the child or whatever it is," he said.

"What do the people say of me?"

"That you were forced by Tauros."

"They do not blame me."

"It seems not."

"And Tauros?"

"He too has gone from Knossos. No one knows where."

"No one is looking for me then?"

"Only Talos."

"I don't fear Talos."

"You should. I tell you he is changed. He is grown to be a giant."

I remembered Talos was well built, but he had certainly been no giant. I pressed Endoios, but he simply shrugged. He was not a speculative man. What he did not understand, he accepted. If Talos had become a giant then that is what he had become. How and why did not apparently concern Endoios.

I thought about it. "I shall return home," I said. I wonder even now why I called Knossos "home" that morning.

And so I went north again and Endoios came with me. Cameira made no complaint. She gave me a little present for Skyllis, a pair of sandals she had made, packed food and my belongings for me, and kissed me. Then she went into her hut and shut the door.

18

Endoios and I walked northward with our packs and on the way I told him what had happened to me in the time since we had both left Athens. It had been a long time and there was much to tell. As for Endoios, he was reticent. All I could learn from him was that he had carved an ivory figure of Athena Alea at Tegea, been married, lost his wife, made another figure of Athena from vinewood, at Ephesus, which had been dedicated in her temple by a man named Kallias.

There are some people who tell one nothing of themselves even though they answer all questions courteously. Endoios was one of these. He lurched along with a jerky, springing stride and covered the miles tirelessly with what appeared to be twice as much energy wasted as he needed to propel him. He walked the way some men stammer. Still, I must say he made me sweat to keep pace with him. He seemed worried on my behalf and kept looking around him as if he expected to see Talos towering on the skyline.

On the fourth day, late in the afternoon, he did. He pointed ahead of us without a word and there, as if on fire beneath the lowering sun, stood an armored figure like a bronze fortress. It limped stiffly toward us, bellowing.

"Run," said Endoios, but I couldn't run.

It came on. Half its body was hidden by a tower-shield bossed with the image of a partridge. The top of this shield was curved upward to guard the face, while the base of it scraped the ground. What I could see of the figure's legs and feet was booted and clothed in leather and, like the padded leather tunic which covered its body and arms, these leggings were sewn with overlapping scales of bronze. It wore a slashing sword and dagger of bronze suspended from a bronze belt, a bronze plastron high in the neck and a helmet crested with two curved bronze horns pointing forward. This helmet had long cheekpieces tied below the red-bearded chin and between these, a beaten bronze mask covered the rest of the face above the lips. If this walking mound of metal were really Talos, he was indeed a foot or more taller than Talos had been when I knew him, and broad in proportion.

The thing shook a long spear in its covered right hand and made a great combination of noises, a clanking of bronze and creaking of leather combined with hoarse war cries which came from behind its clenched teeth. Those teeth and the bearded lips were the only parts of the whole which were visibly human and the mouth was set in a rictus grin which reduced that humanity and would have chilled the blood but for a sort of idiotic cordiality registered in the grimace. I was so struck with this caricature of a welcoming smile, brandished at me to inspire terror, that I started to laugh. I stood where I was on the road and laughed, frightened out of my wits and laughing wildly. The thing Talos had made stopped, grounded shield and spear and went on grinning at me. I went on laughing. The noises ceased to come from Talos, except for a heavy breathing.

"Who made the armor, Talos?" I said. "It must be hot in there." And I went off into laughter again, like a lunatic.

At this moment Endoios elected to start running. He broke to the left and went off over the dry ground in a shower of earth and pebbles, his odd springing gait wildly exaggerated by his efforts to gain speed. He jerked like a drunken magpie crossed with a three-legged hound. Talos ponderously rounded on him, pivoting like a heavy cart, and hurled his spear in the general direction of the capering Endoios. It skidded between his legs, tripped and somersaulted him and he came down flat on his back. A great cry of victory rang from the lips of Talos, as if he had just slain Ares himself. Endoios clambered slowly to his feet. He was so angry that his fear had left him and he was as angry with the sound of my laughter as with the indignity of his fall. He picked up the spear and flung it back. The point struck the top of the shield, glanced off and the turning haft struck Talos squarely across the upper lip and nostrils, below his bronze nose. He fell like a cypress tree and his shield fell on top of him, catching him under the chin. Prone, in a cloud of dust, he looked exactly like a long kiln burst from the pressure of gas in the mold.

Endoios came back and both of us looked down on the fallen giant. His boots stuck out from under his shield and I realized why he had had such height. The boots were set in thick short stilts, tied at ankle and knee, and those stilts were masked by the long leggings. One stilt had been deliberately made longer than the other.

We lifted the shield off Talos, took off his helmet and mask and wiped his bleeding nose. We strapped his legs with his bronze belt and relieved him of his sword and dagger. Then with the ropes from our packs we tied his arms behind him, propped his head on his helmet and waited for him to recover.

Poor Talos, he had filled out since we had parted in haste under the Athenian acropolis all those years ago. His face was blotched and thickened above the sprouting beard and his eyes were pouched. Most of his hair was gone. He was not frightening except perhaps for the fixed grin he wore. Even the blow on the head had not shifted that.

"I have not seen his face since that night in Athens," said Endoios staring down at him. "No one on Crete has seen him like this." And Endoios began, quite silently, to weep.

We sat there in the dust, Endoios with tears streaming down his face and I myself slowly recovering from shock. Talos lay stunned, still grinning, and when he opened his eyes they were mindless. He began to struggle, grunting and sweating like a netted bullock. Froth and more blood burst from between his teeth and dribbled into his beard. He bucked, so that his metal scales clashed, and drummed his stilted boots against the ground.

"Talos," I said, "Talos," and he whined and screamed through his grin. But even with all this grim and fearful change he still looked enough like Talos to make my eyes sting, too. There was enough of him left to bring back the day on the beach when together we had discovered the tongs, the compasses and the fish-spine saw.

"What shall we do with him?" said Endoios.

We tried to lift him and could not. We dared not untie him. We left him where he was and went for help to the nearest village. When we had guided the villagers to the place, we slipped away and left Talos to their care. We knew that, being mad, he would be tended carefully. The mad are very sacred to villagers in Crete.

I must tell you that before we went for help, I slipped the bronze-plated coverings from Talos' fists. They were curiously made things, leather pouches, shaped like hollow hands with palms and backs which extended to cover the wrists. On the back of each, bronze plates were sewn, overlapping, like the scales on a bird's foot, so that these leather hands were as flexible as the rest of his scale armor. I had never seen such hand-coverings before and have since learned that they were originally invented in Egypt. How Talos possessed himself of an Egyptian invention unknown in Crete I do not know. I believe that he must have conceived the idea independently. Things are often discovered in more than one part of the world at the same time and Talos was no less inventive than I am. I think that before his mind went dark and while he was making his grotesque armored disguise, Talos made this last invention. I believe that his skills went from him gradually because although his helmet and sword were beautifully made, his body armor and his shield were botched and of rough workmanship.

Questions of this sort came to me as we went on toward Knossos. At what point did Talos become convinced that I had murdered him? Did he make the great bronze sheath, his new persona, because long ago we had worked in bronze together? I am in no doubt he made all the armor, even those parts which were badly made. They had his individual touch.

There is a crazy logic in the transformation of a great metal worker into the metal work he makes and an irony, of the kind beloved of the gods, in a madness which makes a bronzesmith believe himself bronze. Perhaps the protection of the hands was a final irony, when it was the brain that needed protection,

111

and the helmet was such a masterpiece. Later I made myself a pair of leather hands to use when pouring metal. They are not difficult to design. You simply cut four pieces of leather to the shape of your hands and sew them together in pairs.

Endoios and I went five miles from the place where we left Talos and then slept in a ditch. Next day we went on to Knossos without speaking much on the way. Endoios was uneasy. He kept glancing at me.

About midday he said, "Talos was a good man."

"Yes. A fine man."

"I suppose he made the armor himself."

"I am sure of it." Then after a while, I said, "How does he live?"

"They say Minos feeds him and uses him as a watchdog to guard the coast. He is faithful as a dog to his master and when he senses an enemy of the king's, he kills. That is what I have heard."

"You mean he thought I was Minos' enemy?"

Endoios did not look at me and my fears returned and knotted in my belly. "I don't know," he said, "it may not be that. Talos believes you murdered him in Athens. Perhaps it is that and nothing to do with Minos."

"Perhaps," I said, but I was not reassured. "Do you know why he made the stilts of different lengths?"

"To be lame of course," said Endoios, surprised.

I could not see why this should be so obvious.

"Hephaistos is lame," said Endoios, "All great masters of metal work are lame and so Talos, being bronze, must needs be lame." He glanced down at my legs. I am slightly lame, as I have told you. "Besides, it is the partridge," he said.

There did not seem any reply to make and we walked some way in silence.

"Talos has told the Cretans that he is lame because you threw him from the acropolis, in Athens," said Endoios doubtfully, as if he partly believed it.

"But you were there," I said, "in Athens."

"I do not remember it clearly."

Curious that when a man's mind goes dark, others can come so easily to accept the substance of his private shadows. Endoios knew perfectly well what had happened in Athens, yet he denied Talos' version of the story reluctantly.

"Do you think I murdered him?" I asked.

"No," said Endoios. "You did not murder him."

After that he would not meet my eyes. I suppose that even knowing the truth does not disqualify a man from accepting a fable. I felt sure that, given a few months of tavern talk, Endoios would come to believe the popular version of the tale in contradiction to his own experience.

That evening we reached the palace.

Of course you know some version of the occurrences **19** at Knossos during my absence. Pasiphaë had borne the Minotaur, a creature of terrible strength and ferocity, a monster with the body of a man and the head of a bull. That is true. You will also have been told that Minos confined this creature at the center of the labyrinth I had made and that too is true, although it has been falsely suggested that I made the labyrinth for this purpose. It is also false that Minos, in his rage and jealousy, imprisoned me there. The traditional testimony is faulty. What is left out is that it was not Minos who imprisoned me, but my own alarm.

I did not advertise my return to Knossos but within a day it was known. The palace is large, but it was not large enough to prevent that. I had hidden for eleven months and those months had been of no more use to me than eleven hours. In fact, I would have been wiser to have remained, but flight has become a habit with me.

When I left, opinion had been divided between those who had celebrated the queen's intercourse with the bull as an act of piety and those who condemned it as sacrilege. Now all combined to condemn her. The birth of the Minotaur had seen to that and he, poor beast, was described with pleasing horror as feeding upon human flesh although at that time he was a suckling calf. Tauros had returned and contrived to silence all criticism of his part in the drama. He was much in evidence with his white bodyguard and was thought by some to rule in place of Minos. In fact he did not, but Minos had withdrawn. He was not to be seen in public. As for me, I was now suspected of fantastic crimes and every rumor about me gave birth to another. I was described as responsible for Pasiphaë's lust, as the murderer of Talos, as a manufacturer of monsters and a threat to Cretan peace. It is amazing into what confusion political discussion can drive people. Public opinion often displays a poetic wildness as intoxicated as any Dionysiac celebration and politics are largely conditioned by the brevity of public memory.

In Attica, or anywhere on the mainland, this public hatred of me would have been lethal. In Crete, although on all sides people spoke against me, nothing happened. No one spoke to me except Dipoinos and Skyllis and they were guarded in what they said. Naucrate was not to be found, but then at Knossos people can absent themselves mysteriously for long periods without causing much comment or curiosity. No one came to arrest me, no one tried to murder me and this was somehow more frightening than the clamor. I waited, conceiving and discarding methods of escape and as the days passed I began to accept my peril as ordained, as part of a pattern of divine persecution. I think in time I should have come to accept my own guilt and resigned myself to my fate, whatever it would be. Then Icarus returned to me.

I could not at that time explain his motives. He believed everything that had been said against me. He believed I had murdered Talos and to this he had added a complicated gloss about Perdix. He even accepted the notion that I had fathered the Minotaur on Pasiphaë. This grotesque rumor had spread since my return and I think it possible that the Cretans found the idea so dreadful that they grew afraid of me and dared not lay hands on me. It was a tale to the effect that not only had I manufactured the cow but had made myself a bull by the same means and thus had committed the ultimate sacrilege of possessing the queen.

That both she and I should have consummated this fearful union disguised in cumbersome model animals did not seem improbable to the Cretans nor to Icarus, but merely horrible beyond human credence. The Minotaur was apparently the loathsome extension, not of our lust, but of the travesty we had chosen in which to enact it. Icarus therefore believed the Minotaur to be his half brother. This being the case he felt so far defiled that his only course was to join me in my degradation. He saw us both as outcasts beyond hope and chose for himself the scapegoat role.

In growing up, Icarus had developed a most displeasing arrogance. When he spoke he aped the bards in their lofty contempt for men who were not heroic. He seemed incapable of thinking or speaking in anything but the sort of verse he believed suitable for heroes, so that by way of a general expression of his distaste for humanity he addressed me with:

"All men are lizards trapped in time by dust
To scuffle in it with their crumpled hands.
They write their lives by marking on the crust
Of earthbound time, their symbols in the sands.
Dirt is their cluttered kingdom where they grind
The harvest of the years, sloughing their sheaths.
Scraping their paper off to free their kind
From mortal limitations. He who breathes
Only the sallow lees of midday in
Lies splayed upon this midden where the flies
Tease him and whine and spurn the blinded grin
He wears to watch their spinning as they rise."

When he chanted this to me, I was in no doubt that I was included among the lizards. I even glanced down to my hands and guiltily put them behind me like some urchin being taken to task for dirty paws. Then I was angry with myself and spoke sharply to him and he said no more.

I must admit I could not at the time understand any of it. I am a rational man and my instinct is to dismiss what is obvious nonsense. It has taken me the balance of my lifetime to see that the pattern in which Icarus believed was rationally nonsense but not to be lightly dismissed simply because the facts were other than those in which he believed. Furthermore, the grain of truth which flowered on this dunghill of fantasy sprang from a seed nurtured by divine caprice. In Icarus the tangle of falsehoods, which wrapped him about as impenetrably as any maze, flourished because although they were insane they were consistent. Everything about Icarus was consistent. That is why he died. That is why his death was heroic. That is why the fiction he lived was as true as the facts were false.

To put it simply, the gods employ truths beyond fact and distort facts to fit these truths, whereas man distorts the truth to fit his superstition. It goes against my nature to admit it but, as you will learn, I have the evidence.

So Icarus came back to me and together we went down into the labyrinth I had made and found it completed. I went there to hide. Icarus came with me to act out the drama which he had shaped in his mind and, being consistent, he had no other course.

The labyrinth had been finished in my absence; that is to say, each of the fourteen teams of men had completed a part of it without knowing the whole plan of the maze. They would doubtless have tried to share the secret, but the Cretan capacity to embroider the truth had in this instance served to disguise it. Gossip does not make for an accurate description of topography, and as a construction the labyrinth was naturally intended to confuse. Not only were there fourteen interwoven parts but these occupied different levels. It was not only a maze in plan but a maze in depth, so that paths doubled back above themselves and twisted below each other. Steps and ramps sharply or gently ascending and descending occurred as frequently as horizontal passages. At key points it was necessary to break through certain walls to complete the links and to block other tunnels. Once these final, calculated alterations were made, two people only would know the way to the center. I was one and Minos was the other. When Icarus and I reached each of these points in turn, the alterations had already been made. Minos had therefore passed through the maze ahead of me; the Minotaur had therefore already reached his prison, attended by whatever wet nurses or milch cows he would need in his infancy.

At its center, the labyrinth contained two chambers separated by a maze within the maze, as Minos had commanded, and these rooms were conceived as symbols of the juxtaposition of the sun and the moon. The maze between them took exactly as long to penetrate as the time when sun and moon may be seen in the sky together on the day at the center of the year. If the Minotaur was already concealed in the labyrinth, it would be in the chamber of the moon. He could scarcely be anywhere else, if I understood the king's conception of ritual. In the chamber of the sun we should be safe except from Minos himself and Minos had made no threatening move against me. Icarus and I went toward the chamber of the sun. As you see, it was not Minos who imprisoned us but our own fears, and these fears were quite different from each other. I feared for my life. Icarus feared the wrong death.

It was dark in the maze at Knossos but not **20** airless. The vents and pipes I had incorporated in the fabric worked well enough, although the wind gusted and whined through them alarmingly and our torches flared and spat as though the earth's breathing was troubled. In places the walls were wet and it was a cold and comfortless journey. I do not remember exactly how long it took and for the matter of that I do not now remember the path itself and if I found myself there again I should undoubtedly be lost. I knew the way in those days and we moved toward the center.

I did not know how the chamber of the sun would be furnished nor even if it would be habitable. It was. It contained the furniture of the king and enthroned at the further end of the great room sat the king himself. At his feet knelt his daughter Ariadne, but there was no one else in the whole great hall, no armed men, no servants, no people of any sort to guard or cherish the sacred person of the sun incarnate in the bull; Minos, the center of the Cretan world, at the center of the Cretan world, at the center of his labyrinth.

The place was lit by torches and heated with braziers. It remained dark and cold. It was richly decorated and remained cheerless. Minos, enthroned as calmly as I had seen him when he gave public audience during my first days at Knossos, now gave audience to Daedalus, the one other person who knew the way to him in the cavern I had made for him. Only his daughter and my son witnessed our meeting.

"Welcome, Daedalus," said Minos, as if I had been an embassy from Egypt or a Hittite lord.

Icarus fell on his knees. For myself, I did not have the tact or the sense of occasion to do more than gape. Minos smiled.

"Welcome," he repeated. "I have been waiting for you."

I could not think why he had chosen to entomb himself alive in this dark and deeply disturbing place.

"You are heavily loaded, both of you."

I let my pack slide to the floor and Minos signed to Icarus to put down his burdens. It is a curious thing but in any really alarming situation I am always weighed down with bales and bundles. I am always caught humping my equipment about with me. It is destructive to one's dignity.

"Are you setting up shop here?" said Minos, leaning forward to peer at our baggage. He spoke lightly enough but I did not feel easy.

"I see carpenter's tools and wood," he went on mildly. "What are we to watch you make, another cow perhaps, or something to serve a more general purpose?"

My alarm increased. I fell to my knees beside Icarus.

Ariadne giggled. She was a girl who giggled.

"Oh, come now," said Minos, "you cannot think I hold you personally responsible for the queen's eccentricities. You have nothing to fear from me."

I looked up at him and saw in his face that what he said was true. And so it was that I told him how I planned to make wings for Icarus and myself because I believed that it was possible, with adequate study of the pace and direction of the winds, for a man to fly.

"I doubt it," said Minos, "but if anyone can achieve it, doubtless you can." He did not ridicule the proposal as many might have done since, nor did he ask why I should have chosen the bowels of his palace to construct a device for harnessing the wind. He did, however, point out rather sardonically, that this in fact was what I was doing. Ariadne giggled.

As for Icarus, he smiled calmly at me, as if he had known my intentions all along. I think in a way he had.

"Tell me how you will do it," said Minos, and I, of course, began at once to do so. I cannot resist talking about technical matters. I drew on the floor with a piece of charcoal to show how I should build the wings, I explained the principles upon which I based my assumptions, I talked at length about the flight of birds and of how the dynamics of soaring rather than muscular propulsion must be the key to human flight. The air itself must do the work.

On this he questioned me carefully. "No man can become a bird," he said and I agreed with him. The point that I was making and indeed the whole of my premise was that although the human physique prevents a man from rivaling a bird and he can never adapt himself wholly to the dimension of air, he could conceivably achieve some limited mastery of it, just as a man can swim in the sea but cannot compete with a fish. My hopes rested upon my observation that hot winds rise from the surface of the earth and sea and that certain types of bird, taking advantage of these currents of air, can rest comfortably upon them without effort. Soaring birds, rather than flapping ones, appeared to rely on an ability constantly to adjust and minutely reshape their wings in flight. They trimmed their wing surfaces with great skill and subtlety and seemed to use their power to beat the air, as all birds do, only in order to turn or correct their chosen course. This, I told Minos, meant that the hawk's ability to reshape its wings in flight, to warp them in various ways as it were, was as important as any mechanism it used to give it thrust. I added that I had not been able to conceive any human means of gaining enough force to carry a man into the air by flapping wings. I showed the king the assembled skeleton of a pigeon to prove my point. For a man to fly by flapping would require him to possess a breastbone jutting out several feet from his thorax and sinews of a power equivalent to those of the pigeon, on a scale relative to the difference in size and weight between man and bird. I should not therefore attempt to make a flapping mechanism, but rather I should construct a large but light framework of tapered wings, spanning the widest controllable area, to take advantage of the rising winds and hope to control their lift and maintain myself in the air by an intricate web of wires. The harness I had in mind would attach the wings to the shoulders and back, leaving arms, hands and legs free to manipulate the warping and trimming functions of these wires. The light wooden structure, braced and strengthened with gut, would have, stretched across it, a complete covering of the varnished bladders of animals stretched and laminated together. The wings would be translucent and resemble those of a dragonfly in texture rather than a bird but the shape would be based on the model I had flown at Gortyna and resemble a certain kind of fish.

I may say in passing that the myth which has evolved around our flight concerning wax and feathers is totally absurd.

Minos listened patiently to all this and expressed himself sceptical. "I think," he said, "that you will require some intervention beyond human cunning to achieve what you hope."

I said that I recognized the risk. Icarus said suddenly and calmly that he believed that he would fly. He spoke like a man speaking in his sleep.

Minos glanced at him. "You will need the help of a god," he said.

"We shall have it," said Icarus.

You who know so many things which I could not **21** know about the nature of flight can well afford to look contemptuously upon my wings and if you find me, like yourselves, more prone to rely on mechanics than upon gods, you will have either to accept that there are forces beyond your comprehension, as I was forced to admit, or that most freakish weather made our flight a reality. Consider, however, what we do know, even in my time, about the air. We understand the feathering of arrows and how to use the winds at sea to propel our ships. Then, too, although I believe you will find this hard to accept, I had recognized the relationship between heat and air, having made this connection when watching the burning air burst out of the vents in a mold when the hot metal is poured. Heat expands air and drives it upward with great force. It was the hot winds which would sustain us among the clouds, as the clouds themselves rise and change their shapes as they rise. The primary problem was the initial launching.

All this I discussed with Minos while I worked in the center of his labyrinth. During the days and weeks we spent together I came to understand something of this man or god-king when all his outward power and panoply were laid aside with the solemn rituals of his public life which held his people in such awe. Unmasked, unrobed, lacking his sacred gilded horns,

Minos still contained in his person a power beyond that of any man I have encountered. I am not mystical and indeed have been, from time to time, in some danger of the charge of impiety but, if any god becomes incarnate in any king, then Minos showed that incarnation in his person. It will sound strange coming from me, but I believe Minos played a part beyond my understanding in the launching of our flight.

In the maze, he came and went mysteriously. Those who brought food and lights he himself led blindfold to the place and those who remained to serve him had no knowledge of the path they had taken to come there. Only Ariadne went with him and returned again with unbound eyes. She even wandered off alone and continually lost herself. Many times I went searching for her and found her weeping.

What the king ate and drank, we ate and drank and it was very little. What we lacked he sent for, knowing perfectly that all that time we schemed and built and carpentered the means of escaping from his realm. It was a paradox that apparently in no way disturbed him. As for Ariadne, she giggled.

Ariadne was a placid and rather thoughtless girl. I suppose that considering her parentage it was not surprising that she was somewhat bovine. She had her mother's cowlike look, but none of her regal and sinister splendor. Ariadne would stand and stare at me while I worked, as blankly curious as a calf and sometimes she would take alarm for no obvious reason and bolt into the dark passages beyond my workshop corner in the chamber of the sun. When she did this, she got lost and I would go grumbling into the maze to find her mewing like a kitten in some blind alley. After half a dozen such mishaps, I gave her a ball of red twine one end of which I fastened to the bench in my workshop. Then when she went hiding she inevitably paid it out and I could reel her in like a fish. It saved a good deal of time and established a thin red bond between us.

She spoke pleasantly and looked charming and I realize now that I showed off to her. Metaphorically, I bobbed and danced like a middle-aged partridge, with my new wings extended, whenever I was not concentrated on making them. I even took the time to make her a gold wreath with jeweled flowers to please her and everything I needed for this trifle of metalwork was brought to me by blindfolded men. I cannot imagine what strange cult they must have believed they served in the darkness.

So we danced politely round one another, Ariadne and I, but Icarus never glanced at her. He was turned in on himself, brooding on his destiny and exercising his great shoulders for his flight.

We ate, as I say, very little. It was essential to our flight that we should be as light as possible and for myself I dieted strenuously to lose weight; I am inclined to fatness. We trained like athletes, especially concentrating on strengthening our arms and hands. And all this Minos watched.

Much of the time he was silent. Sometimes he asked a question or made some comment on my work. Very rarely he spoke of himself and when he did he was reticent and gentle, speaking like a man who knows his own future so clearly that it hardly bears discussion.

It was this sufficiency, this acquired invulnerability to fortune, which made him at once remote and perfectly contained, impervious and therefore impersonal. Everything about him seemed to move toward the center of his being and at this center his power hung balanced upon justice. He was unlike a man and even unlike all gods except perhaps Ouranos, in that he did not act upon caprice. He surprised me only when this lack of caprice was most evident in the gravity and consequence of his thought and action. There is after all nothing more surprising than justice in judgment except perhaps a true understanding of the long consequence of justice.

The tradition of the ruling house of Crete rested upon a legendary immortality. Like the Pythia at Delphi, Minos, in the popular belief, was a single being constantly renewed, not ageless but passing endlessly through the cycle from birth to death and rebirth.

In remote times he had been ritually killed and reborn for agricultural purposes. Surrogates, dolls hung from trees, and other magical rituals continued to be employed to ensure his continuity. In fact those of his line were born and died like other men, but all bore the same name and the death of each king was kept secret. So too with Pasiphaë; the moon passed endlessly through the proper phases of the months as the sun carried the progression of the seasons with him across the year. It is an efficient way to turn men into gods and thus all the near relatives of the house of Minos passed into myth because it served as the only exit for them. Thus Ariadne became the bride of Dionysus in due time and Glaukos went into the sea, having borne Deiphobe to be the Cumaean Sybil of whom you shall presently hear more. Time had to double back to make Glaukos father Deiphobe unless, of course, as so often happens, it was a Glaukos of an earlier generation who did so. One of the problems of Cretan genealogy is its repetitive use of proper names.

Ariadne, poor child, was all too mortal, all too vulnerable and one of those unfortunates who invite and continually suffer betrayal. I know this bitterly. I was one of her betrayers. I do not know whether in fact she became the consort of the wine god on the island of Dia, as report has it, but her fondness for wine, which she took in quantity to assuage her pain and loneliness, would have made her a fit mate for Dionysus at least in some respects.

She was not openly resentful of her misery nor did she seem truly aware of her hatred. She hated her mother and in consequence her brute half-brother but this hatred neither pricked nor burned her, rather it grew green and sullen in her, like a canker in an unripe fruit, and numbed her like a bruise. She endured it while it consumed her and although she could not know it, her hatred was so powerful that it came close to love, while Icarus endured a love so jealous that it came close to hatred and only the destruction of its object could hope to quench it. Neither Ariadne nor Icarus destroyed the objects of their passion and in this way they mirrored one another.

Minos and I, being dispassionate in our different ways, also mirrored one another as we gazed helpless at our children.

If I am dispassionate it is because my passions are consumed in the exercise of my skills; if Minos was dispassionate it is because he had dedicated himself to dispassion in his passion for justice. We two then, so different in our powers, watched our children burn. Minos must have watched his daughter with comprehension and compassion, although it seemed he could do nothing. For myself, I was too obsessed with my carpentry to understand my son. The mind of Minos was, as I see it, a theorem and he had achieved the sublime geometry of total self-integration. Beside him, despite my embracing love for order and harmony, I was like a boy whittling his first model boat, hoping but uncertain that it would float on an even keel. My failures have always come from being too busy to attend to matters beyond my finger tips. Icarus and Ariadne never spoke nor considered one another beyond the minimal courtesies; they were like twins born back to back.

Minos, for all his gentleness and compassion, was too remote to comfort Ariadne. With him she felt hopelessly inadequate, but then she needed more than justice and less than noble tranquillity in a father. She turned to me and blundering, my mind elsewhere, I did not serve her well. I understood her revulsion from her mother and her horror of the Minotaur, which she had seen born, but in my thoughtless inattention I did not recognize the depth of her hatred for the queen or her physical loathing for her monstrous half-brother, whom I occasionally heard bawling piteously from the chamber of the moon as he grew to quick maturity. Nor did I realize that Icarus, with his facile acceptance of anything which might make the world of his father seem more disgusting, believed me to have got the Minotaur on Pasiphaë. Both Ariadne and Icarus, when they heard the creature bellow out its infant, and soon its adult, misery and hunger, heard its cries as the animal howls of a thing outside humanity which was yet of their own blood. Each sickened and turned inward so that although we spent our days and nights within so many feet of one another, Minos, Ariadne, Icarus and I were like people separately entombed.

We lay, all four of us, well provided with grave goods, at the center of a labyrinth and at night or rather during those hours we thought of as the night, I was often wakeful. Sometimes I talked with Minos and sometimes I envied his fatalism but I could not share it and must reject it even now. I think however that I understand it.

A king whose royal line stretches back unbroken for a thousand years and who, by the nature of the ever-increasing rituals gathered around the maintenance of his line, is wrapped away from ordinary life. He becomes the puppet of his own illusions. He reaches either toward the exercise of power in order to sustain his belief in his own grandeur and is caught up in the luxuries of tyranny and the delights of cruelty or, overwhelmed with an inbred sense of duty, he drives himself to death in the service of the ideal of kingship and the well-being of his people. A warrior king guards his lands or extends them by conquest, an administrator strives for efficient government, a weakling intrigues to maintain his throne, a strong man fights to perpetuate his dynasty and ensure its continuity. All such kings are at the mercy of shifting circumstance and of power, or the absence of it, among neighboring states. The vitality of kingship is enhanced by its exercise. For centuries in Crete these stimuli had been absent. Crete was self-sufficient, unmenaced, an island so far distant from other powers and so highly evolved in the exploitation of its skills and resources that no fits and starts of danger or of triumph disturbed the old age of the house. Only Poseidon sometimes shook the earth or raised the sea to beat upon Cretan ships and Cretan ports, but this divine damage was smoothly and rapidly repaired.

Thus Minos and his forebears had had no ambition in three quarters of a millennium and at the heart of Crete, which beat within the supposedly deathless line of Cretan kings, lay the ultimate canker of boredom. Ritual is not life but a substitute, a formal game played to counteract the more irrational behavior of the gods. It is played with intricate symbols and the prize is power. Rituals were the measure of Minos' life but since he already had the prize, the game had long since lost its purpose.

Despite the depth and quality of his mind, he had never felt impelled to test it to its full extent. Surfeited with the power he wielded and the power which was manifest in him, he had never sought its increase nor met a challenge to it. He was locked in a losing battle with his own boredom and where a lesser king would have found relief in some extravagance of cruelty or some wild ostentation, Minos lived only by the abstractions upon which he speculated, moving the qualities of justice, truth, good and evil wearily about upon the gaming board of his days. Ritual, hallowed by tradition and complicated to pass the time, had been the illusory landscape of his years and to him symbol and reality were indivisible and empty.

He had needed me to build his labyrinth and he had retired into its buried center. Only here could he sit in undisturbed judgment upon his world and upon himself. Here he could make the minute adjustments to the balance he had achieved and put into the scales thoughts so pared to their essence and so delicate that their weight could be calculated only in an aetheric vacuum and no rough facts could jog the elbow. Here, surrounded by a maze so intricate that its countless walls would have reduced a tidal wave to a fishpond, he would make himself his own final symbol and, motionless, contemplate his ultimate ritual. When Icarus and I were gone into the sky and Ariadne had wed her god, Minos would still be here alone, forever, sitting in judgment on the shades. And in the neighbor chamber of the moon, the Minotaur would crouch, forever brought to judgment. That is his purpose, poor beast, for he is a brute part of man and the antithesis of his judge.

When I knew this, I also knew that the wings I had near completed for Icarus and myself were indeed the necessary means of our escape. In the presence of Minos we were in the presence of an immortality indistinguishable from unmenacing death and although it turned out that Icarus would go to his death, it was no part of his pattern to find it unmenacing. As for immortality, he was never in doubt of his share and jealousy prepared it.

Minos had no jealousy. He knew Ariadne would come to me and he accepted our brief intercourse both because he knew there would be no issue and because he accepted her rejection of her royal parentage as temporary. He knew that Ariadne believed that he had let Pasiphaë betray him and that the whole royal house, of which she was the daughter, was thus defiled. I watched him smile at her, accepting her horror of him as easily as any loving father accepts the little chaos of the nursery and waits to put his child's toys away when she has gone to sleep. He accepted her hatred as easily as he accepted and disregarded what he called the eccentricities of his queen.

Knowing that the line of Minos must survive and that his queen had borne a monster who could not wear the bull mask of royal ritual because it already wore the head of a bull, he had calmly imprisoned this grotesque and innocent pretender to his throne who would not have been capable successfully of pretending even to humanity, let alone a throne. Minos possessed a compassion far beyond pity and a strength of will far beyond compassion. It has taken me many years to realize it and to see how he foresaw and related the shapes of all the lives which touched his own. He brought Ariadne to the center of his maze with him because she was the only woman of the blood of his line left to bear his son, because she was his daughter.

I do not know if she did, but I think she must have done notwithstanding Theseus and her eventual marriage to Dionysus. Legend has overlooked it if she did but, knowing Minos, I think he would have achieved his purpose. I may be wrong, but I think so. At any rate, the line continues immortally on Crete for although the legend has it that I murdered Minos in Sicily, I did not, and even this he foresaw.

On our last day in the chamber of the sun, when the wings were made and finished and stowed for us to take them to the surface, Minos spoke to me as if I were a son at his father's deathbed: "Minos you will not see again," he said, "although you will see a Minos in a distant place and know it is not I, but one calling himself Minos. You and I have spoken of power and as I know the nature of yours, so you acknowledge mine. We think we know each other, but you who understand my sickness may believe me sicker than I am and my power so far dissolved away that I am self-consumed. Therefore although my pride has gone beyond the need to prove my power and because grief and hope are only pieces on my gaming board, as you would put it, I will clear that board for you to show you that I am not decayed. You might call it love, my friend, if that too were not to me a quality to be diced with and then returned to its cup to be shaken and thrown again. You have built me my maze. In return I shall put you and your son into my cup and throw you into the air. Prepare yourselves when you reach the entrance to this coil of earth, to go from it into the coil of the sky. Farewell."

So Icarus and I went out from the place and began the long trek upward through the labyrinth. Ariadne came a little way with us and wept and I kissed her and we parted our red twine. Then Icarus and I went on through the passages, twisting and turning in the stone warren below the palace and as we went the air whined and grew hot. In the hours that followed, the hot wind built in the tunnels, howling, so that as we neared the outer world I drew Icarus aside into an embrasure, and there we assembled and strapped on our wings.

The Earth Shaker stamped and thundered under us and I

heard the curious grumbling of the land which signals the restlessness of the bull beneath it. The Cretans call him Poseidon for reasons I am not clear about. He might as well be Zeus or any other god in the bull-shape gods are always assuming. I looked to my walls and they moved, grinding and trembling, but no large rocks or masonry fell. I am a competent architect even in a shaky land and Crete is a country so unstable in its foundations that earth movements are common.

In the shallow shelter of our embrasure, under a rain of small rock fragments and in a cloud of tossing dust, I babbled warnings to Icarus about stress and the adjustment of the wing camber and gave him other useful information which went unheard. We strapped and buckled each other into our trappings, adjusting wires, tautening gut, looping and binding off the cat's-cradle strings of these fragile wired instruments to which we were about to trust our fragile bodies, and I felt my bones grow brittle as we did it. Icarus did not speak to me. Perhaps if he had I should not have heard him against the screaming wind. Perhaps he did and I did not hear him as I bent frenzied to our twines and knots.

He did not look at me but grinned like a hoplite nerving himself in the battle line. His eyes were as blank as Pasiphaë's had been when she lay spread, swaddled in the belly of the cow, waiting on the white bull's thrust, and he muttered "Apollo" over and over again.

I shouted warnings to him about height and distance, about thermal lift and the pressures brought about by the conflict of hot and cold air, as if I knew how far and where we were going, as if I knew from experience what it would be like to swim in the fearful ocean of the sky, which I did not, and we struggled to be ready when the wind reached its full force. It went past us, building in sound and strength and its ragged edges caught at us, unwieldy in the alcove where we pulled and gripped at each other's harness. Then we flung ourselves into the path and the wind took us tangled and hurled us through the entrance into the midday glare. We went out flung in a clatter of slapping spars and in that moment we were off the earth, sick and spinning. I looked down in terror and there a few feet below us, on the baked earth, our joint and jointed shadows joined, merged into one and threw upon the ground the spread silhouette of a winged bull. I saw it for only an instant but I shall never be rid of the image. As it tore apart, we were torn apart and hurled upward on Poseidon's burning breath, raised by Minos as he had promised. The ground wheeled under me and out and the sky was a floor. Rocks and fields fled from me and swung over my head to strike at me. I have never known such fear.

The earth was moving and groaning, as insubstantial as the sky. Above my head a tower crumbled and fell upward. Then I was pivoted and turned over in the smoking wind and below me walls folded and the great terrace above the entrance to the palace sagged and heaved, throwing down its skirting buildings. I saw cypress pillars topple and one split down its center. Little creatures fled to and fro like frantic beetles. They were the palace servants, they were courtiers, they were frightened people running for the open country.

Suddenly I saw Icarus under my left wing tip, shoulders hunched, legs kicking out like a swimmer and then he went past me, upward, and I was sick, vomiting down my trajectory, like a sparrow dropping lime. I clenched, retching, and fell like a stone into a pocket; spread, thrusting out legs and arms, caught the rising heat and went upward like a slingshot. Then Aeolus took me and laid me in the hand of Notus, the strong south wind, whose belly was filled with the fat, white, jostling rams men offer to him, transformed into scudding clouds. Aeolus did this for me or alternatively the wind may have been Sciron or even my ancestral Erechtheid wind come to my aid. Winds are very mixed.

Gradually my terror left me and I felt like one who has dived into a rough sea and surfaced behind the breakers. Ahead and above me, Icarus rose, soaring smooth as a kestrel and behind me a kestrel tumbled down the sky and went into the shadows of the shaking shore. The sea clamored out of control, far below under my spreadeagled limbs, but I was calm. I felt the pull and thrust of the air and warped my wings to hold it. I played my long strings like a lyre and lay easy in the body of the high wind and lazy in the sweep of the sky. Such peace and ease came upon me in that void that I curled in my comfort as, at the point of sleep, a child rolls in a soft bed, and there was quiet about me, a quiet as dense and safe as childhood's rest, while the land quaked and shuddered behind me.

The sea was kicking as I went out over it. Even from the height I had reached I could see the water boil and beat over the harbor walls at Amnisos and ships were flung about, colliding and breaking upon each other. A galley was whipped out of the bobbing clutter below the sea wall, rose, turned over slowly and splintered against the roof of a warehouse beyond the dock. Inland, above the palace, black cloud was gathered, tossing and thick as dirty tow. Dust, thick as cloud, spouted from the town and the bulk of the palace seemed for a moment to tremble impatiently. In my unsafe security, childishly cheerful to be gone from the perils of the earth and unthinking of my new and future perils, I feared for the safety of Minos and then took comfort from the knowledge of his deep shelter in the labyrinth. Its springing, complex shape would cushion his sanctuary from shock. I had, without knowing it, contrived a buried baffle against such earth-shaking when I built the maze. Minos to be sure would have known it. He prefigured every contingency. And so Icarus and I went out from Crete and left the long and broken bone of the island behind us wallowing in the struggling sea. Its palaces had been battered before and rebuilt. They would be again.

Moving effortlessly across the sky, I felt with wonder the sun stroke my back and knew Apollo **23** moved above me, bending the long bow of his passage slowly downward toward his night-hide beyond the sea rim. I did not then look up but saw, reflected in the sea, the god's smooth leaning through his afternoon toward his gradual setting. Crystal, invisible and silky skeins marked out the temperate sky and as a man long practiced runs a rope I held my balance in it. With moving through that lucent labyrinth, with learning fingertip adjustments to my wings, my time was passed on that first day as I flew northward and set my course a little toward the west.

Softly the sky darkened and began to bleed into the evening. High above me I sensed Icarus break his steady sweep and begin to wheel and flutter, dancing in the sky as if he had been born to the measure. He fell past me suddenly, spinning, joyously, went into a flock of gulls and burst through them so that they veered and plunged, spraying away from him. Coming out of the dive, he went whirling upward, flying like laughter, as if to toss the puffs of cloud about as children toss up tufts of wool at a shearing. He strutted the sky, brandishing himself in the sun's face and shook his weapon-wing's defiance at the god. And the god went calmly down toward the edge of the sky in his accustomed fashion.

As Icarus reeled and rocked, gesticulating at the setting sun, he left no doubt that he was acting out a triumph over a falling foe. For some time I could not grasp these futile gestures and then in a rush the overwhelming hubris of his behavior was plain to me and the clear purpose of his insane dedication fitted the parts of his life together in my mind as if he had broken open his deadly privacy before my eyes and confessed it all to me in simple words. He meant to couple with the god in the sun and his love was an impiety so vast that my soul cringes when I contemplate it.

I have paid in my turn for his hubris and I shall try to describe it as he described it in his sky-mime which began on that first day of our flight and reached its climax over Delos. Remember how we came by ship from Attica, when Icarus was a child, and how Tros broke the nautilus shell against his oar and crushed to death the shaerwater in flight. Those are frag-

133

ments of the broken life of Icarus. Remember Talos and the partridge trap in which he believed, his fear of darkness and his rejection of his dedication to the moon. Those are shards of his smashed shell of life. Now I knew why I had never come near him and why he turned contemptuously from me, disdaining my skills as callously as a warrior burns a peasant's homestead to the ground with no thought of the weeks it cost to build it.

I looked at Icarus, poised like a double axe against the declining sun, and saw him across the gulf forever fixed between man and hero. Rage came upon me at the waste. Jealousy shook me. I, Daedalus, maker, watched my son begin to make his own death and I who am skillful and an ordered man, I who contrive what is needed for the proper worship of the gods and for the celebration and satisfaction of men, watched my son make nothing out of nothing except his own destruction and this he contrived in so poetic and vainglorious a manner that his fame is deathless.

Icarus, first and last a fool, did not become a man although his name became immortal. I do not think he ever discovered who he was. He had pride, such pride that the god himself could scarcely match it and when Icarus flew to rape the sun and throw him down, the god spurned him as you would expect. Yet before you dismiss what I say as folly, mark that Icarus died in orgasm and that Apollo's responding orgasm, long retarded, still took place. Man has taken the god's seed and you now live in terror that with this semen the world itself may yet be cindered. Mark that when you may be tempted to dismiss a myth and bear with me when I try to describe the paradox of Icarus and the enigma of his conquest and defeat. He died gloriously but being a hero he never became a man. He did not love me nor any man nor woman. He loved only his god and his god he resented. Resentment made him a hero, for this is how heroes are made. What else could he be but a hero? He was my son and he had no talent. He had no love for order and was clumsy with his hands, yet I who bring order,

134

measuring to make harmony, brought Icarus to his disorder, and the god who thrust him down is above all gods the ordered and harmonious one. Icarus was even clumsy in his love, yet he consummated it. That is the paradox. The enigma, as you will presently read, lies in how he came to couple with that love.

On that first day the god disdained his strutting adversary while he pursued his ordained and daily passage into the night. Evening came on, and we were seven hours out from Crete. There in the red-stained sky Icarus saw, as I did, Apollo become scarlet in his sphere as he does every evening, but Icarus behaved as if he had wounded the god to death and bathed in the blood. Whom did he think he had conquered, my coxcomb crowing child? All the days he had lived he had seen each one end like this one, but on this one day he believed he had been personally responsible for driving the wounded god out of the sky.

I am convinced, looking back, that Icarus had no clear idea of reality and perhaps this heroic ignorance served him in his final gesture, for he went out of reality in a fashion which I still cannot explain. But I shall come to that.

The night came up, dredged from the sea and filled with gathering cloud. I looked down and saw the sea scuffed with breakers, ruffled and leaden. There was cold and the sky-maze shifted. I fell suddenly, caught and held myself, lurched among walls of air and began a long struggle, ploughing against the rushing pull of cross currents and falling into pits I could not see. Dragged netted, this way and that, I battled in the swaddling mist and Icarus slid away into his blind ambition, so that I lost him in the dark. Presently the wind took me above the clouds and I was carried into the empty vault.

There were pinprick stars, letting in the light, and without them I should have feared myself utterly entombed and shrouded in the endless wrappings of the wind. The sky was a hollow shell, a nautilus unbroken save for the brittle perforations of those pinpricks and the sudden lambent hole made by the rising moon. Even in my fright I knew that I was in the

135

open, safe in the size of the sky, and yet I knew that in the nautilus of night there were many further nights, each in proportion smaller than the last and each a measured room; I also knew how they narrowed imperceptibly toward the last, toward the curled center of the shell forever shut against the morning. I knew and feared the trap and end of night, where the shell could never be broken, and I felt it closing on me so that I should come to crouch curled like a foetus in the night to come, in a cold beyond the warming breath of god. I cried out and opened my eyes and realized that foolishly I had made my inner night by shutting them. So I recovered my wits and flew on and I remember ordering myself, as is my custom, by taking a practical view of the matter in hand.

Far below I saw the seal-backed shapes of islands sleeping under me. There will be nothing remarkable in this to you, but it was new to me. I was first to see the boundaries of these lands entire. I saw the pale shallows and the mottled deeps, the shreds of misty cloud and under them the uneven bed spread with the covering sea. I saw how islands chanced above the surface and where, but for a fathom or so, there would have been other islands and I recognized the disorder of the earth's surface poured on its core in a flow like bronze escaped from the kiln and spreading cooled and wrinkled on the ground. All this was new to me to wonder at. All moved and yet lay still. The moon, sour as an unripe grape, swung among bunched and creeping cloud and I hated her as Icarus hated her. I thought of Naucrate and of how she had given Icarus to the moon and wondered at a gift so ill directed.

Icarus had at least this much of his mother in him that he had no fear of the sea, his mother's place. For this reason I had warned him, when we strapped on our wings, that he should not fly low and let the breakers catch and drag him down. He ignored this warning too, knowing, I suppose, that the sea would have his wings soon enough and without effort. Looking down, I spotted him, sweeping low across the surface of the sea like a searching cormorant careless of the rolling waves, and seeing him there I asked myself how certain Icarus had been of his life's climax all his life. Clearly he had had no purpose until he came to the time of his flight. Clearly his mind had long been fused to the sun and long before I knew it, he had given himself wholly to his dream of that conquest. Heroes, like poets, being of their nature Dionysiac are unmanageable forces lacking utility and kindness. In Dionysus' grip I suppose it was natural for Icarus to fall in love with Apollo and seek in his madness to destroy and be destroyed by the object of his love. The opposition of Apollo and Dionysus is well known. Being close relatives they are fiercely ambivalent.

I am not impious nor insensitive to the visions of poets and other sacred persons, but in general they are less observant than they think, suffering as they do from revelation, which blinds them. I accept that poets celebrate important things such as honor and beauty and birth and valor and man's relations with the gods but, when you come down to it, what they most celebrate are heroes, which is not surprising. Poets have much in common with heroes. They are neither of them aware of the world, of its true appearance nor its real consequence, its structure nor its marvelous imperfection. They are blind to that and because my methods of gaining experience have been observation, deduction and experiment, I have been no worse off and much better instructed than any poets or heroes known to me. In fact since I am not beset by my own personality I am better off. I prefer cognition to revelation and in my view the valiant act is to live as long and as fully as possible, but then I make things which take time. Honor lasts longer if it is gained by patience rather than by some noble gesture rapidly made.

I am involved in matters which I do not wish disturbed nor interrupted by eloquent activities, the facile assumption of power, speculation on immeasurable phenomena, nor any apotheosis. What I make exists.

137

What I make exists. What Icarus would make in the day to come does not exist and I find it hard to forgive that there was no need for him to do more.

Then it was morning and far ahead of us, other gray-pelted islands crawled together. Of these, one was Delos, the sacred island where Apollo had been born, and it would be over Delos that Icarus would make his climb toward his high love and adversary. He came up from below me, where he had flown close to the water, taking comfort from it against the night and, catching the rising heat reflected from the risen sun beating upon the sea, he filled his wings and went past me never glancing in my direction. His face was joyous and the defeated night faded from us, spattered with new blood. The god rode up behind us through the morning and the sea shone from him. There was a great and simple joy in that morning. It glittered like inlaid armor.

The god passed toward his birthplace and because he had been born there it no longer floated, but lay anchored at his bidding. The story goes that Leto, Apollo's mother, had searched the world for a place to bear him and every island, every mountain on the earth, had been afraid to be the birthplace of an unforgiving god and feared to receive his mother. But Delos had harbored her although it had sailed in terror rudderless during the nine days of the god's deliverance from his mother while she, alone in labor, had thrust against Mount Kynthos and clutched a palm tree in her pain. Delos had been her bed until the god rose from her and took his lyre and his bow and fixed the island forever in its place on golden foundations. This is an old tale and has many variations. I myself do not put much faith in the fables with which divinity cloaks its actions. Nevertheless, the god is evidently golden; that can be seen, and on that day all Delos shone in gold and made its neighbors look like dross beside it.

138

Now, as we came toward the island, the god became a lidless eye and in his glare fixed Icarus with a baleful scrutiny. The air grew audible and a silence burned as in high fever silence sounds as though it moves. Movement, so ceaseless in the normal course of life that we take it for stillness, ceased and there was a motionlessness in all things that seemed to quake unmoving. Suddenly a flight of white doves sprang up from Delos and scattered like paper torn and thrown into the wind. At this starting signal Icarus dipped almost to the land and then began his run at death. The birds flapped frantic from his path and Icarus, poor bird-scarer bird, flew out from them. Doves, gulls and kestrels, born to flight, all fled from Icarus as small perfections fly from the splendor of a great fault. No owl fled him, but then he had no wisdom.

He had no wisdom, but he had foreknowledge. He knew his death and went to it boasting of his way of dying. I watched him rise, swimming the flooding sun shoal, black against the pouring light. His waiting death unblinking gazed on him.

He went up the sky and his pace was far beyond any that his wings could withstand. I had built them. I knew the stress they could bear. I had not designed them for the purpose to which he put them and as I watched him, part of my brain was calculating the inevitable breaking point and I was wrong. Before he went beyond my sight, I knew that no wings I could have made would take that strain, that no power known could carry him upward at that pace. Wood, gut, sheep's bladders, my trumpery flotsam cobbled together had no part in that impossible thrust. Here was disorder, an incomprehensible transmutation of materials, some readjustment of the structure of solids, some conquest of the forces which hold matter in familiar shape. Icarus, my son, went out of my head as he went out of my sight and all I could bring my baffled mind to bear on was the technical impossibility of his act. It must sound heartless to admit it, but it was so.

I have tried to understand what occurred and my explanations seem to me lame. Nevertheless, I must attempt to formu-

139

late them for my own peace of mind. I could not come at simple grief for his loss until I had rid myself at least of some part of the defeat I suffered for his triumph. He made more of his wings than I can understand so that I am tormented by the knowledge.

To make things is my work and to make things is to touch and order materials by the judgment of just proportion and in no other way. Icarus had no such sense of proportion, yet he touched and ordered his being at the last and breathed in death to bring himself alive. Yet I do not see how it was done. Somehow he transformed his wings in flight and by his will transformed himself. There must be some logic in it. There must be an order governing energy which I do not understand.

I must try to describe what I saw as I hovered over Delos, if indeed I saw it. I am not even sure of this, but I experienced the apex of his flight although I did not, could not have seen it. I do not see how I could have seen it. He was far beyond human sight. I am still confused by it. I must describe what happened, but I do not know what happened. I shall say that I watched.

While he remained in vision he moved like a slim line of fire. This vanished and all apparent velocity vanished with it so that in my mind, as he reached beyond speed, he became motionless. Despite this he moved upon the god and as he endured the passage to his summit, his moving without motion changed his mass. His trunk splayed out expanding and the jointed projections of his limbs became the vectors of his energy written white upon the now blackened sky. His proportions altered and the physical structure of his body dissolved and reassembled. The cage of ribs passed through the ribs of wing, each performing an identical function, each affirming the ascent implicit in the descent. The wings of his pelvis spread out from the spine and in their bowl the duration of his flight was contained like a liquid. Time turned in on him so that the sequence of modifications to which he was subject appeared simultaneous. A compact projectile and yet spread across the sky, he evolved in the instant a sequence of related anatomies each designed to succeed and doomed to fail. In these anatomies, the embryo coexisted with the fish, the lizard with the bird and at the apex, where he joined his god, he combined the disintegration of ultimate fatigue with a jolting orgasm compacted of the will to birth.

I watched. I watched the geometry of his impending fall demonstrate the ratio of victory to defeat which had been mirrored in his rise. I watched the disordered forms I once identified with Icarus rest upon the tip of time, in a total repose, where the whole emphasis of his humanity was shifted and embraced the shape of flight. I watched. I tell you I saw this happen. There was no sound but a beat so shrill in burning that it rang in me. Then the sun was covered and there was no day. The god made no sound, but threw Icarus out of his embrace and tossed him from his clenched fist and in that moment Icarus cried out. I could not hear his scream, I saw it and it was not a scream of pain but a cry of dreadful loss. It scored the side of space like an ostracon, a scratch of exile on a shard. It was a splinter, narrow as a wire, and by it the sky was grooved against its nature. The cry fell, spinning and oscillating and seemed to plunge earthward. The air about me swayed and fell slack and suddenly was restrung like a lyre.

Then Icarus fell out of the sky at infinite leisure, long after his cry had fallen. Ashen plumaged, a broken shearwater, he turned, slowly pinwheeling, among the feeble stars and he was wrapped in a pall of smoke which seemed to muffle him against the cold of his journey out of heat. He took a lifetime in his fall; and time, which brings disorder, seemed to fall sick while a disorder beyond time inverted the passage time creates so that in falling he was orderly. Icarus, a random factor, the conqueror of order, gave back his particle of chance in battle coupled with the sun. In sleep he wandered slowly to the sea.

It has been said that I saw him fall into the sea, but I did not. It has also been said that I searched the sea for him and found his body. I searched but I did not find it. I do not know what his body became since I did not find him. I can only remember what I saw it become.

I flew on without clear direction when my son had gone and as I flew I became uncertain of myself. I had not been used to that uncertainty. I had been troubled that Icarus did not love me and now it troubled me that his pretensions, which had seemed to me absurd and all his life in which I had been disappointed, should at the last have come to form so complete and ordered a pattern. He was a hero and such people I distrust and avoid. It is the function of heroes to conquer death and Icarus had done so in his attempt to conquer the sun. His defeat was his victory and his name would conquer the death of years. I must confess that I was disturbed by the shape of his life and death and basely nervous that they would devalue my own. I am not usually given to envy. I felt no grief and was ashamed of it. Unable to believe what I had seen, I felt that in some way I had been tricked. The whole episode seemed fragmentary, part of the shapelessness which often mars the heroic form. I could not piece it together and the sea gave me back nothing of Icarus, not even the burnt fragments of his wings. Instead the waves chopped and spumed as the wind changed and blew hard from the west. Cloud came in thick and driving rain, so that my search for Icarus became hopeless and I had no chance to wrestle with my thoughts as I wrestled to keep myself in flight.

Low over the water, fighting to gain height, I could do nothing but let the storm take me in its stride. Through that afternoon the rain drummed on my clumsy wings and the wind thrashed and flung me where it would. In the occasional lull I was grateful that the sun was hidden, but when the cold screamed and shook me, I thought it Nemesis and cowered in

142

spirit from it. When night came and with it some little quieting of the weather, I gained height. I was dog-tired and leaden in each limb so that I do not know how I survived. I thought of letting go and following Icarus down into the water but I could hardly take so trivial a course as to go flopping draggled into death after being set such an example. Childishly I felt a silly irritation that Icarus had so unfilially made it impossible for me, for very shame, to die of cold. Cold drove out grief and I still felt none. This too shamed me. I beat lopsided down the wind, hobbling in the air much as I hobbled on the ground when I was tired enough. The storm flogged me like a wet and whimpering dog.

By morning the rain had lifted, although the wind still blew strongly westward. Over the southern point of Attica I remembered Icarus as a child and Naucrate when we had fled from Pallas into the hills and I wondered if there would ever come a time when I should not be in flight from some real or imagined peril. Still I felt no grief for Icarus, but only pity for myself and I was more ashamed.

I felt defeated. What I was seemed futile. I had no part of the hero in me and no part of Icarus whose blood was mine. I tried to weep. I urged myself toward grief and all I felt was some personal inadequacy so meaninglessly slight that I could not analyze it. I grew angry, which gave me a certain strength.

Aegina and Salamis lay ahead and then drifted away behind me. Athens was hidden in morning mist. The sun rose on my right and I scrabbled in my brain for courage, trying to think myself to bravery, despising terror, but terror seeped through the cracks in my leaking thought. Icarus had fallen. I had seen it. I feared I could not feel it and began to fear myself incomplete. I feared myself disrupted, that my humanity had burnt out or been quenched and above all, shrilly denying it in my bruised brain, I feared Apollo's advance upon me.

I told myself of my familiarity with intractable materials and of how I could subdue and master the inanimate, that I knew how to use things with precision and employ their power. I told myself I was an ordered and proper man and that gods, who lack precision and belong to a different order of being, are not concerned with the affairs of men. I told myself that feckless and fragile figures like my son live and die deluded, but I did not believe it. I feared the god and did not love him, being the father of Icarus and not a hero. And every moment took me nearer to Delphi, to the god's chosen house.

Nothing happened. Delphi hung high, cupped amid the rocks to the east of me and the god shone blandly on it. I had not been there since my father took me as a child and Apollo had not been there then. Instead there had been snow and a dead child. Now there was sun but there was no sign. Then Delphi lay behind me and I was flying further west. The sun rose above me and moved toward his midday height. Perhaps he accepted Icarus' burnt offering. Religion has never been my chief concern and although I know useful charms for making metals alloy and cleansing the faults in unhewn stone, I have never made a study of the forms of worship most pleasing to individual gods. I am not adept. I am not a priest. That function image makers once had, but it is lost to us.

I was perplexed and spent my next hours of flight in trying to remember prayers forgotten in childhood. The Sky God's opposition to the Mother bothered me because I could not remember the proper distinctions between them and how one must play them off against one another. I regretted my neglect of formal devotions. I had paid scant attention to them since I was a boy. I tried to pray, just as I tried to grieve, and my fatigue was such that I could manage neither. I could only fly. Another night came on and how that passed and how the next day went has become blurred to me with time. I was so dazed in my exhaustion that even now I have no idea how I reached Italy. Each of those days must have been days like any other, in that Apollo rose and moved across the hours. His circle is perpetual and I believed he did not notice how I trudged the air beneath him.

My journey ended when and where it ended not by any

144

doing of mine. Aeolus from his nearby island had the wind put me down a stone's throw from the sea upon the western shore of Italy and where it put me I lay and slept. Curiously I remember very clearly the final fragment of my thought as I lay toppled on the sand below Cumae.

I thought "Grief" and could not remember what the word meant and was vaguely perplexed.

PART TWO

I awoke in the sand and groped about under my **26**
battered tent of wing. I searched for something
I had lost and slept again and woke. What I had lost was
Icarus.

"Grief," I thought, "I have no grief. I have lost it," and I
felt about with my fingers for it in the sand. I tried to move
my legs and pain shot through me. Then I remembered what
I had lost. I wept and as the tears came I knew they were not
for Icarus but for myself. I tried to weep for Icarus and wept
for my own weariness. I told myself that I had lost my son
and was puzzled. Grief and perplexity like little squabbling
half-brothers pulled and pushed at me, each urging me to
play with the other.

Very gradually I crawled to my knees in an agony of
strained and wrenching sinews and the sun was warm on my
aching back, the shining sun. I remembered and was afraid.

The sand stretched away in a great curve, its edge flicked by
an innocent and tranquil sea. The sun-smile sparkled on its
edge. I turned painfully, still on hands and knees, and saw a
vast and sudden rock rise out of the scrub, as pitted with holes
as a wasps' nest and looking scarcely smaller than the rock of
Athens. An acropolis seemingly unpeopled, the rock of Cumae
lay humped upon its isthmus.

I knew where I was; seamen at Knossos had told me of this
place, this mighty honeycomb of stone topped with a temple
to Apollo. Apollo! All my fears returned, first gouting in my
belly and then dribbling detail to my brain. My loss, lonely,
unshared, particular, pricked at me, but I could not keep it

central to my mind. I felt like a gourd split open, clubbed and pulpy, and vegetable pain swished slushy in this broken basin. Fear dropped into it, splashing doubt upon me. I lay down again, letting the god's grin restore me, letting warmth and apprehension crawl together on my drying skin.

I lay with my head clutched in my hands to shut out the light and made such vows and promises to the god as a slave might make to buy himself off further beating. I vowed to rebuild Apollo's temple on the rock, to make a noble house and give it golden doors. I promised him all I had, squirming under my wings, and then remembered that all I had to offer were my wings. It was not rational, but to be rational in such circumstances requires a greater detachment than I had. Nevertheless, I remember I tried to overcome my callow terror and to consider my situation soberly. I tried to take a sober and judicious attitude, even as I knew I should not dare to avoid keeping the grandiose promises I was unable to restrain. And all the time I endured this conflict with myself, I tried to let in grief. I was so anguished in my failure to grieve that I was grief-stricken. My mind cried "Icarus" and waited for the pang. Tears came and I offered them to memory, but it was useless. I managed to stand up and once upon my feet to achieve some equilibrium.

You will understand that it was important for me to preserve an equilibrium, to be balanced and ordered. I had nothing to offer Apollo except my wings, but these were not insubstantial gifts. If they were placed in his temple on the summit of the rock, it seemed to me, the god would find them acceptable. I also thought that if I scaled the rock I should have a vantage point, an adequate height from which to launch myself upon a rising wind and so continue my flight toward Sicily, for I could not fly from the foreshore.

Strangely, I did not consider that if I gave my wings to Apollo I could not continue my flight, but then the preservation of a sober and judicious attitude at such a time is so strenuous that practicalities can easily be overlooked.

150

With these important decisions made, I stood on the fore-shore trying to implement them. On the isthmus between the sea and the pallid lake, I stood in a vortex at the empty center of my life, struggling to keep a balance between the memory of my son lost in the sea and the need to placate the god. There was no sound except the monotonous flicking of the sea, talking trivially at the sand, repeating the wet signature of its brief surge.

When I look at my hands they usually comfort me. I am proud to see them, simply and adequately designed to obey my demands. My hands have always seemed to me more than parts of my body and to be curiously separate and autonomous. When I look down at them I am secure. I know them and I know their competence. My fingers flex, the closing thumb is smooth and perfect in action. Together they deal ably with awkward mechanical problems. My hands are seldom in error and I am content to possess them, for they are all I need. But there below the high rock, my hands hung upon my arms like strangers and I had no purpose for them. To fold my wings was blunt and bungled labor. To stow them so that I could carry them was a fumbling business. I held my hands before my face and no longer believed in their abilities, nor in myself, nor in my grief, nor in my high craft. In order to give my hands some simple task, I took them to the rock. To give them some hoisting function, I began to climb so that they might act for me.

I reached for a hold and moved upward from boulder to boulder and then higher upon the face of the rock, watching my fingers catch and grip the foliage and fasten on the stones. I followed my hands upward away from the sea and from my son's death and from the events which had emptied me. My hands carried my empty mind toward the temple of Apollo, so that I might make an offering to him and Apollo knelt on my back as I climbed. The god's knee pressed me down so that somewhere on the escarpment I rested, lying flattened and pressed face to face with the rock. On bladed chips of shale, held casually by the roots of thyme and cystus, I pinioned myself to a landscape which moved as the scree slid past me. This landscape, a handspan from my eyes, was an adequate world. If I could have entered it, merged with the ochre dust, opened to the appetite of the earth and let it eat me, I should have done so. All men are lizards trapped in dust by time. This dust I felt no need to scuffle in, nor could I write my marks upon it for it was a baked and impervious cake of iron-hard clay, dry to my cheek and unwilling to consume me.

At once remote and immediate, the handspan landscape faded and returned to me with heavy regularity, humming and sighing. The briars of the rock rose, swooped and turned, the sabred sprigs of the junipers clashed among the grass spears. Every fleck of stone, every granule of the clotted dust packed by the passage of the long drained cataract, came looming toward me, peopled with insects, laborious and brisk, crossing their kingdom. Each sought some substance to consume or some dross for building. Those winged spun up and flew the passage of seconds and returned for unknown purposes. Those wingless trouped out of the glare, among the colorless spines of long-dead thistles, and went into the dark groves of the roots of scrub. Armored creatures crept into the cracked and rigid earth to mine invisible corruption.

I lay upon this insect city and it inhabited me. An ant, exploring my disturbance of his polis, entered my head through a nostril and, undislodged by sneezing, went in panic deep into my brain. Painless to me, he passed into my mind and as he went he took the name of Daedalus while Daedalus, his future labyrinth, stared down on his apprenticed brothers as they dragged straws to prop the temples of their deme. One, burdened by a scrap of twig, trudged with it slowly toward the shade and led his fellows with him so that a slim black line of loaded insects wound upward into the forest of the grass. This trail of ants I followed, pulling myself upward with all the strength of my arms and moving as hugely above it as Apollo moved above me. I left the landscape of the stream bed having seen no monsters, neither mantis nor lizard, but only the long day's life in little and I climbed in a single stride beyond the ant track and upward toward the temple of the god who had destroyed my son. Climbing, I remembered suddenly that for those insect minutes in the microcosm, I had forgotten both my sky-god and my son.

The ant, my namesake, flickered in his maze. I climbed through thorns and brushwood and all the while the air sang like the entrance to a hive.

Small stones clattered on Cumae. The temple to Apollo stood rickety on the table of the rock and bees mobbed in its thatch. Warped, a wooden knuckle of worship, stupid, askew, the temple leaned on shoring balks. Gateless, shambling, disordered, a temple stacked from tinder, it was a place dried of the sap of honor by the god it sought to honor and he stared down upon it in bleak white anger.

As I stood there in sweat and dust, I saw smoke rise from the roof thatch and the bees rose in a swarm, thrumming alarm. A flame slipped through the smoke. The god was burning his house and it did not take him long. From this pyre, the god spoke snarling and as the building shrank from silver, subsiding into black and blowing ash, there came a continual sound, pulsing like a high fever. Words cracked like roasting hide. The language of the god spluttered in my mind and congealed into one sporadically repeated word:

"Rebuild" . . . "Rebuild" . . . "Rebuild" . . . The curved god rounded like a wind on the pinnacle, his bow drawn. The burning god burned my breath, as he had burned Icarus, and there was no mercy of water on that riven stylobate, no sea to quench the fallen house. The furnace-day, bright with flying arrows, blinded me. The brandished flames spat in my face. Prostrate below the lip of the summit I watched the holocaust of insects. The oxen of the microcosm curled up and died. Mice, rats, and quails, the giant fauna, ran from the place and in their passage twisted and lay charred. A mantis reared and vanished downward. A snake slid between two hewn stones, downward through singing, singeing grass. Suddenly I was caught and sucked into the rock by a wind as fierce and burning as that which had flung me out from beneath Knossos. I went out of the god's eye like a snake into its hole.

Under Cumae lies Gaia open to the spear. A **27** thousand channels pass through her stone sex, a thousand mouths breathe from her core of rock. Below these mouth-openings, a thousand throats pass to her lungs. She is not shaped mortally, lipped only for double purposes at the extremities of her trunk, but each opening in her is a nether and an upper mouth. Roots and the tangled tendrils of the shrubs, pubis or beard, cloak her entrances and all her openings lead downward to the fretted honeycomb of her thorax. Thus Gaia breathes and in her womb, beyond the estuary of her lungs, beyond her entrail maze and ominous liver, sleep those whose birth is continual. She is earth.

Now I knew why the ant had entered me. It was Apollo's joke. I was as much imprisoned in the earth as the ant was pent in me. Gaia had breathed sharply under the welt of the sun-strike on her brow and I was sharp inhaled. I scrabbled in her nostril and crawled upward into the opening. A lid of flame came down at me. I waited and tried again. It was useless. I retreated, beating the sparks out of my singeing hair. With the fire raging over me and Apollo's tongue lapping at the rock, I knew myself to be his insect and I recognized his joke. The jokes of gods can be very simple. Icarus had been a flying ant and Apollo had spat him out. Now let me try to spit out my insect.

To the macrocosm, the microcosm is a comic midget and nothing will make a god laugh more than the dwarfish. As for myself, I was in no state to conceive that the joke could sometimes work both ways. I was not badly burned. I was not in much pain but I was imprisoned without hope of escape until I could rebuild the temple on the summit of the rock of

Cumae. I did not believe I could even stay alive in the great bowels of Gaia where the dead are held suspended and yet I was not dead. I could not see how Apollo's joke could give him pleasure if I were. Therefore I should not die. Time passed and I was slowly drawn downward. I caught one final glimpse of the world outside, of the blazing sky and the black fringe of charred brush smoking in the opening and then I went into the dark. I wondered when I should see trees growing again and for a moment I remembered the sea, which I had feared so much a short time ago, and I felt a dreadful longing for it.

Time, as I have said, is a liquid, but it can be viscous. Gaia's saliva flows heavy with the slow movement and weight of honey and I hung in it like a fly in amber. As honey runs glutinous or in milky crystals clogs the comb, holding itself opaque, I hung in honey-time blind in the clouded comb and I knew only the sight of memory. This too blurred and I no longer knew on what day Apollo burned his house and laid my task on me. I hung suspended as the dead. The dead, however, do not remain suspended except in men's minds, where heroes refuse to die and therefore will not change. My son is one of these. For all the terrible energy of his act he is held static, enshrined in the fame of it.

Moving imperceptibly downward into the nether labyrinth of Gaia, I entered the tightest revolutions of a helix and in my passage lived deluded, believing in a repetition, a second chance. I came to identify the labyrinth I had built at Knossos with the labyrinth I now inhabited and in the darkness I imagined that the turning passages below Cumae were familiar to me. I believed myself returning, circling inevitably toward a past that would come to meet me so that in due time I should find Icarus as a child, playing with his nautilus shell unbroken, and I should be given the alternative.

In the silken, opiate stream of Gaia's honey-time, I saw all things dissolve to be resolved. Even my perplexity slept and those powers of calculation and deduction upon which I have always prided myself fell like playthings from me. I traveled

155

downward like a man happy to die, but disturbed that he is not doing so.

Were I a hero, or a conqueror of nations, or a warrior destroying for glory, I could have wandered longer in this idiot trance. I should have had no doubts as to my destiny. But being a technician I am goaded with minor compulsions which jolt me out of sleep. The trigger of the mechanism of this disease is invariably an uncompleted task. Self-set or laid upon me, either way if it is not properly begun or cannot be properly finished, it will steal my rest. Such unresolved problems do not wake me, they hook at my repose so that I set to work only to wake later and find my labor was a dream.

Sleep muffled me. All that I could touch with knowledge was the pack of my wrapped wings, tied on my back. All that I could feel was a soft and regular heartbeat which was not my own but greater.

The ant stirred in my brain. His eyelash feet teased tiptoe at my sleep. He ran directionless, starting and stopping, silent in search of his fellow craftsmen.

I had no more fellow craftsmen than the ant. The hooks snagged in my quiet, loosed and caught again. Were I a hero or a warrior I could have fought imagined monsters and returned to sleep, but my task was to build, to build a temple. I had no tools, nor the means to make any, no men to quarry stone, no masons, no carpenters. I was awake, dreamed awake in sleep. The barbed questions plucked at me, each nick an item of necessity. To cast the doors of the temple I should need space, a place to work and light to work by. Item, I should need wax, item, a hearth large enough to burn the modeled wax from the mantle, item, a kiln for smelting and alloying the metals, item, crucibles large enough to contain a sufficient pour, item, tongs, a variety of pairs of tongs, item, copper ore of reasonable purity and tin in a proportion of one to nine to the copper. I should need materials to core the wax, rock chips ground fine and clay. I must make rivets to assemble the doorframe and hold the panels, I should need hammers, an anvil, bellows, or leather to make them. I must have bellows enough to give a smelting temperature and also chasers, burnishers and abrasives for cold work. Each item in this catalogue of necessities was a fish-hook which the ant beat into a rivet and hammered to my brain with small repeated blows. Even as I sought in my mind to list my needs for the doors and for the casting of Apollo's image, there crowded in upon me the recollection that the temple itself would need no doors until I had built it. The tapping ant paused in his compulsive hammering and fell irresolute. Fool, ant-fool that I was, with my six-legged intentions running frantic, I still hung between sleeping and waking.

I awoke. Suddenly I was truly awake, seeing nothing, but awake. Encumbered, stupid among my struggling resolutions, it seemed as if my head were a stone cell filled with jumbled properties. In this cranial outhouse, the tools I needed hung in me on pegs. They were gathered haphazard in piles upon the dusty floor, strewn together with the husks of projects and all manner of failed inventions, false starts and ramshackle contrivances. My life's experience, gritty and partial, was stacked like lumber in a little room. Yet out of this confusion came, clean and sharp, the image of the temple and how it would be.

I saw it standing on the rock. I knew its geometry and the order of its structure. Every detail, each figure depicted in relief upon the doors was plain to me as I should portray them in bronze, in honor of Apollo. And I should make the god himself of bronze, cast hollow, and in Apollo's right hand I should put his bow, but in his left hand I should give him, to hold, the figure of Icarus winged. Then when the building was made and the image of the god had been placed in it, I should leave my wings at the god's feet. This was how I should make my offering and furnish the god's house.

Suddenly the liquid which held me captive thinned and ran smooth and clear and there was no longer darkness. It was as if the sky-god poured me into the uterus of the earth, my future workshop.

The light was slow to come and at first partial. I could see my hands again and my knees, for I was kneeling askew in the passage. It was narrow and turned away to the left. I did not move at first but crouched where I was to think what I should do. Part of me searched like a housewife for some ordered recollection of my list of necessities. I looked to the bundle of my wings and it was intact. I took stock with no stock to take.

Any bronze worker has had to seek his materials in the earth whether or not he is a maze maker, since native copper on the surface is not so common. Alluvial deposits are quickly exhausted and so men dig for metals and have done so for many generations. These men are usually small and wary. They do not mix with farmers or ordinary people, but keep themselves apart and are suspect for it. Thus tradition often turns them into giants like the Cyclopes or dwarfs like the Cabeiri. In either case, they are credited with remarkable and dangerous powers and it is thus that when they band together they can move the cores of mountains. They maintain that they are all sons of Hephaistos, but then, of course, men in difficult trades tend to extol their mysteries by assuming divine paternities and miners obscure the secrets of their calling to give themselves prestige. You cannot blame them; their work is hard and they are short-lived. Nevertheless, their function is vital to craftsmen and there are sects and cults in the mines who claim to have special and divine skills in smelting. Of these, the Telchines of Rhodes and the Idean Dactyli, who boast that they were the first to alloy metals and to make bronze itself, are among the greatest braggarts. I am myself prepared to consider their claims, although I believe bronze smelting came from further east long ago. Someone must have stumbled on the technique and probably Prometheus deserves credit for having instigated it.

There is no craft more demonstrative of mystery than bronze

casting and none, it seems, so impressive to watch, for the process appears more the product of magic working than the work of man's hands. I have had whole villages assemble to watch me cast some little figure of a local god and you would have laughed to see men, women and children stare wide-eyed at the inevitable transformations which the craft makes manifest when shown in practice, even in its simplest form.

To put the matter simply, it is three things that make bronze casting dramatic and therefore a memorable spectacle. One is the use of fire and liquid fire at that, the others are the making, the destruction and the rebirth of an image, and finally the strange changes in the color of metals which alter mysteriously not only during their working but with the passage of time.

If you are not initiated you will need some explanation or you, too, in whatever age you live, will find yourself as dumbfounded as any peasant. Suppose then that you are simple and in your village you require an image of a god or more modestly a votive offering of bronze which you yourself wish to dedicate, as from time to time you must. Suppose there is none readymade and available in some peddler's pack for you. Suppose again that a bronze founder comes to your headman who offers him gifts in exchange for his skill. He will perhaps be a small, dark, secretive man from another country, which will make him strange to you anyway. Also, he will do his best to emphasize this strangeness with much pantomime, for he counts, without need, on being memorably curious.

Watch him and you will see how the mystery unfolds. He will first commandeer your pottery kiln and have sufficient bellows available to raise a temperature high enough to fire pots hard as iron, but in your kiln he will have placed but a single lipped beaker and that already fired, a thick, heavy, porous and fireproof one which he has filled with oddly colored stones. They are rough brown lumps of rock and they look spongy, or they may be crumbled, powdery and a brilliant green. To these, with careful measurement, he adds a small quantity of black sand and with these in the pot and reverently placed in the kiln, he sets men to build up heat. The men blow up the fire with bellows and, hidden from you, the great heat will melt and fuse these lumps of ore, for that is what they are, with the black sand which is kassiterite. These materials are copper and tin and they will become molten bronze.

The metals will not heat quickly nor fuse until they reach a certain temperature, so in the long time to spare the smith will take beeswax and model it to the shape of a god, or of a bull, or whatever is needed. He will make a wax cup at the base of the model and if the figure is more than a finger's length, he will put sticks of wax between the limbs and others will jut out from it, and when this is done he will enfold all but the opening of the cup and the ends of those sticks of wax which jut out, in a paste of clay and stone chippings until it looks like a loaf of rough bread ready for baking. You have seen the image made and then buried in a clay husk. Then you will see him place it in a fire and the wax will burn and pour forth smoking. The image is destroyed and only its husk remains, a hollow loaf of stone and clay, with vents where the cup and the sticks of wax have been. That will be the first mystery you will see and you should not be surprised if the founder makes the most of it.

Now watch the preparation for the second mystery. A pit will be dug and filled with wet sand and in this pit the clay loaf will be buried with only the vents left visible. Then the kiln will be opened and with tongs the smith will lift out the pot. No longer filled with lumps of rock, it holds liquid fire—a cup of running heat—and first scooping the scum from the surface, the smith will pour this blazing redness into the cup-shaped vent left open in the loaf of clay. He will pour in a single swift movement. He will also cry out to the god. Smoke will rise and gases sizzle from the vents and swiftly the liquid fire will rise to follow the smoke until the vents brim. That will be the spectacle of the second mystery.

There will now be much time to wait and much ritual of prayer, incantation and the sacrifice of pigeons or some such small creatures and much murmuring of charms. This will be no part of the mystery but a great part of the mystification, but you will not know that, and so the night will pass.

Now it is morning and the smith will raise the loaf of clay from the pit and hold it up, crying for the god to bless his labor. Then he will lay it on the ground and strike the loaf seven times with a hammer and the crust will fall away from an image which will be set upright on its cup-shaped base and the image will be of imperishable and golden metal. It will be dusty from its clay womb and still too hot to touch with the naked hand, but clearly the very spit of the figure made so skillfully in soft beeswax all those hours ago.

There then is the third mystery, and one is added, for the figure will sprout slender metal prongs like multiple umbilical cords, as if it had had many mothers in the fire. With more ritual the smith will cut these away once the figure is cool and then he will fall to polishing, burnishing and chasing the cooled bronze to make it smooth and make it shine.

Place your votive in the shrine then, for it is finished, but return in later years and it will have changed its color. Bury it in the *bothros* and return in a decade and its color will have changed again, to green or vivid blue, or black, or a combination of all three. That is the final mystery. Is it any wonder that men who can contrive such things come to be much feared and remembered when they have gone, as dwarfs or giants? These are ancient skills and mysteries, but I do not think they will change greatly. They will still be worked much as I have described them, in your time, although it may be that there will be less portentious priestcraft among your artificers.

That I should have digressed here to describe the **29** bronze founder's methods serves two purposes. Firstly, you now know something of what must be done to make images in metal, although I have only described what

you may see when bronze is made and not why these proce-
dures should be followed; nor have I revealed to you the nature
of them, nor the alternatives, nor the subtleties of the facture.
Secondly, as I crouched there in the tunnel taking stock, with
no stock to take, it was thus that I rehearsed the processes of
my profession, together with those of carpentry and stone
carving, of architecture, mechanics, drawing and proportion.
Thus I gathered my skills about me for reassurance and
wrapped myself in the comfort, such as it was, of my mystery.

I knew that it was childish even as I did so, for I could see no
way to employ any of these skills in the bleak mine shaft of
Gaia's throat, but like a child lost in a cave who remembers the
safety of his own bed, I assured myself that all would yet be
well and remembered that I was not helpless, but a sufficient
and resourceful man. Decisions as to priorities, listing of requirements and speculation upon methods, these are my re-
storatives. They are a way of ordering the mind and to me
preferable to other rituals such as whistling in the dark. They
eased me and quieted my fears so that when I looked about me
I no longer saw a channel sinking into an unknown deep, but
rock-strata one seam of which was clearly of copper-bearing
ore. This vein ran obliquely across the left-hand wall, twisting
capriciously like the flight of a spent arrow. I rose and followed
its flight and I knew that one at least of my needs was to be
satisfied.

Everyone fears the darkness in some degree, believing that
death and darkness are ultimately one, and it is generally supposed by simple people that the dead are penned forever in the
center of the earth. This dreadful kingdom, visited by Persephone in winter, is easy to reach, but for all but Persephone
so difficult to leave that only a few heroes, immortals and other
especially privileged persons have ever done so. So deep a rut
has been worn in man's memory by Persephone's winter journey and her invariable return, that the idea of a kingdom of
the dead and dark passages leading down to it is not to be
repaired nor even partially filled by a hodful of logical thought

162

hastily tipped into it. Yet, in my experience, there is no way to defeat fear, unless one is a hero, except to think through it to the other side. Thus, as I made my slow descent under Cumae, I had to find my way not only through the proliferating veins and channels of Gaia's vast and living body, but through a mass of old tales half-remembered from childhood and of half-comprehended beliefs accepted then and thereafter without proper examination. Irrational fears are as awkward to disperse as a rock fall and although my journey was not difficult physically, I perpetually tripped and stumbled over ancient terrors and fell into the deeps of multiple human superstitions as dark and terrible as they were old and bred in me.

Gaia's mighty trunk had its inhabitants. There were other wanderers and other prisoners in her belly, but it occurred to me, even as I went forward, that if the whole gathering of all those who had ever died were packed into her entrails, however incorporeal those spirits of the dead might be, then the Earth Mother would be so painfully afflicted with wind that all her parts would be continually shaken with prodigious disturbances and I should even at that moment be violently made aware of them. I laughed, I remember, even at the time to think of it, for the place was so quiet.

There were mysteries enough in that subterranean landscape to confound any sceptic disbelief in the powers beyond human knowledge. The light which seemed to penetrate the rock as water penetrates limestone was of a crystalline texture. It dripped slowly and as endlessly as if it meant to form stalactites of sight and I who have lit my way through many caves and worked underground for long periods, know no precedent for this luminosity. I have generally worked in the choking smoke of oil lamps which are frequently snuffed out from lack of air. Mines, like mazes of any depth, are exceedingly dangerous for this and other obvious reasons. There was no obvious danger, nor was I short of breath, below Cumae. Then too there was evidence that men had mined metals here. I could tell from the surface markings on the walls and from the fact that my

163

vein of exposed copper had been partly tapped. Men had been here, yet I knew no report of mines self-lit nor had I ever heard described, in all my wanderings and in all my many encounters with metal workers, of mine shafts which throbbed and changed color as if life lay pulsing in them.

I thought the chemistry of the changed earth had come about through Apollo's penetration of the Mother. In this I was right. I thought that this epic copulation was in order in some way to give birth to the temple I should build and this was a childish conceit, as I now know. A drunkenness had come upon me so that I sang and shouted like a fool, cavorting behind Gaia's larynx or in whatever stretch of one of her multiple vents or gullets I found myself. And thus I went on downward, tracing the vein of copper with my finger-tips, dipping where it dipped, rising where it rose and leaping upward to touch it when it stretched beyond my reach.

The passage curled and twisted, sometimes it thrust away at acute and then veered at obtuse angles, ran uphill, dipped and swung. Not only did I dance as wildly as any wine-filled satyr, but the very earth leaped and ran with me like wine from the jar. When I had first detected the seam of copper it was so slender and unobtrusive that only one experienced in metals would have noticed it. Now it gleamed and flashed red as the vintage yet like russet gold, so that in my frenzy I thought I heard it clash like the shields on Ida which deafened Cronos to the birth cry of Zeus.

Quite suddenly the vein petered out as if its metal blood had ceased to flow. So sudden was its retreat that its absence caused a sort of silence and my voice howled foolishly and alone, like that of a singer left stranded and absurd when the flutes and drums cease abruptly to support him. My song trundled to a silly halt and I stood still. I had lost all notion of my whereabouts, lost it so utterly that I stood stunned like an ox driven out of the quick sunlight into the blank dark of the byre. The red cord of the copper vein had been like Ariadne's thread but now it remained only in my mind. I was mewed up and my

164

fears returned. On my knees I crept about in the tunnel patting at the ground. I was no longer sure that anything I could see was actual. I felt the walls advance, dip and recede. The ceiling arched and then sagged. The floor tipped and swayed. I knelt there motionless, a fixed point, an island in a tempest. Then I lay full length on my face and mixed prayer with appeals to my own reason and presently I slept.

I had not eaten since I began my flight with Icarus and I had slept on the shore below the rock, but only briefly. Even wonder is eventually overcome by exhaustion and I slept with my head on my corded wings and dreamed, but I did not remember what I had dreamed. I remember that just before I slept, I spoke out loud to myself. "You must remember who you are," I said. "You are Daedalus and you are familiar with mine working. You are simply tired. There is nothing alarming here."

A man, sitting on a ledge, said, "You have now slept for many hours." He was a small man, pale and heavy browed, a very small man.

"I was very tired. You see, I flew here with my son from Crete and he flew into the sun and was burned. I was very tired. You must forgive me." What I said did not sound sensible.

The man got up. He was naked and wizened. I could not tell his age nor his race, but it was clear that his profession was to dig for metals. Standing at his full height he looked like a child of eight or ten who had been long entombed, but it was difficult to believe that there had been mourning at his burial. However, he seemed in no way menacing and he spoke Greek of a sort. He asked my name.

"My name is Daedalus."

"I have heard of you. You are an Athenian."

"I am an Athenian, but I have come from Crete. I came on wings through the air."

He did not reply and I repeated what I had said. This man was certainly not a Greek. After a long pause, he said, "You have slept many hours. I have watched you sleep and I have heard what you said. You spoke in Greek."

"I am an Athenian."

"Yes, you spoke in Greek."

"We Athenians normally speak in Greek."

"You spoke in Greek while you slept. Do Athenians always speak Greek while they sleep?"

To judge from his delivery, this man did not speak frequently, awake or asleep. His next statement he brought out even more slowly and with great solemnity.

"This place is sacred."

"To whom?"

"To the Mother and to her relative the sky-god Apollo who it is said lives above and is a golden disk."

"Do you serve Apollo?"

"I have not seen him in all my life. I have not left this place since I was born. I serve only the Mother and I am her child. I inhabit her."

"Alone?"

"Not alone."

"You must know," I said, "that I did not enter this sacred place of my free will but was driven by the Sky God. I serve him and shall build a temple to him if the Mother will aid me."

He looked calmly at me and said, "All that may be, providing that you are not mad. You have the signs of earth madness and behave strangely."

"I was very tired."

"This I know, for you have slept many hours. You spoke in Greek while you slept."

I am a patient man but circular conversation wearies me and I could see no reason why our dialogue should not circle again. Since much that has happened to me in my life has seemed circular, I attempted to make some progress with the formalities. I asked his name, but he did not reply. Presently, and quite courteously, he asked,

"How does a man fly, what is it to fly?"

"I flew on wings."

"In the air?"

"Yes."

"What are wings?"

I pointed to my pack.

"You are a stranger," he said, "and an Athenian, but we are not fools here. A man cannot fly in the air by clutching a corded bale to his belly." With this he went down the passage and out of sight. I went after him but could not find him. The passage branched at that place and led away in three different directions.

The small man's departure was so abrupt and so unexpected that I had not had time to enlist his help. I was hungry, ravenously hungry, and my drunkenness, although it had not been provoked by wine, had left behind it all the discomforts usually earned by drinking wine unwatered. My head ached and my thirst was even greater than my hunger. Even an Athenian can feel himself a fool and I felt one. I called down each corridor in turn, but there was no reply. So with my corded bale of wings clutched to my belly, I chose the central passage and toiled on down it. It forked and since the choice had no real significance to one so lost, I took the right. It forked again and this time I took the left. It was still light enough to see but the tunnels were no longer shot with colors nor incandescent, nor did they pulse. They were rock and earth and as ordinary as those in any mine, except that their plan was not deducible. The passages appeared wayward, patternless and arbitrary. Here and there I found evidence of working at the face; patches of oxidized manganese, black as pitch, had been scraped. There was iron ore but no use had been made of that. Even in Crete, iron was not then understood although I had seen samples of it which had been wrought in the mountains in the east far beyond the sea and beyond Troy.

Distance has not much meaning underground unless you know the extent of the workings and are used to them. I do not know how far I went except that such rest as I had had from my restless sleep wore off and my legs ached. It was hot and humid.

I came then unexpectedly into an open space, a junction of six or more passages. The light was better there and the air a little easier to breathe. In the center of this space, an oval cavern, there stood a stone table or altar and on it, to my enormous relief, was laid a jug of water, two loaves, cheese on a vine leaf, and a piece of honeycomb on a shaped, wooden trencher.

I was not surprised. Surprise requires some departure from normality, and lacking any norm from which to depart, I was not surprised. Nor was I precipitate. I did not at once attack the food. I poured out a libation from the jug, naming Apollo. I broke a fragment of bread and crumbled it, naming the Mother. Racking my brain, I also called upon every earth deity I could remember, by every name and in every tongue which I could muster. A piece of honeycomb I offered to Persephone and another to her mother Demeter. Roast pork is her favorite dish but she is said to like honey. I mentioned Cronos, made general obeisance to gods unknown to me by name and cautiously sought to leave no member of any pantheon who could conceivably be offended, unpropitiated. During the course of this elaborate performance which I conducted, I must admit, with increasing hunger and growing irritation, I became aware that I was being watched.

"I thank also my hosts for their generosity and give myself freely into their keeping, knowing now that they treat a stranger as handsomely as a guest." I said this loudly and without looking about me before I squatted down and ate and drank. The food was fresh and it was excellent. The jug had a certain sophistication, it was heavy and thick compared to the palace pottery of Minos, but it was well painted and well fired. If it had been made locally, then I had one more tool available for my building. There must be a kiln and at least one person here who understood the firing of ceramics.

The clay of the jug was pinkish like that of Attica, but it was not Attic, nor was it Cretan nor the creamy clay of Corinth nor Chalcidian nor from the east, to the best of my knowledge. Holding it in my hands, I began in my mind to design acroteria and revetments for the temple roof. If good stone was not available at Cumae I should have to make extensive use of terracotta. I should need cypress wood for the supporting members, large trunks, set root uppermost to hold the king and tie beams, I should need to cast bronze saws and adzes, I should need . . . and once again the ant began to run helter-skelter about my brain, listing necessities, contriving, meeting difficulties and overcoming them. I forgot that I was imprisoned in the rock and that I was under surveillance by who knew how many small occupants of Gaia's maternal bulk. I forgot that I was not the master of the works and that there might be little or no willing labor to aid me in fulfilling my obligations to Apollo. However consequential this god might be to me, he was a golden disk known only by hearsay to the small man with whom I had spoken.

I set the jug down on the stone table. Six men, apparently identical, were standing about me, one in the entrance to each of the six passages. Each held his right hand to his forehead and each stood very straight. They looked absurdly like faïence votives in a shrine. All were naked.

I did not know how to proceed. I was not sure that any one of these six stiff little figures was my previous acquaintance. I stood up, assumed a noble stance with my right hand upon my breast and said:

"My name is Daedalus, I am come to build a temple to the god Apollo who brings light even to this the core of the earth."

"This place," one of the small men replied in slow but recognizable Greek, "is sacred."

169

Now Apollo give me patience, I thought, we are about to repeat the whole conversation again, and it struck me at once that Apollo had not shown any patience himself in my recent encounter with him. Compared to some gods he must be considered an ordered and reasonable one, but probably no gods could be called patient, for if time means nothing to gods they may as easily want the vows made to them instantly fulfilled as be prepared to wait a millennium. Gaia give me patience, then, and may her golden relative be patient on his own behalf.

"I know, for I have been told, that this is a holy place and I honor the Mother whom we also worship in Crete. I ask your help, for I am vowed to Apollo and I ask the aid of the Mother in this sacred enterprise with which I am charged."

"We have spoken of this," said the small man, who now stepped forward from the entrance to one tunnel, "and are undecided whether you are mad or not, but we shall not harm you." The remaining five men remained standing rigidly in the attitude of votaries, each in his own doorway.

"I am grateful," I said.

The small man who spoke I now recognized as my earlier acquaintance. A wizened silvery figure, he looked as if he were eroded from limestone, which gave him a certain calcined dignity.

"I am the Greek Speaker," he said, crossed his legs and sat down. "I am he who speaks Greek. These, my brothers, do not."

I too sat down. "How is it that you alone speak my language here?" I asked him.

"Men come here for metals and I have spoken with them in trade."

"You trade in metals, then?"

"It is our trade and how we live, we are the children of the Mother and live in her. She gives us metals from her breasts and her milk feeds us."

"Her milk then is liquid?"

"It is her milk."

This was not a conversation to be conducted with any but the most tedious formality, but rhetoric is no problem to me. I therefore made once more what seemed the necessary sequence of nobly phrased statements as to my intentions and in the course of an interminable colloquy conducted in terms so measured that even Gaia's eternal calm must I felt have been ruffled, I learned certain things.

I learned that these metal workers never ventured out into the sunlight. I learned that they had come originally from the north, but how long ago and why, no one knew. I learned that as a race they were much feared by those who lived upon the surface and that despite the mysterious or metaphorical nutrition they received from Gaia's breasts, they got their honeycomb, their corn and a more prosaic milk than Gaia's left for them as offerings to the Mother, at the various entrances to her body. In this, like priests elsewhere, they received their staple diet as a by-product of the fear of simpletons. Acting upon this, I promised an offering to the Mother sufficiently grandiose and unusual to ensure that I should be respected. I promised to make her a honeycomb in gold.

My purpose in this was twofold. To be respected and as a result to obtain both materials and labor was my primary need, but I had also to know the extent of their skills in metal and with what metals they were familiar.

There are those who can work copper competently, but lacking tin cannot make bronze. Copper is a difficult metal, quick to cool and therefore short in the pour. It is also very soft. Tools made with it will not hold an edge. It is perfectly possible to make large copper images by beating the metal in thin sheets over a wooden or bitumen core, but it is exceptionally difficult to cast any object larger than, say, a human hand. The pour cools, the metal contracts violently and the mold fails to fill properly. Tin is essential to any ambitious project because even a proportion of one to fifteen of tin to copper prevents these disasters. This, I discovered to my great satisfaction, the small man knew. He and his race were not simply miners. Copper they had as I knew, and smelted copper ingots they exchanged for a variety of necessities. It was the basis of their economy. They needed hardwoods to shore up their diggings, charcoal for their kilns and indeed many of the tools and materials which, in my waking nightmare, I had conjured in my mind to order my thoughts.

Most important of all, they traded copper for other metals. Tin was brought to them and gold. They knew silver but used it rarely and as an alloy of gold.

"Tin," said the small man, "comes from the north wind."

"Your knowledge of Greek," I replied, "is remarkable."

"There is one here," he said, "who speaks only in Greek."

"One who lives here?"

"One who has lived here since before my people came. She wishes to die, but cannot."

"She?"

"She is more than a woman."

"How so?"

"She is sacred and this place is sacred to the Mother, but she is not of the Mother. She is of the Sky God and he speaks through her."

I felt the ant move in my brain. He had been so little apparent during my negotiations with the small man that I had dismissed him as one of the illusions to which I had found myself prone in the aftermath of my flight. But he moved.

The silence which fell between the small man and myself was not disturbed. The small man himself seemed to prefer silence and he sat crosslegged and mute. On the table between us lay an uneaten piece of honeycomb and the empty jug.

In the silence, the small man's information jostled earlier experience. I thought of my son's death and pictured again in my mind our flight and his fall. I saw the implacable sea ruffled and heaving, yet at the same time I felt myself dovetailing and sorting the information the small man had given me, planning to organize the other small men and set them tasks, calculating the possibilities and sequence of a schedule of their work under my supervision. Across these streams of parallel or juxtaposed thought, the idea of the unknown, unexplained immortal somewhere near at hand, cut sharply. Was she alone? Who saw to her wants? Had she wants? Was she a reality or some image the small men endowed with imaginary life?

"We have yet to be sure, Athenian, that you are not mad," said the small man. "I have watched you and believe you are subject to madness, although you speak sanely enough, if rather boastfully, about practical matters."

"I am not mad," I said, "but in these last days I have experienced events which would drive most men mad. As for what you call boasting, I shall make good my claims. I am Daedalus . . ."

"An Athenian," broke in the small man. "We have heard of you."

I would not say he smiled. At no time could the expression of the Greek Speaker, nor his companions, be described as mobile enough for that but perhaps some slight rictus was operative behind his lips.

"What is your name?" I asked him. He did not reply to this, but stood up and I saw that his five companions had gone.

"Flying," said the small man, "will not serve you here."

The ant ceased his patrol and lay dormant and when the small man re-entered the tunnel, I followed him.

"You are not the first to visit us," said the Greek Speaker suddenly, "although you are the first to involve us in your problems."

"What problems?"

"You can hardly build anything on the rock without our labor," said the small man, "and since we know enough of your reputation as a builder to expect the grandiose from you, there is little doubt that you plan to have us mining, smelting, fetching and carrying for who knows how long?"

31

173

"Are you prepared to help me in this?"

"That will depend, Athenian, upon several things."

"What things?"

"Principally upon the nature and extent of your talents and your ability to extend to us your knowledge of technical matters. Nor will we work for nothing but knowledge."

"What will you want?"

"That depends."

"On what?"

"That depends."

I did not wish to press him. I was surprised to have my intentions so briskly understood, and at the same time a little ashamed of having underrated my hosts.

"Tell me," I said, "who were or are these other travelers who seem to have been so discourteous as to disclaim your aid?"

"They were usually Greeks," replied the Greek Speaker, "that is how I learned your language. Greeks are both inquisitive and indomitable and I admire them although they are contentious and can be remarkably arrogant. Many have come here and several remain. We learned much from them although they paid very little attention to us."

"Why did they come?"

"They were invariably looking for dead relatives."

"Did they find them?"

"No."

"And those who remain?"

"Those you will see."

"Why did they come?"

"The answer to that you surely know. You Greeks believe the dead inhabit a place in the center of the earth and there are those among you who will not leave the dead alone. You are also inconsistent, for you believe that it was her son Cronos, and not Gaia, who swallowed children. Since Gaia has never been accused of this crime why should you expect to find the dead alive in her belly, especially after so long a period?"

174

I could think of no reply to this simple and absurd question. "We bury our dead in the earth," was the best I could do.

"Everything returns to Gaia and is shortly born again, but it is not sensible to suppose that the spirits of all men are imprisoned in a kingdom ruled over by a god whose woman visits him in winter, as if Gaia had no control over the contents of her own belly. Besides, she moves her bowels, as who does not?"

"Has she, have any of us, god or mortal, control over our inhabitants?"

"That is foolish. Those who live within Gaia worship her and sacrifice to her. She loves and protects us. Others she excretes."

"She knows then that you are here?"

"That is foolish, Athenian."

"And the others, what became of them?"

"Some died here. Many are lost. Perhaps they found other ways to leave."

"Then to leave is not difficult?"

"There are many ways, many doors. The earth is vast. Even we, her chosen children, know only one aspect of her great variety."

I was not quite clear if this was metaphor or fact. Religious and metaphysical exposition usually leave me in doubt. However, it was clear that the small man, while committing himself to nothing in his cryptic and rather high-flown speech, was not ignorant nor hostile, and although clearly as enthusiastic and argumentative as any Greek, he was also liable to be as devious.

"Not only do you speak excellent Greek, you think like a Greek."

"I do not flatter you, Greek, do you seek to flatter me? Greeks are illogical and impetuous. In religious matters they accept absurd contradictions, worshipping a plethora of deities whose interests obviously conflict. I have also heard that the Greeks are in perpetual conflict with one another. Those who

175

come here, if they are not seeking relatives, are usually trying to rescue comrades in arms."

"We are some of us warlike, I agree, and our beliefs are more heterodox than some. We are speculative and therefore flexible. For myself, I have no interest whatever in war."

"Speculation in religion is not something we trouble with here. As for war, our interest is confined to supplying metal to belligerents. We are craftsmen."

"I too."

"That much we know, or I should not talk to you. I am by no means sure that your religious beliefs are tenable, but of your abilities we have heard such great reports that we suppose them much exaggerated."

"Doubtless they are."

"Do you accept the Mother as supreme?"

"I cannot say for sure. I owe allegiance to Apollo and I suspect that the gods are interdependent. I revere Gaia."

The small man shrugged irritably and did not reply. Instead he reached into some niche in the wall of the passage and brought out a small metal figure suspended from a thong.

"Wear this," he said, "at least you should show your reverence."

I took the figure and examined it. Two inches long and excellently cast and chased, it was not unlike Cretan work. The figure was female, big breasted and wide eyed, her arms outstretched. It was of bronze with a high copper content but well alloyed.

"This was made here?" I asked.

"I made it in honor of the Mother."

"It is finely made."

"Naturally. Metal is our craft—and metals are sacred to Gaia through whose veins they run. They are the Mother's blood."

"Her blood is my craft also."

"That we shall see."

Much encouraged by this, I followed him. If I were to be

tested in metal work and other crafts by these small and some-what inflexible people, I should have a contest with the odds in my favor. I slipped the thong of the amulet over my head and let the image of Gaia in human form hang on my chest. It clicked against the crystal lens I had worn there since my first year at Knossos.

"To return to your confused ideas about reality," said the small man, "by which I mean your notion that a liberal and speculative heterodoxy will give you the truth if you are pa-tient and open-minded, I must tell you that those as close to Gaia as we are have long passed that milky stage."

Clearly the small man was as full of pent-up polemic as he was full of a natural desire to practice his Greek. I looked attentive.

"You personify," said the small man. "You give any dilemma a god's name and having named it believe in it. Since the factors which give rise to problems are naturally opposed, you make your gods opposed and, as I understand it, you are content to have them squabble and resign yourselves to the lack of any positive outcome to their bickering."

"And what do you propose?"

"We do not propose. We live within Gaia's force. We have no need to propose."

"What is Gaia's force?"

"Her pull. She holds us to her by her pull and also every known thing on or in earth. There is no reason else why we should not fly off the earth into the sky."

"I have done so."

"So you say."

"I have done so."

"There are three other forces."

"What are they?"

"One is the sun's pull, a power of heat, an energy of which we are ignorant. Nevertheless, we accept that it exists and thus accept Apollo."

"I am glad, for I know his pull better than most. And the others?"

"One is central but dispersed. It holds even the earth and sun in equipoise. It is constant but multiple. It is so vast that all circles round it, yet it is also so small that every minute particle of matter circles its own center identically. This force is so multiplied that we have no name for it, but it is as if every grain of sand were a hive of bees and in the center of each grain the queen dwelt and the bees circled the queen."

"I do not follow you."

"Perhaps not, but you will recognize that the large and the small are identical. Nothing is inert, and motion, being the one absolute, is not affected by scale."

I was, I admit, disturbed by this philosophy which came in spate from the small man. It seemed a vague, priestly contention, but I had some uneasy sense that it contained a truth. The ant trudged in my skull as I trudged in Gaia's. Icarus had been to Apollo as a moth to a lamp. I too was drawn to identify the small with the great and find a pattern.

"What is the fourth force?" I asked the small man.

"We do not know what it is, but it is present."

"And the rest?"

"The rest is simply that which is moved by these forces and that which resists change of motion. It is called mass."

"Then you have men and four gods in your world?"

"We have everything in our world," he said, "and four forces. We worship the Mother since we are nearest to her and understand her best."

This seemed a simple pragmatism, but I could find no obvious fault with it. For myself, I have always wanted to get on with my tasks and be as little beset by supernormal complications as possible. I had not succeeded in this, being a witness to the event when the sky-god's force was greater than the earth's. My son had died of it.

The small man's pantheon contained four gods. Two were named and understood, two unnamed and mysterious. The rest was matter moved against various degrees of resistance by the pull of these four gods whose function was impersonal, unlike the capricious relationships, antagonisms and affections to which our more numerous gods were subject. I found the Greek Speaker spoke sense and I said so. He looked at me as if the compliment were meaningless.

"What else?" he said.

"Death?"

"You have seen the dead pulled down into Gaia. Unburied, they yet pass gradually into the earth upon which they lie. You say you have also seen your son pulled into the sun and burned. Death is the time when all living things succumb to one pull rather than another."

"And life?"

"Life is the equipoise maintained in the multiple circling round the multiple force. A living thing is held briefly in balance by the counter pull of the other contending forces. These forces vary in strength. In innumerable variations of strength, they move all matter perpetually between them, like a game never to be won. So a man is pulled into birth, held compact in his body for a span, but subject to age and change throughout his life. Then he is pulled down to his death, and dead he is pulled apart. Each part separates into a multitude and each rejoins the dance of particles around the multiple centers. They fuse to form other lives. It is like metals."

"Like metals?"

"The forces you choose to call gods smelt and alloy the particles at will. As we can forge or pour and cast metals, so Gaia and Apollo can, with the unnamed forces, alloy all matter to make the inhabitants of the earth and all else."

I suppose that a people who live by metals must forge their gods of metal just as herdsmen make bulls into gods. Metals, as I have described, are very strange and magical substances. Soft they can be quench-hardened, solid they can be melted, fused, transformed and returned to solids. Brittle they can be made

179

flexible, pliable made rigid, blunt made sharper than flint. Fire, ores and patience are the rituals. Chance also plays a part. Perhaps these were the four forces or names for them.

I was aware that we were no longer alone and I **32** could hear familiar foundry sounds. I could hear the grind of rifflers and files almost drowned by the clangor of repeated hammer blows, bronze on bronze, and the roar of fire responding to the bellows. I could feel the heat and knew the home hearth noise.

"You have a smith-god, you Greeks," said the small man, "we do not need one, for Gaia gives us fire and is our kiln. We mate in heat, are born in heat, tempered in blood and as we cool we harden. When we grow finally cold we die."

I could not fault that proposition either and so left it, for I had had enough of metaphysics and was concerned to learn how much these people knew of their trade. They knew enough. I had my craftsmen here if I could find the means to bribe them, and not only metal workers, for there was evidence of proficient carpentry and stone dressing in the cavern. The great foundry held in its center a stone shrine to Gaia, shaped like a tholos and containing an image of the Mother. This image was of copper beaten in sheets and riveted to a wooden core. The face, hands, breasts and pubis were sheathed in gold. It was clearly of great age.

"Here you will offer your golden honeycomb when it is made," said the small man. "If it is made, and if when made it does not disgrace the shrine." He looked sceptical, with his wrinkled child's face bland but uncompromising.

To cast a honeycomb in gold is not easy, but it is less difficult than it might appear. I shall explain why and reveal a small mystery, one of those upon which my fame rests, for it was this task successfully accomplished which bound the small people to me and made the construction of Apollo's temple possible.

I asked for a perfect piece of comb from a well-kept hive and after much delay, it was brought to me. I asked for privacy, saying that I must invoke the gods' aid with secret charms, and my demand was treated respectfully, for all metal workers hedge their craft about with mystification. I was taken to a small but adequate cave and there supplied with wax, fire, tools, a bench, a kiln, bellows and all the necessary impedimenta of the goldsmith.

Fist to forehead, I invoked the Mother and the small men reverently withdrew. It was important that they should, for I gambled on their failure to make a simple connection between the craft of lost-wax casting and the nature of the honeycomb itself. Honey is sacred to the earth goddess and wax comes from the honeycomb. With wax men make the models cast in bronze, as I have described. The small people had given me a honeycomb but they had also given me wax to make my model. Thus I knew that they had not made the connection. They had not realized that the honeycomb itself, being of wax, is the only creation in nature which is itself a wax model and one more delicately constructed than any a man could achieve.

I ignored the wax I had been given and took the comb. It was necessary to uncap the individual cells and to do this I cut laterally through the comb and drained out the honey. Each cell of comb I now filled with fine ground clay and rock dust in a paste as thin as cream new risen on a pan of milk, so that each cell was filled with core. To the side of the whole piece of comb I attached a tiny pouring cup and thin "runners" of wax. It was solely for the pouring cup and vents that I used the separate wax I had been given. Then, I mantled the whole and when all was hardened in the kiln, I burnt out the waxen comb.

Gold pours thin and quickly. I poured each section while the core was still hot and the gold could run smoothly, and so the honeycomb was cast. Breaking the crust and tapping out the core was long and delicate labor, but in time I had the golden comb clean and had covered all its faults with gold granulations to resemble drops of honey. Finally, I capped some of the cells to emphasize the comb structure. In my success I gave thanks to Artemis and her bees, gave it without thinking, as anyone who brings a tricky task to a successful end breathes in relief and mingles a rubric with his breath.

I leaned against the bench and looked at my golden comb and wondered. The small people would know nothing of Artemis. What was a huntress to those who had never walked in the forest or seen the deer fleeing from her? I had here achieved a trick of craft which put me in debt to Artemis, for she was the sculptress and I no more than her foundryman.

It was then I conceived a sacrifice to her, secret and fitting. I covered my work and called the Greek Speaker. He came, asking if the offering was made. I told him I had need of seven bees and he looked mystified, as I had intended.

"Send for seven bees," I said with heavy solemnity, "for without them the golden comb will never fill with honey."

He went away and by whatever means, at that time not known to me, he made communication with the world outside and in due time brought me seven bees, workers from the same hive as the comb I had been given as a model. Of this he solemnly assured me. Left alone, I made sacrifice to Artemis of these seven bees.

There is another trick of casting which I was certain would not be known to the small people and it is this. Anything small enough and dry enough to be burnt totally, leaving no ash or unconsumed material, will leave its negative impression as perfect in the mantle as will wax. I have cast the legs of grasshoppers into saws for ivory workers and cast real butterflies, wing perfect, by these means.

And so I took the bees from the little box in which they had been brought. I killed each one with a needle and gutted it with the sharpest of my knives and I did so with as much reverential care as a priest would sacrifice seven bulls to Zeus.

I mantled each fragile carapace and burned it out of the mantle and, making each laborious insect laboriously immortal, I poured gold into these tiny molds. When, many hours later, I broke them open there were seven bees of solid gold. Each wing and every leg perfect, they lay on the palm of my hand.

"Here in your honor, Artemis," I said, "the most fragile sacrifice ever made you. Each victim ritually killed, each pyre ritually kindled and behold, each is a votive to last forever." And I fastened the bees upon the comb so that they seemed to be coming and going about their sacred business without which no man could cast the bronze doors of a temple to Apollo nor make any bronze sculpture.

It had been many hours of work, for all had minutely to be accomplished, all blurring of the cast chased out and burnished. I lay down by the bench and slept as the charcoal cooled in my kiln, and had no dreams nor remembered any grief.

The Greek Speaker and his companions woke me with murmuring. They were grouped in the entrance to my little cave and they stared at my work-bench, where, covered with a cloth, I had set down my work. I stood up and without speaking removed the covering and held up the golden honeycomb in my hands.

Even the Greek Speaker was deprived of his metaphysical discourse. He stood silent and motionless. His companions raised their right hands slowly, fists clenched to their foreheads.

"It is sacred," said the Greek Speaker. "Was it made in sleep? You have slept many hours."

It was much what he had said when we met.

"It is a sacred thing, no man could have made it."

"I have made it. I am Daedalus the Athenian."

"We have heard of you. If you have made this thing then all that we have heard of you is true."

"I made it with the help of the goddess."

He came close and stared first at the comb and then into my eyes. I waited silently.

"It is true," said the small man and I knew that I had my metal workers, my stonemasons and my carpenters, and could begin to build, for the summit of the rock, a temple to Apollo, and I thought suddenly that once this was done I should be free. I thought that standing in the open by the temple, I might see, if I looked southwest, the island in the far distance where Hephaistos and the Cyclopes worked in metals. And I went out into the great foundry cavern, with the small people following, and laid the golden honeycomb in Gaia's shrine.

The work went forward. How long it took I am still not sure, for there is neither night nor day in the earth nor pattern of hours. The small people worked, it seemed, without ceasing and it was only gradually that I realized they worked in a complicated series of shifts. These shifts each depended upon the individual. A man would lay down his tools and go. A man would enter the cave and take up the same tools.

For some time I supposed this smith or that carpenter had simply gone briefly away and returned, but in fact he had been replaced. So nearly identical were the small people that until I had worked with them for as long as it took to prepare the materials for the temple, I could not tell one from another. Their women and children I never saw.

None of the small people ever left the earth. At the openings in the Cumaean rock they met another race who brought them what they needed: food, stone, wood, hides, cloth and such small luxuries as wine and honey. These people of the land in turn traded the metals and the metalwork of the small people with the peoples of the North and with the ships that beached below the rock. Tin and gold came from the north.

184

Thus the temple to Apollo was made by men who would never see it, although it would stand above their heads. The site, foundations and ultimate construction of the building I conceived and foresaw by guesswork. I had once stood on the summit of the rock and I had been there for minutes only, before the god burned his ancient house and the flames drove me below ground. This glimpse needed to suffice, for it was made clear to me that until I had planned every component, had made every calculation and caused every nail to be cast, every timber to be shaped and every ornament to be perfected, I should not find my way out of Gaia's womb.

Workable stone was a rarity. There was no marble nor any hard stone and the porous limestone which could be quarried locally was of poor quality. It would suffice to build walls and form a stylobate but for sculpture it was too friable to last long. Tufa was easily available and this I used, although it would have to be dressed and covered with stucco to give it finish, for it was spongy and conglomerate and filled with pebbles and fossils, a rubble pressed into stone by Gaia's bowels. Cypress wood was plentiful and so were softwoods. Clay for bricks and for terracotta sculpture and the means to fire it presented no problem. Great heat, which the small people mysteriously tapped from Gaia's burning fluids, served them for all their works. They had less need of charcoal than surface metal-workers, although they used it for maintaining even tempera-tures. I, preferring familiar methods, used it for the small furnace in which I cast those objects in metal which I did not delegate.

The temple took shape. Surely it is the only house of Apollo ever to be constructed in every particular, deep in the earth where the direct rays of the Sun himself could never penetrate. We built it in a cavern as great as the foundry-cavern and we raised it in such a way that it could be dismantled, carried away and re-assembled eventually in its appointed place.

This seemed in no way strange to the small people. The Greek Speaker inferred that they had built and assembled many wonders in this subterranean world, but what these were I have never learned. That they could have done so I believed, for they were marvelously quick to learn and skilled in different crafts, not only in metal work but in building, in molding for terracotta and even in the painting of it. As for labyrinths, to these people, wandering all their lives in the labyrinth of Gaia the one I made for Minos would have seemed a little game for backward children. I did not speak to them of this.

I am unsure how much of all this was a dream. Fact is easily clouded when familiar aspects of normal life are missing. I worked, slept, woke, ate and worked again, but I had no count of hours, no morning and no evening. I had no woman and in all my long sojourns in the earth, I saw only two women and they were mated. I had no close companions, for even the Greek Speaker was a secret man and of all his race he was the only one who spoke, or perhaps could speak, to me. I worked with him and with his people, to whom he was my interpreter, but he never talked to me of his life, apart from his readiness to expound his religion. Except for this, his one garrulity, I should have learned nothing of the other exiles, those not native to this place who yet lived here, nor would I have encountered them in so vast a territory as lies within Gaia's pelvis. I came to see a god's winter bride and to find, in turn, a horned beast fathered by another god and a horned god. I found also the tormented mistress of a fourth god and one other whose identity remains unknown to me. In some degree all these exiles were related, although remotely, to me and to each other. Therefore the Greek Speaker's remark that Greeks always seek relatives in the underworld was ironically borne out. The pattern formed by their presence was also obscurely a mirror image of my past life. The names of those I encountered have, with one exception, entered the pantheon of the Greeks, although the degrees of their celebrity vary considerably. The exception I shall call Cephalon, for he spoke to me silently, sometimes through the others, and never showed himself below the earth. Who he is I do not know,

186

unless perhaps I am he, but if I am, then there is some dislocation in my mind which I can only explain by accepting that a quirk of chance divided me in two so that I spoke to myself and thought my voice another's. At times I have credited the ant with speech, but I am unsure. That would have been too simple a delusion.

Names in the earth are closely guarded things. If you meet a man above ground and ask his name, he will usually tell it to you. In the earth he will not. Not one of the small people, even the Greek Speaker, ever told me his name. When I asked them, they gravely changed the subject. I believe they thought I abused myself by stating my name. It shocked them and from their looks they implied an unwillingness to hear this, my verbal self-indulgence. Most of the names they spoke, they spoke with contempt and those who might have answered had no occasion to do so. One in particular they named with disgust, and I saw her once although I did not speak to her.

When I had been long at work and the temple had taken shape so that it lacked only the splendor of its refinements and in particular the great doors which were to be the final adornment, I saw a woman walking down the long and twisting passage which linked the caverns housing our activity. As she walked, a chill wind followed her; a gray mist, rain-filled, swept about her.

She was tall and empty, beautiful and white as cloud. She walked with a pride that impressed me in that she wore it with such grandeur that it seemed false.

I had been without a woman longer than I had ever been and yet I did not find any response to this woman rise in me; only a cold revulsion.

I followed her, curious to know why this should be, but she outpaced me and went downward. As she went, she took a winter darkness with her and wrapped it round her nakedness like a cloak of the silver mud washed out of the mountains by the melting snows. Yet she was hot.

Her nipples were sprung up like studs facing an opponent

187

shield and her flanks glittered. Ice-hot she strode, as bitter splendid as the virgin Artemis, yet she had the scent of heat in her cold. And so she vanished in the tunnel and as she went she took a darkness, wet with her, downward.

I lost her and returned to my work. The Greek Speaker came to me and took up some point concerning the revetments of the temple. I asked him who it was I had seen.

"A kind of regular death," he said.

"Regular?"

"Yearly."

"Who is she?" I asked.

"A Greek."

"A Greek and she comes every year?"

"It is winter."

"She comes every winter?"

"And leaves every spring."

"What is she called?"

"Persephone," he said, with loathing. "One of the curiosities of your religion, Greek, is that it is all true but none of it relevant. This creature you regard highly. She destroys her mother every year in order to visit a non-existent mate who does not rule a kingdom which you pretend exists in Gaia's sphincter. Yet doubtless she finds him. Greeks can create truths out of nothing. It is one of their gifts."

"How does she look in the spring?"

"Plant-pregnant, like a green melon."

"She seemed to me to take death down there with her."

"She brings it forth too in March, but makes it look like birth. Her mother is the better woman. She wears the winter, ages every season, but remains fertile."

And that was all he would say. I remembered that the daughter of Demeter had had no name until she began her seasonal mating journeys. Until that time she had been known simply as Kore, "the girl." That she should take a name to go into the earth, and disclose that name, may explain some of the distaste in which the small people held her.

I never saw her return. She is supposed to bring the spring out of the earth with her, but I doubt if she does. Myself, I believe her to be unfruitful and to go into the earth only for warmth in winter, but I may be wrong. She was to me so chill a being that I do not believe her frozen furrow would turn under the plough. She never glanced at me.

There were other times when, while I was working, a great sound, rising and falling, seemed to drive like a drill through the rock. A storm of sound, it would gather heavily below the foundry-cavern, trundle and thrum in the passages under my workshop, roll, subside and roll again for minutes on end. It was a nerve-straining noise and I could not get used to it because it had no rhythm, no comprehensible progression and the conclusion of it always came unexpectedly. This final climax was a shriek so penetrating that it climbed above a man's response to sound. It climbed agonizingly upward into a silence which vibrated even when the cry could no longer be heard. Then, after a pause of uncertain duration, a sporadic, abrupt series of crashes would be the finish of the episode. These crashes were the result of great bronze doors flying open, but I did not know that then. After these sounds the whole rock would seem to exhale and shrink as if it had expelled a great cry—although that cry was inaudible. The earth would shake and seem to draw breath and then the tremor passed and all would be as it was. During these times the small men would crouch or throw themselves down, covering their heads to endure first the sound and then the silence. They would wait and when they spoke again, they spoke uneasily and whispered.

Except on these menacing or sacred occasions they were loud and continual in their talk. I should not say they were cheerful but their speech was staccato and rapid. It was loud enough to carry through the foundry sounds and all the clangor of metal-working.

Whether it was night or day was always difficult to tell, but there were times when few men were at work and there was some general quiet. I would sleep then, or at least I would lie down in a corner of my workshop and sometimes I would sleep. The small men came and went in the passages and somewhere, perhaps in many places in the maze, they slept, ate, drank, washed, mated, cherished their children and, I suppose, privately worshipped their mother-goddess. I learned very little of their lives for they were a secret people and were not personal in their contact with me.

There was much to do and the small men were quick to master what was necessary. As time went on there were periods when, in the slow progress of the work, I had little need to supervise the details of it and no one paid me much attention unless he was uncertain of his task. I would wander the passages, especially in those periods which might be called night when few workers were about, and doing so, I remembered and used the old trick I had taught Ariadne at Knossos to ensure she could find her way back. I carried a ball of twine.

It was during these journeys that I made through Gaia's bowels that the invisible narrator whom I have named Cephalon would speak to me, and it may be that it was he who led me to those places where I met the other inhabitants of this the mother-labyrinth.

Clutching my guiding thread and knowing it secured to my workbench, I tugged myself out like a fish dragging the line. The turns and circlings of the tunnels were multicolored, with the red of iron ore and the black of manganese dioxide predominating. The glitter of the calcined surfaces threw the dim light casually about like a lazy game played by crystals. Cephalon conducted a dialogue with me as various and as fugitive as these changes in the appearance of Gaia's core, or rather it was not a dialogue, for it was not so cut and dried an intercommunication as that. It was as slippery as the wet walls of the maze and words played small part in it.

Into my head came a trickle of knowledge which did not come from experience. It was a foreknowledge of whom I should meet and in one specific case Cephalon spoke in me for a being who said nothing. He spoke for the triple bull and the bull was neither bull nor triple, but I came to think of it by that name.

In all my life I have had some sense that I lived a circle. I learned in Gaia that life is not a circle but a helix and I also learned that the distance between places on the surface of the world and equally the time it takes to move between them, are different in the core of the earth. At Knossos I had built a little travesty of Gaia's great maze and left the Minotaur imprisoned in it. I had flown across a wide sea from Knossos and descended to Cumae; and the Minotaur, long left behind in Crete, was still near me. I sensed him even though I could not at once grasp how he had come there. I held Ariadne's thread again and looked down at it in my hand. It was red. I heard the roaring of a bull and started at the sound. Gaia moved under me. Gaia is never still. She churns and writhes beneath that carapace we call the solid earth. When she moves, her entrails follow a pattern as ordained as the circling of the seasons. To us, her pattern of movement is too vast to be understood and our time is not hers. Even now I was only beginning to recognize how she digested place and time and passed them through her as though she modeled and remodeled them at will.

In her those men and women, whose changing shapes and powers had changed and shaped me, were rolled back into a single mass of clay. It was as if some modeler, tired of trying his art, had kneaded his still-damp figures back into a shapeless mass. Or perhaps not quite shapeless; perhaps the bull, thumbed carelessly into the pulpy lump once shaped to Pasiphaë, made a new form of both so that twisted together the Minotaur re-emerged; and Talos the inventor, having been

191

banged idly on the bench of his madness, was flattened and squared off by the impact, to make the shield-shaped warrior he had become when he found me on Crete. The memory of this haunted me.

Others I had known were hidden in this ball of clay. Ariadne haunted here and Naucrate too was deep buried in it and I suppose that could I have delicately dug and separated all the component dolls from their sodden matrix, I could have reassembled everyone I had ever known except, it seemed to me, my son.

In Gaia time moves as the Great Year moves, in opposition to the normal course of the months, and in her it may be that the sign governing each span of time lasts two thousand years or so, as those who study such matters believe. In my era the Time of the Bull is passed and I live in the Time of the Ram, yet the Bull does not give up and I am still beset by bulls as Cretans are and the peoples in the East. The gods, who are invariably old-fashioned, continually take on bull form and if they no longer do so in your day, at the conjunction of the Fish and the Water-carrier, I envy you. You are lucky if you are spared a proliferation of bulls and half-bulls and bull-gods in unexpected places.

In the depths below the Foundry Cave, I heard **35** the roaring of a bull. Perhaps Cephalon had guided me to the place: perhaps I had wandered there, brooding on the matrix, on the remodeling of the clay figures of those I had known. I was in some part of the earth I had not seen before. The walls of the passage seemed hand-hewn. They looked familiar. They looked like the walls of the labyrinth of Minos. Yet how could they be? The red thread in my hand pulled tight, like a fishing line taken by a shark.

I was aware of horns but not of who it was who wore them.

192

Minos in his ritual bull-mask rose in my mind, then Zeus, Poseidon, Dionysus, all those gods who assume the bull in violent epiphany, and I was afraid. I knew the place. It lay below the palace of Minos, yet I was not in Crete. I was afraid. I sensed Talos in his brute-bull guise, but it was not Talos. I was near the Minotaur. It could only be the Minotaur. I unwound the red thread further and went toward the sound of the bull despite myself. Cephalon urged me on. I spoke aloud, I think. I said "He cannot be here, he is in Crete . . . he cannot be here." Still I could not see him.

The Minotaur did not speak and yet he spoke, he did not think and yet I heard his thought through Cephalon, for this displaced narrator spoke from within the slack trunk or from the horn-heavy skull of this bull-masked thing and yet remained outside him. He spoke in my mind and yet I do not think he inhabited me except when he chose and then he squatted with the ant in my brain and both teased me.

The Minotaur cannot think clearly. He does not know where he is or why. Without Cephalon he would be mute in his anger and misery and Cephalon can couch as easily in his bowels as in my mind. Cephalon is unusually gifted, sharp and cruel. He permits no peace to his involuntary hosts and could be named in a sense the very spirit of the labyrinth, for whether he moves among the intricacies of my cerebral cortex or walks inward from the anus of the Minotaur he yet wanders in a maze no less entangling than that of Gaia, which I involuntarily inhabited.

Superior to humans and animals Cephalon may think himself, but the poor disembodied thing treads the same path as the rest of us. A small parasite armed with a needle, he is lost in the involuted confusion of a situation which frequently muffles his voice. Cephalon, for all his powers, is uneasily aware that he in turn may be inhabited by some being, even more impalpable than he is, who lives in his invisible gut.

On my behalf he went into the Minotaur as interpreter and

193

thought for the half-bull to express him to me in gusts blown out of the windy and pulsing belly of his unhappy host.

You will know from common talk the general appearance of the Minotaur, this half-man, half-bull, this demigod sprung from the seed of Poseidon in bull form, when that earth-shaking god took Pasiphaë on Crete. His body is part human yet he begins as bull at the loins and he bears a hump of sinews upon his shoulders which carries the great horned skull and the cattle-brute mask of his head. His belly however is human and into this Cephalon, at once contemptuous and alarmed, for a sufficient breaking of wind would catapult him downward, had burrowed.

The Minotaur moved restlessly and I heard his hoof scrape on the rock floor of his byre. This fissure in the rock, his sanctuary, was scarcely larger than its inmate, a cone-shaped fault set back from a cavern. It was one of many that opened suddenly from the narrow passages of the maze and he, I suppose, had chosen it for stable and found some special comfort there. The cavern itself was circular like an arena and its circumference was crowded with the great boulders of past rockfalls.

I heard his hoof scrape on the floor and a rough abrasive sound as he rubbed his hide against the wall. I heard the click of horn against stone, an abrupt snort, a whistling breath. These, the sounds of the Minotaur, were ominous because they were such normal cattle sounds. They came to me in the same instant as his alarm. His uncertainty naturally coincided with his instinct to stir. His private darkness, hung like a ragged curtain before his brain, was lit with a quick unease and this caused him, so far as he was able, to think.

I felt his fears jolt him and his response was to gather the great mass of muscle on his crest. It was instinct, but perhaps something more.

I stood still in the entrance to the arena, remembering the bull-game and poised to avoid injury. I have watched it many times and marveled at the spectacle of young men and women with no better way to spend their time than in courting danger. I myself take no such unnecessary risks for sport, or glory, or whatever these rituals involve.

The Minotaur moved suddenly into the light.

You, who have a certain aesthetic interest in him, perhaps because you have seen his picture, will know approximately how he looks. You will not know the details of his structure and should you encounter him, it would be best to know the particular advantages and disadvantages his hybrid shape gives him. He is no taller than a man and his legs are light and sinewy. He is very fast over a short distance, but the weight of his crest and skull are such that his balance is very uncertain. His shoulders are enormously thick and he has hands which can crush stones in their grip. In contest with him it is well to remember that although much of him is bull, his hands and arms are those of a man of superhuman strength. His chest too is deep and he is not quickly winded. He can throw a fully armored warrior twenty feet with a single toss of his head and his horns will penetrate three inches of seasoned wood.

There are however two flaws in his design which can defeat him because he is neither bull nor man. One is the setting of his eyes in the great shield of bone he wears for forehead. His eyes are set obliquely in his malformed skull. He cannot focus both at once upon an object immediately in front of him. He cannot look straight ahead, but must turn his huge mask and glance sideways at his objective; therefore he looks to right or left depending upon which eye has his target in vision. Secondly, he is uncertain how to attack and this confusion is central to his condition and gives an opponent the advantage.

A bull is equipped perfectly to fight as a bull and a man may be adept in battle between men, although I am not such a man, but the Minotaur is marvelously made to kill in either capacity except that he cannot decide which. His instincts are double and in perpetual conflict. If he grasps his enemy in his arms he can break him like a twig or tear him apart, but he cannot bring his horns into play and if he seeks to gore his victim his arms and hands are of no use to him. He is not humanly intelligent, but he is also less simple than his animal nature, so that his reflexes are not so certain as a bull's. He is capable of enough thought to frustrate his impulses. His urge to murder is not a lust but his response to the uncertainty by which, so far as his slow brain permits, he is tormented. To understand him is, with luck, to defeat him and I, who am neither athlete nor warrior, did so either because I made quick deductions or because I had entered his mind. I am not sure which.

I stood very still and watched him hunched uncertainly in the entrance to his hide. I saw his crest twitch and his muzzle wrinkle. His spatulate nostrils opened and closed and he blew a spume of saliva which hung in a slender skein from his lolling tongue. Unlike a bull, he bared his teeth. His head swung heavily to right and left and, oxlike, he seemed to look backward out of the side of each great slab of cheek in turn.

As his spittle dropped I knew his thought to spatter and drip with it. Menaces took shape for him and vanished among the landscape of stains upon the walls of his prison as each eye registered and rolled. To him every crack in the uneven rock face, however shallow, could become large enough in an instant to hold a potential danger. These shifted and melted into one another under each dull glance. Nothing was secure.

He opened and closed the squat, stub finger of each hand, opposing the thumb, aware of this approximation to a human gesture. Suddenly he spun round on his heels and, off balance, struck one horn against the wall with a sharp sound like the crack of a splitting timber. Shale came away and slid rattling to the floor. He twisted back, moved forward crouching, his head weaving and a little raised so that I saw, swaying and sagging, the great folds of hide which rose from his chest to join his under jaw. He bellowed and the sound was full of doubt and the will to overcome it. Still he had not seen me.

Splay-legged he moved forward again with the waddling motion of a toad, stopped, spun, fell to his knees groping with both hands, seeming to plead for sight of his enemy. He came springing to his feet like a wrestler and suddenly saw me in his right eye. His head dropped and his shoulders and crest rose. His arms went back and I knew on the instant that he would attack in bull form, favoring the right horn, turn, if he missed his charge, and bring his hands into play on the turn. He came at me fast and I threw myself to his left. His momentum carried him on and when he turned, reaching out, he was ten yards away. He came at me again but uncertainly, trying to be bull and man at once, searching for a hold. I ran straight at him and twisting as I ran, I passed to his right, leaving him stock-still. This unexpected maneuver left him rooted and he lost me. I was behind him. He picked up a stone the size of his own head and crumbled it to powder between his hands. He screamed, raised both his arms and gripped his horns, wrenching and pulling at them. Such was the enormous power of his shoulders that it seemed for a moment that he would tear himself in half. He screamed again, lost his footing and fell rolling and jerking. His mouth sprayed foam, his trunk struck the stony floor, thundering against it like a drum. He made a grotesque leap, stood swaying, fell again and remained heaped where he had fallen in a sudden quiet. He had forgotten me.

Step by step I edged back into the comparative safety of the boulders, leaving him at the center of his bull pen, a mound of sullen muscle and leaden bone. Those few seconds were the extent of the contest and I was in great fear, but that was all there was.

He was the color of weathered bronze and in the sudden detachment of my relief, I saw him as beautiful in his majestic absurdity. I saw him indomitable and ridiculous in all the grandeur and all the fragility of useless physical strength. Icarus, in his foolishness, had once believed himself half-brother to the Minotaur and believed me the father of both. In that moment I felt I could have been and in that moment I heard the Minotaur begin to weep.

He had found his enemy and lost him, found another in himself and fought to destroy the foe he was, and all to no purpose. He had killed neither me nor himself, and failed to wrench off the pitchfork-badge of his fate, upon which he had turned his fury in the absence of a victim. Each combat in which this wretched demigod took part he turned upon himself in frenzy and each time he lost.

Crouched and cramped pupate in the chrysalis of this loathsome immortality, Cephalon spoke in him or in my mind. I heard or did not hear, or believed or thought a monologue within the bone-weary brain of the Minotaur. I felt him try to raise his head and fail. I felt his tears and his hopeless grief in what he was. I write here how it was and record that his silence contained a soliloquy oddly couched in the third person. "His hand no hoof, horn skinned not cloven hand no hoof is thumbed." He gaped at his right hand, opening and closing it. "Skin hard and flakes but fingers curl, his thumb opposed, his palm is hand not hoof."

He crawled a little across the floor, making toward his byre. "Trunk, gut bag, blunt encumbrance, not bull's but bull shaped man. Man's belly tops tripes groaning and slopped." He voided casually in the act of coming to his feet and spattered his hooves. "Bull below yet . . . bull weight of balls swing bagged, stiff pizzle, cowless. Horn, horn, twin tines gripped to his brow impede. Horn tines, thorn sharp, stab nothing. Bos graft. Bull. Beast."

These disjointed images seemed to fall out of his brain as the turds fell from his trunk. He was near his byre now and a snuffling calm descended on him, heavy as a damp blanket. His thoughts straggled on momentarily cohesive: "He is cud, his crest is crusted cud. Once wet and warm, now dried to bone, a sack of sinews dried to plates of bone is all he is. Hide hangs below his throat, a hide to hide a man, a man, a man, a harness on his head, a totem head. Thrust off. Wrench off . . . man, man, not slobber, speak."

He groaned, a straining, anguished sound and stumbled. Shambling now, he sank into his hide and his eyes, reading the walls of his prison, registered again their double image. The walls of his cell were his landscape. The hills and river-beds he saw were little faults and gullies worn by time in the rock; the trees he saw were the scribbles of moss and lichen on the stones. In the broken straw on the floor he saw the scrub of open country and for him droppings of dung doubled for the plough land of the outer world.

"Cud gags, cud gags, mounts in his mouth, gags speech, man's speech, cud, cud, no man makes cud, no man near man no man, no man."

The cud rose in his mouth and he began to chew in a slow, placid, inevitable rhythm. His landscape dimmed for him and clouded. His hoof scraped once on the rock floor, stamped and was still. He snorted, blew brisk and bubbling, once or twice. The man within him slept.

The god did not. The epiphany of which I had had some premonition now took place, in the center of the arena, at the spot upon which the Minotaur had fought out his aimless and solitary combat.

I had been badly frightened. I was shaken and breathless, for I am not used to violence and am a sensible and cowardly man. I can only describe what I thought I saw. At the center of the arena was a boulder, a pitted sphere in some sort different from the other rocks which littered the place. I had not noticed it before but now I was aware of its difference. On it was seated a figure with the head and crest of a bull.

I was startled into hysterical laughter, just as I had been when I met Talos in bronze form. This ludicrous and grotesque multiplication of hybrid monsters crowded out all drama. Farce superseded. I laughed like a fool, reeling and stumbling about and the bull-headed figure joined me in my laughter. Rising from his stone seat, he leaped and danced before me howling, and I, howling with equal enthusiasm, followed him round and round the stone.

I was suddenly tormented with thirst and still I laughed. I was filled with energy and well-being and yet tormented with thirst. The crazy dance increased in speed and I, who am not given to needless exercise, continued to breathe easily even as I continued to laugh. My thirst grew in me, expelling all other feelings. I could have drunk a skin, a dozen skins, of wine. I could have drunk blood!

The figure now faced me, dancing backward as easily and surefootedly as those who play the bull-game. His laughter rang in the cave and yet when I looked into his face he was not laughing but had upon his lips only an enigmatic half-smile and his face was no longer the stupid and yet familiar countenance of a bull but that of a kouros carved from marble, the eyes blank before painting. The eyes were empty and yet concentrated like those of a leopard and like a leopard he moved. Bull, leopard and kouros and in all these eliding shapes beautiful. Ivy and myrtle garlanded his horns, which were gilded. A fawn skin, dappled to parody the leopard, was all he wore. This skin was so tied that it displayed and set off his sex as devoutly as an image in a shrine. His rigid phallus stood erect and it curved back like a drawn bow.

I found myself violently aroused in turn, but not for my partner in the dance. Close to me as he was and nobly potent, I felt no physical urge toward him, but rather I conceived a rout of women and boys leaping and beckoning with him and to all of these indiscriminately and gluttonously I responded. I knew they were not there and were all fantasies, yet like a boy urgent for a woman, I conjured up circumstances, pictures, actions in which I had them all. I licked them, spread them and rode them in a game greased with oozing cruelty. To rape must be to kill by tearing.

This race to pain from lust came as I stared at the great flashing penis of the dancer and when I raised my eyes to his face his beauty was nauseous. Yet he had beauty and a bestial dignity. Such dignity of carriage he had, despite the wild abandon of his capering, that my laughter trailed away, or it may be that I stopped laughing when I scented him. He stank. He stank of blood, of wine dregs, of sperm, of the rankness of lions. The bull-smell of dung and sweat was comfortable scent compared to this and the odor of this dancing thing filled me with more fear than I had felt when the Minotaur charged.

The fumes of his musky exhalation rose and made me drunk. I fell down. I fell clownishly on my bottom and sat stupidly grinning up at this second bull who was no bull with his reek and his small, sweet smile. And he, seeing me incapable on the ground, stopped dancing and stood still.

I was suddenly and violently sick. The vomit rushed into my mouth and nose and it was wine. I was sick-drunk, retching and grunting, and the wine jetted out of me. The wine rose into my mouth and this liquid cud gagged speech. My bowels opened. I heaved up my shoulders, my neck swelled and the tears of strenuous retching clouded my eyes. I rocked my head to and fro to clear my vision but without success. I groaned and cried out, I rolled about. Sweat poured from me. I held my head and in my distress pulled at my hair, trying to relieve the pressure in my forehead. And I remember that as I clutched at my head I had the peculiar sensation that I was holding a pair of horns.

The end to this was what you might expect. I fell into stupor and when I recovered I was alone. There was no sound but my own breathing, no smell but my own vomit and excrement, no one to be seen, neither man nor bull nor god, nor any thing with any combination of these attributes. I had no horns when I put my hands to my head, but somehow or other I had acquired a wreath of ivy. This I took off and left upon the stone.

I picked up my thread and followed its course out of the place and back down the long passages toward the foundry and my workshop, where, although it was only a crowded hole deep in the earth, there was some sense of order, familiar tools and materials and a place to work and sleep. I washed; it seemed to take me hours to cleanse myself.

In my workshop I slept and dreamed that I was a child again and with my father in the snow at Delphi.

Naturally I have tried to interpret what happened **36** and what if anything it meant. In some degree I have come to believe I imagined the whole thing or had given birth to an illusion which then gained unusual momentum. I have called this triumvirate, of whom I was one, the triple bull, and placed the dialogue at the direction of Cephalon who is, after all, only a voice in my own head, although he speaks independently of my conscious thought. Or at least, I suppose this is a rational explanation. My unnatural constriction in the rock, my fatigue from the burden of my task, my son's loss, my solitary condition deprived of normal companionship, all may have served to send me mad for a brief period so that I projected from myself two other selves, divine and bestial, and then saw myself mirrored in their shape.

In Crete they identify the bull with everything, including the sun, and thus Apollo is joined into this bovine pantheon. There is really no end to this identification of gods with bulls and in Crete they placate them by tearing a live bull to pieces and eating him raw. Even poor Talos, who is now no better than a brazen idiot, is identified with the sun and wears horns on his helmet. Cows are of course identified with the moon, which places Pasiphaë at least in her proper context. Knossos is as studded with symbolic horns as it is with ritual axes.

I do not wish to weary you with all this confusion of symbols but I should point out that the Minotaur himself is named Asterion, whose name means that he gives celestial light, and that as the son of the sun and moon he is a star, apart from being a poor monster. The violence and virility which course through humanity do suggest that a vein of bull's blood runs through most men and causes them to behave as they do from time to time.

The temple took shape in the great cavern. Grad- **37**
ually the parts were assembled. The bricks were
fired and so were the gutters and roof tiles. Limestone and
tufa blocks were cut somewhere in the depths of Gaia and
column bases were shaped, each of a height slightly greater
than half its diameter. Orthostats were cut to fit with one
another. Gypsum was prepared dry to be used as covering for
the brick and tufa and for the paving of the interior. Cypress
trunks were shaped to become columns and all were numbered and stacked and stored against the time when the final
assembly should take place above. The small people were
puzzled by the rectangular shape I had planned. To them
sacred buildings were circular *tholoi* and they questioned me
closely, fearing some blasphemy. I told them that Apollo
favored the rectangle as Gaia favored the cone and they
seemed content. I cannot say I spoke with much authority in
this matter, but I had seen the temple whole when first I
conceived it and I had seen it rectangular.

All went well enough until gradually the weight of objects
increased. It was as simple as that, although for some time I
assumed that we were all weary and that lifting cypress trunks
and blocks of stone tired us more quickly than it had when we
began. The work slowed. The small people accomplished less
and less.

I was wrong and I discovered this as I was working on one of
the bronze hands of the cult statue of Apollo. I used rasps and
burins and from time to time I paused to fill small casting
faults by tapping minute bronze pegs into the little holes left
by air bubbles which had been caught in the cooling of the
metal flow. For this I used a small hammer. With the job half
done, I reached for this hammer, where it lay as usual on my
bench, grasped it and found I could hardly lift it. To take it
from the bench needed all my strength, yet I was not ill. I felt
perfectly well. I tried again and could not even raise it.

The Greek Speaker was in the great cavern talking to the

masons. No one was working. Men were crouched and sitting on the floor. The foundry clangor was silenced.

The Greek Speaker walked toward me and we sat together on a balk of timber.

"The Mother sulks," he said.

"Why?"

"She has done so before. If she believes our work is not in her honor she lays her weight on it."

"Why now, why not when we began?"

"It is the statue of your god she resents, now that you have cast the head and hands."

"How do you know it is that?"

"We know."

I was silent for a while. I had not forseen this obstruction, nor could I see a ready solution to the problem. If Gaia increased her force, pulling downward on every part of the construction, not even the labor force they had available in Egypt could shift so much as a roof tile. My powerlessness was a curious sensation. Clearly Gaia laid no weight on human beings or we should all have been flat on the floor. She merely increased her weight on inanimate objects and only upon objects intended for Apollo. We could walk, breathe easily, talk, perhaps eat and drink, although I was not certain if we should be allowed to lift a jug or cup. We simply could not move any part of the work in progress.

I asked the Greek Speaker what we should do. He shrugged.

"Can we placate the Mother with offerings?" I asked.

"It is possible."

"Is there one who will speak for us, if I am not acceptable?"

"There is one."

"Who?"

"I do not speak her name."

I was used to this. It must be taken slowly.

"Why will she speak for me?"

"She is of your god."

"And lives here in Gaia?"

"Forever."

"Why?"

"She is female of the Mother, but bride of your god."

"And she lives here?"

"In the sanctuary from which she speaks."

"Will you speak to her?"

"No, that is for you to do."

The Greek Speaker as usual was cryptic and ponderous of speech. As we talked, in what seemed to be gradually decreasing circles, he allowed it to be known that somewhere in the heart of the rock lived an immortal female who had been there before the coming of the small people and would remain for all eternity.

Only on rare and enormously significant occasions had she ever been seen by the inhabitants of the rock and only when some question was in dire need of answering was she consulted. She was regarded with deep awe. To ask her intervention in the matter of the temple to Apollo would mean rituals, sacrifices and all the solemnities of religious exercise. Sacred objects would have to be carried to Gaia's shrine. This however was permitted.

I could pick up a knife to sacrifice a heifer, even if I could not lift a burnisher to work on bronze. I performed, as I was required, before the image of the Mother, sacrificing a white calf which was unexpectedly produced by the Greek Speaker from some subterranean pen and when he too had purified himself, he led me out of the cavern and we began almost at once to pass downward, deeper into the rock.

This word rock comes too easily to me when I record the deep maze I then inhabited, for this **38** word does not describe the place. To you who walk about the earth it seems founded upon stone and even you who live in lush and fertile country know that the soil is only a thin pelt stretched upon the surface of the unyielding ground. This skin is worn away in the mountainous places and in drought it blows to dust and is carried off in choking storms. Yet you think the earth is both hard and soft together, hard in its poverty and soft in its richness, and you are right.

The carapace of Cumae is hard, and so I call it the rock, yet this is in part an illusion. In its depths it softens. Like a living creature its viscera are protected by an unyielding skeleton. I am not sure to this day what parts of Gaia are her bones and where their joints press hard through her membranes. I know her rigidity and have taken metals from her with much labor of chipping and hammering at rigid strata and yet her variety of texture is incalculable. I swam in Gaia as often as I walked, and waded through deep ooze as often as I trod dry ground. I do not know why I did not drown nor why the terror of the place did not send me mad, for I was never certain of the composition of this enveloping nether world nor what it would do.

The rock, where it is unquestionably rock, is the acropolis you may see from the seashore. You may also see where Gaia becomes water and empties her full bladder into the lake you call Avernus, but between rock and water such changes occur and with such unexpected consequences that words like "hard" and "soft" are insubstantial. Conceive a pulsing stone or an iron mud. Imagine an armor made of spittle or a soup of granite. In such paradox you must seek the nature of the Earth Mother's flesh and bones. And so it was, as the Greek Speaker and I went downward to speak with the immortal who could intercede for me with Gaia, if she were so disposed.

Diplomatic relations with gods are the business of priests, indeed that is the primary function of priests, and I, although I am a subtle man, am not trained in the kind of flattery nor in the application of that necessary unction which I have learned is the balm to be laid upon capricious deities. It seemed to me that Gaia had chosen a strange time to manifest her displeasure. She could as well have prevented the work from the start as played practical jokes upon me just as the end of it

206

came in sight. If it is not men who conspire to add to one's difficulties it is gods. Except in my work for Minos, I have never undertaken a task for either which was not in some degree frustrated or modified by inconsequent changes made late on in the endeavor. That I suppose is the fate of craftsmen, who are essentially more serious and clear-sighted than their employers. The client, I sincerely believe, is invariably wrong whether mortal or divine, and patience is perhaps the first lesson a craftsman must learn, not patience with his materials, for that comes naturally with practice, but patience with his patrons. It was, I felt, for Apollo to make the necessary accommodation with Gaia in the matter of his temple and not for the master of the works to waste his time in disputes of this kind.

A priest would have been useful but there was neither priest nor priestess to confer with the gods, unless the unknown immortal was in fact a priestess. She was a priestess and much more than that.

The Greek Speaker and I, after many hours of **39** traveling deeper and deeper into the earth, came at last to a door. It was of bronze and cast in a single majestic panel. Undecorated, smooth as glass and with neither rivets nor joins, I found it to be one of the most extraordinary technical achievements in metalwork that I had ever seen. There were no faults in it, no filled air pockets, no plugging, and so far as I could see, no chasing either. The great slab of metal had been poured with such skill that no contraction in cooling seemed to have occurred. Not even hairline cracks were apparent, nor was there any web from the mold. The alkalis and other chemicals which aid Gaia's digestion had so patinated the surface that it gleamed in green and black, shot through with azure blue. I have not seen such color in metal above ground.

I was examining the surface of the door closely when the Greek Speaker began to chant. There were no words in the noise he made, only a strange ululating cadence of sounds. When he had finished he said: "I can come no further. You will find your way back if you are successful." And with that he disappeared in his customary fashion, walking swiftly backward into shadow, until I was left alone.

The sounds the Greek Speaker had made were taken up beyond the door, but in a higher key, and suddenly in a great rush of wind the door flashed open. The clangor it made was repeated. Other doors, door after door it seemed, opened almost in unison with it, and each crashed back with a brazen shout. The wind that rushed past me from the open door was filled with smoke and sound. When it had passed, the silence was as hard as the bronze door itself. Either that or I was so deafened I could hear nothing.

The chamber beyond the door was not large and its walls were as smooth and faultless as the door had been. It was a room shaped like a cauldron and furnished solely with a hearth, a pitted boulder identical with that which I had imagined I had seen after my contest with the Minotaur, and a bronze tripod-cauldron so shallow as to form a stool. The stone duplicated that upon which the horned god had sat. Upon the tripod sat a woman. She was naked and she held in her right hand a branch of laurel. Smoke from the hearth gushed about her. The light was thick as if it were being filtered through the cast skin of a snake.

The woman did not speak, she changed. She passed through a series of transformations not in any sequence but capriciously as if to demonstrate her variety, so that she bloomed, withered, extended and contracted, rose and subsided, died, disintegrated and took shape again, a curled foetus in a placenta of smoke. Her age passed before me, not logically from youth to senility, but abruptly, in disorder. Her presence seemed to flicker in a broken rhythm. She was a child, huge eyed and slender, a kore with tip-tilted breasts, a woman full of the child

208

kicking in her belly, a matron ripe as autumn, a child again, clutching bay shoots sticky in her hand, a crone twisted and wizened as a dead shrub and again a maiden. Fragments of her persona were shown to me falling as wayward as leaves so that I could not see her whole, nor did she cease to alter.

The woman turned to bronze, each limb flattened and pulled to marry with her tripod. She shaped herself to a fetish, lost her humanity and became an implacable idol. Her features slipped from her face and she was visored. Her arms clove to her and joined into her sides. She became a snake and reared coiling from the bowl of the tripod.

Then again her hands sprang out from her and became a girl's, her arms lifted like greenstick twigs, Daphne athwart the sun, and this metamorphosis opened to permit the woman to re-emerge from the laurel. She withered so that her skin was rough as bark and wrinkled as dried fruit. She filled with sap and opened her thighs to the smoke licking her belly. She closed them and became again as legless as a serpent. Her disorder was dazzling. If she had gone through a gamut of changes which had any ordered ritual to explain it, I think I should have grasped the meaning, but there was none. Her disintegrations and re-integrations were totally haphazard and continued until I could no longer watch them and hid my head in my hands.

When I looked again the tripod was empty and across it lay a branch of laurel. Standing by the hearth was a middle-aged woman, perhaps more than middle-aged, perhaps elderly. It was difficult to tell her age. She was as ordinary, as utterly unmemorable as a cow in a herd. Furthermore, she was dressed with dowdy modesty and her hair straggled as if she had lacked a mirror to dress it by. This dull housewife addressed me quietly by name. It did not strike me as strange that she knew my name, for she appeared familiar. I felt embarrassed that her name escaped me, but then I am sufficiently celebrated to be known by name to many whom I do not know personally.

I did not identify this unassuming person with the frantic figure on the tripod, indeed I looked anxiously around for fear of some new manifestation.

"You are Daedalus the Athenian, son of Metion of the Erechtheid house," said the middle-aged woman.

"I am."

"I know why you are here."

I asked her who she was and added that I felt we were known to one another, begging her forgiveness for my discourtesy in forgetting her name.

"My name is Deiphobe, daughter of Glaukos."

This too surprised me; I had grown used to the avoidance of names in this nether world.

"Do you live here?" I asked stupidly.

"I have lived here longer than I can bear."

"I too look forward to completing my task and seeing the sun again."

"You will see him sooner than that."

"You speak as if you know my future."

"At times I know what will happen."

"You are an oracle then?"

It embarrasses me even now to think of the foolishness of my part in this conversation. I could not believe that I was in the presence of anyone in the least supernormal and I continually glanced about the cavern seeking the terrible creature I had seen a few moments before and with whom I knew my business lay. I imagined my new acquaintance to be her servant.

She did not reply to me, but smiled. When she smiled I saw at once how beautiful she had been, and again she looked to me familiar. Unsmiling, she looked like a cow and suddenly this train of thought led me to the connection. She resembled Pasiphaë.

"Pasiphaë."

She smiled again and the cow she looked like, unsmiling now, became that most delicate of heifers, Ariadne.

She turned her back on me and that which is bull even in Daedalus rose for her.

"I am not Pasiphaë," she said, "nor are you the Earth Shaker. If you came from the sea it was not as a bull but as a bird." She laughed, walking away, and when she turned to sign me to a seat by the hearth she was once more a housewife whose hair escaped its fillet and straggled about her head. I followed her into the center of the chamber and crouched near her by the hearth.

"Who are you?" I asked, again stupidly, but I was much confused.

"My father was Glaukos son of Minos and of Pasiphaë. He pursued a mouse when he was a child and, in doing so, fell into a pithos filled with honey. There he drowned. Apollo restored him to life by means of an oracle so that, surviving, he sired me. My own life therefore is Apollo's."

"Then you are Pasiphaë's granddaughter." This, to me new-minted, genealogy left me baffled. Here was a woman clearly older than Pasiphaë, who had lived here a long time, or so she inferred. Either she was mad or I had misheard her.

"How can this be?" I asked her.

"You yourself have said that time is a liquid," she replied. "How do you know when these things took place or even if they have yet taken place, for how do you know which way up you float?"

She must have been mocking me.

"Pasiphaë as I knew her was not old and she was beautiful," I said.

"Pasiphaë is all manner of women, all phases of the moon are Pasiphaë and she is much distributed about. In Laconia she is already an ancient oracle and near Menina, where she inhabits a shrine, she is a girl. It is a family name and you know how confused Greeks become about family names. 'Giver of light,' as I am sure you know, is the family name."

"The most improbable people are called that."

"You mean the Minotaur? What would you expect? He is a member of the family."

I found myself floundering in this catalogue, not so much because of the names but because the time span made no sense. Deiphobe was clearly speaking the symbolic language of priests who contrive to make proper names flicker backward and forward in time so that everyone can be shown to be someone else. I have never been able to make out the age of sacred persons at any specific moment.

I thought suddenly of the Pasiphaë I had known to my cost. She was indeed like the moon and as remote.

"The moon is at once old and a young woman," said Deiphobe, cutting through my thought, "and as for me, although I have lived here so long, do I look so old?"

She did not. She looked middle-aged and I assured her at once that she looked young.

"I was first mounted in the year the Bull calved."

I cannot work out this sort of thing. I began again.

"I came to ask..."

"I know why you have come."

"Then will she, do you think, speak to the earth for me? I come at the sun's instigation."

"I am she who will speak."

I stared at her.

"You should know," she said, "who I am, and I shall tell you first what I am, for when I come to speak to the goddess from the god, I shall not be as you see me now, nor shall I know you."

I was silent.

"I shall even tell you about the mouse," she said and smiled her sweet cow's smile so that I, who had had no women for so long, looked away for fear she would see me roused.

"You know well that Minos is the name of a line of kings each one called Minos and each Minos is the bull-god on earth who represents the sun. Who therefore is Minos? I am the granddaughter of Minos. Pasiphaë is his queen and represents the moon. Who therefore in all that line of queens is my grandmother?"

"I have no notion," I said with some irritation. I hate conundrums.

Deiphobe smiled at me again.

"In order to know who I am you must accept that everything is duplicated, everything elides, everything has its reverse, nothing is clear-cut."

I said nothing. Deiphobe touched the great pitted boulder in the center of her cavern.

"This stone, the omphalos, is the earth's navel, yet the navel of the world is at Delphi. This stone you saw elsewhere when you contested with the Minotaur, yet it is here. There is also an omphalos at Eleusis. Does it surprise you that so multitudinous a being as Gaia should sport a clutch of navels, all of them at the center of the world? Each one is joined to her center, since she is a sphere, and each has its cord spun out to join the belly of one of her children. Each is also a pillar which props the sky."

I said nothing. My own navel is concave. I pushed my forefinger into it through my tunic.

"I too am more than one. Here I am Deiphobe, at Delphi, Pythia, who once was male Pytho and female Delphyne, two serpents coiled about the navel stone. Your snake, Erechtheid, is a relative of mine."

At this moment there sprang up beneath the tripod two green snakes closely interwrapped. Tightly coiled, they rose out of the earth until their heads touched the cauldron base which they then cradled with their necks. They were so green they looked vegetable, aping the quick tendrils of the vine. And there they remained motionless.

"As this tripod is supported, so the omphalos supports the sky, and when Apollo couches in the tripod he remains in the sky. I, his woman, am straddled open to him here in the earth and yet he never leaves his ordained circling of the world. He

213

wears me round his sex as you wear your serpent emblem round your wrist."

"You are of the earth?" I asked, to gain time, for I am slow to digest this kind of information.

"I am also Themis. Apollo breeds heat through me to fertilize my mother."

Laden with paradox piled on improbability, I felt like an overburdened mule.

"Patience," said Deiphobe, variously called Pythia and Themis.

"Are you mortal?" I asked lamely.

"To be that would be my release. Then I could die."

She said this with such a weariness that I was moved to touch her hand. It burned me. When I looked later at my fingers they were blistered, although I did not feel any pain at the time.

"Gaia is very old and as she ages she grows cold. Apollo's fire passes through me to warm her. My menstrual blood is oil and feeds her dying fires. My pregnancy is earth's. What I conceive she bears."

However complicated Deiphobe's relationships might be with the divinities, her power was not in question. She was the one person who could intercede for me with Gaia on Apollo's behalf and enable me to release the earthbound tools of my trade from Gaia's pull. Without Deiphobe, Apollo would get no temple and I should be buried in the Mother all my life. I tried to relax.

"I shall tell you the rest," said Deiphobe, "for I seldom find anyone to talk to. Those who visit me, and they are rare enough, want only my oracles, but heat is your medium too and your use of it, although so different from mine, has its value. We are in sympathy, I think."

I was much flattered by this remark. Praise is never unwelcome to a craftsman and one is pleased to be accepted by immortals.

"See how my room is furnished. This hearth is cleft and

from it runs a channel to Gaia's center below the omphalos. Into this cleft I flow. This tripod and its cauldron are my marriage bed. Here the god takes me and when he does I speak, if I do speak, not as I speak now but in orgasm. What I say then I do not know, for it is not my voice but Apollo's and I am charged with his divinity. His semen jets through me and his ejaculation makes me cry to his rhythm. In this cauldron my apotheosis manifests. In its boiling bowl my flesh is consumed and flows downward. In the steam lies whatever prophecy may be found and when that steam condenses into words you will learn what you already know and be confirmed in it. The condensation takes a little time. All will be over before you hear words."

I could not see how I could tell her that prophecy was not what I had come for. Prophecy as to one's personal future is hard to resist, by my primary need was not reassurance as to my future career but rather an intercession of a practical nature which would permit me to enjoy a future career of any sort. I changed the subject as politely as I could.

"What," I asked, "is your reward for these terrible labors?"

"My reward will be mortality."

"Death?"

"Death."

"Why?"

She laughed at me.

"When will that be? I mean, how long must you suffer?"

"You misunderstand. I am a woman, immortal, but a woman. The penetration of the god is an ecstasy no mortal knows and in its train it carries an exhaustion no woman ever knew. I am tired with eons of bearing the brunt of the lustful sun, tired beyond death and now want only death."

"Will you be granted death?"

"I pray for it and I believe a time will come when I shall be given it."

She fell silent and I too could think of nothing more to ask. This woman who looked so ordinary in her drab chiton, who seemed newly risen from bending over cooking pots and pushed her hair back from her damp forehead with so familiar a gesture, was herself continually cooked and on such a fire that molten metal would dissolve in steam at its lightest touch.

In the silence my thoughts wandered to practical matters. I began covertly to examine the tripod and cauldron in which this blaze of coupling took place. The melting point of any alloy known to me could be achieved in any furnace capable of containing a reducing rather than an oxidizing heat. Normal cooking took place on fires so mild they could not even bake clay adequately. Any metal cauldron would naturally be undamaged by normal fires. But given bellows and a tightly enclosed kiln, such heat could be generated as to melt and fuse rocks, for ores are parts of rock in one sense. The tripod and cauldron looked normal enough bronze to me. I was intrigued and puzzled.

"You are a man so absurdly practical," said Deiphobe, "that even in the presence of divine mysteries you can only mind your own business."

For so taxed an immortal she had a rare humor. It must be unusual in such circumstances as hers to find anything comic, yet I believe she found me so. I am not used to this and indeed at another time might have taken some offense, but I could not. She was so natural to me that I could have loved her. For a moment my blasphemous thoughts trembled on the edge of seeing her as a wife.

"What about the mouse?" I asked, to shut out such hubris.

"Presently," she said, "for the moment you would prefer to know why the tripod can withstand the heat of Apollo's orgasm."

I nodded. Really there was so easy communion with her that I had no need to speak at all.

"Your friend the Greek Speaker, as you call him, has described to you how the four forces act and how each particle of matter is a sum of dancers joined in a dance around a center.

216

All things are thus particular and each visible thing is a concordance of dances.

"Metals you know are fused in a liquid dance in the furnace, yet when they cool and harden those invisible particles dance still. Only their measure is altered. Conceive then how a god, by choosing a different chain of steps can so change the structure of any creation as to make its dance as impervious to heat or cold as to time. Even Gaia herself, with all her crushing pull, could not crumple up those slender tripod legs nor dent the cauldron and when the sun himself sits in the bowl it does not even glow with his heat."

"And you, spread beneath him?"

"I too am made in a different measure and when I come to die that measure will change its pace and I shall be consumed utterly. I shall no longer know the music of the round but go into a quiet. Only my voice will stay here, only my voice."

I did not question this.

"As to the mouse," she said, "he is Apollo's creature, like the snake who eats him. Apollo is a most diverse god. He gives health by his warmth and yet his arrows carry pestilence. Pestilence however is so often cured by Apollo's own son Asklepios that there is a story of complaint in certain quarters for the lack of deaths by sickness. This is of course balanced by man's ability to injure and destroy his fellow men for purposes less admirable than that which causes the snake to engulf the mouse. I know, for you have often said so, that you find balance and order paramount. Apollo, however capricious he may appear to you, is concerned above all else with balance and order. He ripens the wheat upon which his mouse lives, provides his snake to control the number of mice and by this principle holds all things properly related."

I felt at that moment more sympathy for the mouse than I should have dared to voice, but I remembered that it was a mouse who had temporarily drowned Deiphobe's father in honey and accepted that there might be an element of prejudice in her apparent preference for snakes. The twin snakes under the cauldron flicked their tongues and coiled about each other lazily.

I touched my Erechtheid bracelet.

"I have something I must ask of you," I said. "I am here to ask your intercession with Gaia so that she will allow me to complete my task for Apollo."

"I know that, I shall ask."

"And in return?"

"Pray for my death."

I looked at her and tears started in my eyes. I sought, even at the risk of being burnt, to touch her hand, but she drew away.

"You are in the right place to ask anything of the Mother," she said cheerfully. "You are in her vulva and who can deny a man when he is there?"

It is strange that I remember Deiphobe's laughter more clearly than anything else about her, even the terrible sequence of her transformations which I had glimpsed and would hear but not see again.

I began to feel a warmth, a choking warmth envelop me and the sweat started from me. I looked up from where I was crouched by the hearth and saw Deiphobe rise. She seemed taller and to be growing before my eyes. Her own eyes were wide open and glazed.

"Go now," she said, "and wait beyond the door."

I knelt before her and then got to my feet. The walls of her room were wet. No longer at rest they were contracting, moving like gripping flesh toward the tripod. The cleft in the hearth opened and the pitted stone swelled, turning red.

I backed toward the door and saw for the first time that there were other doors, uncountable doors all opening in the flesh of the chamber.

The light changed. Golden, yellow as midday, it increased and heat blazed through the ceiling of the place.

At the door, at one of the doors, I looked back. **40**
The twin snakes uncurling from below the
cauldron had twined about Deiphobe's arms and legs. Lifting
her, they spread her in the cauldron bowl, her thighs extended,
and she was naked and beautiful. Her mouth opened and her
head fell back as the door closed, cutting me off from her, and
I was outside. I stood sweating, facing the shining surface of
the great bronze door which had closed so silently that I had
not known it had moved. From behind it a sound rose, cry after
cry, each one greater than the last and added to these cries was
a sharp but vast breathing like the panting rush of air one never
hears but somehow expects to hear in the moment before a
great storm breaks. It was as if a mighty silence was shaken
behind sound.

I do not know how long it lasted, this coupling, but the earth
rose and shook and threw me from wall to wall of the passage.
I could see nothing but whiteness and as the sound went beyond human hearing I could hear nothing but the beating of
my own blood behind my eyes. I clung to the ground, trying to
hold myself down on the heaving floor and I felt blackness
swimming up through the white sheeting my senses. Then the
doors crashed open, not in unison but in rapid and uneven
sequence like a rockfall spraying boulders, a broken clattering
of dented gongs, and I looked up.

In the basin of the cauldron there was no woman. There was
a brazen, extended throat rising from a drum which had become part of the tripod cauldron. It was an entity, boneless as a
snake but rigid as metal standing upright on tripod tangs. This
image, topped by a head as featureless as an axeblade, spoke in
words condensed from scalding steam. Each word came sibi-
lant. The pythoness was whispering. Then her speech thickened and the words stuck mollusc in the mass of sound. Words
came from her that rang, others that fell plummeting like
stones, and through it all the serpent hissing breathed through
the sense.

I do not to this day know exactly what she meant, for I think she spoke of my future in your time and of another coming of Icarus and of great peril to man, but I do not know this for certain. What she meant I must leave to you, but this is what she said:

> "My speech is split, suck at my thistle speech
> My spittle swells to sweeten surety
> See where my mouth is eyed and sees in smoke
> Your summit sky in sallow solstice sleep.
>
> Wax in that summit sky burns out to bronze
> This wax, your waxing lost, you are not lost
> But molten propagate the eagle's clutch
> In bronze out-bronzed blatant to blot out blood.
>
> Know that the fish shall fully hatch the hawk,
> Who in the egg fed on the ram's rod yolk,
> In water springs the pinions to take wing,
> And wingless wheels above the crawling gull.
>
> At such a time your son is multiplied
> And burning, bristles at his burning god.
> The fish sign's season sinks into the dark
> And he who carries water carries light."

Oracles make it their business to be obscure, or else they cannot help it. In any case, it would have been stranger still if the strange configuration of humanity, divinity, metal and serpent, which I saw in that brief span while the door stood open, had said anything readily comprehensible. If, in her voice, the god spoke through her, then it is even less surprising that I did not understand what was meant. There was no priest there to interpret for me. There was no one there but Deiphobe daughter of Glaukos, who was the granddaughter of one Pasiphaë or another and who was also Themis, Pythia and the mistress of the god. The door now shut upon her with such finality that I knew I should not see her again. I was alone outside that bronze door and for the first time since I had entered the earth I was utterly lonely and bereft.

The light was dimming. I was uncertain of the outcome of this high business, this diplomatic mission which I had been forced by circumstances to undertake and which I felt had changed me and left me lonely. I am not usually much disturbed by being alone.

As to the oracle, I understood it only in part and it seemed very remote from me. The time of the Fish and that of the Water-carrier who brought light must refer to the great astrological year which would bring the prophecy to fruition in your time and not in mine. Flight was to bring Nemesis with it eventually. I had known the first part of that. You will know the rest.

As to myself, I was wax and burnt out, as Icarus had been, and deathly tired. How long should I be in becoming bronze and tireless? Talk of millennia brings cold comfort to the individual. My tasks seemed trivial.

The Greek Speaker stepped out of the shadow and held up a hammer. It was one of those long light picks with which metalmen chip for ore samples, and he lifted it easily. "Come," he said, "you have succeeded," and he said no more for he was a taciturn man. I could see that Gaia's pull had been released either at Deiphobe's intercession or Apollo's insistence. None of us could have so much as lifted the hammer from his work bench before.

The weight had lifted from the work. Why did it not lift from me? I thought of Deiphobe and her **41** duality, her mystery and her normality. She had given me more than I asked and told me, however deeply embedded in the obscurity of her chant, that my son would live and multiply and that my fame would not die. I suppose these were the two things I had wanted to hear.

As a woman I thought I could have lived with her and that is true of few women I have met. She was tolerant and intelligent, if not especially handsome. That I should have thought such a thing showed how great was my dislocation from reality. My left hand began to throb and I saw that the tips of all the fingers were raw and blistered where I had touched her and been burned. The sun had been in her even in his absence. She was not a woman to live with but the bride of Apollo who rode her in passing and used her for his voice. My folly made me laugh and yet, immortal or not, she was a warm and likable woman. And again my thought was comic. She was indeed warm.

I have seen what men can do to women casually. I do not mean in passion but in its absence. I have seen the chill tedium they create by lack of love. Now I had seen what a god could do in the furnace heat of his lack of love and I wondered if, without the spectacular element, the effect was so different. I had seen Deiphobe transformed, twisted, reshaped, distorted beyond any human possibility but I have also seen women withered out of youth into nonentity, reduced to bone by bitterness, swollen from overeating to fend off boredom, wrinkled and unripened fruitless, bent by overbearing. These processes are lifelong among unloved mortals, rapid and repeated for a god's woman and it occurred to me that all the ecstasy of congress with a god whose touch could shrivel stone and whose glance parched away the summer yearly would not be less a monotony than the gray embrace of habit. Men cramp women with cold, gods cripple them with heat. There is contempt in both and it also occurred to me that Deiphobe probably hated Apollo, for he shared nothing with her of his true divinity.

Maybe Prometheus, with whom I am sometimes confused, knew something of this when by his theft he sought to raise up man, for men using divine attributes circumspectly, if not well, can make life warm without burning their fingers or their women. I cannot say they do, but some try. Prometheus certainly paid for his experiment.

Gods are incapable of failure. That is their failure. Deiphobe untransformed was a comfortable companion and could have brought comfort. What comfort did she get and what comfort did Apollo need of her?

Poor woman, poor immortal, I prayed for her death as she had asked me and then I shut out these dangerous and blasphemous thoughts. I went back to my workshop with the Greek Speaker and found the work progressing.

One of the sillier tales told about me is that I can make statues able to see and walk and talk. **42** It has been reported, I am told, that I could make statues capable of performing every bodily function. This is not only untrue but, if you think about it, highly undesirable. A statue which would descend from its plinth at mealtimes and step out into the garden afterward to relieve itself would be a singular encumbrance about the house. I say this because I do not think the statues I make would be pliable nor could they be set to useful work. I think it difficult to avoid a certain arrogance in a bronze or a marble carving, for there is some divinity contained in an image and this is inevitable since statues are made in honor of the gods and seldom for any other reason. A good statue has a fragment of the god in it, but I have seen enough of gods not to want them performing their bodily functions in my courtyard.

It is also reported of me that I was the first in Greece to make statues with parted legs and outstretched arms, and there is some truth in this, for I was the first to employ hollow-casting for monumental bronze sculpture, despite the claims you will have heard made on behalf of the Samians. This was the technique I used in casting the great figure of Apollo for his temple at Cumae.

I have said that I intended to show the god striding forward with his arms raised freely from his sides and that he should carry in his left hand the figure in little of my son, winged, and in his right the great bow which gives him the name of "Far Darter." Now the problem of the free-standing parts of a great statue in stone is the problem of support. An arm of marble held out from the shoulder is fragile and can easily snap off under its own weight or while the figure is being set in place. This can be avoided by cunningly carved drapery used in support of the limb, but this of course is an unwieldy compromise and in any case Apollo must be shown naked. On the other hand, to cast a monumental figure in solid bronze would be absurd. It would be absurd and also impossible, for the pour would take too long and cool too quickly and so fail to fill the mold properly. Such a bronze would in any case be enormously heavy and enormously expensive in metal.

The solution therefore is the hollow-cast bronze. A hollow bronze limb is really a skin of metal, and even one twice the size of life has the tensile strength to need no support and, being thin, contains little enough metal to pour quickly. Therefore a great bronze must be cast in sections for the sake of speed in pouring and the parts riveted together and "sweated on," which is to melt over the joins.

It has long been known that, in the east, founders cast small bronzes in piece molds and make them hollow by coring. To do this they take clay and stone-chippings mixed together, fire the mass, and then insert it into piece-molds which have been coated internally with wax. This gives them a core of fireproof material, the wax coat which would be burnt out and the containing negative mold which has been taken from the original clay model of the figure. To prevent the core from shifting when the wax is burned out, they drive bronze spikes through mold and wax and into the core. For simple forms this process is adequate but the thickness of the bronze is inevitably very variable. Furthermore, they have not conceived that the core

224

would need to breathe, just as the porous mantle breathes, or the bronze would be pocked with innumerable air bubbles.

I improved upon this technique by leaving the mold open to the core at one end and mixing chaff into the core itself to make it porous, but even this can only succeed on a large scale when a figure is cast in sections. My second improvement, which perfected the technique, was to carve the original figure in wood. This I conceived from the *xoana*, those ancient wooden cult figures plated with sheet metal riveted on, which are still manufactured in Crete.

For my Apollo therefore I had first carved the figure from laminated pieces of poplar wood, dovetailing the limbs in place by joinery. I had made the parts smooth but not detailed as to hair, fingernails and other minutiae. I had taken the figure to pieces and made clay piece-molds for the parts.

There was a pair of piecemolds for the trunk and another pair of molds for the hips, one pair for each limb, two pairs for the face and head and one pair for each hand and foot. These piece-molds I then packed tight with clay, well mixed with terracotta chips to let the mass breathe. I had my core complete and shaped and I now coated each part of it in wax, working the wax up finely, for this would determine the shape and surface of the final bronze. The wax covering the parts of core was no more in any one place than a quarter of an inch thick and these parts I mantled separately, leaving such vents and pouring funnels as I have already described to allow the free run of the molten bronze.

Each of the twelve sections was easy to handle and no problem to pour. I should add that each section was so made as to joint into the whole much as the wooden parts had done. Then, to complete the preparation, there had to be a touch of ritual, as there always is in casting a bronze for a god. As I was casting the core of the trunk, the Greek Speaker brought me a long sliver of iron. "This," he said, "was thrown down by your sky-god—or so I am told." I looked at it and saw that it was a fragment of one of the iron stones which sometimes fall out of the sky. One end was brown and crusted and the blade resembled long crystals, but crystals of bright metal. I took it and pressed it into the still-damp core of the statue's breast.

I have always done this, always enclosed in the core of a bronze figure some fragment of a substance sacred to the subject of the sculpture and this may have been a factor in creating the absurd legend of my giving life to statues so that they walk and talk. I have wondered about this and conclude that the notion was born out of various quite different aspects of my practice as a sculptor. First and simplest of these may have been the jointing of the wooden parts of the figure to simplify the casting problem, as I have described. Simple-minded gossips may have learned of my joinery and come to believe that because each of their wooden limbs was separately jointed into the trunk, all my figures were jointed like men and could therefore move like men. Out of such ignorance fantastic tales can grow as they pass among people who prefer miracles to technicalities. This may be one source of the error. The other is more genuinely mysterious, for as I say, I have always hidden some dedicated substance in the core of each bronze I have made. This I have done out of piety or you may prefer to call it superstition. I am not entirely clear myself as to which is which.

In your time the dedication of sculpture to the gods may no longer be important. It may be that it will be made for less straightforward purposes and I am often in two minds about the significance of the rituals which in my time are normal. Nevertheless, I do not see how life can be introduced into the work without invoking powers beyond the craftsman, whatever they are, and by this I do not mean the galvanizing of posturing and prattling automata to make travesties of living creatures, I mean the calculated secretion of force within inert materials such as bronze or the uncovering of force already secreted in the heart of the stone or the balk of timber. This force is there or is put there, for who can deny its presence in proper sculpture?

It is not, as I have often told my pupils, put there in response to the diligent imitation of the appearance of men or gods. It is a virtue expanding from the force contained within the forms of the image and it expands in relation to the density of its compression.

To me, the practical reason for piety is that it enables a man to cousin gods. By piety and hard **43** concentration a man may induce gods to exercise that useful attribute of divinity, the ability to break off fragments of their essence. Success depends on it, for a minute particle of this essence must be contained in every admirable piece of sculpture. Sometimes in my best work I have, I believe, contained the divine fragment which is the vitality of sculpture. True sculpture, I may add, always turns in upon itself. Its forms move toward its center. It is thus that it has the strength to contain in that center the outward-moving force which emanates from the particle. The nature of this iota of divinity is capricious and perhaps unknowable. Its quality is not restricted to images of the gods themselves, for it may be present in a votive image of any sort. I have myself seen bronzes of goats, lions and bulls no larger than my thumb which glow with a contained power which I cannot otherwise explain. To gain or earn this power of which I speak is laborious and it is so volatile that every precaution may be taken and great labor expended, only to end in the evaporation of the force so that an empty image results.

One strives for perfection and naturally does not achieve it, but compressed as it were between one's greatest effort and perfection itself, trapped in the error which makes the imperfection, is to be found the fragment of the god. If the error is gross and the gap wide the force will disperse. It is under the pressure which lies between the error and the perfection, if the two are close enough, that the power may be held in the stone or in the heart of the bronze.

Now to arrive even within reach of this dynamic error it is necessary to identify oneself with the image. One must be able metaphorically to pass into it and in portraying Apollo one must attempt to enter his nature. No man can do such a thing, but a man may, if the god aids him, turn not only his mind but his will toward this condition by extreme concentration upon it.

To make an image of a mortal requires the same identification and concentration upon that mortal as to make the image of a god. The difference is that one must entreat a god on behalf of the mortal, for mortals do not possess the substance of which I speak unless they are to some extent possessed by a god. In practical terms, this makes life very difficult, for who knows whether such and such a man, even if he is a king, is really so beloved of a god that his image will be given life? Furthermore, kings can behave so arrogantly that gods are frequently displeased with them, and then the work is hardly worth attempting. Time spent on a working model of a cow is more profitable in such circumstances.

I suppose I should have considered this when I went to make the little figure of Icarus for Apollo's statue to hold in his left hand. When I describe what happened, you will see, as I did not see at once, where my fault lay. I have digressed at this length to explain it.

The Greek Speaker and his companions mantled and burned out the wax. They prepared the **44** bronze and poured it successfully and without hesitation or error, for they were the best foundrymen I have ever come across. In due time, the twelve parts of the bronze god were broken out of the mantle and they were well done. Among us we took the parts and began the long labor of filling each imperfection, smoothing and burnishing every surface, riveting the parts together and covering the joins by "sweating on." We

228

engraved the details of the hair and inserted into their sockets the eyes of shell and silver, fixing them in place from within the hollow of the skull with lead plates. This must be done before joining the head to the trunk. We inlaid the nipples and the lips with copper and added all refinements proper to a god's image and it took us many weeks, if weeks could be measured within Gaia.

During those days and weeks, the Greek Speaker cast Apollo's bow and the quiver of arrows which give him his title of "Far Darter" and I, alone in my workshop, tried again and again to make the little bronze figure of my son wearing the wings which took him into the sky and were the death of him. I tried again and again, but each time I failed. I took refined beeswax to make the model and it melted or crumbled in my fingers. I added resin to strengthen it, built an armature of copper wires to hold the forms together and yet the figure fell to pieces in my hand. Each time I began I achieved less. Icarus disintegrated as an image as totally as Icarus had disintegrated as a man in the eye of the sun.

I laid the pieces of my model on the bench and under my eyes, in the cool cave where I worked, the wax curled, melted into a clear liquid, dripped and fell in rivulets onto the floor. There was no furnace alight in the workroom—only the little brazier I used for softening the wax. It was not even comfortably warm, but the wax melted for all that. I picked it up and held the sticky mass in a bowl of cold water to harden it, but it did not harden. My hands in the water stung me and I saw my left hand, already scarred and newly healed from the burns I had had from touching Deiphobe, was broken open and raw, and my right hand was blistered so that I took both hands out of the cold water and held them in my armpits for the pain in them.

The Greek Speaker came with the model of the bow and saw me hunched with my hands in my armpits and he did not seem much surprised. He brought oil and cloths and bandaged me.

"You burn your fingers when you play with fire," he said,

and came as near to smiling as he ever did. Then he reached into the water, took out the still warm wax and caked it between his palms, suffering no blisters from the contact. There have been times when the Greek Speaker has greatly tried my patience.

Time passed and I was idle and restless with my **45** crippled hands. The bronze Apollo progressed, and when I went every few hours to inspect the work, the god's smiling lips seemed to stretch and grin at me. I spent much time in supervising the assembly of the other parts of the temple and as this work, too, neared completion and only the bronze doors remained to be made, the Greek Speaker took me on the long haul upward to one of the mouths of the many tunnels which pass through Gaia.

On the way, he made it known to me that the people who lived above ground had been enrolled as laborers and that I should presently meet their king. We pressed on through the winding, luminescent rock passage and after one of his more pregnantly sententious silences he said:

"We of the Mother do not leave her womb."

"Never?"

"We are not born out of her but born in her."

I acknowledged this.

"We shall bring all the parts of the god's house to the Mother's entrance and those who bring us food will take the parts and place them as you will upon her skin."

"There remain the doors to make," I said, looking down at my hands.

"When you can make them, make them. When they are made, the parts of your building will lie at the entrance to the upper world."

"That is excellent. I shall model the panels of the doors as soon as my bandages are off."

"The Mother will cure your hands."

"I shall be grateful."

There followed another long silence. The light grew dim. In the passages nearest to her entrances Gaia becomes opaque, making a guardian darkness, perhaps to frighten intruders, perhaps because her flesh becomes more dense immediately below her skin. Her musculature is compact where it is most useful.

As the darkness became general, the distant circle of sunlight which marked the cavern mouth grew larger. Its effect was hypnotic. I was aware that the troglodyte Greek Speaker had begun another monotonous exposition, but it seemed I heard his voice muffled and from a distance. I knew nothing but the goal, the white bowl blazing in the center of blackness, which marked the wide world to which I was born.

I had no idea how long I had been in the earth, nor how blind and groping I should be when I left it. In the cave entrance I was painfully dazzled, as if I had been looking directly at the disk of the sun. I put my head in my bandaged hands and heard the Greek Speaker groaning and grumbling beside me.

I let the light filter slowly between my fingers and gradually I could distinguish my own feet, the shale and withered grass on which they stood, and presently I could make out the landscape below me. We were high in the rock. A path twisted upward to the summit and, interrupted by a rockfall, it also led downward to be lost among boulders and scrub. Beyond these boulders, perhaps half a mile away, was sand, and beyond that the sea lay still as the rocks.

I gazed around me. Nothing moved but a kestrel swinging slowly above the long tongue of land which ran south from Cumae and separated the sea from the pallid lake. Behind me the Greek Speaker had swaddled his head in a cloak, which he must have brought for the purpose, and his muffled complaints came thick from among its folds. He was crouched at least twenty yards back in the opening to the tunnel and as the sun crept along it, he retreated slowly into the deep shade. What

231

could be seen of him looked like a long-dead frog, mottled and lead colored, and when I looked at my own arms they were the color of sour milk.

I could by now see adequately if I kept my eyes slitted and shaded them with my arms. I could see small clouds painted on the sky and I could tell the sun shone brightly on the sea and on the ground, but I should not have dared glance up at it.

What I had not seen, in this sharply defined, hard and brilliant place, was a man seated motionless upon a rock at the point where the path curved over onto the summit of the acropolis. I looked at him and he at me, but neither of us moved. He was enormously fat.

I know his name now, but at that time I simply thought of him as the Fat Man. I have never seen a fatter man.

He sat on his rock with his legs spread to allow his belly repose and his belly lay on the rock between his thighs like the omphalos. Indeed, it was as heavy and as wide as the navel stone. He was not soft in his fatness but thick, seemingly constructed of weathered slabs of stone or like a heap of vast sea-ground pebbles, cunningly assembled. His skin and hair were brindled brown and of much the same color; so was the shapeless robe that alternatively strained and hung upon him. He was the color of the landscape and blended perfectly into it. It was no wonder I had not seen him.

The Greek Speaker's muffled talk resolved itself into a series of shouts and they were shouts in Greek, but I could not understand what he said. The Fat Man said nothing. Instead, the voice speaking firmly but silently in my head was Cephalon's.

I looked at the Fat Man and he had not moved. There was a blade of grass in his mouth. Then he began to laugh and the great cairn of smooth boulders, of which I was convinced he was made, began to shake and rumble, yet I am sure there was no actual sound. It became still again and a field mouse trotted briskly out of the grass and sat on one of his feet, so clearly there was not sound enough to alarm it. In my head the laughter was huge.

The Greek Speaker again began bawling to himself under his blanket and the mouse shot back into the grass.

"I do not speak," the Fat Man gave me to understand, "and nor need you, but perhaps you would quiet our swaddled friend by telling him we have met. I can speak, you understand," he added, "but I dislike the sound."

I went back into the cave and sought to unwrap the Greek Speaker, but he bundled himself even tighter in his cloak.

"What dealings are we supposed to have with this fat man?" I said.

"He will see to your temple."

"By himself?"

"No. He has people. He is their king."

"What shall I tell him?"

"Tell him that the parts of the temple will be brought to this spot."

"I gather the parts of your temple will be brought to this spot," came the Fat Man's voice in my head. "When?"

"Shortly, or as soon as it can be managed, or in so many days," is what I presume the Greek Speaker replied, for he said nothing.

It is very disconcerting to hold a tripartite conversation of this sort if one of the participants has no need for speech.

"What did he say?" I asked.

"He asked when," said the Greek Speaker.

"Well, when?"

"I have told him."

"What?"

"As soon as it can be managed. I do not know how long it will take, but as soon as it can be managed."

"Very well," the Fat Man did not in fact say.

"The people out here are impossible," said the Greek Speaker irritably. "When you wish to return, Athenian, this path will bring you back to the normal world." He got up and still swathed in his copious, sight-protecting shroud, he groped and staggered down the passage and back into the darkness.

"He is a worthy man and an excellent craftsman, a sober and excellent man. I am quite sure that the parts of your temple will be delivered in the most correct fashion and as soon as he can manage it. In the meantime, if you are accustomed to the light, perhaps we should examine the site."

The Fat Man's communication was perfectly clear and although neither of us spoke, then or ever, I am in no doubt that my reply was received.

"Perhaps you are tired," came into my head, "then let us sit here awhile before we begin the work. Have you still an ant in your head?"

At once I felt a twitch somewhere behind my right eye. It felt as if I had the ant still with me.

"You are unusually inhabited. You house transients like myself from time to time and of course your son is a permanent lodger."

"Any man houses memories."

"Yours are more potent than most. Your inhabitants push against your abilities. Your mind is overcrowded. So much so that I can barely find room in it."

"Who are you and why should I have you in my mind?" I said aloud in anger.

The Fat Man silenced me.

I thought with growing impatience that I was in no mood for this verbose pedagogue philosophizing in my private mind without a word.

"I am an extension of yourself. I am the Fat Man who has got out. Without me you cannot build your temple nor propitiate the god, nor keep your vows." And he began to laugh again.

"My name is one you chose for other purposes and I function within the pattern you have established. Consider me an extra dimension of Daedalus, albeit an admonitory one. Without me you cannot penetrate the speechless areas of your own intelligence. You could not know the Minotaur, for instance, nor can you grasp your son's true nature, nor come to terms with your reverence for Minos, nor accept the dead Theseus."

Theseus was not a name I wanted named. I had put him away from me forever. I shut out the sound.

"Let us go to the site," I said, and went up the path to the brow of the rock.

Before me the plateau of Cumae lay bare. It **46** was not large, no bigger perhaps than a hall in the palace of Minos. It was flat, sparsely covered with dry soil and with the bare rock showing through in many places. Not even the charred timbers of the earlier temple were visible. Apollo had consumed every vestige of it and burned the place to the bone. By the signs of grass and rock plants newly sprung upon the ashy soil, I had been in the earth at least a year.

I remembered the site perfectly. I had not been wrong in judging the proportions of the temple in relation to it. I was surprised how exact my memory had been.

What I had to build with the aid of the Fat Man and his people was not a shrine such as they have in the palaces of Crete as places of worship for humans, but a temple to house the god when he should choose to enter it.

Temples are not familiar in my world, but they have them far to the east, in the lands beyond the sea, and some of these are vast. The one I had in mind . . .

"Will be a rectangular naos of dressed tufa blocks fronted with a porch and with four cypress columns in antis. This whole will be ridge-roofed with tiles and decorated with terracotta antefixes and acroteria. No frieze, at least no sculptured frieze, below these but the naos will be entered through the great bronze doors you have yet to make and it will house only the cult image which you have nearly completed, on a plinth of worked stone. The stylobate will have three steps and will also be of tufa. All the components of the building are complete and the plans for assembling them. Only the doors remain and you cannot model their reliefs until your hands recover."

Perhaps you can appreciate how insufferable it is to have someone take up your thought and voice it to you silently in your head so that you are forced to learn more than you want about something you already know.

The Fat Man continually did this. He knew my mind, but could not resist reiterating the knowledge and he was well aware of the exact degree of irritation he caused. It greatly amused him. However, since he knew exactly what I required done and I knew I could trust him to organize the work in precise accordance with my conception, he was of the highest value.

"I am glad you are reconciled to me. Your cave-dwelling friend has never managed to be. Whenever I am in his foundry he tries to shut his mind to me."

I sighed.

"You see what he means," came from the Fat Man.

With the Fat Man, or Cephalon in the Fat Man, there was no avoidance of candor. The courtesy one would show to a man in the normal intercourse of speech was denied one, and all subtlety, all reservation, were inevitably prevented.

Cephalon answered questions at the moment they were born in my mind. He answered questions I did not need answered. He was in fact the most continuous, if silent, communicant I have ever known and he well knew my opinion of him, for how could I disguise it?

I speculated mildly on the name of the Greek Speaker's people. "They are called Kimmerians," was the instant reply. I wondered idly about the name of the Fat Man's people. "We are called Myrmidons, because we work like ants. We are human ants in a sense and building is our principal trade. We are related to the Kimmerians, of course, who are also ants, but whereas they exist within the nest, we live on its periphery."

The ant moved in my head. "He and I are one—we are one," the thought came in consort from the ant and the Fat Man, but while I could feel the ant run frantically about in my brain, the Fat Man, when I looked around at him, had not moved, except that the blade of grass now stuck out of the other side of his mouth.

Involuntarily I considered this ponderous ant's appearance. He was the fattest ant ever born. "Chestnuts," said the Fat Man, without stirring or moving his lips. "My people feed me great quantities of chestnuts. They prefer me in this shape and revere me for it. Chestnuts are very nutritious and they are plentiful north of here. I greatly enjoy them."

This person would, I felt sure, irritate me even more than my invaluable Greek Speaker, yet I could do without neither.

"That is quite correct," came the unruffled voice of Myrmex who was Cephalon the fat-man-ant.

We sometimes equate ourselves metaphorically with insects, or at least with certain specific symbolic virtues we impute to them. The bee is synonymous with laborious virtue, an example to all, whereas the grasshopper is the reverse. Yet grasshoppers have a special significance to Athenians. We think of them as indigenous inhabitants of Attica because of some old tale that they leaped straight up out of the earth, emerging complete like Athena from the brow of Zeus. My mother wore gold grasshoppers in her hair to show she was native to Attica. I remember she told me so when she let me play with them. I do not remember her suggesting that grasshoppers make exceptional mothers or indeed do anything but sing in the grass by scraping their legs together, but my mother, being an aristocrat, did very little more active herself. To my mother the ant would have been the proper symbol for a slave.

Chestnuts! What had chestnuts to do with an ant? Laboriously I dragged my wandering thoughts from this speculation. Myrmex was there or Cephalon-Myrmex and in the flesh, a protean bulk of flesh contradicting the very nature and physique of any ant ever hatched.

"I am, I agree, something of a paradox, but you will see that diligence you admire and seek in me will be available if not apparent. All will be done and better done than by grasshoppers."

The voice trundled complacently in my head, a fat but nimble voice, Myrmex murmuring. His repose was not a quality usually to be found in ants.

"It is a joke in a way. You will recall that athletes are nicknamed *myrmekes* in your tongue. It is a joke of sorts."

It was not a joke I much enjoyed. The disparity of scale, the elusive disposition of minute as against copious mass, the disconcerting interchange of three individuals eliding backward and forward in my weary head and at the same time of indeterminate importance to my future conduct, did not make for good jokes.

It seemed to me that thought, in this hallucinatory form, behaved very like metals. One cannot be clear as to the reasons why metals behave as they do, however pragmatically adept one may be in controlling their behavior. For instance, ores respond to temperature in very different ways. At a low temperature oxide films appear on the surface of impure copper. At a higher one, silver oxides and pyrites will begin to decompose in the mass. Heat it more and sulphide ores will begin to roast but, at such a heat, cold-worked bronze would have fully recrystallized and become soft, and so it goes on up the scale. The parts of a lump of ore melt at different temperatures. To alloy they must often rise beyond the melting point to fuse and contain their earthly matter. Equally, to rid them of rocky impurities they must be reduced. That all this must be, metal workers know from experience. Why it should be so we do not know. I do not wish to bore you with these pyrotechnical matters, but I tend to think in this fashion, however confused I may find myself. Cephalon, Myrmex, the Fat Man, melted, reduced, fused and separated in my mind at different temperatures with the memories I had of others, yet they were one metal and all of them melt below the temperature of the slag which in a sense is the final heap one leaves behind when all else is finished. It is convenient that pure metals, except of course iron, all melt and may be extracted from the slag before the slag itself melts into the past.

Chestnut wood makes fine charcoal, if not as fine as the pistachio, and maybe in association with the chestnut charcoal, fed through Myrmex to make him fat, I could reduce the metal Cephalon and cast him usefully.

"Consider us your associates," said Myrmex, slim and running in my brain, his fat melted and burned out in my mind. "Go about your business. It is the god who will be served."

Thereafter there was silence, and with infinite reluctance I went back down the long channel into Gaia to find the Greek Speaker and begin work on the doors. I had seen the shining world above the ground again and was desperate to return to it, freed of Apollo's grievous yoke. I was even earth blind enough not to realize that in the open he would watch me throughout each day and was not yet inclined to mercy.

In Gaia, in the last days of my labor I worked under such pressure and at such speed that when **47** I lay down to rest my exhaustion kept me from proper sleep. Half-sleeping, uneasy, the writhing of my mind made an ants' nest turmoil of my thoughts. Memories, some, wrinkled like the grubs ants carry about, or like dried chestnuts, mingled with others in brindled colors which skipped capriciously like grasshoppers, part green, part gray and touched with red. Memories scraped their dry legs in my mind like the cricket crackling of half-forgotten speech.

I remembered Athens, gray and ochre, the dust the color of peeled chestnuts, scuffed into clouds by the bare feet of runners. I remembered runners in the stadium and men competing in the long jump, grasshopper leaping, and the click of their hand weights on the ground when they landed. I remembered the games with Androgeos competing, winning every event, and those games merged in my mind with his funeral games, for he was killed at Marathon within a day of the Athenian festival. I saw Androgeos dead from the horn wound of the white bull which gored him at Marathon, where Aegeus sent him to rid the country of its trampling. I remembered the grass stamped flat and the churned earth of ruined gardens and the silence, unstridulated by any grasshoppers, when the bull had come at Androgeos, striking sideways and upward with the left horn, and I heard again the thick, dry, quick sound of the breath driven from a man's lungs when the horn went in under his arm and the gasp from the spectators. Those remembered sounds came to me in the darkness below Gaia's outer skin and the quick rattle of the singing grasshoppers returned. The bull tossed Androgeos high and he fell, and the bull went over him and trod him. Icarus was there with his damaged hand, and he started forward, but Theseus took the bull by the tail, twisting it to halt him and turn him off the body. Now I could see it again, Icarus leaping sideways to turn the bull further and a pack of jostling men pulling Androgeos away. Theseus killed the bull that day.

On the day Icarus had been beaten in the pankration. Androgeos had thrown him, kicking him as he fell, a sharp foot under the ribs, and Icarus pinwheeled, spreadeagled, into the mud. The *skamma*, the pit where they wrestled, had been filled as usual with mud, and Icarus fell soft. *Keroma* we used to call the *skamma* mud, "beeswax." Icarus came up slathered with beeswax mud. It spattered about him, slippery as the wax in which I had tried to model his image for the god, yesterday or whenever it was. He came up and Androgeos took his right hand and somersaulted him—the throw called "the whip"—and Icarus went back into the mud and with two fingers broken. Androgeos hit him across the back of the neck and that ended the contest. There had been no defeating Androgeos. Icarus never got the chance to use his shoulders, which were his great strength. He never pinned Androgeos, never even caught him. Icarus hadn't the speed, nor the skill, for the matter of that. I set his fingers and splinted them, and he was covered with waxen mud except for those fingers which stuck out of the dirt like risers from a new mantled sculpture ready to go into the kiln. Somehow Icarus often comes back to me in some such context; some metallic metaphor seems joined to Icarus. Even a wrestling bout left him prepared to be cast in bronze; an ironic predestination.

Theseus lost the wrestling that day, too. No one could defeat Androgeos until the white bull killed him, whoever the white bull was. There has been much misrepresentation of that bull. Myself, I think he was simply a large wild, white bull, but the Athenians have since made out that it was Poseidon in the guise of Pasiphaë's lover, come from Crete, but as usual that theory is mixed up with hindsight and foolishness, for Pasiphaë at that time had never seen the father of the Minotaur.

The funeral games for Androgeos came later, but they seemed merged in my recollection with the day he died. Now that I think clearly of it, those funeral games took place on Crete and the fact that Athenians took part has served to give circumstantial support to the story that each year Minos exacted seven youths and seven maidens from Athens as blood sacrifice in revenge upon us for Androgeos' death. In truth, Minos demanded a heavy indemnity, fourteen times greater than the usual tally for the death of a man of the royal house, but then Androgeos was Minos' son. The payment was made annually in the usual form of tripods and cauldrons and other treasure and in the reshaping of facts, which time and wine and idle talk achieve, those tripods seem to have become youths and the cauldrons, maidens. Chatter transforms materials more finally than any craftsmanship.

The story goes that those seven youths and seven maidens, the most beautiful in Athens, were sent to be devoured each year by the Minotaur, deep hidden in his lair, the labyrinth. How a bull-headed man whose diet, like that of any other bull, was grass and herbs could have chewed up so much meat is not explained. What is true is that Theseus sailed with the tribute, as the son of Aegeus, King of Athens, in order to deliver it to

Minos. That is how he came to be present at Androgeos' funeral games.

At the funeral games, Icarus won the boxing and Theseus the wrestling, for he threw Tauros three times and covered his white skin with mud. That is as near as Theseus got to fighting the Minotaur. The confusion derives from "Minos" "Tauros" and "Minotauros" sounding alike and people's inability to keep their bulls in some sort of ordered sequence when they talk about them.

Theseus was a relative of mine. He has become very celebrated and is much admired for his treachery to Ariadne, which was true, for slaying the Minotaur, with her help, which is obviously untrue, since the Minotaur cannot be destroyed, at least until he evolves into the man he so much desires to be, and that is not yet. Theseus is also famous for his treatment of Phaedra, his accidental—if it was accidental—destruction of his own father by negligence in the matter of the color of the sail, and other heroic acts. Perhaps the most famous of all his exploits is the victory he achieved over a group of women, a large number of whom were killed in battle with him. Altogether, my kinsman Theseus was a notable hero, not of the foolish sort like Icarus, but of the better lasting and less simple type whose deeds are praised for qualities anyone would despise except in a hero or perhaps a god.

He has recently died by suicide and I believe has been much mourned and indeed worshipped.

At the funeral games of Androgeos, he triumphed in the wrestling. Icarus won the boxing, and they were paired for the pankration.

If you are not familiar with athletics, I must tell you that the pankration combines boxing and wrestling, and little is barred except eye-gouging, which is nevertheless common. No break takes place in the contest, and the loser's submission or total incapacity to continue is the only end of it. Dislocation of the joints is the most usual way it ends, but ribs broken by well placed kicks can achieve the same result. It is the pankration which has gained for athletes the nickname *myrmekes*, for it is in these fierce bouts that the ants use their stings.

Icarus and Theseus fought for three hours in the morning of the day of the funeral games of Androgeos and eventually Theseus won, although he was badly mauled and temporarily blinded in one eye by Icarus. The reason Theseus won was, I must admit, that he was the better wrestler. Since his father Aegeus had invented the science, this is not altogether surprising, but it is not generally known, because Theseus long maintained that his father was not Aegeus but Poseidon, a circumstantial boast which has further entangled the skein of his falsehoods. As I have said, I was related to Theseus. We were both Erechtheid, my father Metion being the uncle of Aegeus, and I am thankful to say that I am in no way more related to Poseidon than to any other god, although indirectly Poseidon has caused me as much trouble as if he had been a relative. If I had not made the cow for Pasiphaë to receive his mounting, I should not have had to fly from Crete.

Aegeus taught me something of wrestling when we were both young and such skill as I had, together with some contrivance and forethought, I used to kill Sciron, the Megarian, who liked to force travelers to wash his feet. On these occasions, he kicked them into the sea for their pains, from a high cliff southwest of Megara. The story of Sciron's death is well known, because Theseus claimed to have achieved it, and the great gift Theseus possessed, above all others, was the gift of being believed. In fact, I gained a certain knowledge of the winds by fighting Sciron, which proved valuable during my flight from Crete. A wind which blows strongly at certain times is named after Sciron, and this wind may have helped to carry me toward Cumae.

I do not like to think of having killed Sciron nor anyone else, but it has been unavoidable once or twice in my life to defend myself physically. Theseus, on the other hand, was a murderous hero, which is the common kind, and unlike Icarus, who killed no one but himself, Theseus killed many, including himself. This must be accepted, for killing, like so many destructive activities, is unavoidable to the uncreative. It is their principal demonstration of power.

Ariadne, Theseus did not kill; he simply abandoned her on the island of Dia, having married her out of a sense of obligation and simple lechery. I take this injury personally, for it was I who provided Ariadne with the method and the thread which I have been told guided Theseus out of the labyrinth at Knossos, from which, as yet, you could say, I have not escaped. I have not escaped from Ariadne either, for the thread I gave her binds me to her, and so, in recollection, does simple lechery. Perhaps I loved her. Certainly Theseus did not, although he pretended to have killed the Minotaur to please her.

My quarrel with him, in this matter, is not that he took her. I have nothing against that, for my needle threaded her and from it came the thread which ties us all together. I too abandoned her, in a sense, but I did not uproot her from her natural home or leave her alone on Dia making unconvincing attempts to worship Dionysus, out of good manners, in return for the hospitality granted to her and to her faithless husband.

Ariadne was not a girl you would expect to become a maenad. She was afraid of blood. She even feared to touch the thread because it was the color of blood. She sought to please and did so very capably, and because she was gentle she deserved to be treated with gentleness and generosity. Theseus, being a hero, had no notion of either quality and used not only her body but her life for quick convenience. As for the thread, it ran into Ariadne from me and metaphorically it was fastened behind my navel and is still attached. Therefore I shall say no more of Theseus.

When my hands were healed, the figure of the god was finished and instead of Icarus, I gave him an arrow to hold in his left hand. This the god permitted. Although this winged arrow was my symbol for the flight and

48

fall of my son, it was, I suppose, sufficiently impersonal an abstraction to be acceptable. In any case, the Far Darter could hardly reject the dart. Symbols are useful things, being sufficiently ambiguous to suggest all manner of alternative interpretations.

The doors I began as soon as the bronze Apollo had been assembled, and he stood smiling down on me from his plinth as I worked.

I took clay for this task and set it in shallow wooden frames, each the size of one panel of a door. On the first panel I modeled Androgeos dying, his body rising from the horn of the white bull, who, with its great head upthrust, tossed him from the point. Bull and victim stood out an inch in relief and the spectators were cut shallow from the moist clay. Icarus I did not show for fear of reprisal. The god continued to smile.

The second panel showed Athenians sailing to Crete with tribute, the third, the funeral games of Androgeos, the fourth, Pasiphaë coupled in her cow's guise to the other bull, Poseidon rampant. On the fifth panel I showed Pasiphaë as queen, with her moon symbols, and the sun-bull mask of Minos worn by the king, and here again the image was ambiguous. Ariadne was with them, the royal daughter of the house, with the thread in her hands. The sixth panel would fit high on the right of the door, beneath the lintel. It showed the palace seen from above, the cliffs and sea below, and on this I showed myself winged in flight from Crete. Icarus I did not show, but an arrow incised in the sky above me honored the god.

All the second door I made in sections to form one panel. To read it, the eye was brought to travel from my flight across the apex of the left-hand door and there upon the summit of the right lay Cumae, acropolis and isthmus, sea and pallid lake with Gaia's many entrances shown in the rock and the place of my landing. Here, too, I showed Apollo's temple as it would stand and below it, leading downward, the whole labyrinth which was that of Knossos, doubled and woven with the earth body of the Mother where for so long I had lived.

245

All this door portrayed the labyrinth, stone, gut and brain my prison, and at its center, in the womb, the Minotaur evolving, with the bull loins of the horned god, the horned loins of man; and Dionysus, vine wreathed, seated upon the omphos, identified with bull and man together and Minos masked and horned. This triple image at the center I modeled in high relief, outstanding six inches from the door, so that those who entered the temple to lay their offerings before the god would grasp it to bring the door to open. This image I modeled separately to cast it almost in the round.

Of these clay panels, fired to terracotta, I then took piece molds of clay, and these too I baked. Into these shallow molds, flat bedded, I pressed wax, joined the parts of each mold, mantled them and then burned out the wax. Thus, I cast panels as thin as wafers, each showing an aspect of the story. The great panel of the right-hand door, which showed the labyrinth, I cast in sections, then soldered together, and these casts were a little thicker than those of the left-hand door so that this door would swing open first when the votary touched the triple figure. This I did to make men open the door to the god by first touching the parts of man above and below humanity. Finally, I cast Asterion identified with Minos and Dionysus and welded the figure to the center of the maze.

The carpenters made the doors themselves of cypress-wood planks, each two inches thick, and to these wooden doors we riveted the bronze panels, like the great *xoana* made in Crete. We forged bronze hinges and framed each door with strips of solid bronze, and they were finished. We raised them to see them upright for the first time and they were well made. How long it all took I cannot tell, but during that time the great noise of other doors opening and closing was heard three times as Deiphobe mated and spoke with the god's voice. I heard the rush of wind and felt the heat rise in the rock, but what was spoken was not addressed to me.

Deiphobe spoke to me once more, and speaking showed herself to me, but I did not see her in the flesh. In my mind

246

she came to me resembling Pasiphaë, blurred and became Ariadne, her features altered subtly and she was Naucrate, then Cameira, then Perdix my partridge sister, and in some way in her single image she carried all the women I already carried in my past. She showed herself to me while I lay in my workshop with the bronze Apollo smiling down upon me, armed as the Far Darter, and Myrmex skittered behind my eyes like a twitching nerve. All the threads that are plaited into the blood-colored thread slid through the fingers of my vision and at long last I wept for Icarus. I wept, and Icarus, my flying center, wrenched from my earthbound body, lay in my mind at once high and soaring and deep swimming, drowned below the sea surge. In Cumae he was never near me until that moment when Deiphobe in apparition showed herself, but when she came she carried him in her left hand, and her hand was unburned, for who could burn her?

Scale is a delusion. Deiphobe was a woman and no giantess. She was even a small woman and plump when at rest, like a partridge, yet it was not an image who stood winged on the palm of her left hand, but Icarus as a boy, a *kouros* in the morning light, smiling in his self-sufficiency. Even as I stared at him I saw the little image I had intended for Apollo's hand made flesh in him and yet he was the size of a man, the size he had been in his life. On her hand he remained and yet he was at once below me, drifting above the ocean bed, and above me in the eye of the sun. And then he was no longer in either place and vanished too from Deiphobe's hand. Perhaps he went into the Far Darter's arrow to fly as weapon into your time. I do not know. He was no longer in my workshop under the rock. Deiphobe too was gone, but in her absence, caught in the rush of wind which circled around my cave, she spoke through an invisible maze of twisting air. This hurricane, her transparent thread, unwound the labyrinth and I knew that I was at last released for all time from Gaia's grasp.

Deiphobe, sybil, oracle, god's hearth, woman, once called Calypso and worshipped on the shores of Avernus, now incorporeal, existed solely as a voice, but such a voice that men will hold it sacred for two thousand years, record its utterances in books and rule by them. Even when those books are burned they will remember her and dimly they will perceive that when she spoke her cryptic truths they held some truth for men which each who heard already knew, but wished confirmed. Men will deny her mysteries but will not escape them. She began as a stone and returned to the stones, and that this would be was the burden of the last words she spoke to me:

> "Gold god, the circling sun, now gives me death
> And I am cooled to ash and ashen earth
> My ash chill rest enters the gentle stone
> And this my mantic voice, my circling breath,
> Remains to answer that which gave me birth.
> My task is only gone when yours is done."

Her voice, and it was her voice and not Apollo's, passed back into the wind and for the last time I heard the frantic crash of the doors. One after another they rang out their mounting and definitive preludes to silence. Clangor in sequence multiplied to become a metallic cataract of sound so charged with bronze-tongued thunder, so instinct with brazen power, that when the last door had closed, the echo of the first still hung in air to join with it, and all that sound, dammed up in its ending, opened a silence as dense as the rock itself.

The ant did not move and Cephalon, even Cephalon, had nothing to say. Then gently, like the casual clink of small tools in a pouch or the remote and dusty metal sound of an army marching in the distance, I heard the work begin again in the foundry and I went out to play my part in it.

How entangled the memories of memories can become! I write them down, in an effort to es- **49** tablish some sort of sequence of events and my recollections proliferate and intertwine so that they bind me like a net.

Deiphobe, with her mysterious ability to counterfeit the images of other women in her single person, showed me such an amalgam of memories that in floundering among them for her true appearance she eludes me. I have not forgotten her, yet I cannot remember her; I remember how I came to her, but I have forgotten the path.

When I write of practical matters, I trust I describe them clearly and when I treat of actions, of what they were and how they were taken, I hope I remember them properly, yet it seems that I am so skilled in making mazes that I block the true paths through my own past and wander down false trails. They are trails I planned myself but I lose my way in them. The walls of every path I traverse toward my beginning seem to me covered with carvings in low relief. Some of these are so sharp and vivid that they light the passages of time, but they do not do so over the full distance. Some are rubbed away and are shadows of what occurred. Some are obliterated and some are doubtfully re-carved with an inexpert hand which remains my own. I have forgotten the topography of my own labyrinth and remember only the decoration on its walls. Therefore you must bear with me and excuse my blundering in the fitful light and dense shadows of my reminiscence.

I can remember much that took place when it concerned the technicalities of my self-set task. The termination of it is carved haphazardly and, I suspect, misleadingly upon my memory. I can remember the assembly of all the parts of the temple, the numbered blocks of limestone and tufa, the terracotta tiles made from a yellow clay which shines golden in the sun, the acroteria and antefixes, the timber for the construction of the roof, the cypress columns and even the lengths of drainpipe I had foreseen would be needed. I cannot remember, in the time that followed, how all these things were taken to the surface or how the Myrmidons, working with the inhuman diligence of the ants from which they derived, assembled and raised the parts into the whole. I see them now, in my mind, gathering and dispersing with an insect intensity of purpose to overcome problems which they did not accept existed. There were accidents and these return to me sharply enough as isolated crises jutting up from a sea of activity. Two men were crushed beneath the trimmed trunk of a cypress when it slipped from its rollers in the narrow turn below an entrance to the earth. The great column caught and pinned these men and they died, as silently impersonal as the ants from which Zeus made them, jerking quickly and briefly. I remember that an antefix fell from its cradle, as it was being raised to the pediment, and splintered murderously on the stylobate and the ants re-formed upon the ropes, bleeding from slivers of terracotta, and raised a spare antefix to replace the broken one without pausing in the work. I remember these mishaps, but I do not remember the raising of the walls themselves.

In contrast to the silent Myrmidons, the Greek Speaker's people sweated below ground, making ample noise. What they said I do not exactly know, for I never learned their language, but they were used to working in the clangor of foundry sounds and by habit they shouted, grunted and cursed more stridently than most men, to make themselves heard above a familiar noise, even when quiet momentarily prevailed. To them only the cataclysmic crashing of the Sybil's doors, the rushing wind and her dreadful, mantic cries were sounds not to be ignored or bawled over. It was a time of effort, of heaving and thrusting, and it was conducted by two groups of men, one of which was the most clamorous and one the most silent I had ever encountered. It was like being stone deaf in one ear and deafened in the other.

Myrmex sat motionless in his fat, upon his rock in the sun, and since he had no need of speech he directed his people silently, giving his orders to them as voicelessly as he conversed with me. At least the Greek Speaker spoke Greek and at least he spoke. When he did so, Myrmex, whose access to him was also inaudible, courteously withdrew from my brain. Bland and familiar though he was, Myrmex could be courteous. The enterprise went as smoothly as Myrmex's smooth silence. Even the noise of building seemed muted. In the final hour, when my task was completed, I went back into my workshop to collect the bale of my wings and the pack of tools I should need on my journey. There the Greek Speaker spoke to me for the last time. "The Mother accepts your departure from her," he said, "and she awaits your return."

My thoughts elsewhere, I made my usual formal and flattering reply.

"You will return," he added.

"I shall remember and I shall speak of you with honor wherever I go. You and all your race are mighty craftsmen in metal and in all the materials of building. Your skills are deep and noble."

"You will return."

The tiresome repetition of this phrase partially penetrated the empty pomposity of my speech but I was filled with the joy of freedom regained. These were my last moments in the bleak subterranean workshop where I had spent so long and to me the foundry caves and corridors had changed, becoming impersonal, almost unfamiliar, as places do at the moment one leaves them.

I looked around at the benches and braziers, at the wax-working tools, the knives and spatulae, the little kiln where I had prepared the golden honeycomb and the golden bees, the fragments of molds and all the detritus of my trade, and I thought of the sight of the sea and of the landscape of the upper world which was my natural home.

"You will return."

I wrenched my mind back to him and focused upon the pale, wrinkled little figure who stared fixedly at me.

"Return?"

"You will return," said the Greek Speaker firmly, "yes, you will return."

"To be sure," I said, "certainly."

In Egypt, I thought, there is a labyrinth more complex,

more tortuous and more profound than any I shall ever make and that maze was made to guard the tomb of Asklepios, who was the son of Apollo. In Egypt, where they called him Imhotep, they sacrifice the sacred ibis to him and they have left embalmed thousand upon thousand of these long-billed birds to sleep in his shrine. There, in the entrance to his sacred place, a myriad white wings, each pair wrapped in twisted shrouds, in its linen labyrinth, lie flightless forever and I, though I leave my wings at Cumae and the rest of me wherever it comes to rest, will presently come to lie like an ibis entombed. Of course the Greek Speaker was right, I should return, Icarus too, a cindered ibis, would in time return. That much was obvious.

"You will return," said the Greek Speaker, whose urge toward the repetition of simple statements was limitless. "You will return from there," he said and he pointed westward.

It is curious that while I remember this, my last conversation with him, so clearly, I cannot remember parting from the man himself. I suppose he moved back into the shadow as usual, with his right fist pressed to his forehead.

I remember that I picked up the bale of my wrapped wings from the floor of my little workshop, where they had lain since first I dropped them there before I began the work. I picked them up, remembering the Greek Speaker saying, "How does a man fly?" all that time ago and adding, "A man cannot fly in the air by clutching a corded bale to his belly." Then I went up through the earth and out into the sunlight and laid the corded bale before the bronze statue of Apollo in his temple. The god smiled as usual. How should he not, since I myself had set that smile upon his lips with considerable skill?

"An ibis to the father of Asklepios," I said, as I placed my wings at his feet, and I went out, closing the bronze doors behind me. For a moment I remembered the delicate process of raising them and how they hung in the ropes as they were lowered by the ants onto their bronze hinges. I touched the triple bull at the center of the right-hand door and looked up at my pictured flight and the arrow of Icarus and turned away.

Before the temple, the banked altar still smoked. There had been processions and garland-swinging and much meat-eating, but I do not remember it clearly nor how the sacrifices were made, nor the number of animals killed. No one was there on the platform top of the rock. All was swept clean and the restless ants had tracked away to their secret nest. No priest was there, but I did not concern myself with that. Priests and their rituals are not my business. The god had his house. Doubtless he would engage domestics.

It was midday. Below me in the rock were those who worked there, knowing neither day **50** nor night, and below them the smooth-walled cell of Deiphobe with its eternal tripod and its omphalos. That cell was empty now of all but her voice. The god must rut elsewhere and speak through the hundred mouths of Cumae, without orgasm, or else take a new bride and recreate the Sybil. Gods can easily do that sort of thing. The Minotaur would be moving uneasily in his rock-hewn byre and Dionysus, his divine and bestial mocker, would dance and smile before him and stink to make him wrinkle up his blunt and damp bull's muzzle. Down there, the wine god would squat drunken in his horns upon another omphalos, for Gaia has many navel stones. All these were there beneath me and all elsewhere. Although I should return to them, it would not be here at Cumae. I should not return to Cumae.

I looked back at the temple, as I went down the path and saw that it was well done. Where I had first seen Myrmex-Cephalon, the chestnut fat ant-king, I saw him now, a great pile of immobile flesh, but when I looked more closely I saw only a cairn of stones, like a heap of giant peeled chestnuts, at the place where the path turned. Ants ran in and out among the stones and one flicked behind my eyes.

I walked on down the path towards the beach, with nothing but my pack and the sun on my shoulders but both resting light and warm. Walking, I wondered how I should find a way to Sicily, now that I had no wings.

PART THREE

I had forgotten the changing nature of weather. **51**
Under Cumae there had been none and above,
while we raised the temple, Apollo had looked blandly down
on us so that the days had been of even warmth. I had forgotten
what it was like to walk under rain and how the land looks
and smells when rain has fallen.

I walked south toward Sicily because in the south there were
Greeks and I felt drawn to my fellow countrymen and to hearing my language spoken by men to whom it was native. Cretans
would do as well. They too spoke Greek and they ruled in parts
of Sicily.

It was hot summer moving toward autumn and the land
was baked, not to the hard bread of Attica nor the corn gold of
central Crete but dry and dusty, between the forest and the
sea. The sun shone hard but fitfully and the sky seemed uneasy
and disturbed so that cloud built and dispersed raggedly and
winds rose suddenly, whipping quick rainstorms to brief fury
even while the sun remained uncovered.

In the first days of my journey I watched the sun for menacing signs and felt his gaze uneasy and his eye withdrawn from
me, yet I was often conscious of his sidelong glance. A shower
of rain was joyous in those first days, but the sun's halting of
the rain made me afraid. The wind, making the grass mutter,
chilled me and yet the light catching the foliage of wind-tossed
trees, so that their leaves flashed, gave me such pleasure that I
looked at the landscape guiltily as though I had not deserved it
and the landscape danced and mocked me. Small birds and

lizards flashed among the thickets, like players making brisk entrances and exits. As I walked, the world performed for me; the rocks glittered at the glittering sea, the spangled hills twitched their dark green skins and every pebble, plant and tufted shrub beside my path was new. I was uneasy, but the sun rose and set so regularly that I was almost persuaded it was uninhabited and there were times when I believed my service to the god had proved adequate.

I should have known better, but there is no peace to compare with those times when, after long service to a god, one believes one has escaped his attention. It is a delusion but a blessed one.

Within a week of setting out from Cumae I was so far gone in this delusion that I came to look up at the sky each morning as if it were no more than the world's blue roof. My slight lameness did not trouble me. Oh, I was gay and feckless as a boy, going south along the shore of the great bay under the mountain which guards it.

South of the bay I worked inland to avoid the long promontory which runs into the sea and sought a pass through the mountains. I climbed through chestnut and ilex forest to the high rocks and so went down again to join the coast. I saw no one, although there were traces of men where fires had been lit, and on the fifth day I found an arrow buried in the carcass of a goat. How long it had taken the goat to die of its wound I could not tell, but the carcass had been rotting for some time when I came upon it. I made a light bow and used my arrow to bring down small game, until I lost it. I did not trouble to make another, but lived on fruits and berries until I reached the sea again and could take limpets among the rocks. There I made fishhooks, botched up from a length of bronze wire I had with me, and I remember thinking at the time that the wire had been drawn to make the bow-string for Apollo's bronze bow, for the bow his image now held in its right hand in the temple on the Cumaean rock. I remember this made me nervous for a moment, but the day was cloudy. The sun could not be seen.

South of the mountains and a day's march on, the sky cleared. In the long plain it grew hot, as if the summer clamored to remain when it well knew its time was past. Here the plain was marshy, but beyond, a long sandstone shelf stretched south as if a great dish were laid to the lips of the sea. It was not hard walking although there was no shade and I was too impatient to go inland again to find some. The uneasy wonder of the first days was passing and I had begun to think of my destination.

The sun beat fiercely down, more fiercely than I had known it since the day the god burned his temple. I squinted up at him as I rested in a dry stream bed, sweating and beating off the flies. I was sticky, covered with dust, thirsty and no longer much enchanted with the landscape. I itched and my skin, still sensitive from my long sojourn underground, was red and sore from sunburn. Cephalon, I thought to myself, I envy your peeled chestnut skin. In your company I exchanged the mottled pallor of a dead frog for the angry red of raw meat and still I am uncomfortably half-cooked. I seem to exchange one unsightly color for another.

Tossing pebbles down into the dried-up stream, I began irritably to consider making new wings to fly to Sicily. I began as usual to speculate on materials and how they could be obtained. I should have known the danger. At least I should have had the sense to plait myself a hat from the reeds which I could see growing in plenty between the stream bed and the sea.

The sun crossed the bed and struck at me. My head began to ache and I did not think to cover it. I got up and walked on, my mind half taken up with my discomfort, half concentrated on my plan to make new wings. I felt sick and the landscape not only danced and mocked me, it rocked and lurched so that I stumbled.

A metal thunder rolled in my head, gathering and dispersing disjointedly. I became angry. The sun, ringed with circles of white fire, advanced and retreated and the light bounced against the ground. I could not see properly and rubbed my painful eyes so that a crucible burst in my head and showered molten drops into the momentary darkness.

I tried to focus between slitted lids and still I could not see properly. The ground swam and the air was thick with stinging flies. I ceased to think of wings.

Then there was a river, a thin drool of water between plates of cracked mud. I fell down and drank and threw up what I drank. I put my head into the water and my face sank in mud. When I got up I could not see. Frantically wiping the mud from my eyes, I still could not see. Terror took me. I could feel my hands wiping and slathering at my face but I could not see them and my head was swelling, forcing my eyes out of the sockets. I crawled a little and met a wall head on. I scrabbled at it and the ant in my mind grew huge and bulging and began to kick. It pushed the sides of my skull apart slowly and full darkness came in. The ant kicked frantically, sank into the dark and drowned.

When I became conscious, I was cold enough to be dead, except that the backs of my calves were on fire. I still could see nothing and groped in agony at my eyes. Then I could see a little and gradually, my sight unfolding slowly from the heap of pain I lay in, I realized that I could not see because it was night. The relief was so intense that it could have been comic, but the pain in my head was so harsh that nausea overcame relief. I lay back and went down into blackness deeper than night and dreamed I walked in half-cooled bronze which clogged and burned my legs and yet I was at Delphi in the snow, where a woman thrust my face into the cold bowels of a dead child, slimy with ice, and the stumps of the child's arms were feathered. Where his head should have been there was the butchered head of a calf.

That dream was vivid. I remember little else or for how long I lay there under the bank of the little river. At times I was aware of my plight and at others not. In time I knew where I

was. I lay under a tree which slanted over the river and I must
have found its shade just as the sunstroke took me. Only the
backs of my legs had endured the full force of the sun and they
were swollen and blistered to the knees. For two days I could
not move, but on the third thirst drove me to drag myself across
the cracked mud to the rivulet. Worming my way across the
river bed, I thought I had become a crippled snake twisting on
the back of a greater one. The mud, contracting as it dried,
had broken into scales of armored clay. Confused by a hissing
which must have been my own breath, I was a snake, an
Erechtheid worm coiling among snakes. Each crawling day
from shade to water and back into the shade was longer than
any day had ever been. I thought of food and retched to think
of it. At night I shook with cold. I swore over and over again
to make no more wings and to obey Apollo in all things. I
cried a great deal, far more than I had when my father beat me
with the flat of his sword. Much of the water I drank I threw
up again.

On the fifth day the weather turned fully into autumn; there
was cold wind and the sky was overcast. I no longer needed
shade and lay by the water until at last I could stand up. When
I could walk ten paces I walked them and my lameness added
to my misery. Gradually I could walk further, lame or not, until, on the ninth day, I reached the sea.

Beached on the shore was a fishing boat with great eyes
painted on her prow. She stared at me as hard as I stared at her
and then there were three men staring at me and with all this
staring I became dizzy and fell down in the sand. They fed me
raw fish and bread and gave me wine and if they had not been
there I should have starved to death on the beach.

The three men cared for me. They fed me and **52**
covered me with nets and goatskins and when I
could speak, the four of us carried on a conversation of some
length. I thanked them and they questioned me. I could not

understand one word they said, nor they one word of mine, and such was their simplicity and my condition that we could not understand why we could not make ourselves understood. There was no help forthcoming from Cephalon, no silent interpretation. Finally, we all grinned at one another and made signs. They were not stupid men and presently I managed to convince them that if one of them would fetch my pack from where I had left it by the river, I could reward them and also show them what I was. The youngest of them, a boy of about sixteen, set out to find it and presently returned. He was not gone long and covered the distance I had taken three days to cross in a few hours.

When he returned with my pack, the three of them opened it and picked among my tools. I could see from their expressions that they were delighted and the oldest of them kept popping bits of bread into my mouth to show it. I gave him the bronze wire, Apollo's bowstring, and two chisels. To the younger man I gave two ingots of copper and to the boy I gave my small knife. They refused to take them with such fervor that I knew I had fallen among honest men and for several minutes we pushed the objects backward and forward between us until honor was satisfied and they accepted. Then we drank more wine and they carried me to the boat and laid me in the thwarts, scooping a bed for me among the reeds and osiers they had gathered at the mouth of the river.

I do not know to this day the name of their race or of the language they spoke. They were compactly built, dark men of moderate size who wore their trade as if they did not believe there were other professions, except, of course, the crafts of boat building and metal work. It is because most simple men recognize a bronzesmith when they see one that I have escaped slavery. We are useful and inspire awe. On the whole, I have been better treated by men than by gods, but then gods are not to be awed.

The fishermen launched the boat and sailed south with a cargo of materials for mat and basket making and one sick maze maker, whose clearest recollection of the voyage remains the smell of dead fish. When I was well enough to lend a hand I feebly did so and the little I had learned of ships, all those years ago when we sailed from Attica to Crete, was enough to make me valuable to my hosts despite my weakness.

In the evening we beached and next morning the long beaches of the shore gave place to cliffs. We steered under their lee and took crayfish among the rocks which, considering the broken water, seemed to me foolhardy, but the old man handled the boat with such sureness and elegance that I tried to mime my admiration for him. He grinned and nodded and was so clearly flattered that he gave me back the little Cumaean bronze of the Mother and my Cretan crystal which he had at some point removed from about my neck. The second afternoon we beached again in a little cove under a towering face of sheer rock. Here I gathered driftwood and dry stalks of sea holly and here, to cook the crayfish, I risked Apollo's spite by taking his heat through my crystal to make a fire. He permitted it and it cemented my friendship with my rescuers so powerfully that when the first flame licked from the dry straws, they hid under the boat and covered their eyes. Miracles are an invaluable aid to traveling and after this one I was more than a crew member, I was a cherished magician, so that when we put in at their village the following day, the boy leaped into the water and swam ashore to tell the elders they were required to welcome some sort of demigod.

The beach below the village was heaped with empty shells. They stank. The foreshore was a midden of fish-heads and offal. It stank. The village was a dunghill of mud huts and in front of it the entire population was ranged by the time we had beached the boat. The elders stood before the crowd and beside them two large men with sticks beat off the dogs and pigs who snapped and rooted underfoot. Had I been able to understand the speech of welcome, I should not have heard much of it for the yelping and squealing of protesting animals.

The formalities concluded, I was taken to the largest hut

and installed in it. I was still weak and liable to nausea and I had cause to be. In my childhood and later, during the lean years in Attica, I had been used to squalor, at least to seeing it daily if I did not always live in it. Here dirt was founded on fish and that is a special dirt. Nevertheless, I lived in that hut long enough to get used to it.

The first days were difficult. I was given two women, both of them personable but filthy. Luckily, their ministrations were so generously straightforward that I was able at least to prove myself more or less adequate to one and had they not been so diligent with me I should not have managed even that. I held my breath so hard that word must have gone around about it. When, later on, I had gained the rudiments of their language, I discovered I had been named "purple face."

What there is to tell of these people is limited. They were strong and generous, kind and murderous, intelligent and ignorant. They were also invaluably superstitious, which gave me a high standing among them when I taught them metal founding. The drama and mystery of that demonstration caused them to treat me with as much reverence as they showed their elders.

I discovered quickly that although they had among them four bronze knives, some copper beads and fragments of copper foil, which the elders used to shave their heads but not their beards, they had no knowledge of working metals. The trinkets and tools I had given my rescuers made them rich beyond the dreams of their neighbors and the ingots of copper I had given to the younger man were all we had to cast knives and axeheads, apart from a little tin from my pack, which I alloyed with the copper to make bronze. Since the younger man owned these ingots and unwillingly let me cast them into weapons and tools, he thereafter owned the bulk of the wealth of the whole village and gave up fishing altogether. His father traded in fragments of Apollo's bowstring, which I taught him to hammer into fishhooks, and these he loaned to the villagers on such terms that soon he too gave up fishing and progressed,

264

first to hunting and then to idleness. The boy slid his bronze knife into a rival and subsequently had his throat cut with a sliver of obsidian by the rival's father. It seems this was just. No one complained, but the bronze knife was paid in tally to the oldest of the elders who had no use for it, except as an ornament.

As I moved about, in the odor of urine and rotting fish, I discovered that in some ways these people were more sophisticated than I had expected. They tended goats and sheep, grew patches of grain and vines and they had pottery. The pottery they made was painted in opaque black on a red ground, but they had amphorae and large basins made from a yellow clay and painted with red lines. This clay was not local to them and these pots had come from islands in the west, together with the obsidian slivers, of which they had quite a hoard. In addition, they had three drinking cups of blue faïence which looked Rhodian.

They were skilled in flaking stone and one man was a master of carving bone. He, like myself, was a man whose life was safe. No one could afford to kill him. He owned one of the Rhodian cups, which further raised his status.

A few men hunted in the hills and from some source they had learned that this was socially superior to fishing so that my rescuers turned to hunting, when they became rich and although they were not very proficient they occasionally brought in hares, deer, wild boar and even wild horses. Once they killed a large bear, which was a memorable event. They used its fat in various ways for months, adding a new savor to the air, and the bones produced all manner of implements.

I lived in the village through the winter and I was lucky. It was a hard and stormy season. For weeks the boats could not put out and when suddenly, in the coldest month, I was given fresh meat, I did not like to question what it was, even if I could have done so without discourtesy. I never got so far with their language as to be subtle in it. Mostly at that time we lived on limpets and other shellfish gathered by the women. Also, the number of dead dogs one stumbled on between the huts grew conspicuously less.

However exalted one's station becomes, there is no more difficult and restrictive a situation to find oneself in than that of resident technician in a community which otherwise lacks one. The bone carver, too, may have felt this, but then he was native to the place.

I was grateful to those who had saved my life and glad to have had shelter from the winter, but I did not wish to spend my life stinking and making axes; besides, there was no metal left. On the other hand, I was clearly a prisoner, however highly honored. I did not dare to try and leave and I was watched at all times, benevolently but scrupulously. I began to make it known that my mastery of fire was immeasurable and that I could, if thwarted, release fire enough to consume the village.

The elders conferred and despite the testimony of my rescuers who said that I had kindled a fire on the beach with my third eye, which I wore suspended from my neck, I was not believed.

The village fire was tended by an elder and two virgin girls whose sole task it was to keep the blaze alive. From it the villagers took embers to their cooking fires and kilns, as I had done to my little outdoor foundry. The fire tender said that fire came only from a god and must be found in a dry storm. Apparently the last burning tree had been discovered a dozen years before and once, before that, there had been a time when there was no fire and many had died. The elders called upon me to prove my claim and at that moment Apollo withdrew into cloud and it began to rain. I talked for all that day and half the next. I have never talked so much, especially to people

266

who, however courteously they listened, could not understand what I said.

I am not unskilled in performing and even inventing rituals, it is part of my trade, but I had used up every device I could think of before the sun came out. I had chanted, danced, gestured, prayed and gone into trances and I was desperate. Even the reappearance of the sun did not solve my problem, for I had planned to ignite the thatch of a hut and everything in the open air was drenched with rain. My solution was a cruel one and I regret it, but it was effective beyond my wildest hopes. I took out my crystal and holding it above my head in as godlike a gesture as I could manage, I focused the sun's rays through the lens and concentrated it upon the spindle of a woman who was carding wool in the entrance to her hut. The village watched. A trickle of smoke rose from the tuft of wool and suddenly it flamed. The flame caught the woman's long hair and, even as she screamed and dropped her spindle, the fish oil with which her hair was dressed caught fire and flared about her head. She beat at her head with flapping hands and threw herself into the mud at the threshold, screaming. No one else moved but a sighing groan rose from those who watched.

I cried out: "See, I have done it," and flung myself upon her, still clutching my murderous lens, and I was so wet with rain that the goatskin cloak I wore and the mud in which she lay combined to quench the fire. The woman twitched and moaned. No one would go near her. I carried her into the hut and tried to dress her head but she was horribly burned and that night she died. I hung my crystal around my neck and left her. Crossing the village, I could see no one and when I had gathered my tools and taken a bow and a quiver of arrows, I walked away from the place. No one tried to stop me. In his dark bed below the sea rim, I suppose Apollo laughed.

It took me four days to fly from Crete to Cumae **54** and fourteen months to reach Sicily. Most of the distance I walked, but in the late spring I found another boat beached. She was a trading vessel from the island of Aeolus and since she was undermanned, I joined her crew as a rower.

I have been told that there are more perils to be met with between the toe of Italy and Sicily than any sensible man would wish to encounter. In the narrow straits lives Scylla, the daughter of Phorcys, who is possessed of twelve legs and six long necks each bearing a head armed with three sets of teeth. She inhabits a rock which is said to touch the sky and she is unassuageably carnivorous. Near her in the water lies Charybdis whose name means "The Sucker Down." Three times a day she sucks ships into her whirling vortex and spews them forth as wreckage. I have not myself seen either of these monsters and do not wish to do so. Nor are these all the risks one may run in those parts. Somewhere nearby, but never twice in the same place, are the Planctae, tall islands which are forever shrouded in mist and float aimlessly about, to the great danger of ships. I am not convinced about these, for, as you will have heard, Aeolia, the island of Aeolus, is reputed to float and to be encompassed by a great bronze wall. I can assure you it does not and it is not. The island is solidly anchored and a bronze wall of such dimensions would be impossibly expensive and impractical even for a king as rich and powerful as Aeolus, who rules the winds.

Tales of this kind are widely circulated and it is not advisable to accept them as valid. I do not think I am presumptuous when I suggest that the accuracy of my own reporting, as compared to the stories told by many travelers and further distorted by repetition, is the product of technical knowledge and a respect for facts.

I am not convinced by the stories of such malignancies as Scylla and Charybdis, but being by nature cautious I took ship for Aeolia far to the north of them, as I wished also to avoid various smoking and flaming mountains which I believe jut out of the sea thereabouts and in particular I had reason to steer clear of the great mountain of fire in north-eastern Sicily, where some say Hephaistos has his workshop and, if Apollo has not killed them all, the Cyclopes work for him. Places where Apollo is more than usually active are not for me and he hates the Cyclopes. In any case, I always think it wise to give thanks to gods and indeed to anyone else for favors received, and although it was not directly on my route I thought a visit to Aeolus would be courteous. He had made my flight possible, after all, and saved my life by setting me down at Cumae, when he might easily have dropped me into the sea. Besides, to judge from the ship and her master, Aeolia was comparatively civilized. The captain was personable and dressed with an ostentatious elegance. He wore a great gold necklace which he assured me had been made in Crete by no less a goldsmith than Daedalus the Athenian. I looked closely at it and found that he was mistaken, but I did not say so.

Compared to the villagers, compared to any human beings I had seen since I left Crete, the ship master and even some of his crew were marvelously dressed and scented. I found it difficult to think of them rowing an eight-hour stretch and I never saw them do so, but then the vessel was Aeolian and that made a vast difference.

The Aeolians have remarkable gifts. Their aristocracy converses in Greek and while it seems likely that their island was first colonized from the mainland by a people much like my villagers, their ruling class assumes itself to be Cretan and they behave as if they were relatives of Zeus himself. They are superb sailors, counting themselves highly cosmopolitan and in this they are far more Cretan than any Cretan. One cannot blame them for trying but they try so hard they make themselves absurd.

The captain's name was Ausonias and due to his nativity he could summon any wind he chose by whistling for it. Thus, when we sailed, he whistled low and quavering; the sail filled and within half a mile of the shore we shipped our oars and never dipped them again until we negotiated the harbor of Aeolia. It was no wonder the crew were so well dressed. No bead of sweat ever dampened any curl of any sailor's carefully wind-tossed hair. I wonder Ausonias bothered to hire a crew, let alone oarsmen. The *keleustes*, a plump and placid man, played knucklebones on his drum with a gaunt Samian all the way over and lost everything he possessed. It did not seem to disturb him.

"Keleustes," said the captain, "you are an ass. I should give you more work to do."

"That would be a pity," said the gaunt man, taking a gold band from the keleustes' wrist.

"Oh well . . ." said the keleustes and wagered his dagger, a gold-mounted weapon of excellent workmanship. "So you are a Greek," said the captain, waving a languid hand at me. "You might well be. You speak the language beautifully."

"It comes naturally to me to do so," I replied.

"Of course," he said, "and you are well born. I can confidently assert it. Your diction is most precise . . ."

"Thank you," I said.

". . . but you do not dress at the level of your class, in fact I must assume you have suffered some misfortune."

"Several."

"I shall not inquire of them. I cannot. Manners forbid it and besides it would distress me. How, may I ask, are you called?"

"I am called Dipoinos," I replied with the first name that came into my head.

"Surely not the sculptor in marble?"

"Yes."

"The pupil of Daedalus?"

"Yes."

"I find it difficult to believe. You look too old. Dipoinos is surely a young man."

"I have a son," I said and suddenly remembered that I had

one no longer. I must have shown it by my look because in an instant the foppish insolence dropped from the captain and he looked at me with concern and an unexpected kindness.

"Of course," he said, "of course."

The keleustes lost his knife. "Oh well . . ." he said.

"I remember a lad called Endoios I met in Ephesus," said the keleustes, picking up the knucklebones. "He was a sculptor. He always beat me too."

"You should stick to drumming," said the captain, "you haven't the speed for bones," and he picked up the knucklebones and won the keleustes' knife back from the gaunt man with a five-bone catch as deft as a conjuror.

"Here," he said to the keleustes and handed him the knife.

"Oh well . . ." said the keleustes.

"It's nothing," said the captain, and for the rest of the voyage he won from the gaunt man everything the gaunt man won from the keleustes. Whatever he won he gave back to the keleustes.

"It passes the time," said the captain, gazing at the sky.

"It's circular," said the gaunt man. "I'll play against your necklace."

The captain laughed.

"What will you take for wager?" said the gaunt man.

"What have you?"

"Not much," said the gaunt man.

"I'll take you," said the captain, and won him.

"Oh well . . ." said the gaunt man.

The wind dropped. The captain whistled. The wind rose.

"Not a bad owner," said the gaunt man to the keleustes.

"I know," said the keleustes.

"You are from Athens?" asked the captain, looking at me.

"Long ago," I replied.

"But you have been in Crete?"

"For many years."

"I shall not ask how you came to be here."

"Misfortune."

"Of course," said the captain, "of course. And did you know Daedalus the Athenian in Crete?"

"Yes, I knew him."

"Of course," said the captain, "of course. He made my necklace, you know."

I did not reply.

"Or didn't you?" said the captain and smiled with great charm and sweetness. He flexed his long, quick fingers.

"News travels," he said, "and how else than by ship?"

"I made the necklace," I said, thinking to please him; "You are courteous."

"I have hoped to meet you. I have tried to meet you for many years," said Ausonias, discarding his dignity as captain. "I know a great deal about you and have seen the shrine you built on the rock at Cumae. We sailed past it two months ago."

"You have seen the house I built for Apollo?"

"Only from the sea. To be honest, no one aboard could understand what it was."

"You did not land? You have not seen the building, the bronze doors, the image of the god."

"The crew were frightened and, to tell the truth, so was I. You never know what may spring up upon the shores of these waters."

"I see."

"Your building is very strange and no one makes landfall under Cumae from simple curiosity."

"From deep curiosity, perhaps?"

"For that, yes, and solemnly and with sacrifices, each man to ask a single question."

"Had you no single question?"

"Not on that day. On that day no man in his senses would have gone ashore."

I left it at that.

"I sought you out once at Amnisos," said Ausonias, to change the subject, "but you were absent in the south."

"At Gortyna, I expect."

272

He took both my hands between his own and stared down at them.

"Such hands," he said, embarrassing me.

"Keleustes and you, Samian, and all of you," he shouted to the crew, "this is Daedalus the Athenian."

"Honored," said the Samian, with a sniff.

"Who's he?" inquired a voice from the first oar bank in a thick Arcadian accent.

"Provincial boor," said the captain to me. "Pay no attention."

He took the necklace from his neck and hung it upon mine. "It is your work," he said, "and you will need things to set up a workshop on Aeolia."

"I shall try to make another and better one for you," I replied, looking closely at it. It was unlikely that I could. I cannot match the best Cretan goldsmiths.

"You will need a wardrobe too," said Ausonias, "and some gold ornaments yourself, to set it off, if you do not wish to be taken for a pauper."

Aeolia is a small and lonely island with a large **55** and proud population. Its people are rich, industrious and monumentally conceited. From the king in his fortified palace, whence he dispenses winds wrapped in ox-hides to distinguished guests, down to the lowest freedman on his plot of land, the Aeolians are agreed that no one except the Cretans and possibly the Pharaoh of Egypt are their equals. Having said that about them, I must add that they treated me personally with the greatest respect. They passed over the fact that I was mainland born and, elevating me to the rank of honorary Cretan in respect of my long residence at Knossos, they came to regard me almost as an equal.

Ausonias himself was royal. That was why he could whistle up the winds; a gift exclusive to Aeolian royalty who are as procreative as cats. Aeolus the king had six sons whom he had married to his six daughters. They in turn had each produced six male and six female children and each first-born male was called Aeolus after his grandfather, while each second-born was called Hippotas after his great-grandfather and the third-born was named Ausonias after his great-great-grandfather who had colonized the island. It was a confusing tradition. This wealth of progeny gave rise to the belief that Aeolus could procreate by whistling up his women and when I met him I found it hard to believe that he could have impregnated them in the normal fashion, he was so fragile.

Nevertheless, he was treated with the deference due not only to a king but to a semi-divine one and although his territorial realm was no larger than Athens, his aetheric one as Warden of the Winds extended from one end of the world to the other. It was no wonder he was held in awe and I daresay his successors are too.

At first meeting he was not impressive. For one thing he whistled with every breath he exhaled. This gave his voice an extreme sibilance, and as many do, who have some unconscious trick of speech, he invariably chose words to enhance it. Not only did he sound like the winds he ruled but he was frail and small-boned enough to be blown away by even a moderate one. The moment I set eyes on him I thought that if he had the strength, he was ideally made for flight and the first words he spoke after greeting me were concerned with flight. He questioned me closely and with the expertise to be expected from his vocation, as to the lift of thermals, the intricacy of negotiating cross winds at different heights and the effect they have on the behavior of the sea. He pronounced the word "thalassa" with a whistling force that could have stripped the thatch off a stable and he brought the final "a" up short as if it had hit a door. He urged me to show him my wings and when I told him that I had given them to Apollo and sworn to fly no more, he asked me to make wings for Ausonias. "Surely," he said, "we should see Ausonias soar?"

Ausonias' mask of disdain fell from him and it was comic to see his relief when I told the king of my sunstroke and that I believed Apollo would allow no one in his sky.

"Ah well," said Aeolus sadly, "I am not a god," and he shrugged, adding, "still, my winds sweep his sky notwithstanding."

When he pressed me, I described my flight in detail and was left in no doubt that Aeolus had known and controlled its passage. I had been right in thinking I owed my life to him.

"I had no part in your son's death," he said anxiously and when I assured him that I knew this, he expressed deep sympathy, making the word sound like a long wave breaking on the shore. Then he changed the subject, but not for long and I suppose that was natural. After all, he had made my flight possible and had a proprietary interest in it. Also, I was the only man who had made such a use of his winds; "the sole survivor," as he put it.

Aeolus spoke of his winds as if they were household pets, treating the gentle zephyrs as lapdogs and the great gales as hounds. He praised a wind for its service and blamed another for unruliness, whether it was at that moment bouncing quietly in the skin of an ox, by his side, or stirring up some tempest west of Colchis.

"Sciron," he said, "there's a savage one. I see him swamping shipping while I speak," and he shook his head regretfully. "I must put a stop to this," he went on and for all I know Sciron slunk back into his kennel under the Geraneian Mountain at that very moment, duly chastised.

"If you won't make wings for us, what will you do here?" said Aeolus.

"Daedalus is a bronze master, an architect, a sculptor. He has many trades," said Ausonias.

"Ah yes," said Aeolus vaguely. He had lost interest.

"I think he is tired," whispered Ausonias. "He is very old."

"It's been a gusty day," said Aeolus sharply, "and I am not so old as all that."

We got up to leave and Aeolus asked me to make him a winged figure in bronze.

"I dare not," I replied.

"You are much circumscribed," said Aeolus a little acidly. "Then make me something else," and with that he dismissed us. As we left, a blast of wind blew our cloaks about and rattled the branches of the trees in the courtyard. Ausonias grinned. "He is a beloved old man," he said, "but crusty."

"What shall I make him?" I asked. "I cannot stay here long."

"Long enough to make me a necklace and something for the king," said Ausonias. "If you don't, he is perfectly capable of blowing you to join the Hyperboreans."

So I made a necklace for Ausonias and for Aeolus I contrived a series of tunnels, hewn in the rock of his island, so that when it amused him he could send his winds through them and make them play music for him. I am good at making tunnels through rocks.

Aeolus was generous when I had finished this work and gave me numerous presents so that I set sail for Sicily in considerable affluence. When I think of him and his happy kingdom, of his sons and grandsons, all called Aeolus or Hippotas or Ausonias, I regret the brevity of my visit to his island. I could have been content there but for the fact that I fear I might in time have been persuaded to experiment further with flight. Then Apollo would have destroyed me and perhaps Aeolus as well. Aeolus had so much to teach and he would have whispered whistling knowledge into my ear until I capitulated. That voice could be as persuasive as the Sirens' song.

My clearest recollection of his lonely island is the sound of his daughters calling their children to them. Each lady had a hereditary whistling trill in her voice, a sound as captivating as the sound of flutes. Since all their children and grandchildren shared so few names, no child knew who was being summoned and at all times they flocked about like starlings, looking faintly

puzzled and twittering among themselves. "Aeolussss—Hippo-
tassss—Ausssoniass—yesss, mother yesssss"; I can hear them
even now.

Sicily lies due south of Aeolia at no great dis- **56**
tance. A parting whistle from Ausonias took me
there in two days of sailing and the vessel beached near a fishing village not unlike the one in which I had spent the winter.
The smell was much the same. It was I who smelled different
and looked it too. I had received such gifts from Aeolus that I
hired half the fishermen in the place to carry my wealth for me
so that my journey to Inykon was a progress very different
from my weary tramp down Italy.

We passed among low hills wooded with oak and poplar and
acacia; we passed among fields of corn and cultivated vetches.
Thyme and asphodel sprouted among the rocks and wildflowers
painted the roadside. Except for that of Minos, the kingdom of
Cocalus is the richest I have seen and his wealth, unlike that of
Aeolus, comes not from a particular talent but from the soil
itself. They harvest twice a year in Sicily, as they do in Crete,
and have no need to whistle for anything.

The mountains too are cultivated and vines grow to the
summit. Water is plentiful and springs abundant so that
streams cascade among the rocks and wander everywhere
among the fields. Only the peak of Eryx, where the Mother has
her sanctuary, rose isolated to the west of our road as we went
south through the gentle landscape. Beyond this mountain, the
sea stretches empty to the Pillars of Heracles, so that the
Mother opens her womb here upon the edge of the world. The
summit of her mountain was cloud-capped that day and her
mouths, two thousand feet above the sea, were misted with her
breath. These openings in her rocky flesh are mouths and vents
larger, in a larger bulk, than the Cumaean rock. All those who
live in Sicily know Eryx to be sacred, from the flaming crater in

the east to Cocalus' city of Inykon in the south, and all journey to the place for the spring festival.

I cannot say that I have learned a great deal about this island. Its people are not homogeneous as the Greeks are, but live by choice in isolated communities scattered all over the island. They are secret and have little intercourse between their tribes, but equally they seem to lack the customary rivalry which we Greeks have elevated into a way of life. I do not say there is no raiding but rather that if their states could be called royal, their royal houses do not seem perpetually engaged in destroying one another. It may be that because Sicily is so fertile, when men have settled there they stay where they have settled. It may equally be that I have known the place in a peaceful era and that tomorrow all will be thrown into turmoil by some migration or other. In my time on the island there has been one invasion, but it was defeated and the invaders who survived dispersed about the country, set up their homes, built two towns and so far as I know, live contented.

Only the festivals of Eryx drew the Sicans together and Eryx is too numinous to encourage dispute between the tribes when they are met there. They come and worship and they depart, viewing each other with contemptuous suspicion but apparently without animus. They are most un-Greek. Equally, the Sicans are unlike the Cretans. Theirs is not a nation and their traditions, like their artifacts, are various and primitive. In some places they make fine implements of stone; in others they are savages. Metals are rare and metal workers rarer, but I have seen little metal hoards and treasures in different villages containing implements and ornaments from as far away as Troy and Tyre. The Sicans are puzzling people.

Cocalus, King of Inykon, is also mysterious. I do not know the history of his house nor am I sure of his race but his manners and his way of life are Cretan, as might be expected.

In one sense Cocalus rules Sicily. He is the only king who might pretend to kingship as we understand it. At least he lives like a king and Greek is the language of his court. His city at

278

that time was laid out to the Cretan pattern and his palace was well built, indeed it was the only well constructed building that I saw on the island when I arrived there.

Cocalus rules Sicily in his view and in the opinion of those who visit him from abroad but I doubt if the tribal rulers of villages twenty miles from Inykon would agree. Each thinks himself autonomous and their federation is a loose one.

Nevertheless, Cocalus commands a measure of respect if not of loyalty from the tribes near his city and when his realm was menaced, a fair number of them turned up to aid him. These he rewarded from his store of metal, which is considerable, and I daresay that is what the chiefs had in mind. Their followers are fanatically loyal to them and fought like furies, but within a day of their victory both chiefs and warriors had taken their prizes and vanished into the hills.

The most profound distinction between Minos and Cocalus as rulers lies in their difference of status within their individual realms. Minos is regarded as an immortal even by the most sophisticated of his subjects and by the people in general he is looked upon as in some part divine. All Crete is a single entity and to Cretans no other place is really to be taken seriously, except perhaps Egypt. Cocalus is in no way regarded as immortal or divine and no man I have spoken to in Sicily considers him to be more than an unusually rich, able and peaceful landowner. There is no complex theology centered on his house, no juxtaposition of sun and moon in marriage, no bull cult and no deep-seated malaise. The Mother is worshipped reverently but without conspicuous fuss and the sky is recognized as a twin divinity who is married to the earth in fair and bountiful conjunction. All other deities are treated with the consideration compatible with self-interest. I do not say that Cocalus' palace lacks sects who aspire to a closer approximation to the Cretan religion and others who dedicate themselves to the sky-gods but, if there are, they are left undisturbed and they conduct their ceremonials in private.

In a sense, Cocalus is not a king at all. He does not proclaim

279

himself tyrant and only with the Cretan fleet at point of disembarkation within a few miles of his home, intent on my personal destruction and the annexation of his lands, did Cocalus summon up a martial ardor, which came as a surprise to me. Nevertheless, unwarlike as he is, he is long-sighted and he prepared himself and his people for such an eventuality. With my help he made himself impregnable.

Cocalus was gay, hard drinking, jocular and devious. He was also easy, if perhaps ambivalent, about everything except honey and for honey he had an appetite so remarkable as to constitute an obsession. If Cocalus, who had little general interest in religious rituals, felt any urge toward the involved symbolism so popular in Cretan intellectual circles, it concerned honey. Honey was to Cocalus the mystical substance uniting earth and sky, the sweet center of the nature of the generous earth brought on bees' wings through the air. He mixed it so richly with his wine that the result was to me undrinkable and he would bawl out tipsy and glutinous phrases, clogged on the lips, in praise of honey. The quantity of sweetness he consumed did perhaps make him sweet. I never saw him angered and never heard him raise his voice except in laughter. He liked his fellow men if they would drink with him and share his jokes, providing they were able to appreciate them. He did not like dutiful or empty mirth, nor fools, nor anyone whose wits were too slow to keep up with him in talk. He delighted in women and collected them. On the other hand, I do not think he really liked himself, but his sense of propriety was rigid and his secret thoughts he kept severely to himself. He was not ambitious but would not see himself deprived. He did not feel safe but he did not wish to be disturbed.

After the disturbance with the Cretan fleet, he has not been disturbed again, except perhaps by his women, and I write of him in the past tense not because he is anything but prosperous and at least outwardly cheerful to this day but simply because I know as I write that I shall not meet him again.

On the day I met him, when I arrived with my train and

my Aeolian wealth, he was seated in the shade of a vine arbor, listening to a group of musicians performing a composition of exceptional intricacy. He made me sit down at once with him and drink a vast quantity of a wine far too sickly for my taste. Together we got very drunk indeed.

"Apollo," said Cocalus, seeing me pour my libation to him, "Apollo is highly respectable. I respect him. I do not know what we should do without him."

"No," I said. "No, indeed," and I looked warily at his rays striking warm upon the walls of the garden where we sat.

Cocalus poured out a libation so copious that it spread in a wide pool about his feet.

"I am not sure that Apollo reciprocates in your case," he said carefully, staring shrewdly at me. "Better make him another libation."

I did, and before we had spent an hour together we were both sitting with our feet dyed purple in pools of dark wine.

"So far as I can tell," said Cocalus, "Apollo has no special feelings about me and anyway he likes music. For my part, I like music too except for the noise."

"The lyre is Apollo's instrument," I said.

"Not this one," said Cocalus, picking up an instrument from the floor, "this is mine, but do not let us tell Apollo."

"Your men play superbly," I said. "Do you really dislike the sound of music?"

"Yes and no," said Cocalus, "yes and no."

He plucked his lyre with wonderful dexterity but without seeming to concentrate on it. "Do you sing?" he asked.

"No," I replied.

"Are you sure?"

"Quite sure."

"Well, that is a blessing," said Cocalus. "I have had to put up with more amateur singing from my craftsmen than I can stand. They all have pleasing light baritone voices and sing at their work."

"I do not."

281

"Have some wine," said Cocalus.

"I wonder," I asked, "could I have some wine unmixed with honey?"

"You don't like honey?"

"I like it, but in moderation."

"In what?"

"Moderation."

"Curious," said Cocalus and brooded silently on the matter for some moments. Then he poured me a deep cup of wine so thick with honey that it would scarcely flow from the jar.

"There!" he said, "no honey to speak of in that."

"I suppose not," I said.

"We take honey seriously here," said Cocalus. "We regard it as sacred. It is impossible to sing without it. The six-line stress for instance is symbolic of the hexagonal cell of the honeycomb, quite apart from the fact that our honey is cultivated. We herd bees here and house them, but then you say you don't sing?"

"No."

"Wonderful news," said Cocalus.

He pushed the table away from him, rattling the wine cups and a dozen of his jars of different kinds of honey.

"You know," he said, picking a jar and nosing its aroma, "I had a table made by you some years ago which ran about on wheels. I didn't have it long."

"No?"

"I got it from that dolt Pallas of Sounion. He said it would obey, but it didn't. On the way home it ran all over the deck doubtless obeying Poseidon rather than me. Anyway, he took it over the side and some of my rarest honeys with it. Made me feel a fool."

"I have made a golden honeycomb. I made it for Artemis when I was in the rock below Cumae," I said, to change the subject.

"Seriously?"

"Very seriously. I should not be here if I hadn't."

282

"There you are," said Cocalus and tactfully pressed me to tell him about the golden comb.

"It is," I said, "so exact in its resemblance to the work of the goddess's real bees that I fully believe no man could match it."

"How did you make it?"

"That, my lord, is secret."

"Cast gold?"

"Yes."

"By the lost-wax method?" Cocalus grinned. "I ask no more," he said, "except that I would have you make another in time for the festival of Eryx. I shall ask my personal bees to assist."

He knew, this honey-loving king, he knew how it had been done.

"I shall obey my lord."

"So will the bees," said Cocalus and set up a thrumming cadence on his lyre which his musicians took up. As they wove variations around it, a swarm of bees flew in over the wall and crossed and re-crossed the courtyard where we sat. These insects joined with the strings of the musicians and blended their industrious whine into the music.

"Beautiful," said Cocalus. "Beautiful."

The first gift I made to Cocalus, when I had been his guest for several months, was a bronze **57** krater the height of a man. It seemed a suitable gift for someone of his temperament because a krater is a bowl in which wine is mixed with water, and it occurred to me that given a krater of sufficient size, Cocalus might come to dispense a mixture at once less powerful and less sweet. I was wrong. He filled his krater with wine and honey in revolting proportion and the quantity of water he allowed to be added would not have filled a hand basin. Still, he was delighted with the gift.

I had excellent workmen at Inykon and excellent workshops too. Cocalus' craftsmen, whether they sing too much for him or not, are as good as many in practice though not so proficient as those at Knossos. Most of them are of Cretan stock and many come directly from their native country, so perhaps their ability is not surprising. They beat out the great bowl of the krater from sheet bronze and riveted a rim, frieze, base and handle to it. I designed these parts but they executed them and cast them with exemplary skill. They also made a tripod to support the bowl and a strainer topped with an image of the Mother in her aspect of Demeter, whose votaries give her honey. This figure I modeled and cast myself. The frieze represented the rout of Dionysus, the rim was ornamented with bronze bees and the tripod with my Erechtheid snakes.

On the bowl of the krater I engraved the words: "Daedalus gave me as a present to his host Cocalus" and he in return gave me a farm with cattle and an apiary, several women and my pick of all his craftsmen to direct in any enterprise or manufacture I should choose. On the lintel of the door of my house Cocalus caused to be carved the words: "Cocalus gave me to Daedalus as a hive for his industry."

A magazine beneath the house was filled with blocks of refined beeswax, stored to keep them cool. There was enough wax there to last the lifetime of twenty metal workers and when I thanked Cocalus for his princely gift, I remarked that so much wax would at least have modeled the mythical bronze wall Aeolus was supposed to have raised around his island. Cocalus smiled and said:

"I shall not ask you for bronze walls but I shall need walls of stone from you. I have word that Crete plans to invade us."

"Minos?" I said, unable to believe it. "Minos invade?"

Cocalus shrugged. "From what I have heard of this Cretan Zeus, incarnate in the bull and buried in the ground, it sounds improbable."

"Improbable, it is incredible. It runs counter to everything I know about him."

284

"Nevertheless, I believe the Cretans are preparing to invade us," said Cocalus. "Gods do not behave consistently and I am told Minos is a god."

My courage abruptly deserted me. It was true. Gods cannot be relied on. Yet I still could not conceive Minos emerging from the remote and speculative realm of his own mind to embark on the expansion of his territorial dominions.

"But why should he?" I asked feebly.

"Largely on your account, I gather. You should be flattered."

"I am," I said.

"And alarmed."

"I am."

I began to see Apollo's hand in the matter. Perhaps he had struck at Minos and made him mad, but then I could not see how the god could reach Minos, deep in my sunless labyrinth, until I remembered Deiphobe and the depth of Apollo's penetration.

"Minos would not pursue me," I said. "He pursues nothing but abstractions."

"You never know," said Cocalus.

I felt a dreadful weariness. I could not fly who had spent so much of my life in flight and whose wings lay at Apollo's feet at Cumae. Where could I go? Into the earth again or into death to escape this endless Apollonian persecution? Could Minos really wish to destroy me?

"Have some wine," said Cocalus.

"Dionysus will not help me. I must leave. I must hide again. Why should you risk all your possessions on my behalf?"

"I shouldn't," said Cocalus decidedly, "but I do not think this projected invasion is all that it appears. Besides," he added, "we have time. They cannot sail before spring and when they come I think I shall welcome them."

"Then I must go."

"Do not be so simple. First you will build me my fortress, north of here, then I shall welcome the Cretan fleet to Inykon and then we shall see."

285

I shaded my eyes and looked toward the blinding sun and, hating the god at that moment with all my heart, I was too craven to sustain that hatred and retreated fearfully from it.

"We cannot win," I said.

"I think we can," said Cocalus. "You see it is not simple, but then I am not simple either, not simple at all."

"Apollo spare me!" I whispered.

"What would you do without him?" asked Cocalus.

"Rest," I said.

"Well, there you are," said Cocalus, "what use would you be resting?"

"I am not one of your bees."

Cocalus ignored this insolence. He began to hum softly and slipping his thumb through the handle of his cup he flicked the remaining drop of wine and honey across the room with a backhanded movement of his wrist. The drop hit a lizard sunning itself on the wall, just as the lizard's tongue flicked out to take a fly. It missed and darted into a crack in the wall; the fly never moved. "A direct hit," said Cocalus happily, "and the fly flies free."

I smiled in spite of myself. "The fly stays," I said.

"You are a religious man," said Cocalus. "It is always a problem."

"I am?" I asked, surprised.

"Oh yes. You worship Apollo because you have no alternative. You may not love him but you worship him. Therefore you must justify him to yourself whether you believe the justification or not and pay the price which he demands."

"The price has been my son and my peace of mind."

"The price is the time it takes between asking for the truth and receiving the answer."

"However," said Cocalus, changing his tone, "I do not think you will leave here until you want to and if you have to take some temporary refuge, Sicily is full of safe places."

"Safe from Minos?"

"Oh, let us not worry too much about Minos; safe for

Daedalus at least."

"I doubt it," I said.

"Then let us build an impregnable fortress," said Cocalus, refilling his wine cup. "We shall probably not need it but it will take your mind off your troubles."

I was silent. I did not feel the word "troubles" adequately described my perpetual retreat from the implacable eye of day. Must I accept my disorder, because I knew that Apollo is of all gods the most ordered? Was I his creature because order is my god? Did justice, which Minos set in the center of his mind, wear the impenetrable answer of injustice like Talos sheathed mad in his brazen harness? Mouse, snake and bird, all are Apollo's creatures. Icarus too belonged to Apollo and knew it. Perhaps I do too.

A god is not to be regarded sentimentally. It is not simply given that a god is good because he is divine nor that a bland piety makes a man's life-work valid. Much that I have achieved has been in honor of Apollo and yet in my heart I know that my most powerful impulse is to be revenged upon him. I am still the father of Icarus. Cocalus was right when he said that I must justify the god and what will remain after my death, apart from a few toys, will be my temple to Apollo on the rock at Cumae and the legend of my mastery of the buried minerals and stones which made my building and my sculpture possible. The price I paid has been my son's life and my own fears. Gradually I come to believe that when I have finished all my tunneling, which I have usually begun with the god hot on the back of my neck, I shall find him in the center of my final labyrinth and meet him face to face, where I have prayed only to find a gentle dark and a certain peace. And perhaps that will be the answer when I have paid the price of waiting. Perhaps the harmony which Apollo shows in the opposed curves of his lyre, in his balance of pestilence and cure, his bow and orb, will resolve my equation and let me rest. I am not Icarus. I no more believe that I can be revenged upon Apollo than that Icarus could have conquered him.

At Kamikos, a little to the north of Inykon but **58** within sight of it, I built a fortress for Cocalus. It is my last external maze and I designed it to exclude the might of Crete. I built it to withstand a siege, made it defensible by a handful of men, and this impregnable citadel was scarcely completed when, with the innate perversity of mazes, it reversed its function. Cocalus opened the gates of this labyrinth to its besieger, drew him in and slew him, closed out his friends and slew them, excluded me and saved my life.

A maze is a map of ironies, a pattern of paradox, and its nature is revealed only to the maze maker and not to its inhabitants. Minos required his labyrinth at Knossos to exclude the external world so that he might contemplate the abstract nature of justice beyond the expediencies of human judgement. Installed in its center, he shared his sanctuary with a monster for whom it was a prison. Again, some of those who dwell in Gaia and live safe in the earth's womb enjoying an awesome reputation as dwarfs or giants, lived under Cumae cheek by jowl with a god's concubine who wished for nothing but release from his burning bed. As for myself, I have built labyrinths for others, imprisoned myself in them in the hope of safety and once safe I have instantly begun the struggle to escape from my security. I have even gone into the open labyrinth of the sky to free myself from earth and watched my son die there to free himself from me.

The labyrinth is not merely a dancing floor, nor a complex of passages nor a web of air; it is a field of force. Its architect, as I have learned, embarks upon the construction of a maze, believing that its force lies within his control only to discover that the field is held in equilibrium by opposed forces, at once containing and excluding, and his life's labyrinth has the laugh on him.

I do not count the building of Kamikos a major achievement. Its defenses were comparatively simple, although I consider them ingenious. Time being short, a mere five months, the advantage of a surface maze was obvious; walls are more rapidly raised than mine shafts are driven. I therefore selected a site above the river, a rocky table with a central depression in which I erected a palace for Cocalus, less luxurious than his home at Inykon but comfortable enough and with one remarkable feature. The depression in the rock was split with fissures from which hot springs gave off steam and I harnessed these exhalations of the earth and piped them to heat not only the baths but the whole house in winter. Sicilian winters can be cold and Kamikos was windswept. In the summer the steam could be channeled off to escape below the acropolis. That was the extent of the tunneling. Otherwise, all I did was to build a series of multicarsal walls both round the base and about the summit of the rock, so that attackers were forced to approach each gate by a long and narrow route, with various blank turnings in which they might be trapped. These walls were so calculated as to make attackers bunch together in the traverses. Each defended locality was so disposed that under attack it could be protected from either flank by enfilade and each gate led into an area closed by a further gate set at right-angles to it. To the best of my knowledge, this adaptation of the labyrinth for tactical defense has not been employed before. I believe that properly put to the test such a defensive maze would be impregnable, providing the walls were high enough, because no attacking force, however large, would be deployable and siege weapons of any size would be obstructed in their approach. A system of trenches on the same pattern would also be effective.

Cocalus moved his people, his treasure and the apiary of his beloved bees into the fortress early in the year. It was a cold winter and we were grateful for the steam. In fact, we spent the early spring in experimenting with the piping system and since that took a deal of rock boring, it was both more expensive in labor and took longer in execution than the defenses themselves. Cocalus enjoyed the whole business. He liked the turmoil, the confusion of wagons, men and animals in the narrow passages between the walls, the bustle of moving his household and indeed all those aspects of organizing for war which give rulers a sense of achievement and which I dislike most. He even insisted upon a steam-heated chamber for his beehives, which so disturbed those industrious but conservative insects that they swarmed anxiously and, to the workmen, painfully, everywhere but in the apartment designed for them.

The daughters of Cocalus were numerous and handsome. They too enjoyed the confusion and they too swarmed about the building, taking hot baths as soon as the baths were even partially built, with such enthusiastic frequency that the work of completing the water system was impeded. Golden girls and their perspiring slaves were everywhere underfoot and one of the most memorable privileges of the master builder was his access to them. Taking advantage of this circumstance impeded the work further and I do not think I was alone in doing so. Cocalus only laughed and continued to drink his thick, sweet wine.

In the late spring the fortress of Kamikos was finished and we waited for the threatened invasion. For the rest of that spring and early summer nothing happened. The spring festival at Eryx was celebrated as usual, and had the Cretans arrived during those weeks we might, I suppose, have been taken, if not by surprise, at least at a disadvantage. I did not attend the festival that year. The summer passed and by then I had leisure enough to make toys for Cocalus' daughters, jointed dolls sheathed in gold which could be made to dance on strings. They looked, as I remember, not unlike the daughters of Cocalus themselves and many were damaged when played with in the baths. Winter came and still there was no sign of the Cretan fleet.

Before the cold weather came down, Ausonias came whistling up the long passage to the main gate of Kamikos and the wind blew dust into the gatekeeper's nose and made him sneeze. Ausonias stopped whistling and apologized. His followers, heavily armed Aeolians, also whistled, but not being royal they did not raise the wind. Nevertheless, the gatekeeper looked sourly at them and wrapped his cloak around him.

"No Cretans?" inquired Ausonias, grinning.

"Not yet."

"Aeolus sends greetings. He asks me to tell Cocalus that he has word the fleet set sail three months ago."

"They have not been sighted."

"Well no," said Ausonias, "that is not surprising." He whistled and a blast of air flattened the gatekeeper and his cloak against the gate like a dingy butterfly pinned to a board. The Aeolians' cloaks flapped wildly and one of the bowmen on the wall lost his oxhide shield, which went swooping out over the country like Icarus dancing defiance at the sun.

"Contrary winds," said Ausonias, "contrary winds."

Then we went in and up to the palace and Cocalus made Ausonias and his followers welcome, filling them with wine and honey from his bronze krater until many of them were very sick.

All through that spring and summer the Sicans **59** had come to Kamikos, singly and in groups. A chief would bring in twenty men and swear fealty to Cocalus, drink with him and depart unsteadily with his men. "They will be back when I need them," said Cocalus. Next week another would arrive with six men on foot and two chariots or eight spearmen in a hay wagon. Gradually six or seven hundred came and trickled drunkenly away again so that the total force of men in arms at Kamikos at any one time was perhaps two hundred, including Ausonias' followers. In addition, there were thirty or forty able-bodied craftsmen and palace functionaries and a disorderly group of Cocalus' sons. There were also the musicians, but they did not look likely warriors. I must admit that I was disturbed by the casual methods of recruiting Cocalus seemed to favor, but I had confidence in the defenses of Kamikos and our ability to withstand a prolonged siege if necessary. "It will not be," said Cocalus.

In the autumn I made another golden honeycomb, a replica of the one I had cast in Cumae and Cocalus gave me seven of his bees to sacrifice and make immortal, as I had done before. When the honeycomb was made I gave it to Cocalus so that in the spring he might dedicate it at the festival at Eryx. I also made a golden ram, not of solid gold but of gilded bronze, as my own gift to the Mother. "She will prefer it," said Cocalus, "I have a feeling she has come to resent bulls. Their day is past."

Making these objects and supervising the work at Kamikos, within the defensive walls, passed the time while we waited for the Cretan fleet. Cocalus liked luxury and once the defenses were secure, he spent his treasure and his men's labor on perfecting the palace. Cold springs also spilled among the rocks and these too were piped so that the baths could be regulated at any temperature from steam to icy cold by an arrangement of sluices. Even the palace gardens on the rock were irrigated. I enjoyed these exercises in hydraulics, and Cocalus was shrewd in his suggestions. I believe that in other circumstances he would have made a fine technician.

The sons of Cocalus and the followers of Ausonias trained for war. That is to say, they ran races, wrestled, boxed and competed against one another in all manner of energetic ways and sometimes damaged each other severely. Certain followers of Ausonias also damaged several of the daughters of Cocalus, but not severely. The winter passed.

Early in the spring a small fleet of galleys was sighted at dawn, south of Inykon, and the city was rapidly evacuated. Within a few hours, at least four hundred Sicans had gathered behind the beaches, south of the city, and at Kamikos the walls were manned and the gates shut. I was amazed and gratified. I had not expected such efficiency. "You underrate us," said Cocalus, handing me a large cup of disgusting wine which, because the morning was chilly, I drank with more enthusiasm than usual. "In any case," he went on, "that is not the Cretan fleet they have sighted or, if it is, it is only a part of it. Anyone would think that no one visits us except these bull-bogeys of Minos."

He was right. It was not the Cretans, but three vessels bound for Sardinia manned by the fifty grandsons of Thespius and their Athenian followers. This expedition was commanded by Iolaüs, the nephew of Heracles. Iolaüs was then a stranger to me, having spent most of his life serving as Heracles' charioteer and his lover. He was devoted to this hero, despite the fact that Heracles in a fit of maniacal despondency had killed all Iolaüs' children by Megara. Myself, I should dislike the whole-sale murderer of my children, but hero worship is not intelligible to those who do not experience it and if I do not understand Iolaüs and loathe his brutal bedfellow, it could be said that I am prejudiced. At Pisa, Heracles smashed a life-sized image I made of him, with a single blow of his club. He took it for a living rival and in one sense perhaps it was.

I made this statue at the behest of the Pisans while I was at Knossos and by no means to honor Heracles myself. It was of poplar wood and well made and I remark this here because it has been said that Heracles found the body of Icarus and I carved the piece in gratitude. This is nonsense. Heracles never did me any service and, besides, I made the carving long before Icarus was lost. The Pisans forgave Heracles, saying that he might smash any image he cared to destroy, which was wise of them but no solace to me. They even sent to me to replace it but I had neither the time nor the inclination to do so.

The celebrity of Heracles is founded on his enormous physical strength; his acts and nature are conditioned by his intense self-disgust, for which, in my view, he has ample cause. He is in fact melancholy-mad and his smashing of his own image is like his murder of the children of Iolaüs; they are two savage incidents among many no less brutal. On the credit side, those of his labors which might be said to have served a positive purpose could all be described as a form of grandiose housekeeping. Pesticide, stable cleaning, shopping for golden apples and the like may make for excellent legends but the best that may be said for Heracles is that while he committed innumerable murders he at least replaced the casualties. Hence the fifty grandsons of Thespius.

These fifty young men are all called Thespius after their grandfather, who sent his fifty daughters one by one to Heracles during a visit the hero paid to Thespius in Boeotia. Heracles possessed each daughter and all naturally became pregnant and bore sons. That every one of them should be named after his grandfather was at once so filial and so confusing that it is no wonder that he sent them to found a colony on Sardinia, but it was sensible of Thespius to entrust the expedition to Iolaüs and I suppose generous of Heracles to permit it.

Iolaüs is an exceptional man with a genius for organization and as much diplomacy and charm as Heracles himself lacks. I incline to think that any clear thinking which has gone into the fulfillment of Heracles' achievements may be attributed to Iolaüs, who, because he is self-effacing, has allowed Heracles the entire credit. But then again, Heracles may have insisted on it and who could argue with him?

The fifty young men are all relatives of mine, cousins in fact, because Thespius is an Erechtheid. I can think of nothing particular to say about them. Not only were they all called Thespius but they were all to me indistinguishable from one another. When Cocalus made them welcome he suggested that if they cared to remain awhile, they might be provided with a war. Being Greeks they were much gratified and within twelve hours they were all as drunk as only Cocalus could make them. They even liked their wine as sweet and thick as he did and mixed no water with it. The digestions of the young are remarkable; on the following day they were competing in athletics with the sons of Cocalus and the followers of Ausonias.

As we watched them throwing each other about on the plain between Inykon and Kamikos, I inadvertently made some critical remark which, to my great surprise, Iolaüs took as derogatory to Heracles and I found myself ranged in argument against all three of my friends. Cocalus, like Ausonias, regarded Heracles with almost as much reverence as did Iolaüs. The glamor of this over-muscled demigod is such that even wise and peace-loving men are as dazzled by his exploits as they are envious of his physique.

"The trouble with you, my friends," I said, "is that there is not one creative coward among you. Procreative as you may be, Cocalus, and brave to a fault as you are, Iolaüs, and with a most fertile pair of lungs, Ausonias, your appetite for heroics will frustrate your best designs."

"Fine words from a mere mortal," said Iolaüs.

"We are all mortals here," I said.

"Heracles is not. We none of us rank with him. None of us has earned his fame, nor shall we."

"If we had Heracles here when the Cretans come, we should not need your expensive fortress," said Cocalus. "One sally from him and they would fly as far as you did."

"But not so memorably," I said, nettled.

"You do not know Heracles," said Iolaüs. "He has a glory about him."

Both Cocalus and Ausonias were silent. I suppose they were embarrassed. We were near to quarreling.

"We are all on edge," said Cocalus, after a while.

"Hero worshippers," I said rudely.

"You are probably right," said Ausonias suavely, "but if you have no response in you to heroism, you have something lacking."

"Why?"

"Daedalus," said Cocalus smiling, "you are my most beloved coward and the greatest creative spirit known to me, but to ordinary men like ourselves the quality of the hero lifts our spirits to heights greater than those you attained on wings. Icarus would have understood me."

I thought that there was nothing I could say and so I said, "I have found nothing born of heroism except pain and death."

"And glory and courage and nobility of aspiration raised to the peak of splendor," said Iolaüs.

"Oh Icarus, Icarus. . . ." I said. "Is it true? Is your absurdity so glorious that my life ranks as nothing against your death? And Heracles, you formidable animal, is your club mightier than my ten fingers?"

"Yes and no," said Cocalus, "yes and no."

"I do not think, Daedalus," said Iolaüs gently, "that you understand the comradeship which draws men together in war, nor the compulsion of danger and the intensity of love which shared danger gives."

"No," I said, wishing to end the discussion, "I don't think I do. I am naturally solitary."

"I am sorry for you," said Iolaüs, and we all turned to watch the young men sharing the companionship which would flower for them in the presence of unnecessary death.

"As cowards go," said Cocalus, "I value you so highly that I shall force a further solitude upon you. You are, it seems, one of the prime causes of this impending invasion and I do not want you here when the enemy arrives. I ask you to go to Eryx and take the honeycomb to the Mother for me. The Cretans and her spring festival will probably coincide."

It shows how irrational one is. I was furious. I refused to go. I ranted at this accusation of cowardice, boasted that I would fight shoulder to shoulder with them, spoke of how I had killed Sciron, boasted of defeating the Minotaur and generally behaved like a vainglorious boy. Then Iolaüs slapped me on the back and I realized that all three of them were laughing at me.

Two weeks before the spring festival at Eryx, Ausonias sighted the Cretan fleet at sea approaching from the south-east. He had sailed in his own ship, the one that had taken me from Italy to Aeolia, and after

60

patrolling the waters south of Sicily by manipulating the winds, he saw Cretan sails on the horizon, numbering no less than thirty, and fled before them. When he beached below Inykon they were two days behind him.

"I did what I could with the wind," he said, "but Poseidon aids them. I cannot compete with him."

"It is time for you to go," said Cocalus to me, and despite my earlier ranting, I meekly went.

I left Kamikos fully prepared and Inykon once more evacuated. Before I left, I gave Cocalus, Ausonias and Iolaüs detailed information concerning the best use of the maze-fortress and told them of a defensive device I had prepared which utilized the steam from the hot springs. They understood me and stood looking grim and soldierly in their armor.

"Heroes," I said, mockingly.

"Coward," said Iolaüs and dismounted from his chariot to embrace me.

"Who is a coward?" I said. "Here are you three bound together in your shared danger and bound to all those muscular men clattering around you with the hot blood of battle already coursing through their veins, whereas I am going out alone and doubtless your grandchildren will call me coward for it in a different tone of voice from yours."

"You solitary hero," said Cocalus. "We respect you."

Then as the Cretan sails came up on the horizon I went out from Kamikos and turned north-west, leaving the bustling tumult behind me. I went alone, dressed simply and with my baggage on two donkeys and no one disturbed my journey through the quiet countryside except the occasional little band of shaggy warriors who passed me on their way to fight for Cocalus. These jeered at me but did not stop and every man who passed me I envied. There is an idiotic urge for heroism even in the most ordered of us.

I reached the base of Eryx on the sixth day and **61**
went up the long, winding path toward the sanctuary. The lower slopes are easy but near the summit the rocks
make it slow going and to mount the back of Eryx is as hard
as ascending to the barren realm of the sky-gods.

At Cumae there is no temenos of the Mother. It is held
sacred only by those who live within the rock whereas Eryx is
public and the rites there are conducted with as great and complex a formality as in the great caves of Crete or at Delphi
before Apollo conquered the serpent. Cumae looks deserted.
Eryx appears much inhabited with its cluster of treasuries and
buildings to house priestesses, scattered below the sacred cleft.

The sanctuary is cut into the rock and at the clitoris of this
entrance to the earth a hundred priestesses serve the votaries so
that each man who brings a gift and lays it in the great sunken
bowl at the entrance is received between the thighs of a
priestess, to make his gift of seed. No man is permitted to enter
deeper into the Mother and the cleft which leads down into
her is guarded even from the sight of man. Boys take their
virginity to Eryx and leave it with their fathers' semen in the
lips of the servants of the goddess, and mothers bring their
daughters to become initiates in the holy practice of their
acceptance.

The climax of the spring festival takes place at the equinox
when a group of white doves is released from the summit and
flies south. These doves return in nine days and when they
return they are led by a single red dove which is the Mother's
sign that all living creatures in Sicily will be made fertile.

I laid my honeycomb in the sanctuary and it was received by
the priestess as too fine to be thrown into the bowl. My bronze
ram they placed in the naos of the temple, if that is what it can
be called, for it does not resemble a temple in our terms.

When Deiphobe spoke her oracle to me she said that the
hawk who, in the egg, fed upon the yolk of the ram's rod would
in due time restore Icarus and multiply him. I did not fully

understand her. I do not now, but I have an inkling. She meant the astrological sign denoting the passage of the Great Year. If I then, standing at the opening of the time of the Ram, symbolically gave my seed in the form of a ram to the Mother, then Icarus, my hawk, would be fed and I should at least have contributed to the long fulfillment of the prophecy. You in your time, at the conjunction of the Fish and the Water-carrier, will know better than I the meaning of the oracle.

To complete my gift I lay with the priestess and if she bore a son to me, he serves, as do all those born on Eryx, at the shrine of the Mother, all his life.

On the ninth day the doves returned and the red dove circled the pinnacle of the mountain and went, followed by her white companions, into the sacred place and down into the darkness. So the festival ended and the multitude of worshippers went down the mountain and spread out across the plain, dispersing to their homes.

I remained awhile, after the people had gone, because I was curious about the sanctuary and how and when it had been designed. It was old, as old I believe as any sacred place I have visited, or rather any place where the goddess was regularly worshipped, and to judge by the nature of the work, much of it may have been done by giants. I am well aware that in saying this I add to the legend of those who live in the earth, but then the people under Cumae are very small. Maybe those under Eryx are giants. I never saw them but I saw, in the treasury, huge horns of ivory so large that whatever cattle they came from must have been ten times the size of ours. I have been told that there are such creatures south of Egypt and to the east and, of course, I have seen horns or teeth of this sort at Knossos, brought in trade, but I have a feeling those in Eryx had been native to the place at some time.

When I left the summit of the mountain and began my descent, the path was deserted. It was evening and a bad time to choose; the path was dangerous in places. However, I risked it and went down slowly, planning to lie down and sleep where-ever seemed reasonably comfortable before darkness fell. Rounding a curve against a wall of rock I came upon a motionless seated figure, a heavy, silent mass outlined against the sky and I thought "Cephalon," for he looked exactly as Cephalon, the Fat Man, had looked when first I came out from under Cumae. The ant, so long quiescent, moved in my head.

It was not Cephalon. It was Tros. He sat there waiting for me and he had not changed in all the years since I had last seen him when Icarus was a child and we came into port at Amnisos. The setting sun glinted on his gold-wire hair, thick and shaped like the curls of wool on my bronze ram and his great gray eyes were as remote as I remembered them. In his bone-hard hands he held a triton shell.

"I broke your son's shell, Daedalus," he said. "Here is another."

Suddenly both my donkeys shied and went tearing off as if they had gone mad. The lead animal pulled the halter out of my hand and gave a screaming bray of terror. They both turned and went up the mountain path. Then on the curve above us, where the shelf of rock was narrowest, the leader slid sideways and went over the cliff, taking the other with him. They were there, kicking and screaming, and then they were gone. I did not hear them hit the ground below.

Tros laughed. My legs gave way under me and I sat down in a clumsy heap. The dust the donkeys had raised gradually subsided and the stones ceased to slide and clatter on the path. There was silence except for my own breathing.

Tros held out the shell to me. "Here," he said.

"What should I do with it?" I asked stupidly.

"You have an ant in your head," said Tros. "It is time for him to leave. Therefore set him a task suitable for Daedalus and since he is Daedalus in little, he will perform it."

I am not quite sure why I did what Tros told me except that it did not occur to me to disobey. I unshouldered my pack and took out a bronze awl and a little pot of honey. Then I took the shell from Tros and bored a hole in the point of the shell.

"Daedalus, inhabiter of labyrinths," said Tros, "your name-sake leaves one maze for another, as you do."

I did not know what he meant, although it is simple enough when I describe it. I knew, though, what I had to do. I smeared honey round the great opening in the triton and suddenly the ant was on my upper lip. "Cephalon," I said, but there was no answer. The ant dropped into my palm. I took a cobweb from a bush beside me and the ant took it from me. I took a spool of thin linen thread from my pack and wound the strand of web to an end of it. The ant went into the shell through the awl-hole and began his long circuitous journey through the chambers of the triton.

I sat there holding the triton steady and the cobweb disappeared into the awl-hole. I wondered why I was doing it. I wondered why the ant was doing it. Tros had me fixed and simply smiled. The ant came out into the lip of the shell and ate some honey. I took the web from him and eased the thread through the shell. I do not know how I did it. My head felt curiously depopulated and my mind was lonely for the ant; a strange sensation.

Tros took the shell from my hands and taking the ends of the linen thread, he held the shell string suspended and with a twist sent it spinning round on its axis. The ant vanished into the grass by the path and I, looking anxiously for it, did not notice four men step out on to the path from among the rocks.

"There is Daedalus," said Tros calmly. "Who else could thread this shell? Who else could wind his mind through such a rhyton? He even invented the implement that pierced the hole."

I looked up. Tros went on spinning the shell and the red sun was directly behind his head. The night was nearly come and the four men stood like ghosts towering over me. I looked up at them vaguely, still mourning the loss of the ant and saw that they were dressed in white, in white loinguards and greaves and wearing white feathers in their headdresses. They were dressed in the livery of Tauros and their skins too were white.

301

"Take him," said Tros sharply.

"Tros—Tauros—Talos," I said like a sick child with a wandering mind. But Tros was not Tauros nor Talos, or not exactly. I do not know what I meant.

"Take him," said Tros again.

They did not treat me respectfully and my return to Kamikos, in the hands of the followers of **62** Tauros, was uncomfortable. I am getting too old to be tied up and frogmarched across country or, rather, I have always been too old for such treatment. Also I am lame. They were surly and would not answer my questions, except in rude monosyllables so that I could not establish what had happened while I had been at Eryx. So far as I could tell, Cocalus had refused battle and had invited Minos to be his guest at Kamikos. This did not surprise me. It sounded like trickery of a familiar Greek kind. If I was surprised at anything, it was that Minos had accepted this dubious hospitality—if it was, in fact, Minos.

From the boasts of my captors, none of which described the Minos I knew, I became increasingly certain that the war lord they called Minos was in fact Tauros. This Minos was white-skinned and wore white; he was the mate of Pasiphaë and that I could believe; he was a man of action and his people feared him. Therefore either Tauros had usurped the throne of Crete, with the connivance of the queen, or Minos himself had abdicated his power to Tauros. Either was possible, but if Tauros had usurped the throne then my capture would have been necessary to him. I held the key to the labyrinth and if Minos still lived in that impregnable maze he could not be destroyed without my participation. While he still lived he was a threat to Tauros; therefore I thought he lived. Hence my capture.

The immortality of Minos meant that he changed his appearance over the years. How else could he be renewed? His surrogate died for him and he lived on. If Tauros had not died

302

for Minos then Minos must die for Tauros. Therefore I must lead Tauros to Minos. It was as straightforward as that. The conception had the brutal simplicity I would expect from Tauros and the acceptance of so obvious a substitution of one king for another could only occur among a people whose theology ran counter to their common sense. Tangle a nation in a sufficient complexity of symbols and rituals and they will collectively believe anything fed to them from the throne, no matter who occupies it.

By the time I had been pushed and jerked across twenty miles of country, I was no longer in any doubt that if Cocalus had not contrived the destruction of Tauros I should be returned to Crete and once there, I should last exactly as long as it took to persuade me to reveal the secret of the maze. What I could not understand was the part Tros played in the conspiracy. The words Tros, Tauros, Talos ran together in my head with every stumbling step I took, yet I could not really grasp any connection between them except the alliteration and running rhythm of their names.

Two days later my four frogmarching captors were joined by sixteen more. At least a quarter of Tauros' personal bodyguard now honored me with their unwelcome presence and their white figure-eight shields, each as tall as its owner, made them look like so many small warships under sail. Their plumes tossed, their spears flashed and they made an unpleasantly brave show. Also they moved at the double, a loping trot in close formation, so that I was forced to trot with them, which made me feel ridiculous, hurt my game leg and quickly reduced me to gasping exhaustion. Cocalus and his sweet wine were much to blame. I was too fat to run and I have never chosen to run when I could walk. If I did not trot fast enough I was encouraged to do so with spear butts. I trotted.

At night we rested, if it could be called resting. I was fed and given water, but I was not unbound. I was simply thrown down as I was and suffered horribly from cramp.

Tros—Tauros—Talos, Tros—Tauros—Talos, that jog-trot

grind, with sweat pouring off me and dust clogged in the sweat, gradually drove all thought from my head so that when, on the fourth morning, I was suddenly pulled to a halt so sharply that I fell on all fours, I had no idea what had happened.

There was a taut silence, broken by the sharp sound of a horse hoof striking a stone. Squinting up I saw the bodyguard of Tauros around me bunch together and take cover behind their white shields. Between the braced legs of the men ahead of me, I could see, where the defile opened into a field of wheat stubble, a line of ten chariots and behind them a crowd of Sican spearmen. Alone in the lead chariot, leaning easily on the rail and balancing a javelin casually on his shoulder was Iolaüs.

"I should not advise any violence," said Iolaüs pleasantly. "Just throw down the shields and those expensive swords."

"Move up on them," said one of the white bodyguards.

"It is all over," said Iolaüs. "Your Minos is boiled."

The silence fell again. No one moved.

"Move up," said the bodyguard. The white shields went forward, the spears advanced, and the men, crouched behind the shields, began to go forward in two lines.

"Well, if you insist," said Iolaüs grinning and he put his javelin neatly through the throat of the Cretan in the center.

The man went over on his shield, his legs kicking, and Iolaüs cried "Hup" in the same instant. The chariots came on full tilt from a standing start. I have never seen horses go from standing to full gallop so quickly.

On the right of the line a spearman leaned out of his chariot and drove his weapon through a white shield. Shield and warrior went down and the chariot went over them, shutting the shield over the man on the ground like an ivory box. The man in front of me took a spear through his shield and fell back on me, got up, turned and hamstrung the nearest horse as it passed him. The horse went down screaming, canting its chariot toward me so that the driver shot over my head like a javelin and broke his neck on the edge of the shield behind me. The spearman fell clear, the unwounded horse broke its traces and ran on and the chariot slewed, broke its pole, folded over, bounced and fell back on the wounded horse.

Iolaüs drove through the Cretans, cutting down the man on my left, took the hamstringer on a wheel hub and threw him against me, bringing us both down. Ten yards through the pack, he flung the weight of his body sideways, turning his chariot round on one wheel as on a pivot, swung the horses toward a Cretan who tried to turn and meet him, brought the man down and put his sword through another to his right, as easily as one might cast a pair of dice. "Heracles' charioteer," I thought as I scrabbled to avoid him. "No wonder he drives alone." I worked myself under one of the white shields. From under the shield rim I watched the Sicans run up howling and throwing their spears. Two spears struck chariot horses and one hit a Cretan in the foot. "Clowns," screamed Iolaüs, losing his grin. Again he swung his chariot by the reins wrapped around his waist and drove into the side of the Cretan line. His near wheel took the nearest warrior, breaking his left leg. In falling, shield and all, that Cretan struck his companion who in turn fell sideways. In a moment the whole front rank of Cretans was piled in a heap of weapons, crumpled shields and bloody white feathers, with the remainder of my captors running like white stags and the Sicans standing stock still with their mouths open.

It must have taken ninety seconds all told. To me it had seemed like a slow dance and I had seen every detail of the fight just as I have set it down.

Iolaüs reined in, looking disappointed. "Phooh," he said and unwound the traces from his waist.

There was one of the fifty sons of Heracles dead of a broken neck and two horses were dead with Sican spears in them. "Peasants," said Iolaüs, frowning at the Sicans. Two of his servants were wounded and the hamstrung horse was still screaming. Of the Cretans, four were dead and six badly wounded. Those the Sicans killed. Six got away and two Iolaüs saved from the Sicans, who thereupon killed the hamstrung horse, cut up all three of the animals and took them away. I suppose they ate them. They also took every weapon, every shield and every feathered headdress from the dead, and within ten minutes the lot of them, the whole Sican band, was gone.

"Thank you, hero," I said to Iolaüs.

"A nice skirmish," he said.

I groaned and struggled up. "Hero," I said, "I should be glad if you would cut me loose." He did and the pain was awful.

63

Iolaüs chafed my arms and helped me into his chariot, looping the long reins around his waist.

"Nice little horses, these Sicans," he said. "Very fast on the turn. Very responsive." He clicked his tongue as charioteers do and we moved off, three chariots in the lead, two sullen Cretans trotting and limping behind them and six chariots bringing up the rear all filled with youths called Thespius and one of them dead.

"As I told those fools," said Iolaüs, "there was no point in the fight. Minos is dead. Cocalus boiled him."

"Boiled him?"

"In the bath," said Iolaüs. "His daughters did it. A little accident; too hot for him. Started out white, finished up red."

"Ah," I said.

Iolaüs talks easily enough in social circumstances. In military ones he assumes a clipped delivery and his talk becomes as blunt and brisk as that of Heracles.

"Started out white?" I inquired.

"White as a gull," said Iolaüs. "Never saw a man whiter. Well built, good looking man, but white. Wore white, nothing but white. Personal troops all wear white too." He jerked his head toward the disgruntled captives trotting behind his chariot.

Tauros. It could only be Tauros. I had been right.

As I had the story from Iolaüs and later from Cocalus himself, Tauros had driven off the Sicans on the beach without much trouble when he landed. About thirty had been killed with only six or so Cretan casualties. Then he had disembarked his whole force of some fifteen hundred men and marched on Inykon without opposition. Cocalus withdrew into Kamikos with Ausonias, Iolaüs and their followers and about four hundred Sicans, including his personal servants and warriors while the Cretans sacked Inykon and burned most of it.

On the next day, further Cretan ships drew in so that there were thirty vessels either beached or at anchor in the bay below Inykon and Tauros was entirely confident of his superiority in arms. Early the following morning Cocalus sent an embassy to Tauros proposing terms so slavish and cringing that only a man as unsubtle as Tauros would have been taken in by them. Cocalus offered Tauros the city of Inykon, which he already held, and the fortified palace of Kamikos which, although Tauros did not know it, was a maze. Tauros had then demanded my person, at which Cocalus had denied all knowledge of me. A long and I presume vinous conference had then taken place, during which Cocalus gradually let slip the information that I might conceivably be the traveler who had passed through Inykon on his way to Eryx for the spring festival. Tauros had then entered Kamikos with his retinue and had there taken the daughters of Cocalus and divided them among his followers. The toys I had made for these girls came to light and Tauros had dismantled one of the dolls. I can imagine with what skill and delicacy he discovered how they moved and I can also imagine his triumph when he recognized their ball-and-socket joints. I had invented that device in Athens.

Convinced that I was in Sicily he had sent his men to take me, with instructions that I should be discovered if I could be cozened into revealing my powers as a technician. Tros had seen to that.

I am no longer uncertain of the identity of Tros. It flashes at me like the splinters of the nautilus he broke and when those shards of shell are reassembled in the mind, each is a clue to him. The bow and the lyre are his possessions; death and music. He destroyed a bird to mock a child and show him death in flight. He pretends to come from beyond the North Wind, where the Hyperboreans sacrifice wild asses to the sun, and he hates the night that is closed against the morning. It is not hard to know my persecutor. I shall meet him again in the end. Who knows, perhaps he will smash the threaded triton shell to show me my own pattern or perhaps he will not. They say he does nothing in excess. Wherever he went after my capture, he took the shell with him and my thread with it.

So Tauros had sent to take me and, with Tros to help him, I had been taken. Then I suppose that in his arrogant security as a conqueror, Tauros had relaxed. Cocalus' Sicans were chained and led away. Ausonias, Iolaüs and their followers were not discovered. Kamikos, like any maze I have designed, can hide what it is required to hide.

Cocalus had then set the stage for the last act of his comedy and I can picture it. In the king's megaron, with the great bronze krater I had given him filled with wine and honey, Cocalus would have smoothed Tauros, flattered him, drunk him under the table and drunk his bodyguard under other tables, without turning a hair. There would have been great fumbling of women and boys, a little rape, and Cocalus smiling at all of it. Then there would have been the tactful suggestion of the bath, Cocalus playing the role of the new vassal seeking to please, Tauros' disdainful acceptance, his disrobing, the arrangement of sluices, Cocalus bowing his way out, Tauros luxuriating in the warm water, the water growing warmer, then hot, and then the full force of the steam boiling up through the pipes. With the cold water sluices jammed shut by the daughters, it would not have taken long, the little accident. As for Tauros' retinue, they found themselves suddenly and un-pleasantly sobered by a dense swarm of bees from whose stings, apparently, all but four were at present gradually recovering.

The four will not recover. The bees of Cocalus are no mean insects.

"How do matters stand now?" I asked Iolaüs, when he had told me what I have written here.

"At present," he said, "Kamikos is under siege. The Cretans are camped between Inykon and their ships."

"Leaderless?"

"Their leader is a giant encased from head to foot in bronze," said Iolaüs. "No one has seen his face. He wears the horns and mask of a bull."

Tros, Tauros, Talos, the trotting words now kept rhythm with the chariot horses. Tros unassail- **64** able, Tauros dead, Talos returned. Talos returned, the maze wound up, Talos my first love brazen-mad, Talos returned and Tauros dead. The horses' hooves clicked steadily on across the stony stubble toward Kamikos and now and again a horse would snort as Tauros used to snort and the harness would jingle with the metal sound an armored man makes in his approach.

"How does he look, this bronze man?"

"You have seen the Minotaur?" asked Iolaüs.

"Yes."

"I have not, but from reports I should say this thing looks like the Minotaur."

I laughed.

Iolaüs looked at me. "Doesn't look laughable," he said. "Looks a job for Heracles."

"A friend of mine hit him on the nose and floored him," I said.

"And lived?"

"Yes."

"Bit of luck for him," said Iolaüs. He clicked his tongue and the horses quickened their pace. One of the Cretans fell and was dragged behind the chariot. Iolaüs did not turn his head. The Cretan managed to get to his feet, bleeding from numerous scrapes, and ran on, gasping.

"Soft," said Iolaüs. "They're soft."

"No heroes," I said.

I looked up and saw a kestrel stoop and rise with some small rodent in its talons.

We reached Kamikos at night and went silently through the hidden gate on the landward side of **65** the fortress. To prevent any noise Iolaüs had the two Cretans clubbed and thrown into a chariot. We muffled the wheels and harness and led the horses, holding their nostrils. The Cretan camp-fires all lay to the south and we had no trouble.

"It has gone well so far," said Cocalus when we met. He poured me the usual thick drink. "This Minos fell into his bath like a bull calf and we cooked him."

"It wasn't Minos," I said.

"That's what they called him."

"It was Tauros, Minos' general. Pasiphaë's lover."

"Very hot in bed doubtless," said Cocalus, "but hotter still here. Minos' Tauros was he? His successor looks more like his namesake."

"That is Talos."

"He is a warrior," said Cocalus. "He went through my Sicans like a bull through a wheat field."

"He is not the Minotaur," I said and then I was not so sure. It could be an ironic twist. I had been so sure from my encounter with it, that the Minotaur's sole ambition was to evolve into a man. Perhaps Cephalon had made me think that. Perhaps the Minotaur is double and has a mirror image. Perhaps Talos was a man who, in his madness, was dedicated to becoming a bronze bull.

"I'm tired," I said.

"Have some wine," said Cocalus.

I felt better for too much wine. I often do.

"What next?" I asked.

Cocalus bent forward and traced a rough map in spilt wine on the table.

"Their main force is ranged between their ships and Inykon. There is not much left of that, I am afraid, and it was a pleasant place." He sighed. "You are expensive, Daedalus," he said. He was silent for a while and then went on: "They have the whole area between the sea and Kamikos in their hands and they have frightened my Sicans. Kamikos is surrounded. On the other hand, they have made no move to assault it."

"Then let us wait."

"I can't hold either the Greeks or the Aeolians."

"Why not?" I said. "The Cretans can't take Kamikos. We're all safe here."

"You have forgotten what it's like to be young," said Cocalus, "and besides, we have a plethora of sons of Heracles strutting about there, shouting to fight."

"I've seen Iolaüs in action," I said.

"There you are," said Cocalus. "Ausonias and his men are also raging for blood. They might be Greeks the way they go on."

"Oh, Greeks," I said wearily and went to my bed, aching in every limb.

By the time I woke, whenever that was, the sons of Heracles and every young man in Kamikos had marched out through the main gates. Cocalus was on the wall looking down toward Inykon when I joined him and below us, ranged in two lines, were the Aeolians on foot and half the surviving sons of Heracles. Behind them came Iolaüs' Athenians. They were all trotting forward behind their oxhide shields and drumming their spear-butts on the hide. Ausonias in a chariot was in the lead, dressed in gold armor. Iolaüs had grouped every chariot

311

which Kamikos could muster, above the footmen on the high ground at the right flank.

"I said you were expensive, Daedalus," said Cocalus irritably. "You build an impregnable fortress to keep the enemy out and I can't keep my friends in."

"If they fall back, are there men enough left to cover them and hold the entrance-maze?"

"About thirty old men and twenty disappointed boys."

"It will suffice," I said. "That number could hold an army. I may be costly but I know how to build."

"I hope so," said Cocalus.

The noise increased. The voices of the sons of Heracles were as robust as their father's and as they ran they shouted over the drumming of the shields. A blare of oxhorns and conches added to the din.

"My musicians," said Cocalus, bitterly, "going to get themselves killed."

Then beyond the charred ruins of Inykon, dividing to pass the burnt-out city, I saw the advance guard of the Cretans move forward glittering and clashing their weapons. Earth-red and gold were the predominant colors and the sun, behind and to the left of the mass of men, blazed on their piebald red and white shields and flashed on their spear heads. They outnumbered us by three to one.

The Cretan wings moved in toward the center, curving in two great horns, while out from burned Inykon a solid phalanx of white warriors, tall and plumed, ran behind white shields to make up the line of battle. Between the golden horns, they were like the bristling crest of stiff curls on the lowered forehead of a vast white bull.

"Earthshaker, Earthshaker," roared in unison by the Cretans, joined with the measured thud of feet as friend and foe ran toward each other at an identical pace. The earth did shake. The rhythm of two thousand feet falling together came at me and resolved itself again into the running rubric: "Tros—Tauros—Talos, Tros—Tauros—Talos." It beat into my brain.

Suddenly Ausonias whistled high and shrill and the rising dust blew in a choking storm against the white bull's face. "Aeolus, Iolaüs," our battle cry, joined into the wind and merged with the names of other gods as men called down protection.

"Good trick," said Cocalus, gripping the wall in front of him.

"Tros—Tauros—Talos," I muttered. "Tros—Tauros . . ." and then Talos was there, at the center of Tauros' white bodyguard, running ahead of them. He carried no shield and no weapon, but ran with his arms crooked like a wrestler, hands hooked, just as the Minotaur had run at me in the cavern under Cumae. Like the Minotaur, he ran hunched and, bronze-covered as he was from his great bull-horned helmet mask to his tapering, bronze-sheathed legs, he was no longer the hulking metal tower I had seen on Crete but an animal fined down to kill. Monster malformed, he ran with the grace and speed of a leopard.

The gap between the armies narrowed. I saw Ausonias raise his arm and hurl a javelin over the head of his driver. A white-clad warrior in the front rank fell and the Cretan horde went over him.

"Now," said Cocalus suddenly. "Now." I glanced at him and he was hitting the battlement with both fists. He stopped and pointed beyond the armies and far below on the beach I saw little figures running in from the dunes toward the Cretan ships. Then they were milling on the water's edge and I caught the flash of torches. A smudge of black smoke went up, east of the bay, as the armies closed.

Half a mile below us, fifteen hundred Cretans struck five hundred Greeks, Aeolians and Sicans like a ram. The golden horns closed on them like pincers and at the moment of impact Iolaüs drove his chariots into the base of the western horn. We had the hill in our favor and Iolaüs had a sharp slope to add weight to his thrust. The horn crumpled and twisted, reformed and pressed in again upward, then fell back. The whole battle slewed sideways under Iolaüs' pressure and twenty sons of Heracles joined their nineteen brothers fighting on foot. The bodyguard of Tauros gave way and our center went through them. The golden horns joined at their tips and held like a vise. Only the sons of Heracles went through.

Out of the screaming, shaking mass came Ausonias still in his chariot, his driver gone and the horses running free toward Inykon.

The sons of Heracles formed to turn and behind them, from the dense heart of the struggle, I saw Talos tower up and throw a broken warrior from his helmet horns.

The sun was in my eyes, like a polished rapier thrust at my head. Dust heaved like a blanket over the battle and beyond blackened Inykon black smoke poured upward from the beach.

Then out of the dust I saw Talos alone, facing the shore, with the sons of Heracles coming up at him and beyond, almost among the ruins of the city, Ausonias trying to halt his runaways. He reined in and as he did so, Talos raised both his arms above his head, clutching a rock no smaller than a man. Then like a discus thrower, Talos whirled and flung the stone toward Ausonias. The stone went high and spinning, in a throw no man could make. It spun black over the chariots, whistling above them as they came at Talos and it struck Ausonias below the shoulders like a thunderbolt. The breath went from his body in a whistling scream, a note so high and yet so powerful that it pierced all other noises. Trees from Inykon's gardens hurtled into the air and buildings fell in rubble. Ausonias' death wind rushed across the beach and in that single, fearful gust the Cretan fleet blazed like a bunch of tow.

As when Apollo burned his house upon the rock, all living creatures in the wind's path charred and fell to ash. The flames licked at the sky. Then Ausonias fell. His chariot crumpled under him; even the horses died under the flung stone. In that breathless second, the wind was gone and the battle with it. Abruptly, as if at a command, every man upon the field stood still. Even the chariots halted, grinding at the ground. A silence fell over the armies and for a moment the ravenous, snapping crackle from the flaming ships was the only sound.

Talos bellowed into the silence and that tearing, agonized trumpet-paean of triumph started the rout. The Cretans, to a man, turned and ran down the slope. Not since they fled from Pasiphaë's mating on the plain south of Knossos had I seen such panic. They threw down their weapons and streamed away, some toward the ships, others right and left across the countryside.

Talos cried out again in rage as the bull of Crete died in Sicily and then he too went running toward the beach.

Long, long after that, we were still standing on the wall. Cocalus spoke as if to himself. "At the **66** beginning, Zeus brought bees out of the flesh of a dead bull," he said. We looked down at the Cretan dead and at our own and at the remnant of our warriors wandering like insects among the corpses.

From all sides, little groups of Sicans converged upon the battlefield. Some carried Cretan heads, some, shields and weapons. They passed across the field, stripping the dead and while we watched, they plundered like locusts, rather than bees. "They have new stings now," I said.

In an hour they were gone and still we stood upon the wall of Kamikos, the fortress with no siege left to withstand.

The Cretan dead numbered six hundred and there were no wounded living when the Sicans **67** had passed. We buried them with honor, in a great mound where they had fallen.

Of our own forces, fifty of Ausonias' followers and nineteen sons of Heracles had fallen, while of Cocalus' sons four had been killed and of his men, a hundred and twenty-five. The Athenian losses were eighty dead. Our wounded numbered seventy, of whom twelve recovered. Iolaüs was unharmed.

The Cretan survivors went into the hills and gradually were absorbed into the Sicilian countryside. Probably some were murdered and some enslaved, but I have heard that they built themselves a little city which they call Minoa and another, smaller, town. There is room enough for them in Sicily. Once the excitement had died down the Sicans would not have persecuted them. Sicans are too private and too self-absorbed to interfere with immigrants.

It is a year now since the death of Tauros and since the battle below Kamikos and I am still **68** here. I have built two tombs, one for Ausonias, above Inykon where the winds blow freely from the sea, and one for Tauros cut in the rock of the acropolis at Kamikos. At its entrance I constructed a little maze to protect Tauros' body and his grave goods, for we buried with him all the rich equipment he had left at Inykon. Knowing the Sicans, I am surprised they overlooked so many possessions. Perhaps they forgot to look, but then they had plenty of loot to share at the time.

Above the tomb of Tauros these Sicans have built a temple to the Mother, calling her by an unfamiliar name. I had no hand in it and Cocalus simply let it happen. Thus over a little maze stands a little shrine, almost as if my temple to Apollo at Cumae had been echoed at Kamikos, but with its meaning reversed. The Mother above ground makes no sense to me in any aspect, but of course there are other cults than those I know and cults get tangled. In any case, the curious thing is that a cult of Minos has grown up about this tomb, so that a king, who was not a god, is worshipped here as a god, when in fact it was not even the king they think it was who lies here. How the

316

Sicans reconcile this absurd confusion with the Mother's shrine I have really no idea. If Minos has become a judge beneath the earth, as I hear he has, I suppose the affair is some sort of joke of his making. He has a curious sense of ridicule and Tauros was, after all, an essentially comic figure.

Talos escaped. Somehow he found a ship unburned and sailed west in her with a few followers. It is said that he has gone to Sardinia, where Iolaüs will presently go. Talos is not a comic figure. He is man retreating into the animal, piteous and terrible. If, wound on the spindle of their destinies, Talos and the Minotaur should meet, will they discover they are aspects of one creature, driven together by opposed forces? And will it halt them both forever? You will perhaps know, in your time, how it comes out.

Today I shall end this writing, not because my **69** life is ended, and not because I know exactly what will happen next, but rather, that I am so sure of the eventual outcome. I do not think there will be time to write more. I have agreed to sail with Iolaüs and today they launched their new-built ships. When the wind is right we shall begin our voyage and if it is not, for we no longer have Ausonias to make it so, then those sons of Heracles can doubtless row. Any physical activity pleases them.

Iolaüs goes to colonize Sardinia and I go with him because he asked me to and because he is the only hero I have ever met with whom I have any sympathy. If I can understand him perhaps I shall understand Icarus. Also, I am drawn to Sardinia because I shall meet Talos there and although I have twice seen him in his monstrous transformation, he was my first love and I remember him as he was in Attica. It is probably sentimental to think of it, but I still somehow hope that he lives on as Talos under the grotesque growth of his bronze bull form. I do not believe it, but I must find out for sure. I think I am a fool to

317

hope, but I have not been enough a fool for most of my life and perhaps it is time. My son was a fool.

Cocalus is gone to Eryx for the festival. He left three days ago and wept when we parted. "I drink too much," he said. "It makes me lachrymose. Apollo spare you," and then he drove off in his chariot and did not look back.

Apollo spare me.

Today Apollo shone on me without apparent rancor, as he has done so often, and ceased to do so suddenly when the mood took him. The sky-maze has been as clear as water and cloudless. Now Apollo sets and the moon is already risen. I can see them both from where I sit in this garden in front of the house Cocalus gave me. "A hive for his industry" it says over the lintel.

Perhaps the reason why I shall cease to write now is that, by chance, the symbols of my life seem to have gathered here in this garden since dawn today. A light wind blew from Aeolus, a nautilus shell was brought me by a boy who would not say why he should make me such a present, the bees of Cocalus hum about the hives he gave me, my mother's grasshoppers chirp for me among the bushes and across the path by my table a trail of ants creep laboriously, each insect burdened with some little treasure twice his size. Any one of them could be my late inhabitant, any could be Cephalon. Sometimes I am lonely for the ant and wonder what of me he took with him into the grass below Eryx. Not, I think, my abilities. Perhaps only his companionship. I have had many friends and loved some of them deeply, but I have been alone all my life, when it comes down to it, except perhaps for the ant.

Is the dead bird below the wall another victim for Tros? It is not Icarus.

I have wild garlic in my garden to remind me of Pasiphaë, for it grows only when the moon waxes. Someone has dropped a piece of thread under the window and it is red like Ariadne's cord. The coincidences seem to pile up. There is even a partridge chattering in a holm oak. All that is missing are the

318

bulls. There are no horns, no symbols of Minos nor any of Tauros either. They are in the earth and Naucrate is in the sea, for the moon is fully risen and the sun is gone. I can see Naucrate's reflection in the sea.

I am becoming mawkish and the light is going. I can still see enough to write and see my hands before me. Before it is dark I must put down the omen I have seen today, although perhaps all these things in my garden are omens. Today I saw a hawk wheeling and soaring in the eye of the sun. I saw it stoop to the ground and when it rose it had a snake in its talons and flew north. Sardinia is to the north and I am Erechtheid.

I have called myself Maze Maker with a certain irony because although I believe myself pre-eminent in many crafts, I have been, as Minos described me, first and last a maker of labyrinths. I have made them as simple as a dancing-floor for partridges and as complex as the deep tomb for Minos which was also a prison for the Minotaur. I have inhabited labyrinths I did not make, of which one was the sky, Apollo's web, which I penetrated and from which I escaped, but which drew Icarus into its blazing heart to destroy him. Into another I was driven, and that was the earth maze of Gaia where she confined me until I could placate the sky-god. Then there was the fortress maze I built at Kamikos to exclude Tauros, and within that bastion another maze to frustrate those who might come to rob his grave. Nor am I finished, for I shall build one more and that will be my last. It will be in Sardinia and there I shall dig a twisting path back into Gaia so that the sun will no longer persecute me, for he will have no further cause.

All this long burrowing and building, to protect or to imprison, this flight through the sky and tunneling in the earth, seems to me now to add up to no more than the parts of a single great maze which is my life. This maze for the Maze Maker I made from experience and from circumstance. Its shape identifies me. It has been my goal and my sanctuary, my journey and its destination. In it I have lived continually, ceaselessly enlarging it and turning it to and fro from ambition, hope and fear. Toy, trial and torment, the topology of my labyrinth remains ambiguous. Its materials are at once dense, impenetrable, translucent and illusory. Such a total maze each man makes around himself and each is different from every other, for each contains the length, breadth, height and depth of his own life.

I, Daedalus, maze maker, shall take this that I have written with me to Sardinia and dedicate it at the entrance to the maze which leads to death. Then you, before you follow me down into Gaia, who is the Mother, will know what is to be known of my journey and the fate of my son, Icarus. Before you follow me, look into the sky-maze and acknowledge Apollo who is the god.